Novels by Hilma Wolitzer

Ending (1974)

In the Flesh (1977)

Hearts (1980)

In the Palomar Arms (1983)

Silver (1988)

Tunnel of Love (1994)

TUNNEL OF LOVE

TUNNEL *of* LOVE

HILMA

WOLITZER

MICHAEL DI CAPUA BOOKS

HARPERCOLLINS PUBLISHERS

Copyright © 1994 by Hilma Wolitzer.
All rights reserved.
Printed in the United States of America.
No part of this book may be used or reproduced in any manner
whatsoever without written permission except in the case of brief
quotations embodied in critical articles and reviews.
For information, address HarperCollins Publishers, Inc.,
10 East 53rd Street, New York, NY 10022.

HarperCollins books may be purchased for educational, business,
or sales promotional use. For information, please write:
Special Markets Department, HarperCollins Publishers, Inc.,
10 East 53rd Street, New York, NY 10022.

FIRST EDITION

Library of Congress Cataloging-in-Publication Data
Wolitzer, Hilma
Tunnel of love / Hilma Wolitzer. — 1st. ed.
p.   cm.
"Michael di Capua books."
ISBN 0-06-118007-6
1. Stepfamilies—California—Los Angeles—Fiction.
2. Pregnant women—California—Los Angeles—Fiction.
3. Widows—California—Los Angeles—Fiction.
4. Los Angeles (Calif.)—Fiction.
I. Title.
PS3573.O563T86 1994   813'.54—dc20   93-51064
94 95 96 97 98 ❖/HC 10 9 8 7 6 5 4 3 2 1

For Gabriel and his Grandpa

TUNNEL OF LOVE

1

The New World

As Linda Reismann approached the city limits of Los Angeles in her late husband's laboring Mustang, the slow procession of rush-hour traffic slowed even more and then came to a dead stop. Linda leaned out the window and strained to see what was happening ahead. It was a fiercely hot June day, and all she could see were the other cars, glimmering and melting in the sunlight. In her eagerness to arrive here before dark, Linda had been driving steadily for hours. She'd had to shut off the air conditioner miles back, when the engine started to tremble and an odor like burning Teflon began to seep through the vents. Now she was sweaty and exhausted, and the pebbly pattern of the vinyl seat was embossed on the backs of her thighs, yet she told herself she didn't really mind the delay. This was the final destination of her long journey, and a personally historic occasion, one that probably required a commemorative pause.

There was a book called *Turning the Bad Times into Good Times* tucked into her suitcase in the trunk of the Mustang; it had been a farewell gift from a friend in Newark, and Linda was trying desperately to live by its upbeat philosophy. What else could she do? If she allowed herself to truly reflect on the recent past or to consider the immediate future, she might feel compelled to drive off a cliff into the Pacific Ocean. If she could get through the traffic. If she could find the ocean. Instead, she closed her mind to everything but this still, singular moment of arrival and said, "Robin! Guess what, we're here!"

Linda's thirteen-year-old stepdaughter, who'd been sleeping, openmouthed, on the backseat for the last sixty miles or so, was jarred awake by Linda's announcement, made in the weary but triumphant voice of an explorer discovering the New World. Robin opened her eyes and sat up, but it looked like the same crappy old world to her. No matter how many times Linda had exclaimed during the past two weeks over this sight or that—the sparkling surprise of a lake on the right, the sudden appearance of snow-capped mountains on the left—their trip was mainly a blur, in Robin's memory, of monotonous highways and cheap motels. She'd slept in the car whenever Linda shut up for a minute and let her, waking when she was hungry or thirsty or needed to go to the bathroom. "Aren't we *there* yet?" she had grumbled from time to time, while Linda urged her to admire the gorgeous view or to breathe the glorious air.

Robin wanted badly to be somewhere, although she couldn't have said exactly where. Certainly not back in Newark, where they'd started out, and where her father had recently died. And not in Glendale, Arizona, where her mother lived with that asshole she'd run away with. Linda had dumped Robin's father's ashes at some rest stop off the highway a few days ago, and now the two of them were as homeless as he would be for eternity. "Big deal," she muttered about Los Angeles, which lay stretched out indifferently before them, the same opinion she'd had of those boring mountains and lakes. "Turn the air on, will you," she added. "I'm frying back here."

"Now, I'm just as tired and hot as you are, Robin," Linda said, with that false note of patience Robin hated.

What Linda didn't say, but was surely thinking, was, "And I've been doing all the driving, you little brat, and I'm pregnant, besides." As if Robin had told her to get knocked up in the first place. And as if she'd asked to go along on this endless, stupid trip. The only high points had been those amusement parks and carnivals she'd made Linda stop at. The wimp never wanted to do anything that looked like fun. She kept yapping about the disgusting ingredients in hot dogs, and she wouldn't try any of the rides, except once, in the Midwest somewhere, when she made Robin go into the dumb Tunnel of Love with her. They sat in the last little car, as far apart as Robin could manage. As they jerked and glided their way into the darkness, all the regular couples began moaning and making kissing sounds. Talk about disgusting! Later Linda stood on the sidelines turning green while Robin hung upside down on the Human Fly. "We can't keep wasting our money on nonsense like this," she said when Robin staggered happily back to the Mustang, clutching a Sno-Kone. "Who died and left you boss?" Robin would have asked if she didn't already know the awful answer. Now she lay back again and shut her eyes.

If they could have spoken of such things, Robin would have discovered that Linda also yearned to be in a place where she belonged. For the past nine years, since she'd been on her own, she had moved around a lot, mostly from one furnished room to another. Those six weeks in Newark as Wright's bride had given her a rare and pleasurable sense of permanence, even if most of the furnishings in their garden apartment had been chosen by another woman who was long gone. And even if that other woman's forsaken child wasn't overjoyed to have her there.

Now Linda was on the move again, but coming out here after everything that happened had seemed as natural as the migration of birds. She was reminded of the song she'd first learned to tap-dance to, the one about leaving your worries behind you and crossing to the sunny side of the street. If California wasn't the sunny side of the street, she didn't know what was. And if her worries weren't exactly behind her, life had to get better, didn't it? In any event, she knew she would gradually get used to things and adjust. It was Robin she foolishly worried about, as if that pigheaded girl were a tender sapling whose roots had been ripped rudely from the earth and might slowly wither in this harsh light, hair by delicate hair. Yet everything was supposed to flourish in Southern California, and Robin had always acted sort of homesick, even back home. She'd made her standard pronouncement—"This place really sucks"—about every motel they'd stayed in across America, and some of them had been clean and pretty comfortable.

Linda wasn't sure why she cared that much about Robin when her own mother obviously didn't. Miriam Reismann Hausner had her second chance at motherhood when Linda tracked her down in Glendale the other day and reintroduced her to the daughter she hadn't seen for more than twelve years. But she gave up that chance, by acting more curious about Robin than happy to see her, and she seemed almost relieved when Linda took her away again. Her very own flesh and blood! Not that Robin was easy to take. Most of the time she behaved like someone awakened too soon from a nap, someone who always got up on the wrong side of the bed. And she was especially hostile to Linda, who had taken responsibility for her after they'd come together through the merest fluke of fate. Of course, the same might be said of any two people, or even any *one* person, whose very being depended on a random collision of sperm and egg. Linda often pondered the mystery of accident, especially in relation to her pregnancy, that other enduring consequence of her brief marriage. There were days and nights when she could hardly remember Wright's face—they were married for such a short time—and now she was alone in an alien place with his alien child, and with another one growing inside her.

Still, Linda was determined to establish a real home for her accidental family. The trunk of the Mustang held a few reliable treasures from her old, fractured life, and as soon as they settled in someplace, she would pull them out and spread them around to create an instant lived-in atmosphere. The yellow-and-lavender double-wedding-ring quilt opened over an unknown bed, one of

Wright's Sunday landscapes hung on the facing wall, that small jagged prism Linda had since childhood set on the windowsill of every strange kitchen. When she lay under the quilt's fairy weight, staring at those doglike cows grazing on what might have been Astroturf, or sat in the kitchen the next morning considering the rainbow of sunlight thrown by the prism, she'd firmly repeat the word "home" to herself and wait for the magic of transformation. It was an old trick her mother had taught her, from her years as a baby nurse in other people's houses, and it usually worked.

But in the meantime they had to find a place to spend the night. The traffic had started snaking forward again, and the usual motel signs beckoned from both sides of the road: *Low rates! Waterbeds! Kitchenettes! Color TV!* Linda found herself driving past them with a sudden resistance to the seductions of temporary shelter. She became determined to find *living* quarters this time, instead of just another rented bed, one that probably still held the contours and heat of its last occupants. Even if it took them all night.

Eventually, the traffic eased and the pink-and-turquoise sky began to darken in a spreading, smoky stain. Linda was almost ready to give up when she noticed a cluster of low, modern buildings in the near distance, and the word "Paradise" spelled out above them in an arc of violet neon light. It seemed like a mirage, but she drove resolutely toward it, and then through the wide-open wings of the wrought-iron gate, thinking "Home, home" with the last remnants of her energy and will.

2

A Fool's Paradise

The rental office of Paradise Apartments looked like a travel agency specializing in Club Med vacations. The walls were hung with poster-size photographs of gorgeous young men and women, most of them blond and bronzed and skimpily clad, and all of them apparently having fun. Some were playing tennis, while others cavorted around a pool or sank blissfully, in two-somes and threesomes, into a simmering hot tub. Music seeped gently into the room from hidden speakers: Jeffrey Osborne singing "On the Wings of Love." Although Linda had never played tennis or been in a hot tub, either alone or in mixed company, she couldn't help thinking, with a pang, of her own mis-placed social life. After so many weeks alone with Robin, she wondered if she still remembered how to talk to someone her own age, if she could have a normal conversation with anyone at all.

The rental agent, a short-winded, overweight woman, who wore several extra pounds of gold jewelry and a gold-plated nametag identifying her merely as "Marlene," didn't seem like someone you could test your conversational skills on. "Make it snappy, I was just closing up," she said in greeting when Linda walked in. Then she tapped on her desk top with lethally long, red fingernails and looked impatiently at her watch while Linda glanced around.

If Linda had any doubts after examining the photographs that Paradise was a singles complex, they would have been dispelled by the sign on the wall behind the agent's desk that said PLEA-SURE, PRIVACY, PARADISE! in commanding letters, and underneath, in smaller print, ABSOLUTELY NO CHILDREN OR PETS. As if they were the same thing! Linda was afraid to ask what the cutoff age for childhood was, and she was much too tired and dispirited to consider getting back on the road. So when she asked if there was a vacancy, she simply failed to mention Robin, who was asleep again in the back of the Mustang; it was a deliberate oversight on her part, rather than a direct lie. Besides, this was just a place to crash for a while until they got their bearings. That's why she signed up for a "tastefully furnished efficiency suite," at the weekly rate, without even asking to look at it. The security deposit was steep—four weeks' rent—but Marlene said it would be fully refunded whenever she moved out. Linda selected an apartment model from floor plans you couldn't read without a magnifying glass, and she made her other choices—a conventional king-sized bed, rather than a round or heart-shaped one, and a view of the pool, as opposed to a view of a maintenance building— by thumbing hastily through an illustrated brochure. The latter choice soon proved to be a wise one. When she drove past the maintenance building on the way to Building C, with a copy of the lease, a map of the complex, and her apartment keys piled in her lap, Linda heard a weird humming, like the sound in science-fiction movies when the Martian spaceship is approaching Earth. It was probably only a generator or something, but it gave her the creeps, and she imagined that the softer, more congenial noises near the pool, of laughter and playful splashing, would be a lot easier to take on a daily basis.

The efficiency suite in Building C turned out to be a smallish square room with a pullman kitchen on one side and a tiny bathroom on the other. There was hardly anything efficient about the place, except that the refrigerator was tucked neatly under the counter, and you weren't likely to lose your way to the bathroom in the middle of the night. The king-sized bed, with its cascade of fringed and flowered pillows, monopolized the room, crowding the few other pieces of furniture into the corners. Still, the bed, too, seemed like a good choice once Linda woke Robin and smuggled her inside. The girl groggily claimed the side she'd sleep on, her usual tactic, and then threw herself onto it without any complaints or questions. God knows what confusion a round or heart-shaped bed might have caused. Linda emptied the trunk of the Mustang by herself, making several trips back and forth to the parking lot. Even though they wouldn't be here very long, she draped the double-wedding-ring quilt over Robin's inert body, placed the prism on a windowsill that might get the morning light, and propped one of Wright's paintings against the vase of artificial flowers on the bureau. The place still didn't seem very homey, though. And when Linda lay down next to Robin, pulling an edge of the quilt over her own chest, she didn't have the conviction or the strength to start reciting her mantra.

It turned out that Robin was five years shy of the minimum age required at Paradise. Linda had to keep her under wraps, prepared to say, if necessary, that she was her eighteen-year-old sister visiting from the East to look at colleges. An unlikely story, given Robin's mouthful of braces and her careless grammar. Robin wanted more than anything else to use the pool, which was, of course, out of the question. And she was dying to start working on her tan, the only point, in her opinion, to being in Southern California. Given her extreme fairness, she would have only burned to a crisp in that brutal sunlight, but it was an argument she'd have strongly rejected, as she rejected any other sane advice Linda offered her. Linda, too, would have liked to swim and sun herself, but she knew it would be blatantly unfair to go out while Robin was forced to stay indoors. So they hid out together in the darkened, air-conditioned chill of their room, where Robin mostly lay on the unmade bed, sipping Cokes and watching television, while Linda stood at the window, peering through the blinds at the boisterous singles gathered around the pool, the ones unencumbered by children or pets. An interchangeable cast of men and women sprawled sweating on the chaises, rubbing one another so vigorously with baby oil it seemed they would ignite from all that friction and be incinerated before Linda's eyes. No one had touched her for ages, even by accident. Sometimes she would rub the goose bumps on her own arms and think, with an exceptional absence of charity, that every one of them would probably be dead within a year of skin cancer or some sexually transmitted disease. She tried to dismiss such loathsome thoughts by engaging Robin in conversation, but after a few moments Robin, whose eyes had never left the flickering screen, would say something like "Okay, be quiet now, this is the good part."

Some nights they snuck out and amused themselves by driving around and gawking at all the other people driving around. To indulge Robin and to save money, they stuck to a fast-food diet: burgers and tacos and pizza and fries. But Linda kept a supply of milk and cheese and other nourishing snacks alongside Robin's cache of Coke in the little refrigerator; she had to think of the baby, who was still pretty much of an abstraction. Only someone who'd known Linda for a while would have noticed the subtle new changes in her body. If she really showed, she would never have gotten this apartment, as awful as it was, and she certainly wouldn't get a job at the Whittier branch of the Fred Astaire Dance Studios. She had a letter of recommendation to the manager there from Simonetti, the manager of the Newark studio. She'd been one of his best and most popular instructors, and even though she'd resisted his repulsive advances, he had said positive things about her in his letter. She'd steamed the sealed envelope open before they headed west, to make sure. "Good smile, good dancer, great build," Simonetti had written. But if she didn't look for a job before the abstraction started to become an obvious reality, she'd be out of luck.

One afternoon, after they were in the apartment a little more than a week, Linda gave up on Robin's reluctant company and tottered out to the poolside, just to escape from Kojak or Pat Sajak or somebody trapped in that squawking box, and to restore her normal body temperature in the sunlight. She'd put on an old, stretched-out tank suit, and stood in the middle of the bed, next to the recumbent Robin, to try to get a look at herself in the bureau mirror. It was a headless view, which allowed her to be somewhat objective. She still had her muscular dancer's legs and that startling but not unattractive fullness everywhere else. She tugged here and there on the suit, and stuck one hand inside the top to redistribute her burgeoning breasts. "Well, that's that," she said, as she climbed down from the bed. "Bye-bye," she called to Robin, who continued to ignore her, and then feeling guilty about her own relative freedom, Linda added, "Listen, we'll treat ourselves to a really nice dinner tonight, okay? And we'll even take in a movie if you want to. The heck with the money, right?" The heck with *what* money, she asked herself bitterly as she opened the door. Their meager savings were dwindling fast, despite the low-cost junk food, and nothing else was coming in; she really did have to get over this lethargy soon and look for a job. Right now, though, she was going to the pool. "Bye-bye," she said again, and Robin grunted something incomprehensible and waved her away.

Outside, as Linda perched on the edge of a chaise to remove her sandals, at a distance from the clustered sunbathers, a bearded man rose like a god or a devil from the Jacuzzi's steaming foam and stood before her in a bikini brief that appeared to be laminated to his genitals. He was handsome, in a horrible sort of way, with too much curly body hair and too many large, perfect teeth bared in a relentless smile. "Hi, there. You're new," he said, and expertly flicked a few drops of water from his shoulder onto hers.

It might have been some kinky benediction or baptismal rite.

Or maybe that moment of water play was considered an entire courtship around here. Not being with anyone for so long must have defused Linda's desire, or maybe it was only another side effect of her pregnancy. Lately, aside from her body's general loneliness, she'd only experienced an occasional, mild carnal itch, which she could, so to speak, scratch herself. But now she was both aroused and repelled, which made her glance shyly away, and then stare back at him, glance away and stare again.

All that time he waited, looking amused and using up all of the highly charged air around them. Finally, he reached down and ran one puckered finger slowly across her collarbone, making her shudder and clench her teeth, as if he'd dragged a screeching piece of chalk across a blackboard. "So? Wanna get wetter?" he said, and Linda picked up her sandals and scurried back to her tomb.

Robin came awake when Linda fell into bed beside her. There was a tantalizing odor of sunshine emanating from Linda's hair and skin—even, it seemed, from her breath. Why should *she* get to go out and have a good time while Robin had to stay locked up alone in this stupid place? There was nothing on television she wanted to see anymore and nothing else to do. The minute she shut the set off, unbidden images of her father rushed into her head: the way he'd been when he was alive, with his tender, oppressive love for her—his Roblet, his Redbird—and the way he was now, strewn among the pine needles and beer cans at that rest stop off the highway in Arizona. She'd have to turn the TV back on or escape into sleep, without any guarantee that her dreams wouldn't be worse than her waking thoughts. Linda had fallen asleep almost immediately, and her monotonous breathing, the simple, solid fact of her *being* there, was getting on Robin's nerves. She crept out of bed to the window, lifted one of the slats, and looked out at the pool. This was siesta time at Paradise, and there wasn't anyone out there now. They were probably all in their rooms boinking their brains out. Nobody would know or care if she took a fast dip, if she jump-started her tan.

She ransacked the bureau drawers Linda had so neatly arranged until she found her blue bikini. The apartment keys were on top of the bureau, where Linda had dropped them, right next to the painting Robin's dad had done last year of that park in Rahway. A bunch of fake-looking trees next to a fake-looking stream, and a couple of cartoony rabbits chasing each other in the foreground. Was that the flat way he saw things? Was that the way he saw *her*, like something Disney might have dreamed up? She wriggled into the bikini and stared at her three-dimensional face in the mirror. It was too round and babyish, and it was still that sickly white color, just like the rest of her, whiter than the Jersey snow she'd probably never see again. Well, she thought, grabbing the keys, she'd soon take care of that.

She swam several furious laps. Then she floated on her back with her hair streaming around her like seaweed and her face tilted up in sun worship. She'd found a bottle of baby oil on one of the abandoned chaises and had basted herself with it until she slid right off the chaise. Now, floating near the deep end, she felt a shadow pass over her, as if the sun had suddenly gone behind a cloud in that cloudless blue sky, and she opened her eyes. A fat woman in a flowered dress and high heels was standing there with her hands on her hips, huffing and puffing like a dragon. The flash of her gold bracelets and rings and neck chains was blinding. "What are you doing here?" she demanded, and Robin thrashed around and went under in an effort to right herself. When she came up again, flailing and sputtering, the woman was still standing there, blocking the sun. Robin hoisted herself out of the pool, not even bothering to swim to the ladder first. She grabbed her flip-flops and the keys and ran in the direction of Building C, without looking back. She thought she heard the jangle of jewelry, though, and the clatter of heels on the concrete path behind her. When she let herself into the apartment, Linda was still asleep. She looked dead lying there like that with her hands folded across her chest. Robin peeked out through the blind; the woman was nowhere to be seen.

Linda woke up to find Robin lying next to her, watching a game show. "I must have dozed off," Linda said, yawning and stretching luxuriously, and Robin smirked. "You look a little flushed," Linda told her. "I hope you're not coming down with something." She reached out to touch Robin's forehead, but the girl shrugged her off.

"Leave me alone," she said. "It's just hot in here."

The room was actually freezing, but there was no sense in arguing with Robin when she was like this. Instead, Linda went in to take a shower, thinking that the shower curtain or something in the bathroom smelled strangely of chlorine. It was probably only her imagination, or a sensory memory from that unpleasant moment near the pool.

That night, Linda kept her word to Robin; they had a good seafood dinner and went to see *City Slickers* afterward, a movie so hopelessly silly they laughed at it together, a rare and relaxing occurrence. But in the car going back to Paradise, while Robin kept spotting movie stars through the dark windows of passing limousines, Linda felt compelled to focus on more practical matters. The dinner and movie had been a big extravagance, and although an evening of such harmony was worth every penny, she knew that her days of idleness were numbered.

When they got back to the apartment, Linda found an envelope under the door. She hoped it wasn't from that man at the pool; an unwanted suitor was the last thing she needed right now. She picked the envelope up before Robin noticed it, and tucked it into her pocket. Later, she locked herself in the bathroom and took it out and opened it. There was a typewritten note inside, with the apartment-complex logo and motto— "Pleasure, Privacy, Paradise!"—on top. The note itself was brief and impersonal. "Come to the office without fail at 9 a.m. tomorrow," it said, and it was signed, "The Management." No "Dear Tenant" or "Please," or "Sincerely yours," or anything polite and friendly like that. Linda wondered what they wanted, but it hardly mattered. She'd intended to go there first thing in the morning, anyway, to check herself out of this prison and back into real life.

The next day Robin's good mood continued, and she helped Linda gather and pack up their things. Then Linda instructed her to lay low in the apartment while she walked over to the rental office to cancel their lease. "Don't get lost now," Robin teased, and she even wiggled her fingers at Linda in farewell.

Robin had hardly been at the pool at all yesterday when that fat witch showed up, but she still had a pretty impressive sunburn. If you squinted at it in the right light, it looked more tannish than pink. After Linda left, Robin knocked the ice cubes out of a freezer tray and ran a handful of them up and down her exposed skin, where they quickly melted, making her shiver and moan with pleasure.

Marlene was sitting at her desk, just as she had been that first night, but she looked up at Linda as if she'd never seen her before, nor hoped to ever again. "Yes?" she said.

"I'm Linda Reismann? Apartment 2, Building C?" She wished she could drop the questioning tone from her speech. "I got this note? But I really came in to say goodbye, anyway. You know, to check out?"

Marlene began clicking her nails on her computer pad. She stared at the monitor's screen. "You've only been here nine days," she said finally.

"I know," Linda agreed. "But I think we need to move on now, to get something more . . . permanent."

"Who's *we*?" Marlene asked.

"Pardon?" Linda said. "Oh . . . I guess it's just a habit I have. I was married for a while."

"Paradise has a two-week minimum, you know," Marlene said.

"It does?" Linda said in dismay. She had hoped to work out a pro-rated fee.

"Didn't you read your lease?" Marlene asked.

Linda shook her head. She remembered scribbling her initials and her name in several places, each time Marlene pointed with a blood-red fingernail and said, *"Here,"* and *"Here,"* and *"Here."* And she remembered carrying a copy of the lease into the apartment that first night, but she didn't read it then, and she hadn't seen it since.

Marlene walked herself in her swivel chair to a file cabinet at the side of her desk, opened the top drawer, and pulled out a stapled sheaf of papers. "Here," she said. "If you'll look at page 4, clause 3, part F, you'll see that underage occupants are strictly forbidden."

"She's only my sister visiting from the East—" Linda began weakly.

"Nor are outside overnight guests who are not registered with the office in advance," Marlene said. "Next clause, part B."

Linda went through the pages of the lease now, belatedly, mesmerized by the wordy clauses Marlene had mentioned, and by a multitude of others, about floods and firearms and willful destruction, all endorsed by her own careless signature.

"You realize you've forfeited your security deposit by not complying with the terms of the lease," Marlene said.

Linda labored to clear her constricted throat. "Oh, but listen, Marlene," she said, leaning earnestly over the desk. "I really *was* married, but he died, I mean he just dropped dead—his heart. We didn't even get to use some of our wedding presents. And now I have his child to take care of, and there's another one on the way!"

"We all have our troubles," Marlene said. She rolled the lease up and slapped it against her palm, like someone slapping a rolled-up newspaper in warning to a bad dog. Linda stepped back. "And in case you were wondering, this lease is airtight," Marlene went on. "Our attorney goes over everything himself, personally, with a fine-tooth comb."

Why did that word "attorney" have a much more terrifying authority than "lawyer"? "But can't you make an exception?" Linda pleaded. "Just this once? For human error?"

"This is a business, Ms. . . ." She paused and unfurled the

lease. "Ms. Reismann. If we started making exceptions we'd soon be out of business, wouldn't we?"

When Linda went past the humming maintenance building on her way back to Building C, the noise seemed louder than ever, as if it were following her, and she put her hands over her ears and began to run. By the time she got to the apartment, everything had fallen into place: her own selfish, abbreviated outing yesterday; Robin's telltale sunburned face; that smell of chlorine in the bathroom.

Robin came to the door of the apartment carrying Wright's painting of the park. "So are we sprung yet?" she said.

Linda glared at her. "You deliberately disobeyed me, didn't you?"

"What? What did I do?" Robin asked.

"You know what you did. And she saw you, didn't she?"

Robin's eyes widened and then narrowed again, registering her understanding of what Linda had said. Still, she doggedly held out. "Who?" she said.

"Marlene, that's who! And it cost us almost a thousand dollars!"

"What do you mean?"

"I mean, I lost my security deposit. Four weeks' rent! I *told* you you couldn't be seen outside. I *told* you there were rules here against children. There ought to be rules against having them in the first place!" Linda shouted.

"What are you yelling at me for? I didn't ask to come here. And I didn't ask to be born, either!"

"I didn't mean that part," Linda said. "Oh, God. I'm just upset."

"I bet you are," Robin said. "You threw away a thousand dollars of my dead father's money! And you drag me across this whole stupid country so I can hide out in this dump and watch TV until I go blind!"

"Okay," Linda said wearily. "I'm sorry. Let's just drop it, okay? It's over and done with."

But Robin couldn't let it go. All those accumulated days and nights of silence seemed to have led directly to this moment of release. "It's *not* over," she said. "Why can't we just *live* somewhere, like normal people? I hate this place," she continued, gesturing wildly with Wright's painting, "and I don't want to keep moving around like a bunch of gypsies. I want to have somebody to talk to, and I'd like to stay still long enough to get a tan. I'm sick and *tired* of this!"

"Me, too," Linda said quietly, taking the painting from her, and all the air went out of their argument.

Later, after they found the place in Hollywood, and had put most of their things away, and sat down in the kitchen to eat supper, Robin said, "I should have drowned that fat bitch when I had the chance. Like her jewelry alone probably would have sunk her."

"Let's try and forget about it, Robin," Linda said.

"She deserves to die."

Linda had a vision of Robin's mother, standing in her bathrobe in the doorway of her house in Glendale, with her bathrobed husband in the background, waving goodbye and telling them to keep in touch. "Right," Linda said. "Fine. Now, do you want any more milk before I put it away?"

"If I had a gun, I'd go back there and shoot her," Robin said. She pointed her trigger finger at the carton of milk Linda was carrying back to the refrigerator, and sighted it down the length of her bright pink arm. "Bang! Bang! Bang! Bang!"

Linda flinched at each sharp explosion of sound, as if Robin held an actual gun and she was the intended target of her rage.

3

Homesick

Linda hated to admit it, even to herself, but sometimes she was as miserable as E.T. longing for his lost planet, or as wistful as Dorothy wanting Kansas again. In her own, more perverse case, it was New Jersey she missed. People back home used to tell her she'd miss the changing seasons out here, but that wasn't it, exactly. When September came, she didn't give that much thought to autumn leaves, or crisply cool air, or the way the pyracantha would always seem to catch fire about now. The steady heat in Los Angeles was sort of soothing, like being perpetually submerged in a warm tub, and the palm trees she could see from her living-room window had a certain tropical glamour. The Hollywood apartment was pretty similar to the garden apartment they'd left behind in Newark, with its pleasant, well-equipped kitchen and modern bathroom. And they had two small bedrooms, so she and Robin were able to get away from each other when they needed to, like fighters going to their separate corners until the bell rang for the next round.

Linda did wish she didn't have to drive everywhere, that there was more public transportation, especially for Robin, who got so stir-crazy, but that wasn't the principal problem, either. Of course she missed her old friends in Newark, but she was making some new ones here, which was more than Robin seemed to be doing. She'd started high school, though, and for several hours a day, at least, Linda knew where she was and that she was safely, if not happily, occupied.

Linda wasn't that happily occupied herself. She had known that the job at the Whittier branch of Fred Astaire's would only be temporary, under the circumstances. All she'd hoped for was to earn enough to see them through the worst of it. And of course she intended to go back to work again after the baby was born. She was a nervous wreck when she went for her interview, bearing Simonetti's letter. She was badly out of practice, unfamiliar with the latest steps, and about eight pounds over her usual weight. But dancing was the one thing her body knew by heart, and when the manager put a Tito Puente tape on and held out his arms, she cha-cha-chaed right into them.

As she'd expected, the job wasn't that great. Aside from their splashy sport shirts, California men who sought distraction and companionship in the arms of strangers weren't very different from the ones back in Jersey. Their breath was just as hot and anxious, their hands as cold and slippery in hers, and their inner rhythm every bit as out of sync with the rhythm of the music. Before she started working, Linda had visited a low-cost maternity clinic at a nearby hospital, where she was pronounced perfectly healthy and given special prenatal vitamins. But her fatigue seemed to grow along with her pregnancy, and being whirled around the room several times a day in some dumb new dance craze called the Whiplash left her reeling with vertigo. So when Vicki Wheeler, another instructor, told her about an opening as a cocktail waitress in the Western bar where she moonlighted, Linda switched jobs.

She didn't like leaving Robin alone until all hours of the night, but she kept in touch by phone whenever she could. Robin would growl about being checked up on, like a baby, but Linda was sure she detected relief in her voice as well. She was probably spooked by every little thing—the play of shadows on the wall, and real and imagined noises—the way Linda was at that age, when her mother was off somewhere taking care of someone else's child. It was a time when tree limbs grew fingertips to scratch at the windows, and the closets became breeding places for murderous creatures.

Linda's pregnancy was beginning to be burdensome, although that general sickish feeling had passed. She was into her fifth month and going to the clinic now for regular visits. In a booklet she'd found in the waiting room, she read that a pregnant woman sitting in a chair expended more energy than a man climbing a mountain. If that was true, Linda figured that standing in high-heeled cowgirl boots in the smoke and noise at Lucky's Last Roundup, with bombed men trying to hit on her, was like scaling Mt. Everest on a nightly basis. She always longed to fall into bed afterward and sleep for about a hundred years. Still, if Robin happened to be awake when she came in, Linda forced herself to stay awake, too, and use that time to foster some closeness between them. To begin with, she wouldn't mention the overpowering smell of pot in the apartment, or the incense burned to mask the smell of pot. "What kind of evening did you have, honey?" she would say, or "I didn't even ask you about school yet today, did I?" Although questions about school always sounded insincere, even to her own ears, and Robin gave them short shrift.

School was consistently "okay." She never seemed to have any homework, or she claimed to have finished it and put it away moments before Linda asked. She refused to invite any of the kids from school home with her because they were all "wimps" or "fags," or they hated her for being "wimpy" and "faggy."

"You've got to give people a chance," Linda told her. "Friends are very important at your age, at *any* age. Gosh, when I was in high school, my friend Dee Dee and I were inseparable. That friendship saved my life."

"Oh, yeah?" Robin said. "So where is she now?" And Linda couldn't answer that.

"I wish we never came out here," Robin said, echoing Linda's own unspoken thoughts.

Turning the Bad Times into Good Times had a chapter called "You're in Charge!" which was devoted to the importance of a positive attitude in reversing unsatisfactory situations. Linda read aloud from that chapter to Robin, following her from room to room, trying to ignore her bored face and melodramatic sighs. When Linda was finished, Robin said, "I got a positive attitude already. I'm positive that's bullshit."

Linda lost her self-control. "God, what's *wrong* with you?" she shouted. "Here I am, practically *killing* myself to support us and give us a decent home, and all I want in return is some common courtesy and a little affection! Is that too much to ask?" Once she got started she couldn't stop. She went on and on about Robin never picking up after herself, and that her face wouldn't break if she *smiled* once in a blue moon. Then she said, "And what's that terrible stink in here, miss? Do you want to end up in a reform school with scrambled brains and no future?"

Robin, who'd managed to seem comatose until then, sprang miraculously back to life. "Yeah, right," she said. "Like *you* have a great future, waiting on those losers in that cruddy hole!"

Linda tried to contain her own anger and get to the heart of the matter, to what she believed was the real source of Robin's discontent—her unexpressed grief for her father. Wright and Robin had been an intense and enclosed little family unit until Linda showed up in their lives. Miriam had abandoned them before Robin even learned to talk, and Wright had raised her alone, with valor and overbearing love. When he died, it was Linda, who Robin already despised and mistrusted, who had to break the news to her. Robin had acted as if Linda had *caused* the news. Together, yet apart, they'd watched as Wright's body was cremated, and then they carried his ashes practically all the way here in the trunk of the Mustang. Believing that they both needed the relief of completion and ceremony, Linda finally scattered them in a lovely gladed rest stop off I-10 on the western

edge of Arizona. She delivered a fast, improvised eulogy, while Robin stood there, wordlessly, clutching a tree. Afterward they fled the scene like a couple of litterbugs.

Cautiously now, Linda approached the subject. "You know, Robin," she said, "I miss your dad an awful lot."

Silence.

"I know you do, too."

More silence, which triggered Linda's need to keep talking. "He would have really liked it out here, I'll bet." What was she saying? Wright would have hated L.A. He'd loved Newark, with its skies darkened by churning industry, not car exhaust, and with its proximity to the lush parks and meadows where he painted his earnest landscapes. Robin's stubborn, appropriate silence eventually shamed and stilled her.

Things might have remained at an impasse if their opposing schedules had continued much longer, and if they'd never met Manny Green. But then Linda's job at Lucky's was forfeited the night she showed up wearing her first maternity top. Lucky said he was sorry but that real life wasn't anything like *Cheers*; if his customers wanted to look at pregnant women, they could stay home and look at their wives. Vicki and the other waitresses stomped around indignantly in their cowgirl boots and hot pants, and urged Linda to sue the bastard for sexual discrimination.

But Linda was glad to just get out of there, and to get off her swollen feet at her third job in less than three months, as a cashier in a discount liquor store. She'd found this one on her own, through the want ads in the newspaper. It occurred to her, as she went up and down the columns with a red pencil in hand, that in twenty-seven years she had hardly learned to do anything practical. Most of the jobs listed in the paper—accountant, book-keeper, controller (whatever that was), draftsman, editor, right down through the alphabet to X-ray technician—required skills and specialized training she simply didn't have. And almost all the ads, even for the most menial kind of work, mentioned a preference for previous experience or a college education.

Robin watched Linda scan the ads without marking any of them, and she finally volunteered to quit school and get a job herself. What she said, precisely, was, "Who's going to hire you, anyway, you look like an elephant. I bet I could get something great if I could work full-time."

Linda immediately said, "Absolutely not, Robin. That's out of the question."

"Why?" Robin persisted. "Why can't I?"

"Because you're still a child," Linda said, "and there are laws against children working."

"Sure," Robin said. "They'd much rather torture us by keeping us in school. Well, I'm going to quit the second I turn sixteen. I can, you know. That's the law, too, you know."

"Not without your parents' permission, you can't," Linda told her.

"I don't have any parents, remember?" Robin said.

"Don't say that," Linda said. "You have me. And don't even think about quitting school. If you get a good education, you'll be able to have a real profession someday. You could be a doctor or a lawyer or even . . . an astronaut! You won't ever have to settle for being just a . . ." She paused and searched the want-ad columns for a suitable example of a compromised life. "A cashier in a discount liquor store," she said at last. And then, after another thoughtful pause, she circled the ad.

The first wonderful thing was that the Liquor Barn was pretty close to their apartment, and hardly anything in L.A. was close to anywhere else you wanted to go. The store's owner-manager, Manny Green, was fiftyish and paunchy. He had a pencil stub behind one ear, and his thin wiry gray hair looked as if he'd scribbled it on, himself, with the same pencil. He greeted Linda with a wide smile and dragged a couple of wine cases to one side of the store for them to sit on during the job interview. "Step into my office," he said, with a grand gesture, and he seated her on an upended case, like the maître d' in a posh restaurant. "So why

would a lovely young lady like you want to work here?" was the first question he asked, after her name, as if she'd had dozens of other, better offers.

"I don't have much formal training or education," Linda admitted. "I'm a dancer—a dance instructor, actually. But I'm pregnant right now."

"Yeah, I noticed that," he said. "What about your husband? What does he do?"

"Nothing. He died," she hastily added. "Back in New Jersey. It's a long story."

He looked around the store. It was ten in the morning, and besides a cashier and a stock clerk, there were only two other people: a well-dressed woman loading a shopping cart with bottles of gin, and a scruffy-looking man contemplating a pint of whiskey. "Go ahead," Manny said. "I have time."

The quiet, patient way he said it reminded Linda of Wright. She took a delightfully deep breath and proceeded to tell him everything.

She gave Robin the good news that afternoon, as soon as she came in from school. "Our lives are about to turn around," Linda began, although she knew that she often said things like that—"This is our lucky day" was another favorite—and that it really bugged Robin.

Robin moaned and rolled her eyes up until only the whites showed.

"Please don't do that, Robin," Linda pleaded, and then she said, "I met the nicest man today."

Robin looked at her with a bewildered blend of panic and scorn. "Is he your new boyfriend?" she asked.

"Robin!" Linda exclaimed. "He's going to be my *boss*. I'm not looking for any boyfriends right now." She patted her bulging belly. "The thing is, I've got a good day job now, and I'll always be here for you after school."

"Great," Robin said glumly.

But that night, when Manny dropped by to give Linda a crash

course in cashiering, Robin was instantly taken by the roll of bills and the cigar box filled with silver he'd brought. "The cash registers are computerized," he told Linda, "but I like my people to be alert. It makes the job more interesting, and even machines can fail sometimes." He proceeded to put her through a rapid-fire drill of making change. It was something she was perfectly capable of doing, but she was nervous at first, especially with Robin breathing down her neck that way. Why did she have to pick this moment to become so interested in Linda's life?

As it turned out, Robin was a whiz at simple arithmetic, something she'd never bothered to reveal before. Now, whenever Linda committed a little error of addition or subtraction, Robin made a grating, buzzerlike noise, and then yelled the correct answer right in Linda's face, like some obnoxious game-show host. Linda would have been elated by this display of talent at any other time—she often despaired about Robin's lack of ability and enthusiasm—but now it was driving her crazy. Finally, she jumped up and shouted, "Robin, do you *mind*? I can't even think straight with you standing right on top of me!"

Robin gave her a contemptuous smile, and Manny touched Linda's shoulder in gentle restraint as he said, "Robin, if you aren't a famous movie star or a math professor by the time you're twenty-one, I'll have a job waiting for you at the Liquor Barn. But in the meantime," he added with a chummy wink, "let's give poor old Linda a chance, okay?"

"Sure," Robin said, benevolently. "Why not?" And she floated out of the room.

Linda turned to Manny and said, with true awe, "How did you *do* that?"

He laughed and said, "Oh, years of experience, I guess. I have three daughters myself, all grown now, but they were once that age, too, God help me."

Then she asked why he was hiring her, pregnant and all, and he said, "Hey, I'm an equal-opportunity employer, that's why. And I pride myself on being an excellent judge of character."

Later, over coffee, he told her that he was widowed, too, for about five years now, and he knew how lonely and difficult it could be. He thought she was very spunky to take care of her little family this way.

Linda would never have applied that word "spunky" to herself, but when Manny said it, it felt oddly accurate, and like a blessing. She carried it with her all the way to bed that night, and she believed it helped her to relax, and to fall asleep. What she'd missed so much, what she was so achingly homesick for, she supposed as she drifted off, was approval, that small but essential aspect of love.

4

Love and Work

How are you today, my friend?" Manny said in greeting to just about everyone who entered the Liquor Barn: panhandlers counting out their quarters and dimes for pints of Ripple, caterers ordering house brands by the truckload, housewives needing cooking sherry, construction workers thirsty for a cold beer, and even the old ladies who bought only lottery tickets and ginger ale. He took the time to kibitz with all of them, but the wine browsers were his clear favorites. They came in search of treasures, like those hard-to-find vintage years and unadvertised sales on first growths. Manny led them to the enormous rows of wine bins, arranged by country of origin, and helped them make their selections. He removed the pencil from behind his ear and wrote down their orders, without ever losing a beat in the ongoing discussions of "nose," "fruit," "tannins," and "finesse." Linda's cash register was close enough to the Australian and Italian sections for eavesdropping, and sometimes it seemed to her that they were speaking a foreign language. Once she heard Manny refer in somber tones to the merits of oak over stainless-steel casks, and thought, for a single morbid moment, that he was talking about coffins.

Linda confessed one day that she didn't know anything about

wine, that aside from the obvious differences between the reds and the whites, they all seemed pretty much the same to her. Manny promised to give her a mini tasting course after the baby was born. He admitted that wine connoisseurship could be a little narrow and pretentious, but the thing he loved most about the people who haunted those bins was their passion. Passion about anything that moved you, he often told her—baseball, poetry, gardening, members of the opposite sex, members of the *same* sex—was the greatest saving grace. But he was only preaching to the converted. Passion, it seemed to Linda, was the quality Robin most conspicuously lacked, the deficiency that kept her at an emotional distance from everyone and everything around her. Passionate was the way Linda remembered feeling about dancing before she'd turned into the Goodyear Blimp. And, she suspected, it was the way Manny was starting to feel about her.

They had been going out together sometimes after work, to supper or the movies, usually accompanied by Robin, who sat between them in the movie theater like a chaperone, passing the popcorn and Milk Duds back and forth. And when Manny dropped by the apartment on the weekend to visit Linda or to do some small household repairs, Robin hung around listening to their conversations, and putting her own two cents in every chance she got. Manny was consistently sweet and funny with Robin, but he'd look over her head at Linda once in a while with what she soon recognized, with mixed emotions, as a lovesick smile.

One Sunday night, he suggested they leave Robin home this time, and he made reservations for just the two of them at a waterfront café in Marina del Rey. As he took Linda's hand across the table, in the festive glow of the patio lights, she understood his intentions without his having to say a word. They had already fallen into the habit of friendly good-night hugs and kisses, and she felt genuine affection for Manny—how could she not? Now it was only a matter of going on to the next logical step in their friendship. If she didn't match his ardor right away, she could always blame it on shyness, on her pregnancy, on the sadness she still felt about Wright, released forever to the elements in his roadside resting place. Linda's mother used to say that you could learn to love any man, if he had a good heart and a good income, and that passion will fly out the same window it flew in. Linda had certainly loved Wright, but even when they were newlyweds their passion was quickly spent, as if they had gone to bed with the window left carelessly open.

After their dinner in Marina del Rey, Manny and Linda drove to his house, where she'd never been before, and where he had lived all those years with his wife and their daughters. Linda was touched to see that he had been optimistic enough to prepare for her arrival. Everything was strikingly neat; you would swear someone had fussed with it only moments before she stepped in. The living-room rug still wore the tracks of a vacuum cleaner in its pile, and the sofa cushions were plump with expectancy. The bathroom was as pristine as a motel's, with a fresh bar of soap in the soap dish and fluffy white towels hanging side by side in perfect alignment. The only thing missing, as far as Linda could see, was one of those paper banners across the toilet seat.

She was nervous and couldn't stop talking, fixing on every artifact in his living room as a point of interest, from the numerous photographs of his family to a spindly, waterlogged philodendron. "This is so nice. I keep thinking I have to fix our place up more," she chattered. "I saw some really cute ideas in a magazine. Like using wallpaper samples to line your dresser drawers? And making a collage of colorful food labels for the kitchen?"

Manny put some music on the stereo and held out his arms to her. She hadn't danced with anyone since her days at the Whittier Fred Astaire's. When she went into Manny's arms, their bellies bumped, and they both said, "Oops, pardon me!" at the same time, and then laughed. Manny patted his gut and tried to suck it in. "At least you've got a good excuse," he said ruefully, before placing his hand again where her waist used to be. The music was from the big-band era, all yearning saxophones and the slow, sliding plaint of trombones. Manny was from some-where around that era, too, the kind of dancer who bends to dance cheek-to-cheek and executes extravagant twirls and dips. She could see the excited pulse in his neck and hear his hum-ming breath in her ear. He smelled so good, a mixture of floral fabric softener and minty after-shave. As he led her into his bed-room, she slipped her wedding band off and transferred it to the ring finger of her other hand. Despite what she was about to do, she was still married to Wright in some abstract but final way.

Yet it was surprisingly easy after that, except for the awkward instant when she first saw Manny naked, and he saw her. Linda had not consciously intended to take a lover during her pregnancy; she couldn't imagine anyone finding her attractive now. But Manny was in awe of her stretched and rounded splendor, and as grateful as a starving man called to a banquet. "Oh, God, oh, God," he kept saying, worshipful and irreverent at once. He paused only long enough to worry about hurting her or the baby, but she assured him that it was fine, that it was lovely, as in fact it was. Only the week before, the doctor at the clinic had said, out of the blue, that intercourse was permissible until the final two weeks of gestation. As if she had asked him, as if he didn't know that she was widowed, and big beyond anyone's wanting. Now, the lonely places on her body that Manny touched and kissed responded like flowers to sunlight.

In Linda's opinion, all men's bodies were dear and comical, with their basic planes and showy baggage, and Manny's was no exception. His midsection gave evidence of gravity's pull, but his arms and shoulders were ropy with muscle, from so many years of lifting heavy crates and boxes. He had two significant scars, whose origin she would learn about afterward, a wrinkled pink splotch on his chest from a childhood collision with a boiling teakettle, and a smaller white depression on his shoulder, where a bullet had grazed it during a holdup at the store years before.

If you can't feel desire for every man who desires you, Linda thought, the very least you can feel is fondness, pity, kinship. She felt all of these things as she gathered Manny in. At one point, he groaned and said, "Linda, honey, I'm old enough to be your . . ." And Linda put her fingers to his lips and finished the sentence for him. "Lover," she said. "You're old enough to be my lover."

It was much better and simpler, she told herself later, than rabid sexual heat, with all its crazy complications of obsession and jealousy. Back in Newark, when she was safely married, she used to listen in wonder as a couple of other instructors at Fred Astaire's complained about men who cheated and bullied and lied, and with whom there was a constant furor of breakups and reconciliations. "That bastard," one of the women once said. "I'll cut it off him before we're through." But she came in the very next day with her eyes shining and her lips bruised from kissing.

Manny assured Linda that his three daughters—who were all married and lived in various places around the country—would be crazy about her, which she couldn't imagine, since she was two years younger than the youngest one. They'd probably think she was a gold digger, or worse. She had a clear memory of the icy reception Robin gave her when Wright brought her home for the first time, the way she'd refused to make eye contact or lower the music blaring from her stereo. Linda dreaded ever having to meet Manny's daughters almost as much as she dreaded Robin's reaction to this latest turn of events in her life. But to her surprise and relief Robin didn't appear to mind at all. She seemed to take Manny's being both boyfriend *and* boss right in stride. They hadn't said anything to her about their physical relationship, and Manny never stayed overnight at their place, but there were still plenty of clues, especially a new playfulness between Linda and Manny, a habit of innocent touching that intimated something less innocent. And he was there more than ever, bringing silly and lavish gifts and the welcome bulk and noise of his presence. Linda wasn't allowed to drink alcohol, so he chose sparkling non-alcoholic treats for their at-home dinners, and he always brought little bags of taco chips and peanuts from the store for Robin.

One evening in early November he arrived at their apartment

with a dusty, beribboned bottle of champagne. "My wine mavens tell me this is good stuff," he said, holding the bottle up. "We'll pop it open in January and drink to the little fishie." For a few silent seconds they all gazed into the pleasant, blurry vista of the future, but in the meantime the bottle needed to be stored somewhere, lying on its side. Somewhere cool and dark where it wasn't likely to be disturbed, Manny said. Robin volunteered her closet floor, and the champagne was laid to rest on a tangled nest of sneakers, blue jeans, and dirty socks. "Perfect," Manny pronounced, as he peeked in. "I can see that nobody's disturbed this place in years. What a photo op for *The Wine Spectator*!" Robin actually chuckled and punched him lightly on the arm.

Linda would never have gotten away with teasing her like that, any more than she could get away with honest praise. If Manny said something flattering about Robin's skin or hair, she might stick her tongue out at him, but she'd still flush with pride and toss her glorious white-blond mane around. If Linda offered her an identical compliment, Robin would bemoan her inability to tan "like every normal person in California," and she'd threaten to shave her head. And if Robin ever happened to punch Linda, she was positive it would hurt. Manny had mellowed Robin, had civilized her; that was his special brand of white magic, and he had worked it on both of them. When Linda was convinced she was hideously huge, too grotesque to even be seen in public, he told her she looked radiant. Radiant. Spunky. He was reinventing her.

The job was working out well, too. Men buying their whiskey by the bottle didn't seem to mind the bloated sight of her as much as the ones who'd bought it by the glass at Lucky's. And Troy and William, the two stock clerks at the Liquor Barn, and Rosalia, the other cashier, were all helpful and friendly. Their lively banter, the jangling of the sleigh bells on the door when a customer came in, Manny's hearty greeting, and the computer beeps of the cash registers had become the gratifying sounds of Linda's daily life. Manny insisted that she take a maternity leave, with pay, beginning a month before her due date. And whenever she decided to come back to work, she could keep the baby with her behind the counter, in a basket. He hinted at marriage, without actually proposing it, and she deflected that possibility without completely discouraging it. It was something that couldn't really be properly addressed until after the baby was born. Each day, Linda's attention was drawn more and more toward that event, the way she imagined the terrified and exhilarated passengers of a space shuttle narrowed their concentration as they counted down toward liftoff. She had packed her overnight bag and shopped for baby furniture and nursing bras and a layette. Manny instructed Robin to call him when Linda's time came, so he could drive her to the hospital, and Linda's friend, Vicki, had volunteered to be the backup driver.

Vicki told Linda she was a lucky dog to have someone like Manny waiting in the wings for her. "He may seem a little on the ripe side to someone your age," she said, "but then your average chick doesn't come equipped with a teenage kid and one in the oven." Vicki, who wouldn't divulge her own age, except to say that her parts warranty hadn't run out yet, had been a showgirl in Vegas, and then a blackjack dealer, before coming to L.A., and Fred Astaire's and Lucky's. She'd been married three times, but, as she put it, "none of them ever took," as if she were referring to organ transplants from donors who weren't the right genetic match. "I can never seem to love the guys I pick half as much as they love themselves," she said, sighing. Lately, she'd been seeing a married man, at his convenience, an arrangement that troubled Linda. She saw it as both a transgression and a dead end. Her father, she suspected, had cheated on her mother, another source of anger and sadness in their household.

Vicki said, "But all the single guys I meet are either gruesome or gay. And I've used up my own husbands. If I don't sleep with someone else's, I'd have to sleep alone forever. Wouldn't that be sad?"

"Yes," Linda said, "but this is sad, too."

Vicki told her not to worry—she could take care of herself. She worried about Linda, though, bopping from job to job like that while her bills piled up and her belly grew. Manny was what Vicki's mother, back in Akron, would call a real good catch. If Linda's mother were alive, she'd probably have said the same thing. "If you don't want him, honey," Vicki said, only half joking, "I'd be happy to take him off your hands."

But Linda *did* want Manny. There were plenty of other saving graces in this world besides passion, weren't there? Manny was the perfect antidote to Robin's bitterness, and the only rational solution to Linda's irrational wish to have Wright restored to their lives. He was the second chance hardly anyone ever gets, and she'd be a fool to pass him up.

5

The Good News and the Bad News

When Linda went into labor, Robin didn't call either Manny or Vicki, as she had promised to do. It started at about two o'clock in the morning on December 28, almost a week before the baby's official due date. Robin woke from a crazy dream in which she was swimming frantically across the Pacific Ocean, dodging sharks and submarines, when she heard Linda shuffling down the hallway to the bathroom. For the past couple of weeks, the baby seemed to be dancing a jig on Linda's bladder, and she'd been going back and forth to the bathroom all night, finding her way there with her eyes still shut, like a single-minded sleepwalker. Robin, who used to sleep through everything, from Linda's restlessness to random screaming in the streets, was alerted somehow lately, and would jerk awake at the slightest noise in the apartment. Then she would lie there in a semi-doze until she heard the toilet flush and Linda's bare feet padding back to her own bedroom. This time, though, Robin realized that several minutes had passed and Linda had never left the bathroom. "Linda?" she called. "You okay?" There was no answer, so she went to the bathroom to investigate. She found Linda sitting on the toilet, with her head resting against the tiled wall. Her face was greenish and sweaty and she didn't look up when Robin appeared in the doorway. "You okay?" Robin asked again.

"Ohhh," Linda moaned. "I guess so. I just keep feeling as if I have to go, you know, move my bowels, but then I can't."

"Could it be the baby?" Robin asked, feeling a slight push in her own bowels.

"Oh, I doubt that," Linda said, as if her due date was still months away, or as if she was thinking: what baby is that? But after sitting there for a while longer without feeling relieved of that peculiar pressure, she asked Robin to call the doctor. By the time the doctor called back, Linda had discharged a little bloody plug of mucus and her contractions had begun. She was advised to wait at home until they became regular and were ten minutes apart.

That took almost three hours, during which Linda and Robin played numerous hands of War, Spit, and Stealing the Old Man's Bundle on Linda's bed. The few times Robin had deigned to play cards with Linda before, when Robin was the one in bed, with a bad cold or her monthly cramps, Linda had contrived to let her win most of the hands, a practice that Robin quickly recognized and resented. Did Linda think she was playing with some stupid little crybaby sore loser? Robin, who held her cards close to her chest and played with genuine strategy and a killer instinct, would have won fair and square, anyway. And the few times she couldn't win, because of incredibly bad luck, she cheated, which was cinchy to do, with Linda exposing her own cards like that, and thinking over every move for about a year. Now, though, with Linda propped against two pillows like a fat, invalid child, Robin felt grudgingly inclined to let *her* win a couple of times.

When the contractions were fifteen minutes apart, Linda showered and shampooed her hair, while Robin sat on the closed toilet seat, timing her progress with the big, noisily ticking alarm clock. The pains couldn't be too bad, Robin figured, because Linda was singing over the water's gush, as usual, loudly and off-key. She sang lively, upbeat numbers, "Finally" and "Something to Talk About," really belting them out, and occasionally hitting high notes beyond her normal range. It was a wonder none of their neighbors called to complain, the way they did whenever

Robin turned up the volume on her stereo. When Linda emerged from the shower, though, she grew strangely quiet, as if she were listening for something far away. The contractions were coming closer now, about eleven or twelve minutes apart, and they were also deeper and more urgent. "You'd better call Manny," she finally told Robin. "This doesn't feel very good."

Robin went to the telephone, but instead of calling Manny, she called for a taxi. She liked Manny a lot, but they hardly knew him, he was just a stranger, when you really thought about it. This business of the baby had nothing to do with him; it was between her and Linda. When Robin told the taxi dispatcher their destination and that he'd better hurry up, he said, in a suspicious voice, "You're not having a baby, are you?" The asshole was probably worried they'd mess up his cab. "No," Robin told him. "I'm having a heart attack."

In the taxi, Linda's labor accelerated rapidly, and she was sure that she and the baby would both die. She couldn't help thinking that Robin would be her last link to this mortal life, and in the midst of a particularly fierce contraction, she gripped the girl's equally icy hand and gasped, "Robin, honey, always remember . . . you're my . . . bridge!"

"Huh?" Robin said, bug-eyed and pasty-white. "I'm your *fridge*? What do you mean by that? Linda?" But the taxi had arrived at the hospital, and Linda had passed onto a higher plane, beyond ordinary communication.

After they took Linda away, a nurse directed Robin to the maternity waiting room. Two men were already sitting there, smoking, when she came in, both of them needing shaves and a comb. One of them wore what looked like a pajama top over his trousers. The other one, in a leather jacket, had a motorcycle helmet on his lap. Robin wondered if he'd brought his wife there on his Harley. They both glanced at her and nodded, but didn't say anything. She curled up on a couch and closed her eyes. After a minute or two, one of the men said to the other, "Did you hear about the guy who goes to his doctor and the doctor says, 'I got good news and bad news—which do you want first?' The guy says, 'Give me the good news,' and the doctor says, 'Okay, you got twenty-four hours to live,' and the guy says, 'That's the *good* news? What the hell's the *bad* news?' and the doctor says, 'I was supposed to tell you yesterday.'"

The two men laughed a little while Robin just lay there, pretending to sleep, and after another minute the same man said, "Then there's this other guy goes to his doctor and the doctor says, 'I got good news and bad news—which do you want first?' The guy says, 'Give me the bad news,' and the doctor says, 'You got twenty-four hours to live,' and the guy says, 'What's the good news?' and the doctor says, 'See that cute nurse at the desk? Well, I screwed her last night.'"

This time the men really cracked up. Robin opened one eye and stared at them. She didn't get it. They must have gone nuts, she thought, from waiting there so long.

Meanwhile, upstairs in a four-bedded labor room, when another woman screamed her husband's name in sworn vengeance, Linda screamed Wright's name, too, but mostly to conjure him up, to bring him back where he belonged. After many hours of hard labor and escalating regret, she was taken to the delivery room, where a healthy eight-and-a-half-pound baby girl was born, like everyone, in unfair proportions of agony and joy.

Robin called Manny at work to tell him, and he rushed right over to the hospital. When he asked why she hadn't called him much earlier, at home, as she was supposed to, she said that she'd tried, but his line was busy. "In the middle of the *night*?" he said, but Robin merely shrugged.

Soon they were summoned together to the nursery window to see the baby. A nurse scooped her from one of the bassinets, unwound her receiving blanket, and held her up for their inspection. Her eyes were open, all inky iris, and she was frowning, as if she was inspecting them, too, and found them lacking. She was as long and garishly pink as a skinned rabbit Robin had once seen in a butcher-shop window, and her head was bald and bullet-shaped.

But when Manny said, "Look at that, she's the spitting image of you, Robin," she felt an uncommon surge of happiness.

That night Robin slept at Vicki's apartment, as prearranged, although she wanted to stay home alone. "It's nice and peaceful there for a change, and I don't need a babysitter," she'd told Linda when she and Manny were allowed, at last, into her semi-private room. But Linda, lying there pale and spent from her labor, insisted that she go to Vicki's, and Manny squeezed Robin's arm as a signal not to argue about it. "I have to go back to the store tonight, but I'll buy you a great dinner first," he said. "Taco Bell, Pizza Hut, the Colonel—you name it—price is no object."

They ended up at a small Chinese restaurant near the hospital, where Robin discovered that Manny liked exactly the same things she did: chicken chow mein, egg roll, barbecued spareribs, pork fried rice. It was easy to share dishes with him, which was impossible to do with Linda, who always scanned the menu for way-out items like thousand-year-old eggs and bird's-nest soup. "If we don't try new things," she'd say, "how can we tell that we don't like them?" Robin could tell by the very sound of them, and was invariably proven right by the sight and smell. Linda usually wound up picking around the edges of those repulsive dishes and eating all of Robin's leftovers, but she'd insist it had been worth taking the risk, that life was an endless series of exciting and instructive risks. That really killed Robin, who'd seen Linda sniff her glass of milk suspiciously before drinking it, and watched her drive across the country like a nervous snail, honking at every intersection, and using her turn signals even when there wasn't another car in sight. Robin couldn't wait to drive, to show Linda what risk-taking was all about. That was the other great thing about California, besides the climate and the beaches—you could get your learner's permit here at fifteen, two whole years earlier than you could back in Jersey. Robin had only six more months to go. Now she let a sparerib droop from her greasy fingers as she thought dreamily again about the baby, how it had seemed to look back at her in solemn recognition through the nursery window.

Manny said, "I remember when Deanna, my first girl, was born. She had this little capelet of brownish fur around her shoulders, like a baby bat."

"Get out," Robin said. "She did not."

"No, she really did. And it's not that uncommon, they said. It's called lanugo hair, and it's all supposed to fall out way before the baby starts dating. But, boy, I was worried stiff. I kept thinking, what if it *doesn't*? This poor kid's going to need piano lessons."

"And dresses with sleeves," Robin said.

"Yeah, that, too. But it did fall out a few weeks later, right on schedule. Sort of like moulting? And like my hair," he added cheerfully, patting himself on the head.

It occurred to Robin that she was deprived forever of any similarly interesting recollections about her own birth. Once, long ago, when she'd asked her father to tell her about the day she was born, he only mentioned the weather, that it was the hottest July 7 since 1898 or something. She supposed that all memories of that event were connected to her mother, and were much too painful for him to recall. Even most of their early family pictures were badly faded or had been lost somehow. When she was little, she was positive she remembered being born, the sound of cheering in the delivery room as she skidded out, like the roar of the crowd at a baseball game when someone slides safely home; the hot, brilliant lights on her naked skin and unused eyes. And her mother's triumphant, tender, smiling pleasure. But as time went on, she realized she'd made it all up. Maybe her mother had wanted a boy instead, or a different girl, one who was beautiful and good enough to deserve her love, and to keep her home.

Linda had decided to call the baby Phoebe Ann, which had been her own mother's name. It was something Robin thought only Jewish people did, naming their babies after somebody dead. "Maybe so," Linda said, "but it really seems like the right thing to do, doesn't it? I mean, then something of the dead person lives on after them."

Robin wondered, if it had been a boy, whether Linda would have called him Wright. It wasn't a good name for a girl, of course. In fact, it wasn't such a great name for a boy, either. Once, Robin's father told her that when he was a kid and gave the wrong answer to a math problem in school, a mean kid yelled out, "Wright is wrong again!" Everybody laughed, including the teacher, and it became a regular schoolyard chant after that. Robin would have killed that kid if he'd done something like that to her, but her father had done the biblical thing, turned the other cheek. Not because he was wimpy or even that religious, Robin was certain, but because his own parents had been very strict, meaner than that mean kid, and probably would have beaten the crap out of him for fighting, even in self-defense.

Another time, when she'd gotten a good report card (in first or second grade, when she still got good report cards), her father said, proudly, "You sure didn't get your brains from me." He didn't go any further than that, though, didn't say who she *had* gotten her brains from. He seemed to go out of his way never to mention her mother.

Phoebe Ann. The name was intriguingly new on Robin's tongue when she tried it out in a whisper in Vicki's bathroom that night. Manny had told her over their pineapple chunks and fortune cookies that there was a bird called a phoebe, which Robin thought was the most amazing coincidence. She and the baby both had bird names! Until then, she'd been disappointed that Linda hadn't chosen something more current and popular, Tiffany, or Ashley, or Brittany, or Samantha, which half the girls in school seemed to be called, or something exotically lovely, like the names of some of the black girls—Lateesha, Lawanda, Vondella—that rolled right out of your mouth like music.

Vicki's bed was one of those monster jobs, as big as the bed Robin and Linda had shared in their Paradise apartment, so Robin had plenty of room to stretch out without having to get too close. Vicki did some sit-ups, grunting horribly from the floor, a little like the noises Linda had made in the taxi that morning. Then, as she climbed into bed and leaned over to shut off her lamp, she said, "Remember, no snoring, no kicking, and anything I say in my sleep is strictly confidential."

Robin was completely bushed from the excitement and from being awake all those hours—she'd only taken a couple of catnaps in the hospital waiting room—but she couldn't fall asleep right away. The room was too dark, for one thing. She often fell asleep with the light on at home, something she would never admit. And her head was overflowing with images and thoughts: Linda on the toilet seat with the baby still trapped inside her, and the way she'd looked in the taxi, as if she was the one who was trapped. The taxi's headlights cutting an illuminated path through the dark streets. The good news and the bad news. A cheering crowd. The baby being held up by the masked nurse, and what Manny had said about how they looked alike. Phoebe Ann, little bird. Sister. The boy who had teased her father. The words Wright and wrong, over and over again until neither of them made any sense. Sitting next to Manny in his car and then in the restaurant. The deep soothing tones of his voice, the agreeable scrape of his cheek against her forehead when he hugged her good night. The tiny strip of paper in her fortune cookie that said, "Your file will soon be changed." Manny saying it was a typo, that it was supposed to be her *life* that would change, and wasn't that great? Big deal, whose life *didn't* change? The slant of moonlight in the room, and Vicki's even breathing as she slept, like the comforting sounds of a reliable machine. And then, as Robin finally let go of everything and dozed off, too, the sensation of flying toward sleep, of gliding— dipping one white feathered wing and then the other—so that her passage was perfectly smooth, almost effortless, and her landing guaranteed to be safe.

Across town, in the hospital, Linda slept, too, the serious, hard-earned sleep of new mothers. Down the hall, in the nursery, Phoebe Ann sucked her fist under the merciless lights and dreamed of floating in darkness. And at the Liquor Barn, as he was getting ready to close up for the night, Manny heard the jangle of the sleigh bells on the door, and turned and said, "How are you tonight, my friend?" and took a bullet through his left eye.

6

The Scene of the Crime

Sometimes Linda looked into the baby's indelible eyes and asked, "Who are you, really?" She didn't expect an answer, of course, but she was truly mystified by this sudden, intimate connection to a stranger. For some reason, her connection to Robin was clearer, if not nearly as satisfying. Robin still considered her the wicked stepmother—minus the crucial, interesting wickedness—which deeply wounded Linda's feelings. She was doing the best she could under the circumstances. And hadn't she saved that ungrateful girl from a worse fate, from some institution filled with other angry, abandoned teenagers? But Robin's disdain seemed to bear out Linda's own darkest fear about herself, that she was a seriously flawed—no, worse!—an unfinished person, someone not adequately prepared to live in the world. Yet how could *anyone* be prepared for so many terrible surprises?

Robin had actually seemed to be softening recently, smiling more often, and helping a little around the apartment. One day, a few weeks before the baby was born, she even brought two friends home from school with her. They were sisters, tall and slender black girls named Lucy and Carmel Thompson. Linda had been resting, but she got up to greet them, and she tried to draw them into conversation. Did they live nearby? Were they all in the same grade? Would they care for a snack? The sisters answered politely—"Yes, ma'am, no, ma'am, thank you, ma'am"—but they kept exchanging furtive, amused glances with Robin, and soon they all escaped into the bathroom, where they slammed the door and locked themselves in. Linda stood outside and listened hard for a while, but all she heard for her efforts was the flushing toilet and an occasional scream of laughter. When they finally emerged, reeking of sweet smoke and Linda's White Shoulders, they began whispering to one another, just out of earshot. Linda hadn't experienced such social loneliness since her own adolescence. What if you never outgrew it? The important thing, she kept reminding herself, was that Robin seemed much happier and more relaxed.

But she'd gone back to being her old miserable self again after Manny's death, which, like Wright's, she simply refused to discuss. Once more, Linda had to break the bad news to her, a task she dreaded but couldn't let anyone else assume. She decided to take her cue from Rosalia and Troy, who'd come to the hospital to tell her about Manny the morning after he was killed. She would never forget their faces, the way their eyes had skittered around the room before they looked directly into hers. "I have to tell you something very bad, Linda," Rosalia said. "Manny is gone. In a shooting, a robbery at the store."

Linda gasped, then lay very still, but Troy began sobbing as he related his side of the story. As Linda knew, either he or his cousin William would hang around the store until closing time to help Manny lock up. But that night there had been a family party, an aunt and uncle's silver wedding anniversary, and Manny told them both to take off early and have a good time. Rosalia was there when the guy came in, Troy said, but she was in the back, in the lavatory. Otherwise, she would have been killed, too. He cried even harder after he said that, as if he'd just envisioned that narrowly escaped double tragedy.

Rosalia had worked for Manny for twelve years, and had loved him, she said, "just like mi familia," but her voice was calm and she kept patting Troy's hand, and Linda's, as she spoke. "I was in the bathroom," she said, "doing my business, but I heard the bells. You know how loud they are. It was past ten already, but Manny hadn't put down the gate and locked the door yet, or even turned the sign around. Then I heard him say something—you know, 'How are you tonight, my friend,' and all that. And then, madre de Dios, I heard this bang."

Linda was sobbing along with Troy by now. Rosalia continued: "And I knew right away—no backfire, no box falling off a shelf. I was sitting there, excuse me, with my underwear down, but I stood right up, maybe too fast, and then I guess I must have passed out. When I came to, the guy was already gone. Both cash drawers were open and empty, and Manny was lying there. I took my compact and held the mirror to his mouth, just praying, praying, and then I breathed into him, but it was only my craziness, it was already too late."

When Linda was able to compose herself, she asked them not to say anything to Robin until she had a chance to talk to her, and they promised they wouldn't. She extracted the same promise from Vicki when she called that afternoon. If there was anything about the holdup in the newspaper, Linda was pretty sure Robin wouldn't see it; she hardly ever read anything but the comics, the advice columns, and her daily horoscope. She'd phoned in Phoebe's very first reading before breakfast: Capricorns, watch out for ambitious business associates, and avoid unnecessary travel.

Linda and the baby were discharged from the hospital two days later. Vicki had brought Robin to visit the night before, and when the girl remarked on Linda's dismal face and puffy, red eyes, Linda said, "Oh, I'm just feeling kind of blue," and Vicki added, with a dismissive wave, "Post-partum depression, it happens all the time. She'll be fine as soon as everything snaps back into place."

Robin had made a welcome-home sign for Linda and Phoebe, using Magic Markers and a magazine photograph of a mother and baby, and she'd readied the crib in Linda's room with a fitted sheet and the pink-and-blue bumper. Various stuffed animals were arranged in the corners of the bumper and a musical mobile was clamped to the crib's railing. When she came home from school that afternoon, Robin went right past Linda to the bedroom. "How you doing there, Feeble?" she asked, and she set the mobile spinning out of control over the sleeping baby.

Linda had trailed in after her. "It's Phoebe," she said automatically, reaching to still the mobile. And then she said, "Robin, honey, listen . . ."

Robin looked up sharply, the way she had just before Linda told her about Wright, as if she had an instinct for bad news. If it were possible, she grew even paler than usual. "What?" she asked, but her shoulders hunched against the anticipated blow of Linda's answer.

"It's about Manny . . ." Linda said. "There was an accident at the store the other night. I mean a holdup. He was shot. Oh, Robin, it's awful . . ."

"You mean he's dead, don't you?" Robin said, with a queer little smirk.

"Yes," Linda admitted, and she rummaged in her head for some way to moderate the dreadful, final fact of it. But what could she say? That he didn't suffer? It was what she'd told Robin about her father, whose hospital bedside Linda happened to be attending at the moment of his death. It seemed like the truth when she said it—Wright had looked a lot more amazed than agonized. But she didn't know that for certain about Manny. And what else could she say? He's at peace now? Manny was one of the most peaceful people she'd ever known. And death had never seemed that peaceful to Linda, anyway. She imagined it, when she could bear to, as a permanently restless state, a desperate, thwarted yearning to come back. How could anybody ever be reconciled to all their unfinished business among the living? "Robin," she said, which was the best she could come up with, but Robin had already left the room and disappeared behind the locked bathroom door.

Manny's three daughters came from three different cities, in the East and the Midwest, for his funeral. Under other circumstances it would have taken place much sooner—that was Jewish law—but with the scattered daughters and the police and coroner's work, he was dead almost a week before they buried him. Linda hoped Robin would go to the graveside services with her, that something might be said there that would ease their hearts and minds. But when Linda approached her about it the night before the funeral, Robin said, "No way, I've got school tomorrow." You'd think she was a dedicated student, that Linda hadn't already received a few notices from the attendance office at Northside High about her repeated cuts and lateness.

Linda took the baby with her to the cemetery, carrying her from the parking lot in her Snugli. It was too soon for them to be apart, even for a few hours, and she derived a sense of consolation simply from holding her, from having something to do with her hands besides wring them. She had not been in a cemetery since the week before she left New Jersey, when she'd made a solo trip to Pennsylvania to visit her parents' graves. After all, California was so far away. There was a thick, spiny weed in the sparse grass on her father's side of the family plot, and she knelt to pull it out, but it wouldn't budge. She pulled harder, scratching her hand on the spines, and it still wouldn't come. She had the unsettling idea that he was holding on to it from the other side, the way he used to hold on to something she wanted, a toy or a piece of candy. Did people only become more themselves after they were dead?

Manny's family had chosen a plain pine coffin, and when Linda got to the grave site, the daughters and their husbands were surrounding it like a human fence. She recognized them from the photographs Manny had shown her. A few other mourners—men wearing hats and women in dark dresses—listed toward one another, the way some of the older tombstones around them did. Linda stood to one side, near Troy and William and Rosalia, while the rabbi spoke briefly about Manny in what seemed like pretty general, impersonal terms. He said that he'd been a loving father and a respected businessman, cut down by senseless violence in the prime of his life. He urged the bereaved to put violence out of their own hearts and find peace there instead, as Emanuel Green had. Then he said some prayers, first in Hebrew and then in English, and finally he recited the Twenty-third Psalm. When he got to the part about the valley of the shadow of death, Linda noticed her own elongated, motionless shadow lying across the grass. It was like a negative image of the chalked figure the police had left on the floor of the Liquor Barn. She had gone there a couple of days ago, in the middle of business hours, to see for herself if Manny wasn't really still alive, if the whole thing wasn't some kind of horrible hallucination or hoax. The store was gated and padlocked, and there was a sign on the door that said: CRIME SCENE. DO NOT ENTER. L.A.P.D. She shaded her eyes and looked through the grillwork into the window. All the lights were on, as they always were, but there wasn't a living soul inside. Only that crude outline of Manny on the floor between the cash registers, to show where he'd fallen.

At the cemetery, Linda shifted her feet a little just to see her own shadow move. As the Psalm ended, one of the daughters glanced over her shoulder at Linda, and then she poked her nearest sister, who looked back for an instant, too. Only the shortest daughter, whose face was hidden in a wad of Kleenex, seemed entirely absorbed by her grief.

The very last thing the rabbi said was that the family would be receiving visitors at the home of the deceased, immediately following the interment. The coffin was lowered, in slow, swaying motions, by four men manipulating two heavy straps, and then everyone stepped up to the grave, one at a time, and threw a shovelful of dirt into it. When it was Linda's turn, she stood clutching the baby and the shovel with its moist clump of earth, and studied the double gray-marble monument. The left side was engraved with Manny's wife's name, Esther, the words

"Beloved Wife and Mother," and the span of her years. The right side was blank. Linda hadn't meant to, but she looked down into the hole as she tossed the dirt, and suffered a moment of vertigo. Then she found herself thinking of the space between Manny and Esther as the narrow aisle between twin beds. If she had married him, too, would they have lain three abreast someday? But that was idiotic; the family would have been scandalized by such a notion, and it was a Jewish cemetery, anyway—they probably wouldn't even have let her in. She felt a sharp pang of exclusion as she passed the shovel to the next mourner and started walking down the path toward her car.

Twenty minutes later, she drove up to Manny's house and saw a pitcher of water on the front steps, and everyone rinsing their hands before going inside. Linda hesitated at the steps—was she about to wash her hands of Manny forever? The short daughter came up behind her and touched her arm. "It's all right," she said. "You don't have to. It's only a custom."

There was a lavish buffet waiting in the dining room, and the family and friends quickly surrounded it, as they had surrounded the grave. Linda went down the hallway to use the bathroom, stopping briefly at Manny's closed bedroom door. She almost expected to see another sign like the one on the door of the Liquor Barn. CRIME SCENE. DO NOT ENTER. As if love was the criminal act that made you mortal. She thought again about his chalked ghost on the floor and imagined lying down on it, fitting herself into his body as he had fitted himself into hers.

On the way back to the living room, the baby woke up and began to fuss. Linda took her into the little den where Manny had done his paperwork for the store, and sat down on the love seat to nurse her. About fifteen minutes later, one of the daughters who'd turned to look at her during the funeral came into the room and said, "I hope you're not planning to tell us that's his child."

For a second or two, Linda was confused. "Pardon?" she said, and then, "You mean Manny . . . your father? No, no, of course not."

"Well, thank heaven for small miracles, at least," the daughter said. After a pause, she continued. "The family is selling the store, as you may have already guessed."

Linda hadn't guessed; she hadn't really thought about it. But she nodded her head anyway. The daughter bore only a superficial resemblance to Manny—the wiry hair and brown eyes—but she reminded Linda strongly of someone else, someone she couldn't quite place right then and there.

"So any arrangements he might have made with you are completely null and void," the daughter said. "But we've decided to give you two weeks' severance pay."

Linda didn't say anything. For the first time since Manny's death, she faced its practical implications, not just her sorrow, and Robin's. She was out of a job. The baby began to squirm and mewl and Linda hoisted her to her shoulder for a burp. "There, there," she murmured, as she patted the baby's back, not sure who she was trying to comfort. When she looked up again, the daughter was gone. They hadn't even introduced themselves.

Linda put the baby down next to her on the love seat and changed her diaper. "There, there," she said again, although the baby seemed contented enough, was almost asleep again. Linda began to put her back into the Snugli, eager to get out of there, to just go home. Then she remembered: Marlene! The rental agent at Paradise—*that's* who the daughter reminded her of! Poor Manny, she thought. Poor me.

As she stood up to go, another daughter came to the doorway, the short one who had been so bereft at the cemetery, and who'd touched Linda's arm on the front steps of the house. "I'm Leslie," she said, "the middle one. And you must be Linda."

"Oh, I am!" Linda said, like an amnesiac who'd suddenly remembered her identity. She held out her hand and Leslie shook it.

"Dad called and told me all about you," Leslie said, and she smiled, remembering. "He was so excited, like some high-school kid."

"He was really so . . . so *nice*," Linda said, thinking she was as inadequate as the rabbi had been in evoking Manny's special qualities. And the rabbi, she suspected, had probably never met him.

"He was, wasn't he?" Leslie said. "I just wanted to say thank you, you know, for making him so happy." Her eyes filled with tears, and the two women embraced, with the baby squeezed between them.

Robin did go to school the morning of Manny's funeral. She had to, because she knew that Linda was watching the bus stop from the kitchen window. But she sneaked out again right after homeroom and hitched a ride practically all the way home with some guy in a pickup. Linda would have a cow if she knew. She was always warning her about hitchhiking, about all these "disturbed men who prey on young girls like you." Linda knew every horror story that ever happened, and a few that probably hadn't, about girls who were never seen or heard from again or were found in too many pieces to count. But Robin wouldn't get into a vehicle with a weirdo; she had built-in radar for guys like that.

Funerals were such a sick joke, she thought, as she let herself into the empty apartment. People saying all those great things about somebody they probably hated like poison, who couldn't hear them anyway. When Robin died, they could just stand her up in a dumpster somewhere, for all she cared. What a neat surprise for some creep scrounging around in there! The only reason she did consider—for about a second—going to Manny's funeral was to get a look at his daughter, the one born with all that fur on her shoulders, just to see if it ever grew back.

There was a message blinking on the answering machine. It was for Linda, from the attendance officer at the high school, asking her to call him as soon as possible to arrange an appointment. Robin rewound the tape, erasing the message. Then she wandered into the kitchen and opened the refrigerator; there wasn't anything good to eat, just healthy stuff like yogurt and fruit. She wasn't hungry, exactly, but she poked around in there for a few more minutes before she closed the door. She wandered into Linda's room next and leaned over the empty crib. A sweet baby perfume rose up from the sheet. As she inhaled it, Robin wound up the musical mobile. The fuzzy ducks and rabbits went around in circles, while the lullaby repeated itself over and over again, even after Robin left the room and went down the hallway to her own, smaller bedroom. There she put a Guns N' Roses tape on the stereo, flopped onto the bed with her arms under her head, and stared up at the ceiling. She was bored to death, that was the problem. She hated the morning shows on TV, and there was nothing else to do.

Since Linda quit work, near the end of her pregnancy, Robin hardly ever had the place to herself like this. Now she wished she had a joint or something, so she could enjoy being alone for once. She jumped off the bed and opened her closet. Not really expecting to find anything, she went through the pockets of a few pairs of jeans that were tangled together on the floor. That's when she discovered the bottle of champagne. "Oh," she said, and she could feel her heart beating.

There was gold foil covering the top of the bottle, and after she peeled it off, using her teeth and a pair of scissors, she sat down on the edge of the bed, with the bottle clamped between her knees, and contemplated the wire cage surrounding the cork. It took her only a couple of seconds to figure out how to untwist the wire, and a few more seconds to actually do it. As soon as the cage was released, the cork shot up with a bang that made her scream and then laugh, while the warm foam spilled over onto her hands and down her legs. She licked some of it off her fingers and knees before she lifted the bottle to her mouth and took a drink. It tasted like beer a little, and also something like the pale, bubbly ginger ale her father always gave her after she threw up.

Linda used to sing this prehistoric song that started "I get no kick from champagne," and Robin wondered if that might be true of her, too. She took another, longer drink after shaking the bottle vigorously with her thumb pressed over the top, to liven up the foam again. She liked the way it stung her tongue and palate as it went down. Axl Rose was still going strong, but Robin was humming that champagne song to herself as she lifted the bottle to her mouth again, and again. When Manny brought it over that night, he said they would open it in January and drink to the little fishie. Well, it was January, wasn't it, and Phoebe was here, even if he wasn't.

She wondered if any of his daughters were going to name one of their kids after him. Robin hadn't been named for anybody, dead *or* alive. It was just a name her mother and father had liked. She was never going to have any children herself, but if she ever did, she wouldn't call them anything some retardo could turn into "Robin Redbreast," which had happened to her in the sixth grade. She held the bottle up and saw with surprise that it was almost half gone. Phoebe Ann, she thought, and then she had this amazing flash, the kind of thing other people always said happened to them when they were stoned, but had never happened to her. The name "Ann" was inside the name "Manny"! Wait until she told Linda—she'd probably croak, too. "Fishie," she said aloud, in a sort of toast, before she lifted the bottle again.

Linda let herself into the house. "Robin?" she called. "Yoo-hoo, we're home!" She went down the hallway with the baby in her arms and knocked on Robin's bedroom door, behind which she heard the stereo blasting away. "Anybody in there?" she shouted, knocking harder. "Hello?" Asleep, no doubt, Linda decided, or finally deaf from all that noise. Why didn't she ever listen to music that was mellow and melodic, something to soften her outlook? Something by Kenny Loggins, for instance, or Elton John, Linda's own favorite when she was a teen. She took the baby back to their room, and hummed "Your Song," sadly, under her breath, while she undressed her and gave her a sponge bath. Robin hadn't made an appearance yet, so Linda put Phoebe in her crib and went down the hall and knocked on her door again, still competing with that so-called music. When there was no answer, she announced, "Ready or not, here I come!" and opened the door. The blinds were shut, as usual—it was always twilight in Robin's room—and Linda saw in the shadows that things were in their normal disarray. It stank in there, but not of pot. It smelled more like one of Lucky's rest rooms after a busy Saturday night, of stale alcohol and vomit. Once or twice a few months ago she'd been sure she detected beer on Robin's breath, although Robin vehemently denied it, swore it was only cough medicine, or Linda's wild imagination. She hoped this wasn't another occasion for a serious lecture; she was much too tired and heavyhearted for that right now, and she had to feed the baby pretty soon, besides.

Robin was out like a light on the bed, although it took Linda a moment to locate her in the snarl of bedding. Oh, it was *definitely* beer this time! How could anyone sell it to a minor? Linda punched the power button on the stereo, and in the abrupt silence she said sternly, "Wake up, miss, I want to talk to you!" There was only a hoarse answering groan from the bed.

Linda went to the window and yanked up the venetian blind, and sunlight crashed into the room. More groans from the bed. Linda was about to really lose her temper when she saw the cork on the floor, next to the dresser, and a twist of silver wire a few feet away. The bottle, she discovered, had rolled under the bed. Linda fetched it out and then knelt there, holding it tightly with both of her hands. Oh, God.

Robin tried to sit up, floundered, and fell back again. "Ohhh," she moaned, "I'm sick . . ."

"I'll bet you are," Linda said, and she put the bottle down and stroked the girl's damp hair back from her brow. Her hand might have been a sledgehammer, given the violent reaction that gentle gesture evoked. Robin cried, "No! Don't!" and wrenched herself away, out of reach.

Linda got up and went back down the hallway to the bathroom, where she filled a basin with warm water and dropped her own brand-new pink bath sponge into it. With a towel draped over one arm, she carried the basin to Robin's room. There she knelt by the bed again and slowly, carefully ran the warm, wet sponge over Robin's face and neck and arms. The same way she had bathed Phoebe a little while ago. "Robin?" she whispered. "We're not going to talk about this today. Someday we'll have to, but not right now, okay?"

Robin didn't answer, but she gave her body over limply to Linda's ministrations.

"Do you feel like talking about anything else?" Linda asked. "About something that's on your mind?"

After a long pause, Robin said, "No," in a small voice.

"Okay, then," Linda told her. "You just lie there and rest, and I'll go into the kitchen and get you a nice cold, refreshing glass of ginger ale."

Robin looked up at her with stricken eyes. *Now* what have I said, Linda wondered.

7

Two Kinds of Men

Then it rained, and rained. Not the standard seasonal showers Linda remembered from Newark, which might be broken by spells of simple cloudiness, or even glimmers of sunlight, but rain of such intensity and duration she began to believe it was divine punishment, and that it might never stop. What am I doing here? she'd think. And when the baby cried incessantly at night, or Robin whined and complained, she would ask herself, Who are these people, and what do they want from me? It wasn't like that happy rhetorical question she used to ask when she looked into the baby's fathomless new eyes. Now she felt cranky and bewildered, and she needed some real answers.

To make matters worse, Robin seemed to hold Linda accountable for the weather. "I thought this was the land of *sunshine*," she'd say accusingly, or "*You* said it was going to let up!"

Linda didn't know why, but she felt guilty, and unable to resist the urge to offer further false hope. "Maybe it will be nice tomorrow," she told Robin during breakfast one Saturday morning, raising her voice over the battering noise of the rain. "And don't forget, all that gorgeous greenery out there needs a drink once in a while."

"Yeah, right," Robin said, staring gloomily through the window. "So why don't they just pour the whole stupid Pacific Ocean on it?"

There was no talking to her, really, about anything. The only time Robin displayed normal human responses was when she was with the baby. They looked so much alike, with their pale hair, invisible eyebrows, and opalescent skin, they seemed to be the true mother and child, and brown-haired Linda merely a caretaker, of another, lesser species. Robin's affinity for Phoebe was what Manny would have called her saving grace.

But Linda, too, was saved by the baby. When she lay under the shelter of the double-wedding-ring quilt, nursing Phoebe, her various tensions gradually unwound until she fell into a mindless state of rapture. She didn't bother herself then about who any of them were, or why they were all here, on this planet, in Los Angeles, in the same household. Riddles about existence and more urgent concerns about poverty and loneliness didn't exactly disappear, but they receded into the fuzzy distance as she and the baby became one and the same again, milk and pulse and flesh and spirit.

Linda had been officially out of work for two weeks now—the two long weeks of the deluge, and the two short weeks of her severance pay from the Liquor Barn. She'd glanced through the want ads without applying for anything, and she had investigated a few day-care centers without making any decisions about them, either. She was frightened of ending up on welfare, or even out on the street, but she couldn't seem to make a definite move. It was as if she needed someone to snap their fingers in her face and say, "Wake up! *Do* something!" Her friends tried to perk her up. Rosalia, who had taken a part-time job in a plastics factory, dealt privately with her own grief about Manny, and became a surrogate of Linda's mother, saying things like "Life goes on," and "You have to think of the children." Vicki tried to make her feel better by reading worse stories aloud from the newspaper, about the victims of a terrorist's bomb in Peru and a tidal wave in Japan. Of course, that only made Linda feel worse, but she appreciated Vicki's good intentions. Robin didn't even attempt to lift the dreary mood of their household. One morning, Linda found that the girl had left a gallon of milk out on the counter all night, where it had soured. "Do you think we have money to throw away, Robin?" she said. "You are totally irresponsible!"

Robin narrowed her eyes and said, "Oh, yeah? Well, you're the kiss of death."

Robin had called her plenty of other names in the short time they'd known one another—wimp, jerk, bitch, and asshole were only a few that came to mind—but nothing she'd ever said had given Linda such an acute sense of horror and recognition. "What do you mean by that?" she demanded when she could find her voice, and Robin hadn't backed down the way she usually did. Instead, she stood her ground and said, through a cruelly curling mouth, "Everybody you love dies on you, don't they?"

"That's not true!" Linda cried.

"Oh, no?" Robin said. "What about my father, huh? What about Manny?"

"But I loved them!" Linda exclaimed, and at Robin's instant, twisted smile, "I mean, I never did anything to hurt them. They just died, that's all! It was just very bad luck!"

"Yeah, *right*," Robin said.

Linda sighed. Maybe someone like Robin, whose father had been taken against his will, and whose mother had abandoned her by heartless choice, could never believe in anything as random as luck. Why did Linda feel so stricken with guilt, though? "I love you and Phoebe, too," she persisted, "and you're not going anywhere." But Robin only shrank back at those words. And Linda shrank back into her shell.

But then, yesterday, for no apparent reason, she started to come back to herself. Right after breakfast, she prepared a complicated casserole for dinner, and in the afternoon she called to answer a want ad, for a dental assistant. The remarkable thing was that the ad said, "Will train, no experience necessary." Not only that, the dentist, who answered his phone himself, sounded so friendly, and he agreed to interview her the very next morning, on a Saturday, when the office was officially closed. That meant that Robin could babysit while she was gone. And it meant that Linda was going to get out of the house by herself for a couple of hours. Even the rain seemed less oppressive as she finished breakfast and got dressed. She'd been wearing blue jeans around the apartment, with one of several milk-stained T-shirts, and she either went barefoot or wore a pair of floppy flowered house slippers. Now she put stockings on, and the one wool skirt that still fit, and she eased her feet into the silky leather of her good black pumps. After peering at herself critically in the mirror, she pulled her ponytail from its rubber band and brushed her hair into submission and shine.

She gave Robin instructions about defrosting the packets of expressed breast milk in the freezer, and about checking the baby from time to time while she slept. "When you change her diaper, try not to let the tape stick to her skin, Robin, okay?" Linda said. "And when you put her back down, see that she isn't lying on her face."

"Yeah, yeah," Robin said, wearily. "Just go, already, will you?"

Then Linda was out of there, running under the drumming umbrella through the flooded street to her car. It had been giving her all sorts of trouble lately, stalling and backfiring, scaring her half to death. And now the wires had to be soaked. But the engine turned over smoothly after only the second or third try, which Linda took as a good omen for the day, maybe for her entire future. She would get the job, the rain would stop, their lives would start to turn around.

The dentist's name was Dr. Gordon Alan Leonard. He had three first names! Linda found that sort of elegant, like the names of royalty. The four-story building in which he had his office didn't seem very regal, though; it was pretty seedy, in fact. The whole area, at the outer edge of Culver City, looked deserted and run-down. Maybe Dr. Leonard was young and just starting out, or was one of those humanitarians who treated poor people for low fees, and had to keep his expenses low, too. She scanned the lobby directory, which was arranged by floor number, for his three names, and noticed that no other professional people were listed. A palm reader, an importer of Indian spices, and a pet-food supplier shared the first floor. The lobby smelled exotically of the spices. There was a novelty distributor and a domestic employment agency, called Maid to Order, on the second floor. For the third floor, the directory said, "Space available, call Donna." Dr. Leonard was listed as being in room 401, right before the Movie Institute of Health and Beauty, in 402.

Linda wiped her wet shoes with a Kleenex and gave herself a last-minute inspection in the smudged glass of the directory before she rang the bell for the elevator. The building was very quiet; she could hear the elevator cage descending slowly on its creaking chains. Maybe nobody else came in on Saturdays, either. It was so nice of Dr. Leonard to accommodate her this way. As she rode up, she remembered her interview with Manny, the two of them sitting on the wine cases, how he had encouraged her to talk about herself, and then hired her on the spot.

There were no signs of life behind the frosted door of the Movie Institute, but a light was on behind the door of 401. Linda didn't see an umbrella stand, so she stood her dripping umbrella discreetly against the wall next to the door. Then she hesitated; should she knock first or just go right in? She decided to play it safe and do both, tapping lightly on the door and then opening it before anyone could answer. She found herself in a tiny waiting room, with three shabby leatherette chairs and a table with a few magazines scattered on it. No paintings or prints on the walls. No canned music, either, which was certainly a relief. The inner door, to what had to be the dental office, was shut. Linda wondered if Dr. Leonard had heard her come in, or if she was supposed to knock on that door, too. She put her ear against it and thought she heard the murmur of voices. She hoped no one had beaten her to the punch for the job, but maybe it was just a patient with an emergency. Linda sat down on the nearest chair and picked up a magazine. She glanced at her watch; she was ten minutes early, despite the rain. If nobody came out in five minutes or so, she would knock then, making a good impression by being on time, without seeming overanxious.

The magazine was a year-old copy of *People*, in a plastic binder marked "American Airlines." A soap-opera star featured in an article had actually died suddenly since then, in real life. They'd had to kill him off on the show, too, Linda remembered, and now it felt eerie to read about his career plans, and look at pictures of him smiling and lounging near his pool, and sharing a slice of pizza with his wife. It was as if she could still warn him that he would have a heart attack soon if he didn't get some exercise and watch his diet, the way Robin used to warn his onscreen character that his girlfriend was double-crossing him. Linda was almost at the end of the article when she heard footsteps that came closer and closer until they stopped and the inner door opened. A disheveled-looking woman about her own age came out and shut the door quickly behind her. After giving Linda the once-over, she adjusted her wrinkled skirt and finger-combed her hair. Linda was about to say something sympathetic about toothaches, when the woman gave her a bitter little smile. "Good luck to *you*," she said sarcastically, and went out the door. Another job applicant, after all, and obviously a disappointed one. When it was too late, Linda wished that she had said, "If you really wanted the job, you should have remembered that good grooming counts."

The inner door opened again, and there was Dr. Leonard, at last. He wasn't the young, clear-eyed do-gooder Linda had hoped to see. He was at least sixty, wore half glasses, and was kind of portly in his white jacket. But he looked both pleasant and serious, like those fatherly dentists in TV commercials who sit on the edge of their desks and push denture adhesive. "Ms. Reismann, I presume," he said in silvery tones that matched his hair.

"Yes. Hello," she answered, as she stood and shook hands with him. His grip was firm and encompassing. She thought of Manny again, of the unexpected kindness of older men.

"Shall we go in?" Dr. Leonard said, and he held the door open for her.

There was a single treatment room inside, and a small, adjacent consulting office. She started for the latter, but he took her elbow and guided her into the former. "Oh, but I'm here about the—" she began, but Dr. Leonard interrupted her. "I know, dear, I know," he said. "Now, why don't you have a seat and we can chat."

The only seat, except for a chrome stool on casters, which he had already appropriated, was the reclining examining chair. Linda perched sideways on it, facing him, with her purse held primly on her lap. It was awkwardly quiet, and she realized she missed the gurgling of the little chairside sink, which she was used to from a lifetime of dental visits. But of course this wasn't a regular dental visit. What *was* it, though? A little alarm was ringing remotely in her head.

Dr. Leonard scooted his stool closer to the chair, so that his knees almost touched hers, and shuffling through some papers he'd picked up somewhere, said, "Let's see now. You have no experience, am I right?"

"Yes," Linda said. "But I thought—"

Once more, he interrupted her. "Not necessary, not necessary. What counts around here is attitude. Attitude, and personality, and a willingness to learn. I assume you're willing, uh . . . Linda?"

"Well . . ." Linda said.

"Good. Very good," he said absently, and rubbed his hands together. Then he began staring at her so earnestly over the tops of his glasses she almost expected him to say something about her overbite. Instead, he put one hand on her shoulder and said, "Would you mind if I steal a little kiss?"

"What!" she cried, jumping up so abruptly her knees banged into his and he rolled back a few feet.

"Wait," he said, starting to rise. "Don't get the wrong idea."

"Too late, I already did!" she yelled, making for the door to the waiting room. As she ran through it and opened the outer door, he called sadly after her, "I would have taken care of that overbite!"

She didn't wait for the poky elevator but headed for the fire stairs, taking them two and three at a time, although she looked back and saw that he wasn't following her. She knew by the spicy smell that she was getting close to the lobby, and when she got there she walked right through it and out into the rain. She'd left her umbrella upstairs, of course. "Jerk! Idiot! Fool! Imbecile!" she pronounced as she ran toward her car, alternately addressing Dr. Leonard and herself.

She drove away so fast she'd gone two or three blocks before she noticed that she hadn't put her seat belt on. As she was buckling herself in at the next traffic signal, the Mustang's engine shuddered convulsively a few times and then died. There was a red warning light glowing on the dashboard, something to do with the battery or the alternator or something. Had it been lit before the engine conked out? She kept turning the key in the ignition and pumping her foot against the gas pedal, but all she heard was a series of clicks and the pummel of rain on the roof. "Oh, *great,*" she said.

She looked in the rearview mirror; there was no one behind her, no one anywhere on the wet, pockmarked, two-lane street. Now Linda knew why all those people in Mercedes and Jaguars who passed her on the freeway seemed so devoted to their car phones; she would have given anything for one at that moment. There weren't any public telephones as far as she could see, and she didn't know where she would even go if she abandoned the car and tried to look for help. "Help!" she said, just to hear the sound of her own voice again. Then she put on her distress blinkers and continued to sit there, still belted in.

The traffic light changed four or five times and only two cars went by, both of them heading in the other direction and neither of them even slowing down. Linda leaned on her horn when she saw the first one approaching, only to discover that was dead, too. She opened her window and received a faceful of rain as the second car sped past. She was thinking that she might be worse off if someone did stop, some maniac or mugger, when a sleek red Z pulled up alongside the Mustang. She opened her window again as the passenger window of the Z lowered, and she saw a dark-haired young man sitting behind the wheel, leaning toward her. "Hello, in there," he said. "What's the problem?"

My whole rotten life, she thought, but only said, "I'm not sure. It just conked out."

"Aha!" he exclaimed, as if she'd said something more specific, and he started to get out of his car. She rolled up her window and locked all her doors as he came toward her. He was both muscular and slender, with snakelike hips Linda couldn't help glancing at with a pinch of envy. He tapped on her window. "Can you release the hood?" he mouthed, and when she did, he pulled it up and disappeared behind it.

A Good Samaritan. Linda felt ashamed of herself. And she didn't think it was fair of her to be sitting so cozily dry inside the car while this stranger was out there getting drenched on her behalf. She knew she couldn't be of any real assistance—she didn't even have her umbrella to hold over the parts of him not protected by the raised hood—but she got out, anyway, and stood beside him, looking in at the mysterious clutter of machinery as he tinkered with it.

"I think it's the battery," he said, finally. "No lights, no horn or anything, right?"

She nodded.

"That's what I thought," he said, "and I don't have my jumper cables with me. It looks like you flooded it, too," he continued. "Were you pumping the gas to try and get it started?"

She had to admit that she had been.

"Then a boost wouldn't help much now, anyway. It's got to dry out, maybe overnight." Then he looked at her and said, "Hey, you're getting wet."

"You, too," she answered. His black silk shirt was plastered to his back and he was standing in a puddle.

"Come on then," he said, slamming the hood down so hard it made her heart leap. "Let's get inside." He guided her to the passenger side of his car, and when he opened the door she stood there hesitantly for several seconds, as both of them got wetter. All the warnings she'd ever given Robin about getting into cars with strangers came back to her now, especially her emphasis on the seductive charm of most psychopaths. But he really *did* seem okay, even if he was a little slickly handsome, with the black shirt and tight pants and those neck chains and everything. And what was the alternative—going back to Dr. Leonard and trading kisses for the use of his telephone? She ducked into the Z and sank deeply into the black leather seat. He slammed her door, causing another vault of her heart, and ran around to get in on the other side. There was a mixed fragrance in the car: the scents of new leather and carpeting, and something delectably musky she couldn't name. *Him*, she suddenly realized, and edged toward her door, with her fingertips poised on the handle.

"Nathan Diaz," he said, flashing a smile and shaking out his wet curls. Linda noticed a tiny gold hoop in his right earlobe, the flawless spiral of the ear itself. "And it's okay," he added. "I'm only wanted in a couple of states."

She blanched, and then blushed deeply. "Linda Reismann," she said. "Thanks a lot. Really."

"Wait, I haven't done anything yet," he said. "You got towing insurance?"

"No," Linda said. "And I really can't afford to have it towed right now."

"Maybe I could help you out," Nathan said.

"Oh, thanks, but I just couldn't," she told him.

"Then we're going to have to get your car over to the curb, and pray it's still here tomorrow, and in one piece. Come on, it's easy, I'll push and you'll steer. And then I'll drive you home. Don't worry, I'll bring you back here first thing tomorrow morning to pick it up."

On the way to Linda's, they exchanged stories. Nathan, it turned out, was a dancer, too. She should have known from the fluent way he moved. He used to be part of a Latino dance team, he told her—Delila and Diaz—doing club dates and private parties, but they'd split up about two years ago. He'd held a lot of different jobs since then, but now he was a dancercize instructor at a swanky women's health club called the Beverly Body, where, among other things, he led the salsa workout. "What about you?" he said.

She didn't tell him every last detail of her life the way she'd told Manny. This was different; they were only killing time, only making casual conversation. She mentioned the dancing, of course, and that she'd come from the East originally, and was out of work at the moment.

"You're kidding," Nathan said. "We're looking for someone at the Bod right now! Could you teach a few jazzercise classes? Of course you could," he answered for her.

"Listen," she said. "I haven't danced professionally in a long time."

"So what?" Nathan said. "The body doesn't forget anything."

That was true; her own body was a veritable warehouse of memory. Still, she tried not to get too excited. "I had a baby a few weeks ago," she told him, and for the first time he became still and thoughtful.

Then he said, "You're married?"

"No," Linda said. "Not anymore."

Nathan brightened immediately. "Then it's all settled. You'll come in this week for an interview and an audition. Do you have references? Hell, I'll give you a reference myself."

"But you don't even know me," she protested.

He turned and looked into her eyes. "Yes, I do," he said.

When the Z pulled up to her building, Linda saw Robin's face appear at the kitchen window and then quickly disappear. Linda knew she'd be grilled like a prime murder suspect before the day was over. She said a hasty, grateful goodbye to Nathan, who kissed her hand when she offered it for a friendly clasp, sending a charge all the way up her trembling arm, as if she'd stuck her fingers into the toaster. "See you tomorrow, Linda mujer," he said, and she hurried off.

"Who was *that*?" Robin demanded. "What took you so long? Where's the Mustang, anyway? And why can't we get a cool car like that, instead?"

She didn't ask a thing about the job interview, and Linda was both relieved and a little hurt. She had decided not to tell Robin any of the ugly details of her encounter with Dr. Leonard, just that the job wasn't right for her and vice versa. Linda didn't want her to get the idea that there were only two kinds of men in the world, the good ones who died young, and all the others, who lived to make women miserable. Even if it was true.

8

Lost in Space

Star *Trek*. That was the first thing Linda thought of when she stepped into the lobby of the Beverly Body Health Club and Spa. Maybe it was the ultra-modern architecture and all those pulsing computer screens around the circular desk. Or maybe it was the two silver-blond receptionists in their matching black spandex bodysuits, looking like the twin pilots of this black-and-white spaceship. If Linda ended up working here, would she have to bleach her hair, too, in order not to clash?

Nathan had said the club was "swanky," which didn't begin to prepare Linda for the gleam and glamour of it, the softly perfumed air, the piped-in semi-classical music, and the cooler whose double spigots dispensed Perrier and Evian water. And of course there was valet parking—she hoped her poor Mustang didn't die of disgrace among all the Bentleys and Rollses out there. This certainly wasn't anything like those fly-by-night health clubs she remembered from Newark, the ones that advertised specially reduced membership deals one week and closed their doors the next. Linda once lost four hundred dollars that way, had used the exercise equipment at Shapely Lady only twice before it disappeared from the face of New Jersey.

The receptionists at the Body weren't very receptive. They

were like those scary saleswomen in boutiques who can tell from a mile away that you don't belong, that you don't have the taste and money that entitle you to enter the premises. Nathan had said to ask for the general manager, Mr. Rembrandt. "Whom shall I say is calling?" one of the blondes inquired coolly. And after Linda told her, she said, "I'll see if he's in," in a tone that indicated it was highly unlikely, although Linda had mentioned that she had an appointment.

As she sat waiting tensely in a black suede armchair, leafing through one of the club's brochures, a few clients strolled through the lobby, carrying their squash racquets and sports bags. They were all impeccably groomed women in their thirties or forties, whose designer athletic shoes probably cost more than Linda's entire outfit. She had thought, when she left home, that she looked especially nice in her safari suit and patent-leather flats, that she had managed to effect a satisfying balance between sportiness and style. Now she wished she'd worn something flashier, or simpler, and that she had more hair and longer finger-nails. The brochure she held was printed on heavy creamy paper that made her hands look work-reddened and rough. "Welcome to California's acropolis of health and beauty," it said on the opening page. From the captioned photographs that followed, Linda saw that the club was equipped with continually updated, state-of-the-art body-building machinery, and that there was a swimming pool and three Jacuzzis on the glass-enclosed roof deck. Massage of every persuasion, from Swedish to shiatsu to reflexology, was available to members, and so were numerous kinds of therapeutic baths and wraps. And in Aphrodite's Place they could be coiffed, manicured, pedicured, and sloughed of their dead skin cells in a single Afternoon of Indulgence. According to the brochure, a medical doctor, assisted by a licensed nutritionist and a renowned Rumanian esthetician, supervised all of the club's treatments. Linda could see that mere floor exercise, although offered in great variety, was only a small part of the Body's agenda.

Mr. Rembrandt *was* in to her, as it turned out, and she was directed up a spiral staircase to his spacious office. That manic salesman, Dave, who'd signed Linda up for Shapely Lady, had delivered his pitch in a cluttered cubicle about the size of an airplane lavatory. She remembered how fast he'd talked as he explained the savings on a two- or three-year membership, and that he began to write up the contract before she'd agreed to anything.

Now, Linda thought, *she* was the salesperson, and she was going to have to sell herself quickly to this dapper, pin-striped executive, who was already glancing at his watch. The language of praise in the stained and frayed letter of recommendation from Simonetti of the Newark Fred Astaire's suddenly seemed cheap and insufficient, too much and too little at once. She opened and closed her purse a couple of times without withdrawing the letter. It might be better to just talk about her work experience, stressing her natural abilities and her willingness to learn.

But Mr. Rembrandt appeared more interested in extolling the virtues of the Beverly Body than in hearing about any of Linda's. What she had to understand, he said, was the *exclusivity* of the club. "We only accept women for membership who are recommended by current members," he said, "and *then* only after a careful screening process. We cater to the epitome of Beverly Hills society here, to some of the biggest names, people who are used to the best of everything. So you can imagine that they, *and we*, do not tolerate inferiority of any sort."

Linda, who had suffered from a sense of her own inferiority most of her life, had to remind herself that she knew how to dance and how to teach dancing, that they were the only two things she was genuinely *good* at. As if to prove that unspoken claim, and as if they had a life of their own, her feet tapped out a silent little tattoo on the black carpeting beneath them. "Oh, yes," she responded automatically to whatever Mr. Rembrandt was saying. "I understand. Of course." Robin, she was sure, would have been disgusted by her bootlicking, and would have told Rembrandt promptly and precisely where he could stick his lousy job. But in her outrage she probably would have forgotten the essential thing, that Linda desperately needed work. Besides, if she got this job, she would be doing what she loved to do best. But why hadn't Nathan warned her that the place was this . . . this *grand*, and intimidating? And where was he, anyway? He knew that she was coming here today—he had called her a couple of days ago to find out—and she'd expected him to show up and offer some last-minute coaching and encouragement.

Linda changed into her leotard and tights, and went to one of the exercise rooms to be auditioned. Two stone-faced staffers, clones of the receptionists, awaited her there, but Nathan was still nowhere in sight. As she did her warm-up stretches, her anxiety increased. Every time she encountered her own image in the mirrored walls, she glanced uneasily away, as if she kept running into someone she had hoped not to see. But as soon as her tape of the orchestrated highlights of *West Side Story* began playing, the music poured through her body like a lubricant, loosening all her joints and soothing the nervous muscle of her heart. She was as ready as she would ever be. For the past few days, ever since Nathan had driven her back to Culver City to pick up her car, she'd been putting together and practicing dance routines that would be easy and fun to follow, and would constitute a thorough workout. She knew the basics of aerobic and body-toning exercise, and she had added the joy of free movement to them. On Sunday, Nathan had given her some advice for the audition. "What they look for most is pep and drive, you know, like a cheerleader or a drill sergeant. You can't slow down for a second, and you've got to really *scream* out those commands. I swear, those women are all into domination." He offered to come over later that evening, or any evening before her interview, if she wanted to try something out on him. But she was afraid that Robin might get the wrong idea, or that Nathan himself might.

When the tape ended, she was flushed and sweaty and very

hoarse. The two staffers, who had been busily taking notes during her performance, like judges at the Olympics, merely told her to shower and change, and that Mr. Rembrandt would be speaking to her shortly. She rushed to get ready, not quite drying her hair, and stuffing her hopelessly tangled panty hose into her purse, and then he kept her waiting for at least twenty minutes. But when she was finally readmitted to his office, she was given the job, which had decent hours and fairly decent pay. She might have to work one or two evenings a week, but Robin would be able to babysit then. For the morning and afternoon sessions, Linda was going to have to find a day-care center for Phoebe. It was awful to think of leaving her with strangers when she was still so little, and it would be one more expense to juggle, but she had no other choice. Linda was in the parking lot, mulling all of this over and reclaiming the Mustang, when Nathan came running out of the back of the building, calling her name.

"Hi, I didn't think you were here," she said. "But guess what? I got the job! I start Monday!"

"Hey," he said, "congratulations! I told you you could do it. I knew you'd knock 'em dead."

His confidence in her was flattering and flustering at the same time. "Where were you before?" she asked, mostly to change the subject. "Did you have a class?"

"No, today's my day off. I came in just to see you. But I didn't want to make you nervous before the audition, I didn't want to jinx you."

"I can't get over this place," she said, looking back toward the club, and away from his penetrating gaze.

"Yeah," he said, and he whistled a few bars of the *Star Trek* theme.

"I had the same thought!" Linda exclaimed.

"But instead of being lost in space," Nathan said, "we're stranded on the Planet of the Rich and Famous." As Linda opened the door of the Mustang, he put his hand over hers and said, "Do you want to go somewhere for a cup of coffee?"

Linda didn't answer right away. The sensation of Nathan's hand pinning hers to the car door was pleasantly disturbing. It was only a lower-voltage version of the kiss on her hand the week before, to which, she had since decided, she'd overreacted, probably because of all the stress that day. But what was her excuse now? Oh, no, she told herself, not again, not yet. She needed Nathan's friendship, was truly grateful for it, but she was afraid of becoming romantically involved with him. It was much too soon after Manny, and she didn't feel very lucky in the love department. There wasn't enough time for even a harmless cup of coffee today, anyway. The interview and audition had taken longer than she had expected, and she still had to pick the baby up at Vicki's, and then go get Robin, too, at her friends' house. Linda remembered her mother saying that too many good excuses usually add up to one bad one, so she only said, "That sounds lovely, Nathan, but I really have to be going."

"It's all right, querida," he said, releasing her hand, along with the rest of her. "We'll be seeing each other. There's no rush. How about tomorrow?"

This was Robin's first visit to Lucy and Carmel's house, a small yellow bungalow on a street of similar bungalows in Echo Park. They'd all gone there together straight from school, and now they were lying around the girls' bedroom, listening to the latest U2 tape and trying to talk. But Lucy and Carmel's kid brother, Garvey, a punky little ten-year-old, kept hanging around and interrupting them, and staring at Robin as if she were some kind of freak.

"Yo!" he'd cried as soon as she walked through the front door. "It's Snow White!"

"Yeah," Lucy said, swatting at him and missing, "and you're one of the dwarfs."

Now he stood in the doorway of the bedroom, gazing at Robin again, and said, "Uh-oh, we haunted, gotta call Ghostbusters!"

"What's your problem?" Carmel asked him, and Lucy said, "Get out of here, fool, before *I* call somebody."

"Who axed you?" he demanded.

"Nobody *axed* me," Lucy said. "If somebody *axed* me, I'd be bleeding all over the place, wouldn't I?" Before he could answer, she slammed the door and pushed a chest of drawers against it, in case he tried to open it again. "Just ignore him," she told Robin. "He thinks he's cool."

"He's pathetic," Carmel said, with a sigh.

"You are so lucky not to have a brother, Robin," Lucy said. "And by the time your baby sister's old enough to dis you, you'll probably be married."

"Or dead," Carmel added cheerfully.

"I'm never getting married," Robin said.

"Oh, yeah, what if Bono asked you?" Lucy asked.

"Sure, like he's coming over right this second to start begging me."

"Too bad you're not home," Carmel said.

"He wouldn't have to beg *me*," Lucy said.

Lucy was fourteen and a half, the same age and in the same grade as Robin. Their last names, near the tail end of the alphabet, had gotten them into the same homeroom, too. Carmel was a year younger and a grade behind them. When Robin first arrived at Northside High School, she felt like a complete outsider. She hadn't had any really close friends back in Newark, but there were always a few kids she hung out with. She didn't know anybody here, and they all seemed to be best buddies since birth. There was so much shrieking and hugging that first day of school you'd think they'd been separated for about a century instead of just a few weeks. Robin had hoped to get lost in the crowd, to sort of blend in and become invisible, but everything about her was conspicuously different and wrong, from her deadly pallor and East Coast inflection to her sexual retardation. People were just starting to pair off in her crowd back home when her father died and she began her long, torturous journey with Linda. She had never had a boyfriend and probably never would; it was like losing your place in a moving line and not being able to cut back in. And now, at Northside, she felt as if she'd landed in some foreign country without a passport, and without knowing the language. In social studies, a couple of smartasses made fun of the flat, nasal way she spoke—"Noo Joisey," they mimicked, cracking themselves up—so she just stopped speaking, for the most part, after that.

All of her old personal problems were nothing compared to the assorted daily torments of high school: the nasty kids, the indifferent or demanding teachers, the cavernous building echoing all day long with voices, whistles, and bells. And later, when she got home, Linda would usually be waiting for her with cupcakes and milk and all those dumb questions. How was school today, honey? Do you have much homework? Did you make any friends yet? Why don't you join some nice after-school clubs? *God.*

Robin skipped out as often as she could without getting suspended; she didn't need to have Linda bugging her about *that*, too. Sometimes she would just stay home if Linda wasn't there, or she'd hitch a ride to the mall or to one of the video arcades. She had to keep a sharp eye out for attendance officers, who, she'd heard, prowled those places disguised as normal people. Luckily, she was never caught. She was caught shoplifting once, though, at a sneaker store in the mall. The guy took her name, but he let her go with just a warning. Big deal, she'd only copped a pair of glow-in-the-dark shoelaces. She never lifted anything that great or that she actually wanted or needed: the shoelaces, a crappy plastic key ring and a lipstick from the five-and-dime, a black lace bra from The Broadway. The bra wasn't even her size.

Then, one Monday in December, she went to school, and a girl in her homeroom accused her of stealing a ballpoint pen. It was a total lie; Robin had actually borrowed the red-and-silver pen she was doodling with from Linda's purse that morning, when she couldn't find her own Bic. "Just bug off, okay?" Robin told the girl. "It's my pen."

But the girl said, right in Robin's face, "Bullshit! It's mine, and you'd better hand it over."

The homeroom teacher was out in the hall, trying to round up some kids still goofing off near the lockers. In the classroom, other kids were starting to gather around Robin and the girl, hoping to see a good fight, when Lucy Thompson, who had glanced at Robin from time to time on other days but had never spoken to her, intervened. "Chill, girl," she said to Robin's accuser. "It's *her* pen. She's been using it all term." Robin was so surprised by this unsolicited and enterprising lie in her defense that she didn't say anything, but she really *looked* at Lucy for the first time. She saw a tall, skinny light-brown girl with elaborately plaited hair and huge, innocent eyes. Robin was reminded of the illustration of Queen Esther in that book of children's Bible stories she used to have. Who wouldn't believe her? Robin was almost persuaded herself.

"Oh, right," the girl said to Lucy. "Like *you* really know." But you could see that her heart wasn't in it anymore. And then a boy who usually waited to see which way arguments were going before joining the winning side said, "Yeah, I've seen her using it, too, every day." Immediately, other voices chimed in, agreeing with him, and as easily as that, Robin's social exile was over.

After school that afternoon, while they were waiting to board their respective buses, Lucy introduced Robin to Carmel, who bore as strong a resemblance to her older sister as Phoebe did to Robin. "Want to come over sometime?" Lucy called to Robin as she was getting on her bus. And Robin shrugged, and said, "Maybe. I'll see," without betraying at all how stupidly happy she felt.

She made them come to her place first, though, as a kind of test, and also just to get it over with. Linda was still pregnant then, as big as a barn, and she went totally bananas when Robin walked in with Lucy and Carmel. Like Robin had never had a friend in her life before. She didn't stop yakking and falling all over herself until Robin hauled the Thompson sisters into the bathroom with her and locked the door. There the three of them shared a joint Robin had bought from a guy on the football field that morning, and tried out some of Linda's makeup and perfume.

Lucy invited her home again, but first Robin got the flu and then Lucy did. And after the baby was born and Manny died, Robin didn't feel like doing much of anything, except play with the baby and mope around. Lucy and Carmel kept asking her when she was going to come to their house, but Robin managed to sidestep the issue by inventing alibis or by making dates she didn't keep. One day, Lucy confronted her at the lockers and said, "If you don't want to be friends, Robin, why don't you just say so."

"It's not that," Robin mumbled.

"Did your mother tell you not see me anymore?" Lucy asked.

Robin snorted. "Are you kidding? She likes you more than she likes me. And she's not my mother, anyway, she's my *step*mother."

"So then is it because Carmel didn't inhale?" Lucy asked.

"What?" Robin said. "Look, forget it. I'll come to your house, okay? When do you want me to come?"

And now here she was, walking down the hallway from Lucy and Carmel's bedroom to the kitchen, to look for something to eat. A bent-over old lady was standing there, stirring something at the stove. The sisters took turns kissing her. "Hello, Ga," Lucy said. "We thought maybe you were sleeping."

"Dead folks couldn't sleep with that racket," the old lady said, squinting at Robin.

"Ga, this is my friend Robin from school," Lucy said. "Robin, this is my grandmother, Mrs. Pickett."

"Will you look at that hair," Mrs. Pickett said.

"I'm going to braid her later, Ga," Carmel said.

This was the first Robin had heard of it, but the idea instantly appealed to her. She loved when someone fooled with her hair, combed it or touched it; it made her feel like lying down at their feet and going right to sleep. And Lucy's intricate network of braids and beads—Carmel's handiwork—was really beautiful. In fact, Robin had tried to do something like that to her own hair just the other night, but she'd only made five or six fat, lopsided braids, which kept unraveling as she worked, before her arms grew weary and she gave up.

She followed the girls back to their bedroom, where Carmel kept her word and arranged Robin's hair in about a hundred tightly woven, precisely aligned braids. Each one glistened with the gel Carmel applied, and was neatly tied off with a tiny blue rubber band. Her hands moved like a magician's, but the whole process still took almost three hours. When she was finished, Robin's scalp tingled violently from the pull and scratch of the comb; in the dresser mirror she saw that it was as pink as a baby pig's. She stared at herself for a long time, trying to decide how she looked without her usual camouflage of hair. Sort of *naked*, she thought, like bald Phoebe right after she was born, although Lucy assured her that she was the image of Bo Derek in *10*. You didn't have to take the braids out for months, she said, patting her own head; you just shampooed it the way it was.

Garvey was lurking in the hallway, and he started laughing the minute Robin emerged, pointing helplessly at her and doing a crazy little stomping dance. The girls pushed past him and went back to the kitchen, where Mrs. Pickett's only comment about Robin's hair was "Lord!" Soon Mr. and Mrs. Thompson came in together from work. There were more introductions, more talk, laughter. The clatter of dishes and pots. Then a tall, very dark woman in an apron walked into the kitchen from somewhere. She might have stepped out of a cupboard or come right through the wall. Without saying a word to anyone, she took a bowl out of the refrigerator and began beating whatever was in it with a fork. Did she live here, too? Nobody said. In a few minutes, Garvey reappeared, looking meek and small in front of his parents. The house was pretty small, too. Lucy had once said there were only two bedrooms; where did everybody sleep? The kitchen was so crowded and busy with cooking and cross-conversation it made Robin's head spin. She remembered having to share a room with Linda at all the motels they'd stayed in across the country, some of them so teeny you could always feel the other person's breath on your skin. She didn't know how Lucy and Carmel could stand all this closeness and commotion. To make matters worse, Garvey started laughing about her hair again, and although his father shook him a little to make him stop, Robin saw that Mr. Thompson's eyes were watering, too, and that he was hiding his own laughter by coughing repeatedly and beating himself on the chest. By the time Linda came to pick her up, she was looking forward to going home, to the relative peace and privacy of their apartment.

When they got there, though, it seemed strangely big and empty. Robin went into her own room and shut the door. She put on the House of Pain tape she'd borrowed from Lucy and stretched out on her bed. But no matter which way she turned, her tightly braided head ached from its contact with the pillow. She supposed she'd get used to it eventually, but now she got up and shut off the stereo. The sudden quiet was startling. She went to the door and put her ear against it. All she could hear was Linda singing something—was that supposed to be the music from *Star Trek*?—her voice sounding wavery and far away. Robin wandered down the hall to the kitchen, where Linda was preparing supper and Phoebe was lying propped in her infant seat in the middle of the table, like some extravagant centerpiece. Robin let the baby grab her finger.

"Did you have fun today?" Linda asked. "Your hair looks very . . . interesting," she added. She hadn't said anything about it before, although she did a double take when Robin came out of the Thompson house and got into the car.

"You like it?" Robin said, trying to catch a glimpse of herself in the refrigerator-door handle. "I'll get Carmel to do yours, too, if you want." Then she plucked the baby from her seat and danced around the kitchen with her. "And you, too, Feeble," she said, "as soon as you get some hair."

Linda drew her breath in sharply, as if she was getting ready to say something, but then she seemed to change her mind.

9

Sleeping Arrangements

Robin had taken an instant dislike to Nathan, which Linda couldn't understand. He treated her the way hardly anyone treats teenagers, with friendly respect. He never asked her any of those empty questions about school or friends or how she liked living in Los Angeles. When Linda introduced them, he simply shook her hand and said, "Hey, Robin, I'm glad to meet you. Linda's told me so much about you." She pulled her hand back as if she'd touched a hot oven, and gave Linda a dirty look.

No matter how hard Nathan tried to win her over—with good-natured patience, and by driving the whole family to those places Robin had been dying to see, like the La Brea Tar Pits and Universal Studios—she didn't budge in her bad opinion of him. They'd spent one especially pleasant afternoon at the Santa Monica Pier. They all rode the carousel, and Nathan won a stuffed bear for Phoebe by knocking down a pyramid of wooden bottles with a baseball. After he'd brought them home and lingered a while and then left, Robin dropped the bear carelessly in a corner of the living room. Linda picked it up and propped it against one of the sofa cushions. "Wasn't today fun?" she said. "Isn't Nathan nice?"

"God, you are so lame," Robin told her. "Can't you see he's only after you for sex and a green card?"

"That is completely ridiculous, Robin," Linda said. "Nathan is an American citizen!" That was true; he'd gotten his final papers right before she met him. She couldn't bring herself to defend him about the sex part, though. He had said there was no rush, but he didn't act that way. He'd managed to see her almost every day since they'd met. And he was always *touching* her, it seemed, and often came dizzyingly close to kissing her without actually doing it. She tried to dismiss her own ache of attraction by remembering what her mother had said about passion flying in and out of windows, but this time it wasn't much help or consolation. She confided in Vicki, who said, "So what's holding you back?"

Linda explained that the swiftness and intensity of her feelings unsettled her. And Nathan wasn't really her type, in temperament, at least. She needed someone less self-possessed and domineering, someone willing to encourage her independence, the way Wright, and then Manny, had. And how could she not have second thoughts about loving anyone at all?

"Why don't you stop thinking so much and just give in to it, Linda?" Vicki said. "Before you know it, it's all over, anyway."

"What is?" Linda asked. "Life? Love?"

"Everything," Vicki said, snapping her fingers in Linda's startled face. "Poof!"

During a break between classes the next day, Linda stood outside the exercise room where Nathan was leading his salsa workout and watched as he put his students through their paces. They were like the dance troupe of an amateur show, moving in earnest, clumsy unison to Poncho Sanchez's "El Mejor." The best. If Nathan wasn't the best dancer Linda had ever seen, he certainly came close—with his whole body undulating like that while his feet carried out a precise and complicated pattern of steps. His students breathlessly echoed his cries of "Olé!" and "Arriba! Arriba!" as they moved across the floor behind him. He spotted Linda in the mirror and wiggled one raised hand in greeting at her, and then the other. Anyone would think it was part of the routine, and sure enough all the women in the class dutifully wiggled their hands, too. "Linda! Linda!" Nathan cried, without breaking his stride, and the women repeated, "Linda! Linda!" as they labored to keep up with him.

He made her laugh and feel sexy at the same time—nobody had ever done that before. When his class was over, and the students began drifting out, Linda was still standing at the entrance to the room, watching as he wiped his face and neck on a towel and took a long swig from his water bottle. At the club, he was usually in a cluster of women, even when he wasn't working. She supposed they were attracted to his Latin good looks: that satiny sepia skin, those heavy-lidded eyes, and the voluptuously wavy dark hair. And then there was the way he moved, and the way he smiled . . . Why, he's *gorgeous*, she realized with a jarring, below-the-belt thrill, although she must have known it, on some level at least, for some time. As soon as the last woman left, Nathan started the tape again and turned and held out his hands to her. They had never danced together before, had hardly been alone, except for a few minutes here and there at the Bod, between classes. He had asked her more than once to go out with him without the children tagging along, but she kept putting him off. And when she finally decided that she could handle the situation, and asked Robin to babysit for them, Robin refused, saying that she had her own life to live, and that she wasn't Linda's servant.

Linda stepped into the exercise room and into Nathan's arms. They waited in place while the introduction to "El Mejor" played itself out, one of his hands resting lightly at the curve of her waist and the other meeting hers, palm to palm, at the end of their outstretched arms. Linda held her breath, and neither of them moved; they were as still and poised as those plastic figures on top of a wedding cake, ready to waltz off into their newly connected lives. She remembered the dance with Manny that preceded their first time together. She remembered the hundreds of times she'd opened her arms to strangers at Fred Astaire's. And then she forgot everything else as the melody crashed through the speakers and propelled them into motion. She didn't follow Nathan's lead exactly, or try to lead him. It was more as if they had become one four-legged person of exceptional agility and grace, one person who had done this particular dance so often it didn't require conscious thought or memory. She believed that if the music suddenly stopped they would continue dancing, hearing something inside themselves that would keep the rhythm and the energy flowing. Each time she swung away from him, invisible threads drew her back again, and she could see their joined images in all the mirrors around the room, whirling and whirling.

When the tape ended, he didn't let her go, and she didn't try to get away, at least not for several seconds. The music was still playing in her head, in her rapid blood. "Well . . ." she managed to say at last, to break the spell, and when they stepped away from one another, it was like a coda to the dance, a final movement that had been choreographed into its design. Linda had to hurry off to meet her next class, and she left him standing there without saying another word. But that evening, a couple of hours after she'd dropped Robin at a classmate's house for a slumber party, and come back home again, Nathan rang the doorbell. They hadn't prearranged this—not directly, anyway. Linda had only mentioned, earlier in the day, that she was getting some time off from Robin later, and that she intended to use it to catch up on her ironing. But then, right after she put the baby into her crib for the night, she started preparing for Nathan's arrival, pretty much the way Manny had prepared for hers that first night at his house. Tidying, vacuuming, looking at everything in the apartment with a freshly critical eye. She scrubbed the bathroom to surgical sterility, and dragged the rocking chair from her bedroom to cover a stain on the living-room rug where the baby had spit up. She even went into Robin's room and shoved some of her debris under the bed. As if she were readying the place for prospective subletters. Then she took a lingering bath, hardly able to keep her weighted, dreaming eyes open. By the time

Nathan showed up, she was in her fleecy yellow robe, drowsing in front of the TV, on which a hoarsely weeping preacher promised heaven and threatened hell.

When she opened the door, Linda suppressed her immediate impulse to say something moronic, like "Nathan, What a surprise!" or "How nice to see you." In fact, she didn't say anything, for once in her life, only stepped back a little to let him inside. But he began kissing her right there in the doorway, holding her face with both of his hands. She kept moving backward in tiny, faltering steps as he kissed her lips, her hairline, her eyelids, her ears, her chin, her throat. He must have kicked the door shut behind him, because she heard it close and he had not let go of her face. Her own hands were in the thick of his hair, and then her arms blindly found their way around his neck, as his hands slid downward, slowly taking the measure of her body, which seemed to mold itself to suit his grasp and desire. All that time, they kept kissing without a pause, and Linda sucked in his sweet, hurried breath to restore her own, and tasted the rough silk of his mouth and tongue. His hands were on her breasts, on her hips, pulling her toward him, and then opening her robe as she began to struggle with the buttons on his shirt. Oh, oh, she thought, in an avalanche of sensation, so *this* is it, and fought a swooning, losing battle to stay on her feet.

The slumber party was being given by a girl named Stephanie Kraus, in honor of her own fifteenth birthday. Back in July, when Robin turned fourteen, Linda insisted they go out for dinner to celebrate. Robin almost died when the waiter brought in a birthday cake with sparklers stuck in it and everybody in the whole stupid place started singing "Happy Birthday." Fat guys in lobster bibs and old ladies waving their forks in the air. What kind of idiot threw a party for herself?

Robin had hardly ever spoken to Stephanie, who was only in typing class with her, and she wasn't sure why she'd been invited, at least until she got to Stephanie's house. There she discovered that the other guests were four of the most unpopular girls at Northside. Two of them—Heidi and Michelle—were grossly overweight, and another had recently come from Hungary and could only speak about three words of English. The fourth was a brainy nerd named Marybeth Nixon. Robin wouldn't have accepted the invitation if it wasn't for Linda, who ran right out after Stephanie called and bought a present for Robin to bring her, and then said all this stuff about "expanding your horizons" and "giving friendship a chance." When Robin resisted, saying, "I don't even *know* that nimrod," Linda said, "Well, stay home then, Robin. You can help me with the ironing, and then maybe you can clean up your room, before it's condemned."

Robin couldn't even escape to Lucy's; the whole Thompson family was at a wedding that night, so here she was, sitting on top of a smelly sleeping bag on a smelly living-room rug in a strange house, eating fried chicken from a big bucket with people she didn't know or like. Marybeth was trying to teach Halinka, the Hungarian girl, a few choice phrases in English. She held up a piece of white meat and said "breast," and when Halinka repeated it, the other girls howled with laughter. Stephanie's mother, who was divorced, and who'd told them all to call her "Pal," the way Stephanie did, kept peeking into the room and asking if everything was "okey-dokey." Pal sounded like a dog's name, and she was like an older version of Linda, talking too much and trying to be everybody's best friend. Stephanie acted as if she didn't even mind, as if she hoped her mother would get another sleeping bag and join the party. If things were going to continue like this, Robin would just as soon go home, and she began trying to figure out how to do that with the least amount of fuss.

Marybeth clapped her hands for order. It was time to open the presents. Heidi had a pad and a pencil; she was going to write down everything Stephanie said about the presents, and then read it back to them later. That was the dumbest idea Robin had ever heard. Who wanted to hear that retarded stuff twice? She wished Lucy was there, so they could talk about everybody else, and she idly wondered what Linda had bought for her to give to Stephanie. It had never occurred to her to ask when she shoved the heavy, fancily wrapped package into the shopping bag with her pajamas. If it was up to Robin, she'd have given her that black bra she'd lifted from The Broadway.

Stephanie got tapes and socks and stuffed animals from the other girls. She squealed and exclaimed over everything, while Pal kept taking pictures, urging them to "say Brie!" and making the flash go off right in their faces. By the time Stephanie got around to opening Robin's gift, which was last, Robin could hardly see. "It's so big!" Stephanie said, shaking the package. "And hard," she added, as she squeezed and poked it. Everyone but Robin and Halinka was screaming with laughter. But there was a huge, collective gasp after Stephanie tore the wrappings off. "Oh, my God, it's the most beautiful thing I ever saw!" she cried. Robin blinked away the black spots in front of her eyes and saw that Linda had gotten Stephanie a metal sculpture of two children with big, sad eyes, sitting on a park bench, each of them holding a balloon. It was pretty ugly, but it must have cost a bundle.

Then Heidi said, "Okay, quiet, everybody! And listen! Here's what Steph's going to say on her wedding night." After the giggling and chatter died down, she began to read back all the things Stephanie had said while she was opening her gifts. Things like "Ooh, it's so cute, I'm gonna sleep with it every night!" and "Oh, pink, my favorite color!" The girls couldn't stop laughing. Even Halinka, who probably didn't understand a word, got into the spirit of things. Of course, the worst part was when Heidi repeated what Stephanie had said about Robin's gift, about how big and hard and beautiful it was. Robin wished Linda was there so she could murder her.

Before she knew it, they were all changing into their pajamas, wriggling out of their clothes inside their sleeping bags. Pal came back into the room, wearing the same Snoopy nightshirt as Stephanie. Maybe after everyone was asleep, Robin could grab her clothes and sneak out a window.

Linda woke in the dark, under the double-wedding-ring quilt. Nathan was asleep beside her. Carefully, she raised herself on one elbow and looked at him for a long time, before she lay down again. Sharing a bed with someone you cared for was the best of all sleeping arrangements. Why did she feel so restless, though? Nathan had come there prepared to practice safe sex, so there were no regrets on that account. But it occurred to her that she knew nothing about him, really. Right after they'd first met, in the rain in Culver City, he said, mysteriously, that he knew *her.* Is this what he meant? Did he imagine this entire extraordinary night just from looking into her eyes that day? She didn't want her heart to be that visible to him, not unless his was open for her to read, too.

How was she ever going to fall asleep, with everybody in the world breathing around her like this? Heidi and Michelle had whispered and giggled until Robin was getting ready to throw something at them, maybe that heavy sculpture Linda had bought, but when they stopped, the silence was worse. The other girls were asleep, too, and even Pal had disappeared, after a series of blown kisses and a lecture about not setting the burglar alarm off by opening any windows or doors. Great. Now Robin would never get out of here. She remembered that there was no burglar alarm back in her own apartment, no protection *there* against thieves and kidnappers. And if lamebrain Linda left the iron on when she went to sleep, their apartment would burn down, and Robin wouldn't be there to save Phoebe.

She tried to find a comfortable position on the floor, in the lumpy sleeping bag. Every once in a while, Halinka sobbed in her sleep and mumbled something, probably in Hungarian. It was awful to be the only one still up; everything bad you could think of always crept into your mind at night. Sure enough, as if they'd come all this way to tuck her in, here were Robin's father and mother, back from the dead and from the living dead. They were both in their nightclothes, which was the way she'd last seen each of them. Her father in his blue-and-white-striped pajamas, as he was on the final morning of his life, calling after her as she left for school to remember to take her lunch. Her mother in the green satin bathrobe she was wearing when Linda and Robin burst in on her and her asshole husband that Sunday afternoon in Arizona. What had they interrupted? Robin shut her eyes and covered her ears. Still, her mother clearly said, "Don't forget to keep in touch," the way she had that Sunday, and her father whispered, "Roblet, my little birdie" in his sweet, distant voice. Robin moaned and thrashed around on the floor until they were both gone. She didn't intend to get married herself, but if she ever did, it would only be to someone who always let her fall asleep first.

Linda woke once again and looked at the digital clock on her night table, just as the time changed. 3:05 a.m. Phoebe would be up squalling for attention in a couple of hours. And Linda and Nathan both had to go to work soon after that. She told herself to hurry up and go back to sleep. But instead she took off her wedding band and touched it to her lips before slipping it into her night-table drawer. Then she reached out to lightly stroke Nathan's shoulder, and he turned to her.

10

Love Chains

Linda was in love, or in a state of giddy happiness closely resembling love—she wasn't sure which and she didn't really care. Whatever it was, it was certainly different from what she'd felt for Wright or for Manny. Much more sexual, for one essential thing, and more obsessive, too. She thought about Nathan with her whole body, not just her mind, and she thought about him all the time. One morning, when she was in a romantic reverie, Robin broke in, saying, "I'm *talking* to you. Where were you, on Mars?" And she did seem to be somewhere else, removed from her old life on dear, familiar Earth spinning safely under the stars.

Robin was still giving Nathan the cold shoulder and the evil eye. Linda tried to explain that Robin was like that—it took her a little longer than most people to warm up (about a century, she thought, but didn't say)—and he shouldn't take it personally. His latest theory, which he'd offered Linda the other night, as they lay dazed and tangled on his bed, was that Robin believed their relationship insulted her father's memory. He asked if she had minded Linda's previous boyfriend, and Linda had to admit she hadn't, at least not for long. The painful truth was that Robin had been a lot nicer to Manny than she'd ever been to her. "Yeah, well, then there must be something about me," Nathan concluded. "Maybe she just doesn't like Chicanos."

Linda was appalled. "Oh, no," she said. "Robin can be really horrible sometimes, but she's not *prejudiced*."

Valentine's Day was approaching, and Linda began to concentrate on the symbolic aspects of love: Cupid, hearts, flowers, all the words and music that speak for those poor souls stunned into speechlessness by their emotions. She wanted to buy Nathan something wonderful and original that would convey her own confusion of feelings. Except for groceries, Linda bought whatever she needed at one of the many stores in the nearest mall. She didn't like the vastness of the place or the milling crowds, but it was the most practical way to shop, with everything anyone could possibly want assembled under one roof. Robin frequented the mall, too, as much for social encounters as for shopping. The Saturday before Valentine's Day, Linda asked Robin to go with her and help her choose something for Nathan. They could take Phoebe along in her stroller; on previous trips, she'd seemed to be soothed by the canned music and all the people and the lights. When Robin balked, Linda bribed her with a five-dollar incentive added to her usual allowance, for her own Valentine shopping, and she grudgingly agreed to go. Not that she had any intention of buying any presents or cards for anyone; this kind of holiday was for suckers like Linda, who enjoyed making Hallmark rich. In the lower grades, when the teacher encouraged the exchange of valentines with a big, foil-covered box on her desk, Robin never put any inside, and the few she received had insulting verses and pictures on them. *Roses are red, violets are blue. With a face like yours, you belong in the zoo.* But this was just a free ride to the mall, where she might meet Lucy or somebody, and then she could lose Linda and use the extra money to get Cokes and pizza.

The whole place was blooming with hearts, the speakers were expelling love songs, one after the other, and a new perfume called Kiss Me Quick hung as thickly as smog in the air. The items that attracted Robin in the card and novelty store they went into first were gag gifts, in the worst possible taste, like lip-printed toilet paper and a battery-operated, clear plastic replica of the human heart that beat loudly and circulated something that looked revoltingly like blood. Linda headed for the greeting-card section to explore the valentines, hoping to find a verse that could be read two ways, seriously and ironically. She started reading one, about the secret language of love, aloud to Robin, who said, "Ugh. Barf," and looked around to make sure that no one she knew was witnessing this embarrassment. "Feeble and I are going to cut out now," she announced. "I need to go to another store."

Linda looked up from the card she was holding, surprised and pleased. "Sure, honey," she said. She glanced at her watch. "It's ten-forty now. Phoebe won't be hungry for a couple of hours, I hope. Why don't we meet back here at twelve. Will that give you enough time?"

Shit, Robin thought, she thinks I'm getting *her* something. Fat chance—who gave their stepmother a valentine? But Robin merely nodded and left, pushing the stroller with the sleeping baby in it toward the center of the mall, where most of the food places were, and where her friends usually hung out. There was a little stand between the yogurt and muffin shops that sold cheap but nice seasonal gifts, Halloween stuff in October, and stuff for Christmas in November and December. Robin had bought Linda a bread-dough Santa Claus pin there last Christmas, for only two bucks. Linda cried when she opened the package, and she fastened the pin to her maternity top, where she wore it every day until she gave birth. Of course everything made her cry in those days.

Now the holiday stand had a Valentine's Day display of jewelry, topped by a big sign that said: *Love Chains, Stay Together Forever*. A good-looking guy in his twenties wearing goggles and a leather vest, and with snake tattoos on both arms, was engraving an ID bracelet. Sparks were flying from the engraving machine, which made a grinding noise that almost drowned out the amplified strains of "Love Me Tender." He adjusted the machine when Robin approached, reducing the noise to a steady whine, and shouted over it, "See the love chains yet, babe? Wanna be the first in your neighborhood?" He lifted his goggles and showed Robin the bracelet he'd been working on. The plate was heart-shaped and the name "Tiffany," missing only the tail of the *y*, was engraved in its center. Robin shrugged; except for the heart, it looked like a plain old ID bracelet to her. Then he picked up a second bracelet, bearing the name "Joey," and with a magician's rapid-fire motions linked the two bracelets together, a sturdy, six-inch chain between them. "Voilà! Here you go, chained for life," he said, dangling the joined bracelets from one hairy finger. They looked sort of like a pair of handcuffs now. "This is gonna be the hula hoop of the nineties," he said. "Got 'em for ankles and wrists, come in fourteen karat, sterling, and a nice yellow or white base metal, from $2.99 to $69.99 each, name or monogram, up to eight letters, included. So what's your poison?"

"Each?" Robin asked.

"That's right, babe," he said. "But, hey, we can even link up *three* of 'em, if that's your preference," he added, winking and twirling the bracelets in a dazzling silvery circle.

Three, Robin thought. Her and Lucy and Carmel. Together forever. But Linda had only given her five extra dollars—even two bracelets would set her back more than that. And Lucy was her main friend; Carmel was just kind of a bonus friend. "I'll take two," Robin said, "of the $2.99 ones."

He asked her to write down the names she wanted engraved on the bracelets, and he made her pay for them in advance. She was to come back in about ten minutes for the finished products. As she stepped away from the stand, the sparks started flying again. Robin killed time at the muffin and yogurt shops, with a snack at each place. When she went back to pick up the bracelets, the tattooed guy said, "No offense, but what kind of faggot name is Robin, Lucy?"

"Robin's *my* name," she said, belligerently. "What's wrong with it?"

"Hey, nothing," he said, holding one hand up. "Like the little red-breasted birdie, right? I like it." He looked thoughtful. "So then the guy's name is *Lucy*?"

"What guy?" Robin demanded.

"Wait a minute, wait a minute," he said, tapping his forehead. "I think I'm getting the picture now. We're talking two ladies here, aren't we?"

"Yeah, so what?" Robin said, but her own brain was struggling to sort this out at the same time. And then she looked at the sign again. *Love* chains, it said, and she finally understood what he was implying.

"No, that's not—" she began, but the guy interrupted.

"Hey, live and let live, that's my motto," he said, holding out her package. "But the kid's gotta be adopted, right? She sure looks like you, though."

Robin snatched the package from him without answering, feeling her cheeks go up in flames. Six dollars and change, out the window. And she felt as dumb as Linda, who probably couldn't tell the difference between friendship and love, either.

Linda found the perfect card after reading about twenty or thirty of them. This one simply said, "Valentine, I love dancing in the dark with you." There was a drawing of two goofy-looking bears dancing together on the cover, which made it seem light-hearted, if that was the way you chose to read it. She went to a nearby men's shop next, where she bought a beautiful dark red silk shirt for Nathan, and then she wandered toward the center of the mall, hoping to run into Robin and Phoebe a little earlier than arranged. There was a kiosk next to the muffin place that was selling jewelry for Valentine's Day: heart-shaped rings and pendants and charms. A sign saying *Love Chains, Stay Together*

Forever caught Linda's eye, and she went closer to see what they were. A greasy-looking biker type behind the counter said, "See the love chains yet, babe? Anybody you want to shackle for life?" And he demonstrated the quick and easy linking of two bracelets, with only the slack of inches between them. She'd gone way over her budget for Nathan's shirt, but there was something irresistible about the love chains. Like the card she'd bought, they could be thought of as serious or just a cute joke. And they made Linda think of that song her mother used to sing so wistfully when she was dusting or doing the dishes:

> *Alone from night to night you'll find me,*
> *too weak to break the chains that bind me . . .*
> *Something something something something,*
> *I'm just a prisoner of love.*

It was such a strange song for her mother to have sung. If anything, she was a prisoner of poverty, of a bad marriage, of her own lonely child and other people's needy newborns. The love part seemed to be just in her head, but maybe that's what saved her all those years.

Nathan wore only gold jewelry, which Linda definitely couldn't afford, and the base metal looked like something you'd buy in a plumbing-supply store. So she compromised and bought a pair of bracelets in sterling silver, which cost her over sixty dollars, with the tax. Some joke. And there was something official about those engraved names—"Nathan" and "Linda"—like the names on wedding invitations or the monograms on newlyweds' towels. The biker said, "If you ever cool on this Nathan dude, baby, you can always chain me up."

Robin buried her love chains in a dresser drawer under her socks and underwear. The crazy thing was, they did become a big fad for a little while, just like that tattooed guy said. Couples all over school walked around chained together at their wrists or ankles. They took classes and ate lunch that way, separating only to go to the bathroom or to classes they didn't share. Students' handwriting became erratic, the traffic in the halls was notably slower, and the wrists of those wearing the base-metal bracelets all turned green. Then there was a series of accidents. At the end of February, after the fullback on the football team and his girl-friend, the captain of the pep squad, who'd chosen the gold anklets as a symbol of their commitment, fell down a whole flight of steps together, the principal got on the P.A. and announced an edict outlawing the love chains. But the fad was already losing steam by then, as couples broke up and everyone began to realize how much easier it was getting around on their own.

Just as she'd expected, Robin didn't receive any valentines, except for a beautiful handmade card from Carmel, a mushy one from Lucy, signed "Bono," and a nasty unsigned one she was sure was from Garvey. Linda gave Robin that neat plastic heart they'd seen in the novelty store, but about a week later it suddenly stopped beating and the fake blood lay in a gory-looking pool at the bottom of it. Robin felt obligated to get something for Linda, too, after she received the heart, so she went back to the mall the next day and bought the toilet paper with the lip-prints on it. It was on sale by then—fifty percent off—and they gift-wrapped it for free. Linda didn't cry when she opened that package.

Nathan loved the red shirt. He wore it to bed at his place on Valentine's Day night, and Linda wore it afterward. She watched him closely when he read the card with the dancing bears on it, and he smiled, but he didn't laugh. He'd given her a huge bottle of Kiss Me Quick and a single long-stemmed red rose in crinkly green tissue paper tied with a red ribbon. She put off giving him the love chains until much later, when they were sitting up in bed and she was wearing the red shirt. Then she slipped one bracelet on his wrist and the other on her own, and, less deftly than the biker, clasped them together.

"Hey," Nathan said, "what's this?"

"Now you can't get away," she told him, hoping she sounded more playful than she felt.

"Who says I want to?" he said huskily and, sliding his unchained hand inside the shirt she wore, pressed her gently back down on the bed. Then he slid his hand out, and opened his bracelet and slipped it off. Linda felt the sudden weight of both bracelets and a twinge of disappointment. But she didn't say anything as Nathan kissed the pulse point on the inside of her still-encircled wrist and slowly raised her hand over her head. She heard a click and tilted her head up to look behind her, where he'd fastened his bracelet around the bedpost. "Is this okay with you, amor?" he asked.

Linda tested the tether, which was fairly loose, and the idea, which excited her. "Okay," she said, and put her strong free hand on the back of his neck and pulled him down.

11

Proof

The Thompsons picked Robin up one Saturday morning to go downtown to their photo shop. Lucy and Carmel were in the backseat of the family station wagon, and Garvey was sitting up front with his father. Robin had been watching for them from the kitchen window, and she ran outside as soon as they pulled up to the curb, glad to be released from the apartment, where Linda and Nathan were hanging around each other like a couple of lovesick dogs. Whenever Robin walked into a room and caught them in a clinch, they jumped apart as if she'd turned a hose on them. By the time she left, they seemed just as relieved to see her go as she was to get away. Nathan actually hustled her out the door, saying, "It's a really swell day out there, kid," and Linda yelled after her, "Have fun, honey!" the way she always did. She'd probably say the same stupid thing if Robin was on the way to her own funeral, but Linda was clearly the one intending to have fun. It was such an unpleasant thought Robin thrust it from her mind as she plunked herself down between her friends in the backseat of the wagon. At least she was wanted there. Carmel, whose chief expression of affection was physical, patted Robin's braids and plucked at her T-shirt sleeve, while Lucy whispered into her ear all the private news that had accumulated since they'd spoken on the phone late the night before. Robin was practically in a stupor of relief and pleasure. Even Garvey's leering side-glances at her from the front seat didn't spoil things, didn't break that spell of satisfaction.

The Thompsons' long, narrow shop, tucked between a bakery and a check-cashing place, was called Images of You. Mrs. Thompson was already there when they arrived, selling film to a young couple with a baby. Another woman was peering into a showcase of frames and photo albums, and a man waited behind her for service. Mrs. Thompson waved hello and called, "I could use somebody back here!" Lucy and Carmel hurried behind the counter, and Lucy drew herself up and addressed the woman looking into the showcase. "May I help you?" she asked in smoothly adult tones, while Carmel beckoned to Robin to join them.

Robin felt immediately and oddly important behind the counter, and surprised by the new perspective she had of the people going by in the street. She found herself fiercely willing them to come inside, to become customers, and she even imagined echoing Lucy's words, although she had never volunteered to help anyone in her entire life. The only job Robin had ever held was as a babysitter, back in Newark. But that was just a matter of putting up with somebody's brats for a few hours, mostly keeping them from killing each other until it was time for bed, and then watching television and eating snacks until their parents came home. Working in a store, she quickly realized, was quite different. For one thing, the whole dumb, complicated concept of free enterprise, which her social-studies teacher was always going on and on about, seemed suddenly clear and reasonable. You had something someone else wanted, like film or frames, and they bought it from you. With the money you made from the sale, you could buy something else that *you* wanted. Food, maybe, or tapes. And so on. Sometimes you got gypped, like the Indians when they sold Manhattan for a lousy twenty-four bucks, but most of the time it probably all worked out.

For another thing, as a clerk you could be anyone you wanted to be to the strangers who walked into the shop. It was like being in a play, Robin supposed, although she'd never done that, either. Best of all, there was an extraordinary sense of power that came from being on the side of the counter with the merchandise and the cash register. For once her fingers didn't itch to touch, or to take, what was within such close reach—it was enough to be its custodian.

The shop did a lively business, a neighborhood business. The elder Thompsons—Lee and Jewelle—greeted people, and were greeted, by name, or by "bro'" and "sister," as if everybody was related. Robin wished that Linda was more like them, more laid back and at home in the world. She wished that she was, too. Most of the customers either purchased film or brought rolls of it in to be developed or picked up their finished pictures. Robin sneaked a look at some of the prints behind the counter before she handed them over. There were a few really weird ones, just of the sky, for instance, as if the photographer had been lying flat on his back, and some of a dead woman laid out in her coffin. And there was a whole stack taken of some old guy in a hospital bed, hooked up to everything and *about* to be dead. But mostly they were shots of families doing ordinary things, like sitting around the supper table, or standing in the street. They probably saw each other in person every day of their lives; what did they need all these pictures for?

Linda, of course, had a fat album of photographs of everyone she'd ever met and every boring place she'd ever been. In several of the photos from their trip across the country, all you could see was one of Robin's blurred arms or legs against some scenic background, as she'd tried to escape Linda's camera, always aimed at her like a loaded gun. Linda had added captions, neatly printed on narrow strips of tape affixed to the plastic sleeves in her album: "A Memorable Day in Moline" or "Robin at the Grand Canyon," although only Robin's elbow in the foreground, looming larger than the Canyon, attested to her presence there.

Robin refused to look at the album when Linda periodically dragged it out, and she'd managed to lose the few snapshots of herself as a baby that Linda had dug up in the back of a closet before they left Newark. They were badly faded and stained black-and-whites that had been taken with an old-fashioned Polaroid camera. Linda made a big fuss when she found them, like she'd just discovered buried treasure, but Robin was only a bald-headed, bald-faced little blob in a stroller, or behind the prison bars of a crib. And a couple of photos with her mother and father were no better. Everyone's features had practically disappeared, except for her mother's dark lipstick and darker hair.

Lucy showed Robin how to fill out the envelopes for incoming film and tear off part of the flap as a receipt for the customer. Within minutes, she was asking the appropriate questions with professional cool: "May I help you? How many sets of prints do you want? Matte or glossy? Three-by-fives or four-by-sixes?"

There was a darkroom and a photo studio in the rear of the store, behind a black curtain. Mrs. Thompson did the custom developing and printing back there and Mr. Thompson took the pictures. Polaroid passport and ID photos were specialties at Images, but they also did a lot of formal portraits. There were poster-size blowups of drooling babies and smiling brides all over the walls of the shop. One photo in particular caught and held Robin's attention. It was a group portrait—there must have been at least fifty people sitting and standing in the sun on a lawn in front of a large white frame house. Three old ladies sat front and center on folding chairs, with babies on their laps and dogs at their feet, and a crowd of men, women, and children all around them. "It's a family reunion," Carmel explained, coming up behind Robin.

Robin had no living relatives beside Phoebe and her mother, who had elected not to be counted. She didn't even *know* fifty people, and couldn't imagine a family that large. "Looks more like an accident," she said under her breath. But with Carmel, and then Lucy, beside her, she continued to examine the picture, as if it was one of those puzzles where you were supposed to find hidden objects in the trees and clouds. She saw a barbecue near the porch of the house, with threads of smoke rising from it, and some abandoned toys in the grass: a wagon, an overturned tricycle, a doll. The shrubs that bordered the house had bloomed, and some of the blossoms lay in the grass, too, like crumpled Kleenex. Summertime, Robin figured, somewhere else. Then she noticed a couple of familiar faces, first someone who resembled Garvey—with a flattop like his and that same crazy expression in his eyes—and then the girl standing next to him, who looked a lot like Lucy. Why, it *was* Lucy! Her hair was a little different, but she was wearing her Naughty by Nature T-shirt, and that was Carmel standing next to her, half hidden by a boy making devil's horns on the head of the boy in front of him. Two of the other kids—a boy and a girl—seemed to be in the midst of combat the moment the picture was taken; their arms were a flailing blur and the girl was grimacing against a blow. Next to the girl was that woman Robin had seen in the Thompsons' kitchen, Lucy and Carmel's Aunt Ez, wearing the elaborate garb of an African queen instead of her apron. Lucy's grandmother, Robin realized, was one of the old ladies up front. A coolie hat shaded her face, and a corsage of roses drooped on her breast. Robin searched the rows of faces until she found Mr. and Mrs. Thompson, too. Some of the people were smiling, while others squinted in the sunlight or looked dreamily toward the horizon beyond the camera.

"It's *you*," Robin said accusingly.

"Yeah," Lucy admitted. "And that's my cousin Mallie I told you about right behind me, and Aunt Berta behind her. And there's the twins . . ."

"Daddy took it," Carmel said.

"But he's right there," Robin said, pointing to Mr. Thompson, who was standing to the left side of the assembly with his arm around his wife.

"He had to set the timer and then run for it," Lucy explained, and Robin thought now that his smile looked a little breathless, and that she could almost see the empty space he'd filled seconds before the shutter clicked.

"It's in Roanoke," Carmel said, "where our other grandmother lives. We have to go there every July, on her birthday."

Two grandmothers, and a whole army of aunts, uncles, and cousins. The camera probably had to be set up about a mile away to get them all in the same frame like that. The scene was sharply real. It was practically possible to hear people's voices, and to smell the barbecue's smoke and the scent of the grass and the flowering shrubs. Robin had the feeling that if she looked much longer, the picture would come suddenly and scarily to life, and that she would find herself trapped inside it, an intruder in that family spectacle. She turned abruptly away, pretending to be absorbed by another picture, of two children, probably a brother and sister, in their white confirmation outfits, like a midget bride and groom.

"Take a picture of me and Robin," Lucy implored her father as he went by, and ignoring Robin's protests, she maneuvered her into the studio, where Mr. Thompson stood the two girls against a hanging bedsheet painted with a backdrop of mountains. Robin hated having her picture taken. At the sight of a camera, her neck always collapsed under the sudden weight of her head. And what were you supposed to do with your hands, your mouth, your whole twitchy, unphotogenic self? When it was her turn to pose for an individual school picture in the fifth or sixth grade back in Newark, some nerdy boy had warned her not to break the camera with her sour puss. She'd gotten even by digging her fingers into his arm until he shrieked, but the fury was still in her face when the shutter snapped. A couple of weeks later, the teacher sent the photographer's proofs home with them to show to their parents, so they could order copies. Most of the kids had idiot smiles on their faces, smiles made to be flashed in wallets, displayed on mantels, and mailed to distant, doting relatives, but Robin was frowning darkly, and her white-lashed eyes gave nothing away. She looked like an angry zombie, like something just coming awake in a pod. To make matters worse, the word "proof" was stamped right across her face. Proof that she was ugly, stupid, mean. She hid the picture under a pile of junk in her dresser drawer and never bothered mentioning it to her father. Every once in a while, she'd go through the stuff in that drawer, looking for something else, and find her own marked face staring up at her. That picture, too, was misplaced or thrown out in the mess of moving.

Unlike the school photographer, Mr. Thompson didn't instruct his subjects to "Say cheese!" and he didn't ask them to freeze like dummies into stiff-necked, unnatural poses, either. He just kept up some low-keyed patter, almost to himself—"Got to set you up here, got to get this *just* right . . . Oo-kay, ladies, just a minute now"—while he played with the lights and a big white umbrella Robin couldn't figure out the use for. "What are you doing, girl?" he said to Lucy, who was fussing with her hair and trying out a series of peculiar smiles. "This is you and your best friend, right? Now you think about that, never mind your hair," he said. "Just think about going somewhere nice together, and having a good time."

Robin, at a loss for the proper fantasy, nibbled at a hangnail, her sole attempt at grooming. She could only picture herself and Lucy at school, hardly "somewhere nice," or at the mall, where they hung out for want of a better place to go. Then she glanced behind her at the fake purplish mountains that quivered a little under the air-conditioning vent, and tried to imagine walking toward them with Lucy, maybe for a picnic or a campout or something. That didn't work at all, so she quickly switched gears and projected them at the beach, and then at Disneyland. But *nothing* seemed to work, and in desperation she turned to look at Lucy, who was looking intently back at her, which made her laugh in surprise, and she heard the camera click and click.

Later they returned to the front of the store, where they waited on a few more customers. But after a while the fun of it began to wear off—it was only work, after all—and Robin's feet hurt and her empty stomach had started growling. She yawned loudly to cover the noise, but of course Garvey heard it. "Who did that?" he asked, staring straight at her. There were a couple of kids like him in school, kids who always had to name the burpers or farters, to single them out for group recognition and torment. There was this great comeback you could use if you were the one who farted. You could say, "Whoever smelt it dealt it," diverting the laughter and unwanted attention from yourself to the fink. But there wasn't a similar snappy answer for this situation, so she only said, "Don't look at me," which made everybody do just that. She would clobber that kid when she got him alone.

"No big deal, your stomach's only saying you're hungry," Mr. Thompson said, opening the cash register and pulling out a few bills. "You girls go get some lunch now. Go to Henry's and bring something back for the rest of us."

"Something low-calorie for me," Mrs. Thompson said. "But not *too* low." She was always trying to diet, according to Lucy, although she wasn't that fat.

"Hey, what about me?" Garvey demanded. "Why can't I go?" But Mr. Thompson silenced him with a glance and the girls were soon outside, and free. They walked three abreast, with Robin in the middle and their arms linked, like a line of chorus girls. They zigzagged down the street and around the corner, singing an En Vogue medley and bumping hips and cracking up with laughter. Two older boys sitting on the hood of a parked car made catcalls and kissing sounds at them as they went by. One of them yelled out, "Hey, look, it's a Oreo cookie! Hey, mama, wanna gimme a taste?" Robin paused long enough to say, "Asshole," but her friends gripped her arms and pulled her swiftly along.

Henry's was a coffee shop, where they ate burgers and fries and drank bright blue Slurpees. Some of the people eating at other tables and at the counter gave Robin funny looks, but nobody said anything to her.

On the way back to Images of You, they looked in a shoe-store window, admiring stiletto heels you could use as double-duty weapons—to drop-kick and stab somebody at the same time—and then they lingered at the window of a jewelry shop. Lucy and Robin ogled dangling earrings and Carmel chose matching wedding rings for herself and her future husband. They'd brought cheeseburgers and fries for Mr. Thompson and Garvey, and a tuna salad for Mrs. Thompson, who seemed disappointed when she opened it, and defiantly ate several of Mr. Thompson's fries. Garvey complained that everything was cold.

A little later he made a weak attempt to scare Robin in the darkroom, after Carmel had taken her there to show her around. He was hiding behind a file cabinet and he jumped out and yelled "Yo!" at her. But Carmel had warned her he'd probably do that, and she'd heard him breathing in the red darkness, so she yelled "Boo!" almost at the same moment, and then they both screamed a little in the aftershock.

Lucy explained that all of the color film was sent out to a lab for processing, but that her mother did the black-and-white custom work herself. When business finally slowed down, Mrs. Thompson came to the back to demonstrate. The room was small and the girls crowded around her in front of a row of trays. A blank page of paper floated in the first one in a pungent chemical brine. "Pee-*yew*," Carmel said, holding her nose, but Robin liked the caustic smell, just as she liked the smells of gasoline and bus exhaust that most other people hated. Although she had seen something like this in a movie once—when the submerged photograph slowly revealed the identity of a serial killer—it was still kind of exciting to watch the picture magically appear. No killer came into being this time; there was only a cloudy mass at first, which gradually revealed itself to be two figures standing in front of a mountain. The mountain looked like a regular mountain, like somebody really *could* have a picnic or a campout there. As Robin gazed into the tray, the details of her own faint features and Lucy's defined themselves: the very shape of their nostrils and lips, the complicated patterns of their hair, Lucy's delicately etched eyebrows, and every loose thread in the ripped knee of Robin's jeans. If she didn't know better, she would think it was some kind of miracle. At the instant of absolute focus, Mrs. Thompson caught the picture with a pair of tongs, pulled it from the tray and plunged it into the next one, to stop the developing. The picture was dunked twice more, in the other trays, then rinsed at the sink in the corner and hung, dripping, by a tiny clip, from a nylon clothesline overhead. A little while later, when the print was dry, Mrs. Thompson put it into a folded cardboard frame and gave it to Robin to take home as a souvenir.

There were other pictures of Lucy and Robin from that shoot, which Lucy brought to school to show Robin the following week. But that first picture proved to be the best one, somehow perfectly true, yet flattering at the same time. The two girls were looking at one another and smiling, as if they'd just been reunited by joyous accident at the foot of the mountain, after a long separation. They could have been mountain climbers who had lost one another in a blizzard. Or they might have been sisters, mysteriously separated in childhood. Or merely friends, having a good time together somewhere nice, of which Robin now had undeniable proof.

12

Dreamscape

    Linda was having that horrible dream again, the one in which she goes to bed, leaving the oven on, and then wakes to find the whole place in flames. Of course she wasn't ever really awake when she thought she was, and nothing was ever actually burning. Any one of several different things could trigger the dream: a slight fever, a distant siren, her alarm clock ringing, or even the aroma of a neighbor's late barbecue.

    This time it was particularly vivid—sirens again, frantically screaming, and a persistent smell of smoke. "Oh, no!" Linda cried, as she sprang up in bed, coughing, certain of real disaster, and that somehow she had caused it. Within minutes, she was in front of her television set, shivering in spasms while she watched the world go out of control. She'd already seen the coming attractions of this catastrophe in other news bulletins—the beating last year of that black man by those four white policemen, and then their acquittal today in Simi Valley. During the videotape of the beating, she'd leapt up from the sofa and said, "Wait! Don't!" with her hand raised like a traffic cop's, as if she could halt what was happening on the screen, or even reverse it. Afterward, she hated the way she felt, heartsick and powerless, yet responsible at the same time.

Still, Linda was as unprepared as the newscasters seemed to be as they struggled to put words to the terrible new pictures they were showing, pictures of blazing fires, of looting, of absolute chaos. She ran from the room several times to check on Robin and Phoebe, who, to her amazement, slept through everything, slept through history, as she would later think, as all children should be able to do. But right then, while it was happening, she only registered a general sense of horror and a fear that mortal danger was approaching fast, like an enemy on horseback. She had to keep seeing for herself that the girls were still all right. Among the scattered, stammered sentences coming from the TV, she heard "awful, awful," "South-Central," "torching," "raging fire," and "state of emergency." Nathan lived in Compton, practically on the edge of South-Central L.A. Linda had driven through its streets many times on the way to or from his place, as he must have done just as often coming to see her, and they'd gone shopping there together once or twice. They were supposed to have met that very evening for dinner at a Korean restaurant only a mile or so from where all the turmoil was now taking place. But Nathan had called during the afternoon to cancel the date.

It was Linda's day off from the Bod, and she was just sinking into a scented bubble bath when Robin banged on the bathroom door to say that Nathan was on the phone. He told Linda he was getting the flu or something, that he was leaving work early and getting right into bed. She was disappointed about the broken date and concerned about him, and she offered to run over that evening, after the baby was asleep, to bring him some soup. "No, no," he said. "My appetite's really shot, I won't want anything."

She asked if he had any fever, and he mumbled, Maybe, yeah, he probably did. Chills? she wanted to know. Sore throat? Aches and pains? Her questions seemed to exasperate him; he barely answered them. Men and sickness, she thought with fond impatience. Even brave, sweet Wright used to become a martyred monster when he caught a common cold, groaning and honking in bed until she had to drag her pillow into the living room to get some sleep. "Poor baby," she said soothingly to Nathan. "You take it easy, and I'll call you later to see how you're feeling." But he told her not to, that he was going to just try and sleep it off.

Maybe it was only the power of suggestion, or the fact that she was still damp from her interrupted bath, but after she hung up Linda started to feel chilled and achy herself. Robin was sealed inside her room, as usual, deafening herself with a blast of heavy metal, and when Phoebe passed out right after her next feeding, Linda lay down on the bed to take a little nap. When she woke to all that chaos, it was after nine. There was evidence in the kitchen that Robin had made herself supper from an assortment of cans, and she had given Phoebe one of the relief bottles of baby formula. Unlike Robin and Phoebe, Nathan was a light sleeper. When they dozed off together at his apartment after making love, and she got up carefully later to go home without disturbing him, he always felt her slightest movement and came awake. "Don't go yet," he would say in that drowsy, seductive voice, or he'd simply start to kiss and caress her, as if she were starring in an erotic dream he was having, and she would lie down beside him again for a little, blissful while.

Now she thought that he'd have to be *dead* to sleep through all this. She muted the TV and went back to the kitchen and dialed Nathan's number. But there was no answer. She redialed and let it ring and ring this time, but he still didn't pick up. On the third try she heard a series of shrill beeps and then a recorded voice saying that all circuits were busy. In the living room again, she perched on the arm of the sofa and watched the silent mayhem for a few minutes. Then she tried phoning Nathan once more, and got that same recording. What if he was sicker than he'd seemed? What if he needed help? Linda had never felt so trapped and helpless herself. If she wasn't afraid of leaving the children alone, she might get into the car and drive to his place. There had to be a way to bypass the area where all the trouble was. If only the telephone lines were open, if only she could talk to Nathan, or Vicki, or Rosalia, or *someone*. She thought of waking Robin, just for her company, but she knew that Robin, awakened like that, would be miserable company, and didn't Linda want to spare her the horror show still playing on the television screen? So she watched by herself and paced and tried the phone from time to time, and then she opened the front door and stepped outside into the mild, smoky night. The lights were on in almost every window around the courtyard, and Linda could see the nervous flutter of other television screens. Then she noticed someone lurking in the shadows near the apartment opposite hers. She felt a quake of apprehension, but she called out, "Hello? Hello?"

After a moment another robed figure emerged and stood in the dim glow of the coach-style lamps, like a religious statue. "Linda, is that you? It's me, Regina, from 1J. Isn't this the pits?" Linda had met plump, middle-aged Regina Clark several times near the mailboxes, where they'd mostly exchanged pleasantries about the weather. All Linda knew about the other woman was that she worked for a wholesale butcher (she'd once offered to get Linda a break on a side of beef), and walked her pet cat on a leash.

"It's terrible," Linda agreed, "and I'm so worried about my boyfriend."

"Why? Where is he?" Regina asked.

"Home, right near where everything's happening, and he's sick, besides. And I can't get through on the phone!"

"Maybe he's okay," Regina said doubtfully.

"I wish I could go over there and be sure," Linda said. "But I don't want to leave the kids alone tonight."

"Well, I could stay with them if you want me to," Regina offered, "but I think you'd be nuts to go out there. Just *listen* to that." The sirens continued to howl obligingly in the background.

Linda hesitated; after all, Regina was a comparative stranger. But wasn't Phoebe left in the hands of comparative strangers all the time at Kiddie Kare? There, two middle-aged, widowed sisters—Rose Petrillo and Angie Davidson—kept ten small children of working parents in their home. The sisters were licensed, of course, and Linda trusted her instinct that they were responsible and kind. She had no reason to think otherwise of Regina, and she remembered that rainy day in January when Nathan came so gallantly to her rescue and into her life. If their situations were reversed now, he would probably already be on his way. "Are you sure you wouldn't mind?" she said. "I'd just see how he is and come right back."

Regina followed Linda to her apartment, and they stood together watching the rioting on the television screen for several seconds before Linda headed for the bedroom to get her purse and shoes. "I'm not even going to bother getting dressed," she said. "I'll be back in a jiffy." But when she got to the front door, she turned around and ran in to look at the children one last time before she left.

In the car, she took a street map and a flashlight from the glove compartment, and tried to figure out a way to Nathan's without getting too close to the rioting. Against the far-off sirens, her own neighborhood seemed eerily quiet. There was very little traffic, and no one at all walking in the street. When Linda finally decided on a route, and pulled away from the curb, hers was the only car in sight. Before long, though, there were others, especially police cars and fire trucks that sped urgently by. Linda pondered how often fate seemed to put her at the wheel of a car during difficult times, a place she dreaded being even when things were normal. This was like an extension of the nightmare she still couldn't quite shake off. Why else would she be out alone in her bathrobe in the middle of the night, in the middle of a civil crisis?

There was a construction detour on the route she'd chosen, and she found herself in a narrow, bumpy rut of road between trenches, following glowing arrows into residential streets she didn't know and couldn't find on the map when she was able at last to pull over and look. Her flashlight flickered, the sirens went on wailing. She started out again, and soon realized that she'd passed the same house twice. She urged herself not to panic. After all, it wasn't like getting lost piloting a plane; you wouldn't eventually run out of gas and plummet to earth. The worst that could happen was that she would ride in circles for a while, and maybe get closer to South-Central than she'd intended. When another car pulled out of a driveway ahead of her, Linda decided to follow it, and soon she was in another area she didn't recognize, but at least she was going *some*where. She tooted her horn at the car she was following, hoping the driver would pull over and give her directions to Nathan's street, but he promptly picked up speed, and went right through a traffic light and disappeared. The sirens were louder and closer now; they were all around her, it seemed, and searchlights lit the darkening sky the way they did at Hollywood premieres. Linda realized that she was heading toward the conflagration, like a moth seeking the candle's flame. She decided to turn back at the next corner, but there she was caught, in a single-lane, one-way street, in a cortege of emergency vehicles—a fire truck, two police cars, and an ambulance—with their lights flashing and their sirens going like mad. At first, she saw only the fire truck and one of the police cars, but as soon as she slipped in behind them to make her turn, the ambulance and the second police car came up quickly behind her. Everyone was moving so fast Linda had to go fast, too, to keep up and not get in the way. It was insane; with cars parked on both sides of the street, some of them double-parked, there was really no chance to slow down and pull over once she'd joined the procession. Please let me be dreaming, she pleaded, leaning earnestly forward and clutching the wheel. But she was alarmingly awake, all of her senses heightened by the incredible noise and lights. By the time they came to a wider street, where the Mustang could break away from the screaming pack, Linda saw that she was in the middle of the battlefield, inside the very picture she'd watched with such dismay earlier on her television screen. The buildings all around her were burning and people were running wildly in every direction. The air inside the closed aquarium of Linda's car was steamy and hard to breathe. "Oh, God, oh, please," she intoned, before breaking into a spasm of coughing. She drove very slowly, wheezing and crying, through the crush of people. She could feel their bodies brush and bump against the doors of the car. Then somebody banged so hard on the roof Linda jammed on the brakes and threw her arms over her head. When she looked up again, faces appeared at all the windows, shouting and grimacing, and the car began rocking back and forth on its springs. Linda's immediate impulse was to step on the gas, but she was afraid she'd mow somebody down. So she honked, over and over again, as if she was stuck in rush-hour traffic. The horn made only pathetic little bleats in the general din; she could barely hear it herself. Then she tapped the gas pedal lightly, hardly enough to get moving, and the engine belched and backfired—once! twice!—like gunshots, scattering the crowd around her. She drove quickly through the hole they'd left, and out of there.

Later, looking at the news on television, she would recognize the street she'd been on. She and Nathan had been there together once on a sunny Saturday afternoon, to buy a leather jacket for him. Linda remembered the animal smell of the shop called Hide and Seek, and she imagined that when it burned it must have stunk like a slaughterhouse. She was sure she would never be able to wear leather again, never again eat meat. Of course, her revulsion diminished with time. Within a few weeks, she could put on her shoes without thinking of burning flesh, and she could bite into a hamburger without gagging on it. That was the blessing of human memory, she knew, that it allowed the worst images to gradually evaporate, so that your spirit and appetites can return, and you're able to live.

But that night, as soon as Linda arrived at Nathan's street, she jumped out of the car and vomited into a trash can, until she believed the very lining of her body had been shaken out and emptied of everything—food, guts, emotion. She moaned and hugged herself as she made her way to Nathan's building. When she got there, she looked up toward the second floor and his dark windows. If he *had* really managed to sleep through all of this, it would be one of those amazing, ironic anecdotes that people loved to tell. Once she got through this night, it would be something she and Nathan could talk about for the rest of their lives. Right now she just wanted to see that he was safe, and to feel that way herself again, in his arms.

She rang the bell downstairs, and when Nathan didn't respond, she rang all the bells until some poor trusting soul buzzed her into the building. Upstairs, she knocked weakly on Nathan's door. Again, he didn't answer, and she gathered the strength to knock harder. She began calling him, too, with her eyes shut and her face pressed against the cool, varnished wood. "Nathan? Honey, it's me! Come on, open up! *Please.*" But all she could hear when she listened was her own blood thumping in her ear.

She went downstairs to the parking lot and saw that Nathan's car wasn't in its designated spot. Oh, this was even stranger and more ironic than she'd imagined—while she was rushing here to take care of him, he was probably rushing in the other direction to see that she and the children were all right! It was something, she thought distractedly, like that story about the couple who sell their most precious possessions to buy each other Christmas presents they can't use anymore. Staggering back to her own car, Linda laughed out loud, a short desperate yelp, like the sound a skittish dog might make in its sleep.

It took her a long time to get home—there were traffic jams everywhere and some streets were completely closed off by then—but the return trip still seemed easier, because she was calmer now and better able to orient herself. As she ran up the walk to her own front door, it occurred to her that she'd been crazy to rush out like that, leaving the children with someone she, and they, didn't really know, someone who wore a bloody apron and kept a cat on a leash.

Nathan wasn't there, to her acute disappointment, and Regina Clark was snoring loudly on the sofa. She seemed as innocent in her sleep as the children, who Linda hurried in to check. They slept, too, under her burning gaze—her angels, her demons. Back in the living room, Linda had to shake Regina to wake her.

She yawned and rubbed her eyes. "Where am I? What time is it?" she asked. "Oh, shoot, I've got to walk Whiskers. How's the boyfriend?"

"He didn't come here?" Linda asked.

"What do you mean? I thought you were going there. I thought he was sick."

"Yeah, of course," Linda said. "I'm so tired I don't know what I'm saying." Where *was* he?

After Regina went home, Linda tried using the phone again, to no avail. Then she washed her face and brushed her teeth. Still wearing her bathrobe, she got into bed, intending to just rest until she could figure out what to do next. She was startled awake shortly after dawn by the jangling of the telephone, and again she sprang up from that same nightmare of fire. But this time it was true! She groped for the phone and heard Nathan saying, "Hello! Hello! Linda, are you there? Are you okay?"

Two people who'd worked at the Beverly Body Health Club and Spa died in separate circumstances the first night of the riots: one of the cleaners, a middle-aged man named Louis, was killed in a fire, and Kim, a seventeen-year-old shampoo girl who'd wanted to be an actress, was caught in a shootout between cops and looters. There was a discreet notice from management in the locker rooms a few days later, after it was all over, regretting the deaths and suggesting where commemorative donations might be made. Some of the employees clung to one another and wept, but the club's routine of workouts, massages, lip waxing, and earnest laps in the rooftop pool continued as usual. There was a new charge to the atmosphere, though. People avidly exchanged stories and opinions. A towel attendant at the pool held court there as she proudly told a rapt audience of clients and colleagues how she had to be rescued by firemen from her building that first infamous night. Somebody suggested that it would make a great television movie. And somebody else, a producer who had been in Paris during the whole mess, reported how a close friend had almost been *killed* when her chauffeur made a wrong turn and skirted the disaster area. Linda, on her break, was listening politely and thinking how much better (and worse) her own story was, when she suddenly remembered a conversation she'd overheard as a child between her mother and a neighbor about President Kennedy's assassination. They'd been discussing, in terribly thrilled voices, where each of them had been when she first heard the news. The neighbor was in a beauty shop getting a permanent wave that she claimed never took, because of the shock. Linda's mother had been on a job, caring for somebody else's colicky newborn. The baby had cried inconsolably that day, as if, Linda's mother said, it was grieving for the poor dead President. Years later Linda found out that both women had voted for Richard Nixon, and had never liked or trusted President Kennedy. The women at the Bod were divided on the political issues surrounding the riots, and there were little flare-ups about right and wrong and good and evil, but that didn't truly matter. The thing was, something was happening to them, at last! They were a part of, or at least close to, a historical event. That it was bad, even disastrous, seemed beside the point—they were horrified, but they also felt exhilarated, involved, *alive*. To her shame, Linda felt that way, too. People suffered and died in this, she reminded herself, and she slowly withdrew from the excited group and went off to her next class.

At home, Robin acted as if nothing unusual had taken place. Linda still wanted to protect her, but she had decided it was healthier to air things, and to let Robin express her own feelings. So Linda cautiously prompted her. "Isn't it a shame we all just can't get along with each other?" she said. But wasn't she merely being hypocritical? After all, Robin had more black friends than she did.

Robin didn't respond, but Linda went on anyway. "Why must people resort to violence," she asked, "when it never really solves anything?" Robin only slid further into herself, the way she did whenever a touchy or painful subject was raised. And when Linda turned the television on, to let the commentators speak for her in their wise baritones, Robin switched it right off, grumbling, "News, news, and more stupid news!"

Linda contemplated telling Robin about her ride into hell, just to get her full attention for once. She hadn't told anyone but Nathan so far, and he'd only deflected her questions about him by berating her for being so foolish. When he called that next morning, he insisted he'd been home all night, practically in a coma; that was why he didn't hear the phone or her knocking.

"But your car wasn't there!" she exclaimed.

After a pause, he said, "I know, that's right. I lent it to somebody, some guy in my building. His car was in the shop."

That was pretty hard to imagine—Nathan hated anyone touching his precious car. As Linda was getting ready to comment on that, though, *he* challenged *her*: Why was she giving him the third-degree? And what the hell was she thinking of, driving into the combat zone like that? She could have been killed! He was so upset he didn't want to talk about it anymore.

Robin, on the other hand, might simply resent Linda's going off and leaving her and Phoebe in the hands of a total stranger. Or she might further demonstrate her lack of interest in anything related to Linda, who felt too tender about personal relationships right then to risk another blow of rejection. So she gave up, and they didn't discuss any of it, as if it had never happened, as if it all actually was only another bad dream.

13

Blood Will Tell

Early one morning in May, Linda lay in bed nursing Phoebe and struggling to stay awake. She hadn't gotten enough sleep the night before, and there was the hypnotic drone of the endless shower Robin was taking. Then the baby paused in her steadfast sucking and bit firmly with her two premature little fangs into Linda's nipple. At that same moment, the lullaby of the shower stopped in a screech of braked plumbing. "Ouch!" Linda cried, pulling herself free, and then watched in horror as twin pinpoints of blood welled up. The baby, of course, began to wail in the shock of her separateness. Anyone coming upon that scene would think that Linda had bitten *her*.

Indeed, seconds later, Robin, naked and with her hair streaming, trailed talcumed footprints across the floor and yanked Phoebe from Linda's arms. "What'd she do to you now, Feeble?" she demanded.

Linda was certain that if Phoebe could speak, it would be in Robin's fresh, sarcastic lingo. "What *hasn't* she done?" she might have said. "You know that jerk can't do anything right. How come we never have any money? How come she's so dumb, huh? Did she leave her brain to science back in Newark? Huh? Huh?" It was almost as if Phoebe really *had* spoken those words, and

Linda was stuck, as usual, for a satisfactory response.

It was true that they were just about scraping by on her salary, that there wasn't enough left over for any sort of luxury or minor indulgence. And Robin, like all teenagers, was always wanting something: new clothes, tapes, Nintendo games, junk food, money in her pocket. Linda wanted certain things that she couldn't have, either, and before she knew it, Phoebe, too, would have desires beyond mere milk and affection. It was never enough to say you couldn't afford something, and that it was because of bad luck, even if it was the honest truth. God knows it wasn't Linda's fault that she couldn't properly support these two arrogant albino beauties. It wasn't her fault that the cost of living was so high, and that the Mustang needed so many expensive repairs. There were other people besides Robin who would say it was, though.

A few nights before, Vicki had come for supper, and they'd watched the evening news afterward. There was Vice President Quayle on the screen, blaming the L.A. riots on a breakdown of family structure, and saying that Murphy Brown mocked the importance of fathers by calling single motherhood just another life choice. "You'd better listen up there, Linda," Vicki said. "He's talking about you."

"He *is* not," Linda said.

"Oh, no? You're a single mother, aren't you?" Vicki asked. She glanced at Robin, supine on the floor, inches from the TV, with the sleeping baby sprawled across her chest. "This homey little scene sure doesn't look like *Life with Father* to me."

"But I *was* married," Linda said, indignantly. "Wright *died*, remember?"

"Please, please, Ms. Reismann. No excuses now."

Robin looked up. "Quayle's a real asshole," she said.

"Robin!" Linda exclaimed. "He's the Vice President of the United States!"

"Well, don't blame me," Robin said. "*I* didn't vote for him."

"Neither did I!" Linda said.

"You voted for Dukakis?" Vicki asked. "I did, too."

"No," Linda said, sheepishly, "not exactly. I mean, I didn't vote for anybody. I was moving around a lot that year and I never registered." In fact, she had never registered to vote in any election. Voting had always seemed to her like something only bona fide members of families and communities, of society itself, did. Nobody she would have voted for ever won, anyway—or ever lost by just one vote.

"So are you registered now?" Vicki asked.

"Not yet," Linda admitted.

Robin reached for the remote control, aimed it at the Vice President's heart, and in a moment they were watching *The Simpsons* instead.

Vicki was only teasing Linda about her single motherhood, but she hated having to defend herself when she hadn't done anything wrong. After all, she'd never planned on becoming anyone's widow at twenty-seven, or anyone's mother either, for that matter. She had always recoiled at the sight of those harried women in supermarkets and shopping malls, women driven by their own misery to jerk their children's arms right out of their sockets and scream some variation of "Shut up! I didn't ask you to be born!" But they *had* asked, or at least invited the possibility in some wanton, molten moment, when they probably would have agreed to quintuplets. Linda had blindly agreed to her own situation, too, in the quick, glad confusion of love—such an enormous return on such a small investment.

And now here she was, on the defensive again, and with Robin, of all people. "I didn't do anything to her," Linda said, about Phoebe. "She bit *me*. Here, look," she said, aware that she sounded more like a competitive child than a loving mother.

It didn't matter; Robin only muttered, "Sure, *right*," and carted Phoebe off without a backward glance. Faithless Phoebe began trying zealously to latch herself onto one of Robin's tiny breasts, which made Robin cry, "Ooh! Gross!" She flipped the baby upside down, holding her by the ankles with one hand as she strode away.

"Hey, watch it!" Linda yelled after her. "She's a person, remember?" Then the refrigerator door slammed shut, and Phoebe's wailing abruptly ceased, as if she'd been corked, and Linda knew that Robin was finishing the feeding with a bottle. Linda touched her wounded nipple and sighed. Maybe she'd have to think about weaning Phoebe completely soon, before she turned into a vampire. It would probably be a lot easier, anyway, with her own crazy schedule. She sighed again, more deeply, and glanced at the clock. It was seven already, almost time for Robin's bus, and for Linda to get Phoebe to Kiddie Kare and then go to work.

Linda's jazzercize classes at the Bod were supposed to be fun as well as beneficial, but her fitness-crazed clients didn't seem to care much about the fun part, and the early birds were the worst. They could hardly wait to get started every morning. When she got to the club, she'd find them warming up, climbing the StairMasters or running on the treadmills as if they were being chased. And when the class began, they would ignore her frequent pleas to "Smile, everybody!" and "Come on now, relax!" Instead, they glared at their own repeated reflections in the mirrored walls as they moved, and later demanded a heavier concentration on the "abs" or "pecs" or "glutes." It was like learning some repulsive new language. Once in a while, Linda felt a slight nostalgia for the male clients she'd gladly left behind at both Fred Astaire's. Some of them had been real creeps, of course, with roving hands and other parts, but she could almost forgive them now. At least their needs were familiar, and more or less human. Most of her regulars at the Bod were like those one-celled animals that reproduce by dividing. Her fantasy was to make them look at each *other*—just once—and then willingly take partners and glide together across the floor. There was nothing lovelier, to Linda's mind, than the physical teamwork of social dancing, except maybe the teamwork of lovemaking, both of which she and Nathan did together with uncommon success.

She took her own, quick shower and retrieved Phoebe from

Robin, who, it appeared, had had a Coke and a doughnut for breakfast again. Linda followed her around as she gathered some schoolbooks and loose papers and walked her way into her sneakers. "Your shoelaces are untied," Linda said. "You're going to break your neck one of these days."

Robin ignored her. She paused in her preparations only long enough to make a monster face at the baby, who rewarded her with a drooly smile and a joyful squirming of her whole self, reminiscent of a puppy wagging its tail.

Linda picked up the empty Coke can. "All that sugar!" she called after Robin as she was running out the door. "You are destroying your precious body!"

Robin didn't even pretend to have heard her. "Bye, Feeb!" she called back. "See you later!"

"See you later, honey!" Linda answered, as if Robin had really meant to include her in her farewell.

Well, at least her awful behavior was countered by her love for the baby. And the baby, who loved everyone, seemed to have chosen Robin as her favorite, also. There could actually be something genetic that bound them. Perhaps that's what Linda's mother used to mean when she'd say, mysteriously, "Blood will tell." Linda had never had any brothers or sisters of her own. But when she was a child, and left to amuse herself while her mother was working, she pretended to have a little sister she named Allergina, a variation of the name on the label of one of her mother's medicine bottles. Oh, all the mischief Allergina got them into! And all the sacred secrets Linda whispered only into her discreet, invisible ear: how much she missed her mother, away somewhere in her white uniform, caring for someone else's child; how much she feared her father, who had no patience with children, real or imagined. It was Allergina who joined Linda in her banishment to the dark closet or her lonely bed, and who murmured, "Never mind, never mind, never mind," until the punishment was over or Linda fell asleep. She was glad that Robin had the small but steady comfort of a real sister in her uncomfortable life.

When Linda was younger, with both parents dead, she had sometimes used men in an effort to fill the absence of family in her own life. She would try to fall head-over-heels in love, so that she'd become consumed by passion, the way other women she knew were consumed by their husbands and children, by the daily demands and pleasures of their households. Nothing so heartily willed ever lasted very long, though, and she began to look for something less thrilling, something more stable and permanent. Wright flowed conveniently into her life about then, into her modified needs. It wasn't settling for less, she told herself, it was settling down. And they *were* happy, in a reliable and quiet way, during their brief time together.

Linda had hoped that Robin would be a dividend of that solid union, that eventually she would come around to accepting Linda and even loving her. And maybe she would have, if Wright had lived. Even now, there were occasional moments of near-affection between them, when Robin was caught off her rigid guard by circumstance or Linda's dogged determination. She tried to recall these rare instances at other times, when Robin was at her angry, insolent worst.

Linda was ready to leave the house soon after Robin. She put the baby into her car seat in the back of the Mustang, and climbed in front and turned on the ignition. The car stalled, and one of the lights on the dashboard—the one marked "oil"—flickered on and off a few times before the engine finally turned over and the light went out. Now what? She'd just added a can of motor oil about a week ago, when she stopped at the service station to get gas, and the mechanic had poured some carburetor cleaner into the tank, to stop the backfiring. Maybe this was only a loose connection. She would have to ask Nathan about it later, if she remembered, but to be on the safe side she left the motor running while she carried Phoebe into the day-care center.

At the club, Linda called out a cheery good morning to her impatient first class, and then put a Technotronic tape on, turning the volume way up. She preferred mellower music, played more softly, so that her instructions could be heard without her having to scream or bark them out. But the women only wanted this hard-driving stuff, and they were always after her to make it louder, as if they might be driven to further extremes of exertion by the mere magnitude of sound. "Let's go, ladies! Burn it up, burn it out!" she cried over the frantic rhythms of "Pump up the Jam." Linda did short stretches of the workout herself, to demonstrate both the moves and her oneness with her straining, grunting students. In between, she went from woman to woman to correct flaws of posture or form, or just to offer praise. It amazed her to realize that she could never work them too hard, that even when they seemed on the verge of collapse, they wanted more and more and *more*.

At the end of this first session of the day, Linda was worn-out. The baby had been fretful during the night, probably because she was teething, and the only thing that seemed to calm her, for short stretches, was being nursed. Linda was still suffering the effects of that interrupted sleep. She retrieved her tape and wrapped a towel around her damp neck. She had a twenty-minute break between classes, and she decided to forgo a restorative shower in favor of looking for Nathan to ask him about that flickering light on her dashboard. But as she was leaving the exercise room, one of her students stopped her. She was probably the oldest woman in the group, a talent agent in her early fifties named Claire Winston, who never spoke above a stage whisper. It gave everything she said dramatic significance. "That was simply fabulous, Linda," she breathed. "I really mean that."

"Thank you," Linda said. She meant it, too; it was so rare that any of the women took the time to say something nice to her. It wasn't because they weren't perfectly nice themselves, but they were always in such a hurry—rushing off to their next physical torment or gratification, or to the locker room and then their own jobs.

"Do you have a minute?" Claire Winston asked.

"Sure," Linda said, trying not to whisper back.

"I have a friend, someone very big in the industry, who desperately needs a personal trainer." She looked around her at the empty room, and lowered her voice even further. "I'd rather not mention her name around here. The thing is, I told her how fabulous you are, and she could see for herself what you've done for me, and well . . . you're the one!"

The woman said it as if Linda had just won the California lottery. Linda knew that one-on-one training paid very well, especially if you did it independently, off the Bod's premises, but she could hardly handle her current workload and still be a rational, functioning mother. She didn't want to burden Robin with extra babysitting, or be away from Phoebe any more than she already was. "I'm really flattered that you asked me, Mrs. Winston . . ." Linda began.

"Please, it's Claire," Mrs. Winston said.

"But I'm pretty overextended right now," Linda continued. "Claire," she added, after a beat, to soften her refusal.

"She's somebody special, Linda," Mrs. Winston said in her urgent whisper. "And, strictly entre nous, she's been through a very rough time recently. Very rough." She waited a couple of seconds for that to sink in.

"I'm sorry to hear that," Linda said.

"I knew you would be," Mrs. Winston told her. "Look, let me just get a pencil and scribble her name and number down for you. The money would be fabulous, I assure you. You have a family, don't you? A baby, somebody said? And you'd be making a real contribution."

Linda was trying to think of some other gracious way to say no when Claire Winston headed for the front desk to borrow paper and a pencil. And by the time Linda got around to looking for Nathan afterward, he was in the middle of teaching his salsa workout. Their schedules overlapped after that until the end of the day, when Linda had to rush off and pick Phoebe up at day care. She and Nathan only had time to wave at each other and blow kisses. And an old friend of his was coming in from out of town that night, so she wouldn't see him then, either.

The light on the dashboard didn't flicker again on the way home, or the next morning as she drove to work. She was still going to mention it to Nathan, though, and she also wanted to tell him about the extra new job she'd agreed to take, against her original judgment. The night before, Robin had begun to nag her about a great TV she'd seen at the mall. Their set had been bought secondhand soon after they took the apartment, and it had played pretty well until recently, when everything, sound and picture, would suddenly sizzle and disappear in a field of staticky snow. Robin would bang on the set and fiddle with the indoor antenna until it all came back. But then it would happen again, usually in the middle of the same show. And when Nathan offered to look at it the other day, saying he'd once done a little TV repair on the side, he wasn't able to fix it.

"You could just charge it," Robin advised Linda about the new set she'd seen. It was useless to try to explain to her that even charged purchases had to be paid for eventually, and with the added expense of compounded interest. "If you watched less TV, maybe it wouldn't have burned out so fast," Linda told her. "And maybe your grades would be a lot better, too." That line of reasoning didn't go over very well, any more than her follow-up argument that they might both be better off without television. Robin just growled something back, and jiggled the antenna harder until a piece of it broke off in her hand. Linda couldn't help admitting, at least to herself, that the set *was* "crappy and old," and that she, too, would miss the pleasant distraction from real life that it provided. She decided to call the woman Claire Winston had told her about, and see exactly what she had in mind.

Someone with a heavy Spanish accent answered the phone, and soon after, Linda was connected with Cynthia Sterling. Unlike her friend, she spoke in a clear, vibrant voice, and she didn't sound at all like someone in severe distress. Yes, she was looking for a trainer whose emphasis was on dance movement.

But she was a very busy television producer with neither the time nor the inclination to come to a club. She was hoping for evening or weekend sessions at her own home, which she was sure could be arranged at their mutual convenience. And she was prepared to pay more than the going rate.

"The problem is," Linda said, in the wake of all that information, "I have a baby."

"I think Claire mentioned that. Is it a boy or a girl? How old?"

"Actually," Linda said, "I have two children, but one of them . . . well, it's kind of complicated . . ." She trailed off and then began again. "Anyway, it's, *she's* a girl. Five months old, and I don't have anyone to leave her with."

"Well, then bring her along," Cynthia Sterling said. "She can't take up too much room, can she?"

As usual, Linda got the joke too late, and said, "Oh, no, she's real little, and—"

The other woman cut in. "It'll be fine. Lupe, my housekeeper, will look after her for us. Shall we try this Saturday, at eleven?"

And so it was settled. She wasn't crazy about leaving Robin to her own devices any more than she had to, but maybe a new television set would keep her out of trouble while Linda and Phoebe were gone, the set they could only afford with Linda's moonlighting. As she drove toward the Bod the next day, she allowed herself to dream of other things besides a working TV that some additional income could provide. She envisioned new summer wardrobes for herself and Robin. Dinner out together at a restaurant you didn't have to drive through. And an assortment of those expensive, educational toys for the baby. She was still lost in her reverie of spending when she glanced at the dashboard and saw that the same red light, the one with the symbol for oil on it, was flickering again. This time it stayed on. If she tried to find a garage now, she'd be late for her eight o'clock class, and they probably couldn't even do anything about it right away. She wished she had mentioned the problem to Nathan yesterday. Well, she would do it this morning, for sure.

He was in the lobby of the club when she got there, leaning on the desk, talking to one of the blond receptionists, making her laugh. Linda had hardly ever seen her *smile* before. When Linda went up to them and told Nathan about the car, he said, "You didn't keep on driving it, did you?" She nodded miserably and then followed him out to the parking lot, where they discovered together that the car wouldn't start at all.

"Do you think it could be the battery again?" Linda asked, without much hope. Nathan had disappeared under the hood, as he'd done the day they met. He said something angrily in Spanish and slammed it down. "You know what I think?" he said. "I think you've got yourself a seized engine here."

"Is that very bad?" Linda asked, although she already knew the terrible truth from Nathan's face and from the words he'd used. A seized engine. She imagined it wrested from the Mustang, separated from all its vital connections, like a terminally ill patient detached from life support. She remembered Wright, helplessly hooked up in the hospital, and she thought of Manny reduced to his outline on the floor of the Liquor Barn, and she burst into tears.

"Oh, sweetheart, don't," Nathan said, taking her into his arms. They held her in a powerful brace of muscle and sinew, and she could smell his sweet skin and feel the regular clock of his heart against her own erratic flutter. How extraordinary it was to be held at that moment, not for sex or even dancing, but for the elementary and essential sake of solace. "It's only a car, right?" he said. "Hey, niña, what's the matter?"

After she'd wiped her eyes and nose with the back of her hand, she said, "Nothing. *Everything*. I have to have a car. I'm going to have to stop nursing the baby."

Nathan smiled. "You need to nurse her in a car?"

Linda smiled back as she sniffled. "*No*. Oh, you know," she said. "It all keeps piling up."

"Yeah, I do know, but you may have to forget about the Mustang. See?" he said, pointing upward toward a slow-moving cloud. "There goes its soul right now!" Then he said that he was sorry for making her cry like that, and to make up for it, he would be her personal driver until she got another car.

"Another car!" she cried. There went all her daydreams of consumerism. She would need the extra work just to make car payments, maybe for the rest of her life.

"We'll find you something good in a used model," he said. "Don't worry, I won't let you get stung. We can look around on Saturday morning, maybe get you a nice Jag or something, and blow old Robin's mind."

"I can't, Saturday morning," Linda said. "I've got this private job. And then I promised to take Robin for new sneakers after that. Do you mind? When do kids' feet stop growing, anyway? Can we go for the car another time?"

"Sure," he said. "I'm all yours."

14

To Have and Have Not

If Robin's hostility to Nathan was unreasonable, her reaction to Cynthia Sterling was even more extreme and unfair: she hated her before she'd ever set eyes on her. When Linda announced that she was going to start a second job on Saturday, as a private trainer for a woman in Beverly Hills, Robin folded her arms across her chest and said, "Well, don't expect me to babysit, I'm going to the mall that day."

"I had no intention of asking you to babysit," Linda said. "Who are you going to the mall with, anyway—Lucy? And how are you getting there? You're not thinking about hitching again, I hope, are you?"

"So who's staying with the baby?" Robin asked, neatly bypassing all of Linda's questions.

"I'm taking her with me. Cynthia Sterling's housekeeper is going to take care of her."

"Her *housekeeper*? What is she, a millionaire or something?"

"I sincerely doubt that," Linda said. "And I really don't care. All I know is that Mrs. Winston, from the club, said she's a lovely person, and that she's been having a very difficult time lately."

"Yeah," Robin said. "She must of broke her fingernail or something."

"Robin!" Linda cried. "Why must you always be so cynical? I mean, rich people have problems, too, you know. Maybe somebody in her family died, or maybe she's been sick herself."

"I'll bet," Robin said.

Linda regretted having taken Robin to the Bod that once, on a Saturday morning, before regular hours, just to show her around. She had thought it would be fun for her, the way the Universal Studios tour had been. After all, Robin was so star-struck. She was forever spotting celebrities in unlikely crowded places, like the mall or the beach; and when Linda fell for it, spinning around and saying, "Who? Where?" Robin would say, "You just missed him. It was Michael Jackson. I swear." Or it was President Bush. Or Madonna. Once, at a Jack in the Box, it was President Bush *with* Madonna. Many of the club's members were involved in the entertainment business—or, as everyone here called it, "the industry"—although most of them were executives or agents, or the wives of executives or agents. None of them would be at the Bod that early, anyway, but Linda thought the glamorous atmosphere itself would impress Robin.

That Saturday, true to form, she'd looked around the premises with a fixed expression of scorn on her face. Linda pointed out some of the particulars that had impressed her on her own first visit: the futuristic lobby; the rooftop swimming pool, with its exquisite mosaic border and retractable glass dome; and the private treatment rooms—each one a separate little asylum of luxury. One of the nicer masseuses had even invited Robin to lie down on her table for a mini-rub, but she'd curtly refused, as if the woman had offered to chain her to a torture rack.

Later the same day, Nathan drove Linda, Robin, and Phoebe to Rodeo Drive, to complete their Beverly Hills tour. They'd mostly window-shopped there, with Linda exclaiming over the elaborate displays of clothes and jewels. "Robin, look at that!" she kept saying. "Isn't that *incredible*?"

Robin had simply stared at everything and everyone with those laser-beam eyes, especially the bedecked and bejeweled women who walked past them and disappeared into the enticing and forbidding recesses of the stores.

Nathan tried to make a joke out of the whole thing. "Who wants to be rich, anyway?" he said, nudging Robin, who scowled at him in return. "Then somebody's always out to rob you, right?"

Linda knew that wasn't even true; poor people were more likely to rob other poor people, who were conveniently nearby and relatively unprotected. But she didn't see this as the fault of the wealthy, who had somehow managed to earn, and keep, their lion's share of things.

Robin, on the other hand, perceived a strict, totally unfair division between the haves and the have-nots. She persistently wanted what she couldn't have, and, to her mind, those who had what she wanted were all dirty rotten crooks. When Linda tried to reason with her, to point out that America was still the land of opportunity for all people willing to work hard and follow their dreams, Robin looked at her with contempt. Linda gave up. To tell the truth, she wasn't actually that persuaded by her own argument; she had worked pretty hard most of her life and she had hardly anything to show for it. What could these rich women have possibly done to deserve so much? Of course, Linda's life wasn't over yet, and she didn't think it was appropriate or useful to present a negative attitude to someone younger than herself. It didn't matter, anyway—Robin made her own crazy assumptions about everything, and nobody could talk her out of them.

Well, at least Linda was able to convince her to let Nathan drop her at the mall on their way to Cynthia Sterling's house in Benedict Canyon. Just as Robin was getting out of the car, she turned to Linda and said, "If you want me to, I'll take Feeb with me. She likes the mall, and she'd probably be bored stiff with some boring *housekeeper*."

"No, thank you," Linda said. "Phoebe will be fine. You just worry about yourself, Robin, okay? And I hope you really have a ride back with Lucy's father." Linda had managed to squeeze that dubious bit of information out of her during the trip here.

Again, Robin didn't bother to answer. She rapped Phoebe lightly on the head, saying, "Don't let Ms. Rich Bitch get to you, flake," before she strolled off toward the crowded mall.

"I don't know what I'm going to do with her," Linda said, with a heavy sigh.

"Leave her alone," Nathan advised as he drove away. "It's just a stage she's going through."

Like life, Linda thought, sighing again and looking out at the rushing scenery.

They stopped for gas a few minutes later. Nathan pulled up to the self-service island, slithered out of his Z, and headed for the cashier's station. As he walked away, Linda noticed the tinted window of a Mercedes at the full-service island sliding down. The woman sitting there lowered her sunglasses next and stared long and hard at Nathan walking back to his car and then pumping the gas. Linda looked at him, too, as if for the first time, at his dark ringlets and perfect profile, at his tilted hips, which were as narrow as a girl's. He was wearing a gauzy white shirt that fluttered in the mild breeze against his sculpted shoulders and back.

The woman in the Mercedes began a thorough inspection of Linda and Phoebe now, with occasional, calculating side-glances at Nathan. Nathan replaced the gas nozzle and gave her a little mock salute. "Everybody says she can't be my kid," he said, "but, hey, I know my woman's true-blue."

"Nathan!" Linda squealed, but the window of the Mercedes had already slid up, and Nathan slipped in beside her, kissed her gaping mouth, and started the engine with a roar.

"You're worse than Robin," she chided as they pulled away, but she felt suddenly, excessively happy, and less nervous than she'd been about the new job. She even sang along with the radio while they drove, some impassioned Spanish love song to which she had to fake the words, making Nathan laugh.

Linda was still singing as they approached the wrought-iron gate of a walled estate. Then she saw the name *Sterling* etched in silver script above an intercom box and the song disappeared down her throat. "Oh, my goodness. Nathan, stop, this must be it," she said. Nathan switched off the radio and they both grew quietly thoughtful. The closed gate was tall and ornate, like the one at Paradise, and there was a winding, tree-lined gravel road beyond it. Linda leaned out the window to ring the bell on the intercom, and when a voice crackled, "Yes?" she said her name in an awed whisper. In moments, the gate slid open and they drove slowly up the road. The rambling, pink stucco house at the end of it was a pale gem set against a deep-green velvet forest. It had a handsome terra-cotta tile roof and a little courtyard with a turquoise ceramic fountain that splashed and sparkled in the dappled sunlight. To Linda, the scene was like a picture in a magazine, and she had just turned the page and been surprised by it. Nathan braked sharply when he was still more than fifty feet from the circular driveway, where a sleek Porsche and a sporty-looking Jeep were parked. He took one hand from the wheel and hastily crossed himself.

"Why did you do that?" Linda asked.

He shrugged. "Habit," he said, and he leaned over and kissed her forehead, and then Phoebe's.

Linda kissed him back, skimming his ear. "Thanks an awful lot for taking us, Nathan," she said.

"Anytime," he told her. "Just don't go Hollywood on me, sweetheart, okay?" Then he stepped on the gas again, and they drove over the flying gravel toward Oz.

Robin wasn't meeting Lucy at the mall, as she had let Linda think. They'd had a big fight in the corridor at school the day before, and now they weren't speaking to each other. Lucy had started acting really uptight when they kept showing Rodney King getting beat up on the news every night, as if it was all Robin's fault. Then, when the Thompsons' store was torched during the riots, *that* seemed to be Robin's fault, too. In fact, Robin had been so upset by that dim, silent black-and-white tape of the beating, she'd turned the TV off and stopped watching everything for a few days. It was much more disturbing than the noisy, full-color violence on some of her favorite cop shows—the ones Linda was always telling her not to watch—and it only proved what she'd always known, that the whole world, and everybody in it, sucked. And when she heard about Images of You getting burned up, Robin felt as bad as if somebody had died. But Lucy didn't want her sympathy, she didn't even seem to want her around very much.

Later, when they called a special assembly in school to discuss all the issues—the beating, the verdict, the riots, and the beating of that white guy, Denny—Robin had sat in confused silence, while all around her black kids and white kids shouted and taunted each other. The teachers had to patrol the aisles, like cops, to break up fights, and the principal kept screaming for order over the P.A.

Robin and Lucy became friends again, but it wasn't the way it used to be. Lucy was super-sensitive—she'd blow up if you looked at her crooked. Then, yesterday, weeks after everything was over, Robin asked her to cut English and go to the beach with her, and when Lucy wouldn't, Robin accused her of being a goody-goody, the teacher's little kiss-ass slave.

Lucy grabbed Robin's wrist, hard. "Don't you *ever* call me that again, girl, you hear?" she said, her big eyes narrowed and smoldering with anger.

Robin tried to escape, but Lucy held on so tightly Robin's wrist began to burn. "Hey," she said, "let go! I didn't call you anything." Lucy only intensified her death hold, and Robin bopped her with a math book. Of course, Lucy hit her back, and finally two boys had to jump in and separate them.

When Robin was waiting for the bus later, Carmel came by and started to talk to her, but Lucy strutted up, saying, "Why are you talking to that racist pig?" Carmel seemed as shocked and bewildered as Robin, but she walked off with her sister, lagging behind a little and glancing sorrowfully back at Robin.

Robin might run into some other kids she knew at the mall,

and one of *their* fathers could offer her a ride home later, so what she had told Linda wasn't an out-and-out lie. She'd felt much too restless to stay home by herself, while Linda was off sucking up to some billionaire. Every time she thought about Lucy, Robin would start to get mad—she *wasn't* racist, Lucy was crazy if she thought she'd meant *that* kind of slave. And Robin really hated to be called a pig, since that was the animal she privately feared she most resembled. But her anger gradually gave way to a feeling of anxiety and sadness that was almost unbearable. She couldn't stay home, she had to get away. But in the bustling aisles of the mall, Robin still felt anxious and alone. Even the profusion of material goods in the stores couldn't tempt or soothe her.

She didn't try to hitch a ride home until she had walked about a half mile past the mall, to the side of a heavily trafficked road. Then, keeping one eye out for any red Zs that might be coming along, she stuck out her thumb. There were days when she'd stand there for fifteen or twenty minutes before anyone stopped. Other times, it was as if the pickup was prearranged; someone would pull over, she'd get in, and that would be that. A few weeks ago, a police car skidded to a stop alongside her, and one of the cops inside said, "You looking for a ride, sis?" A woman's voice on the car's radio kept sputtering stuff Robin couldn't make out, probably about murders and robberies that were taking place that minute, while the cops were busy bothering someone innocent like her.

"No, thanks," Robin said coolly. "I'm waiting for my father."

"He picking you up all the way out here?"

"Yes," she said. "He works over there." She pointed vaguely toward some buildings across the wide road. One of them could have been the police station, for all she knew, and the cop didn't look like he believed her for a second. But he must have been in a good mood or in a hurry or something, because he only said, "Well, you be careful now, sis," and they drove away.

Now Robin stood there with her thumb out, and cars whizzed

steadily by her. But after about ten minutes she got lucky; an older guy in a Buick convertible pulled up and said, "Where to?"

Robin looked him over quickly but carefully. Despite what Linda thought, she knew what she was doing. The guy seemed okay—friendly, but not too friendly—and she was pretty sure most ax murderers didn't drive around in new white convertibles. She named a street two blocks from home, and he leaned over to push the passenger door open and said, "Hop in."

Nathan waited with the motor running while Linda pushed the doorbell. A series of musical chimes went off inside the house, and she could hear what sounded like a whole pack of dogs barking. As soon as the heavy oak door opened, Nathan's car pulled away behind her. She didn't even have a chance to remind him that she'd call when she was ready to be picked up. She spun around to wave at him, but he kept on going without looking back. When she turned to the door again, a tiny Mexican woman in a maid's uniform was standing there, flanked by two huge black dogs, who were still barking vigorously and wagging their stunted tails. The woman held her arms out for Phoebe, and Linda relinquished her and the diaper bag before she bent down to pat the excited dogs. "Hi, there, cuties," she crooned. "Oh, you just want to say hello, don't you? Don't you?" The woman crooned something in a similar tone, in Spanish, to the baby, as Linda and the dogs followed them into the house.

She found herself in a large vestibule, which had the same beautiful and mysterious quality of light and shadow as the little courtyard. There was an expanse of lustrous blond floor under her feet, with a jewel-like pattern in its center from the stained-glass skylight overhead. Linda turned to give the woman instructions about the baby, but they had both disappeared, and another woman, in her forties, dressed in a black leotard, with silver-streaked black hair and intense dark eyes, was standing at the top of a spiral staircase across the room, looking down at her. "It's Linda, isn't it?" this woman said, in a commanding voice, as she started to descend the stairs. "I'm Cyn Sterling, and you're just in time to save my life."

Robin had combed out her braids the night before, when she was still feeling furious with Lucy. She didn't want to look like her anymore, or have anything to do with her. Linda had been after Robin for months to undo the braids, just for a while. She kept saying that Robin's hair would fall out if she didn't let it breathe. Robin told her that was stupid—hair didn't have *lungs*—and to mind her own business, but she was secretly a little worried that Linda might be right. So when she snipped the rubber bands with Linda's cuticle scissors last night, and ran her fingers through her liberated hair, she was relieved that it stayed attached to her head, and astonished by the way it had thickened and rippled during its long confinement. Even after an energetic brushing, it still fell into an abundant cascade of waves. And in the convertible it blew wildly around her face without losing any of its new, crinkly fullness.

They'd driven about a mile and the driver hadn't said a word since he'd invited her to hop in, which was fine with Robin. She hated the talkers, the ones who made her pay for the ride by listening to them yakkety-yak about their boring lives. Sometimes they dragged out pictures of their wives and kids and dogs, and one joker had even slipped on a tape of his whiny brats singing nursery rhymes. Like she really wanted to hear that. This one just slapped his hand in a relentless tattoo on the rim of the steering wheel as he drove. As if he was listening to some fast-paced music in his head and was keeping time with it. Then, all of a sudden, after a mile or so, he said, "That *cunt.*"

"Huh?" Robin said, not positive she'd heard him right, what with the wind in her hair and his hand slapping the wheel that way.

"The Colonel's fucking, tight-assed daughter," he said. "*You* know who I mean."

Occasionally, Robin envisioned a situation like this, just for the fun of it, and in order to test her survival skills. She would get into a car with some psycho, the way Linda had always predicted she would, and she'd have to figure a way out of the situation. Like, when he slowed down, she would open the door, turn herself into a human ball, and roll safely away from traffic onto the shoulder of the road. Or she would outsmart him with some clever double-talk, the way she'd seen it done in the movies. The girls who became ax fodder were probably all chickens who screamed and pleaded, who couldn't shut up even to save their own lives. Linda was exactly the kind of person those loonies loved to kill. So Robin didn't say anything. The guy didn't slow down, though, and he kept driving in the fast lane; if she tried to get out now, she would be road jelly in about a second. She'd have to outsmart him, after all. "Hey, I just remembered!" she shouted over the wind. "I have to get off here! I have to pick up some medicine for my mother! Hey, mister?"

Linda discovered that the house had a real gym on the upper level, a vast mirrored room with a gleaming dance floor, a barre, and a quadraphonic sound system. The workout went very well. Cynthia (like Claire Winston, she'd insisted on first names) was a willing pupil, with the right combination of natural grace and energy. She had a lovely, willowy figure, which, she told Linda, she intended to keep as long as she was aboveground. Best of all, she'd rejected the kind of nerve-jangling music the women at the club always demanded. Linda had put on a tape by one of those strident young rap groups Robin loved, and although the volume she'd set was moderate, the words ricocheted around the room like bullets:

So he broke your heart and he stole your money
And he gave your clothes to a brand-new honey
Still you're lookin' good, baby
Lookin' real good

So he left you lyin' on an empty bed
With tears and blood gushin' outta your head
Still you're lookin' good, baby
Lookin' real good!

"Jesus!" Cynthia said, hitting the power button on the tape deck and hurling the room into silence. "They sound like a bunch of angry castrati!" She ejected the tape and inserted one of her own: fluid bossa novas and dreamy standards played on jazz guitar. Still, both women managed to work up a good sweat during the next hour. And they did it without any props or aids, like the steps or Dyna-Bands or weights that were so popular with other trainers at the club. Linda believed in using only your own body in space and against the pull of gravity.

"That was *great!*" Cynthia exclaimed, collapsing onto an exercise mat at Linda's feet. She was smiling, glowing. Linda couldn't help thinking that she didn't look at all like someone who'd been sick or bereaved recently. Without getting up, Cynthia directed Linda to a bathroom down the hallway for a shower.

"Oh, but I didn't expect . . ." Linda began. "I mean, I didn't even bring a change of clothes with me. So, if I could just use the phone, I'll call my boyfr—"

Cynthia interrupted. "Don't be a goose," she said. "There's a terry robe behind the bathroom door—you can wear that to lunch. And we'll find something to fit you later."

It was amazing that someone lying down could be so authoritative. Linda went obediently down the hallway, past several closed doors, and one that was opened onto a room where a woman typed noiselessly in the otherworldly glow of a computer. She didn't look up as Linda tiptoed by, feeling like a figure in someone else's dream.

The spacious bathroom was as white as a blizzard—the walls, the floor, the towels, the oversized loaves of soap, everything. The porcelain fixtures looked old and new at the same time, with their sleek contemporary design and antique gold faucets. There was a walk-in linen closet, a sauna, and even a bidet, like the ones at the Bod! The stall shower looked big enough to lie down in. Linda opened the etched-glass door and stepped inside, still wearing her damp leotard and tights. Above her there was a slanted skylight through which she could see a dense bower of treetops and a patch of gorgeous blue sky. She stepped out again, took off her clothes, and faced the full-length mirror opposite the shower. She had not seen her entire naked self in such naked light for a while. Getting dressed or undressed at the gym or at home, she was always in such a hurry. And having a lover again, especially so soon after the baby was born, made her feel self-conscious, almost shy of her own image. What if she didn't like what she saw, what *he* saw? Nathan's body was so beautiful. Now she forced herself to look in the mirror. Her skin had a yellowish cast in all this whiteness and her ears poked out through her dank hair. But working at the club had slimmed her body down, had tightened her stretched skin and softened stomach muscles. Her breasts were unusually full, but not really pendulous. When she stopped nursing, they'd probably shrink back to normal again, but now she turned sideways, admiring their imposing profile. Then she glanced guiltily upward, toward the skylight, as if she were being caught out in her vanity by God or some nosy bird flying by. And she stepped quickly into the shower.

There were three different water jets, one overhead and the other two on opposite walls at waist level. She let out a shocked cry when the water first struck her. But the pressure here didn't suddenly fail, the way it did sometimes at home, and the water's temperature didn't keep changing between scalding and freezing. Gradually she relaxed under its reliable warm drumming. She was keenly, luxuriously alone in this amazing place, and for once she didn't have to think about a single moment ahead of this moment. She held the soap with both her hands. It had a wonderful perfume, like a garden at night, and it made a thick, creamy lather. She soaped her arms until they wore long, billowing sleeves of white. Then she washed herself everywhere with a mother's tenderness, and the soapsuds slid off in foamy rivers that frothed at her feet before they disappeared down the drain.

There were all sorts of shampoos and conditioners on a recessed shelf in the shower wall, but she washed her hair with the white soap, too. And rinsed and rinsed it. She revolved slowly with her eyes shut and let the water pelt her everywhere. Then she sat down on the floor of the shower, under the steam-clouded trees and sky, with her knees drawn up. After a while, she realized she had been asleep and she scrambled to her feet. Miraculously, the water was still warm, but the bar of soap in her hands had dissolved to a sliver, and her fingers were as wrinkled and pink as a newborn's.

The towel she plucked from the heated rack opened into a floor-length cape she wrapped royally around herself. She inhaled her own flesh as she rubbed it dry, her fingers and shoulders and armpits, for the lingering traces of the soap's fragrance. When she emerged from the bathroom, wearing the white velour robe, she felt bridelike, purified.

Linda found Cynthia downstairs in the kitchen, which was probably bigger than Linda's entire apartment. The whole house was enormous, yet Cynthia lived here alone, she said, except for Lupe and the houseman, who sometimes doubled as a chauffeur and stayed in an apartment over the garage. As they set the table together, Cynthia told Linda that her husband had lived here, too, until just a few months ago, when they split up. That, apparently, was the big tragedy in her life, and although Linda was sympathetic, she was also a little disappointed. Mrs. Winston—Claire—had hinted at a darker and more mysterious story. Separations were very sad, but common; Hollywood marriages were always breaking up. According to Vicki and all the gossip at the club, everyone out here played musical beds. And Cynthia seemed far more angry than bereft. Her husband, who she referred to only as "the Director," was now living in Malibu with somebody Cynthia called "the Starlet." Linda wondered if they were famous. Robin, who kept up with things like that, would probably know.

As Cynthia pulled open the vault-sized refrigerator and peered inside at its packed shelves, Linda said, "Wow, it's like a whole other *room.*"

"Yeah, that's so the lamb chops don't get claustrophobia." There was a brief pause and then Linda laughed uncertainly. "Bad joke," Cynthia said. "I have a million of 'em. Let's see now . . . lobster salad okay?" She began pulling things out and handing them to Linda. "And we've got bagels and croissants—and how about some Montrachet, and a little guacamole? We can have ourselves a nice, ecumenical buffet."

Linda was beginning to wonder again where Phoebe was, when Lupe came into the kitchen, carrying her aloft like a trophy. "Aquí está mamacita!" she announced, handing the baby to Linda, and giving each of them a maternal pat on the behind.

"Well, well, look who's here," Cynthia said.

Phoebe, who usually smiled at everyone, stared back at her with sober, unblinking eyes.

To break the awkward silence, Linda waved the baby's little hand at Cynthia, saying, "Say hello, poopsie. Or has the cat got your tongue?"

"What's her name?" Cynthia asked. "It's not actually 'poopsie,' I hope."

"Oh, no, it's Phoebe," Linda said, looking the baby over. She seemed perfectly fine; her diaper had been changed and her neck was lightly dusted with talc. Linda kissed the scented creases.

"Really?" Cynthia said. "After Holden Caulfield's little sister?"

"Pardon?" Linda said. Then, "Phoebe was my mother's name. I'm afraid I don't know those other people."

"Oh, you mean you never read *The Catcher in the Rye*?"

Linda blushed and shook her head. "I don't actually read very much," she admitted, "what with work and the baby and everything."

"It probably wasn't compulsory in your high school like it was in mine. But, quel relief, after *Scaramouche* and *Silas Marner*! Just wait a minute, I'll be right back."

While Linda waited, she exchanged smiles with Lupe, who seemed to take that as an invitation to snatch the baby back. She sat down at the table with Phoebe in her lap and proceeded to amuse her by jouncing her vigorously, and by making a series of noises with her tongue, like the chirping of tropical birds and the clicking of castenets.

Cynthia came back into the room and handed Linda a book. "Here," she said. "But remember, I'm going to ask questions later!"

"Thanks," Linda murmured, staring down at the unopened book in her hands, wondering what kind of questions they'd be, until Cynthia grabbed it back and plunked it down next to one of the placemats on the table.

"Let's eat," she said. "I'm starving—aren't you?"

Linda realized that she was, and since Phoebe wasn't squawking for her lunch yet, she sat down across from Cynthia at the table. Lupe was still sitting nearby, making those noises and jiggling the baby into a golden blur. "Basta, Lupe," Cynthia said, "before she turns to butter. And have something to eat, too. You can't just live on love, you know."

But when Lupe stopped bouncing her, the baby continued the motion on her own.

"Smart little bugger, isn't she?" Cynthia said, and Linda flushed with pride. It was so pleasant sitting there in that velvety robe, eating such delicious food in such friendly company. She realized how hectic her usual daily life was, with hardly any time to relax or even think.

"You have two children, right?" Cynthia asked as she poured iced tea from a crystal pitcher. "Is there a man in all this?"

"*Was*," Linda said. "Their father, my husband, Wright. But he died, back in Newark, before Phoebe was born. Before I even knew there was going to be a Phoebe."

"Men," Cynthia said, with an exasperated sigh, as if Wright had elected to die rather than live up to his earthly responsibilities.

"It wasn't his fault—" Linda began, tired of always having to defend poor Wright, but Cynthia cut her off with a dismissive flick of her hand.

"When is it ever their fault?" she said. "The Director fell for the Stewardess against his will, too. It was like a dybbuk had gotten into him, he said, and what could the poor guy do? But we all know who got into who, don't we?"

Linda didn't think Cynthia's husband's affair could truly be compared to Wright's dying, and she was confused: didn't Cynthia say her husband had gone off with an *actress*?

"It was supposed to be a simple little desk-top fling. You know? But then he knocked her up—can you believe it, when they're handing out condoms in junior high?—and now he wants to *marry* her."

Linda didn't know what to say, so she just nodded in commiseration, hoping that would do.

Cynthia nibbled on some cheese and went on. "You must understand, the Director's a man who never wanted children. We agreed on that before we married. And frankly, I gave him more credit. I mean, she's such a *cliché*. Blond, boobs, and completely banal. If I was casting the part, there'd be a line from here to eternity." She paused to catch her breath. "I don't know why I'm telling you all this," she said. "I don't usually bare my soul to strangers. And Jocelyn, my shrink, gets two-fifty a pop for listening to this shit. It must be something about you that invites confidences, Linda. When your legs go, you could become a lay analyst. Believe me, you'd always make a living in this town."

The baby began fussing to be fed then, saving Linda from any further response. Cynthia led them upstairs to her bedroom, another vast, elegant space, and directed Linda to make herself comfortable on one of a matching pair of apricot silk chaises. The walls were covered in a similar fabric, and there were acres of pale plush carpeting underfoot. Linda felt as if she were suspended in a gigantic bowl of apricot Jell-O. She prayed Phoebe wouldn't spit up anywhere.

Later, after the drowsing baby was carted off again by Lupe, Cynthia, who had lain on the twin chaise reading a book during the feeding, made her amazing proposition. She wanted to hire Linda for one-hour training sessions two or three times a week, and she was offering to pay her a hundred dollars a session! Other trainers at the Bod had said they got as much as sixty or seventy dollars, but they had much more fitness experience than Linda, and she would never have had the nerve to ask for that much money, anyway. The night before, when she had dared to imagine herself actually getting the job, she'd also imagined asking for forty dollars a session, which was twice what she earned at the club, and the possibility of such riches had made her lightheaded. Now she was shocked into speechlessness, which Cynthia took as hesitation on her part.

"I believe that's a highly competitive fee," Cynthia said, "and, remember, the babysitting's on the house."

Linda finally found her voice. "Oh, my goodness, yes," she said. "It's terrific! I mean, I only hope I can—"

That flick of the hand again, and it was as if she'd severed the wires that animated Linda. "It's settled, then," Cynthia announced. "We'll ask Hester to work something out that's compatible with both our schedules."

Hester—that was probably the woman at the computer, a kind of private secretary. "Great," Linda said, "I can't tell you . . ."

But Cynthia had gotten up and was sliding some doors open to reveal a wall of closets that were as generously stocked with clothing as the refrigerator had been with food. She began pulling garments from hangers and shelves. "Try these on," she said, tossing a few items in Linda's direction. "I think the pink jumpsuit would work, with your coloring. Have you ever been colorized? I'll bet you're a spring or an autumn."

Linda demurred—she couldn't borrow such beautiful and expensive clothes, and her own things were probably dry by now. She'd left them on a hook behind the bathroom door; why didn't she just go and see?

"Forget it," Cynthia said. "The jumpsuit's a gift. It was never right for me, anyway. Come on, Galatea, let's see how you look in it."

.

Robin had started to think in headlines: *Jersey girl killed in freeway crash. Blonde's body mangled beyond recognition.* She imagined Linda coming to the morgue to identify the mess of hair and bone and blood she'd be, and it gave her a small thrill of spite. The wimp would be sorry for dragging her all the way out here, just to die horribly like this. And Lucy would be even sorrier for picking that fight and calling her names. But then Robin thought of Phoebe, growing up without a sister to guide and defend her, with only Linda between her and the rest of the world. And she thought of her things, left behind forever. The picture of her and Lucy that Mr. Thompson had taken and that she'd propped on her dresser top. Both of them smiling, leaning together. Those dumb love chains. Her tapes and her clothes, all of which would probably be out of style by the time Feeb was old enough to use them. Their father's painting of that park in Rahway, which Linda had hung on the wall facing Robin's bed, so that it was the first thing she looked at every morning, and the last thing she saw each night. Manny's champagne cork rolling around in the dusty darkness of her night-table drawer. "You better pull over," she told the Buick's driver. "I think I'm gonna be sick." It wasn't exactly a lie, but it didn't matter, anyway—he kept on driving, kept on looking straight ahead, as if he'd forgotten she was there. And he was still punishing the wheel with the palm of his hand. Robin might have been invisible, already a ghost before the inevitable accident. "Stop! Stop the car!" she screamed into his ear while she pounded his arm with her fists. "Please! Please! I don't want to die!"

When Linda announced that she'd better call Nathan to pick her up, Cynthia tried to talk her out of it. "Don't bother," she said. "Mellors will drive you home in the Jeep."

"No, thanks, really," Linda said. "Nathan is waiting for my call." She was beginning to feel a little overwhelmed by Cynthia's generosity. How could she ever live up to it?

Nathan's line was busy. She had to dial three or four times before she got through, and it was awkward, with Cynthia in the room. Linda felt the need to make excuses for Nathan: "It must be a business call," she said. "Or maybe he's trying to get in touch with *me* at the same time." And then, "Gosh, I hope his phone's not out of order!" When he finally answered, he said he'd come and get her, but that he had another quick errand to run first.

Lupe came back with the baby and her belongings and the two big dogs bounded in with them. "Aren't you sweet! You came to say goodbye to me, didn't you?" Linda said, while they lavished her with canine love.

"You make friends everywhere you go, don't you?" Cynthia said.

"Oh, they're just a couple of old pussycats," Linda said.

"Well, Bismarck and Brunhilde are not the man-eaters they were hired to be," Cynthia admitted. "But believe me, they don't take to the mailman the way they've taken to you. You have a rare quality, Linda—you bring out the best in everyone."

Nathan took his sweet time getting there, forcing Linda into further embarrassing conjectures about traffic and car trouble. And when he showed up at last, he honked long and noisily for her, like a rude teenage suitor. Linda said her goodbyes and hurried outside. She was surprised to see Robin sitting beside Nathan in the Z, her face almost hidden by that explosion of hair. When Robin saw Linda, she climbed into the back without a word. Linda deferred her own good news to ask some pressing questions. "What happened to Lucy's father? And where did you two find each other? You weren't hitching again, Robin, were you?" But Robin played dead back there and Nathan said, hastily, that he'd driven past the mall on his way here, spotted Robin, and given her a lift. Linda thought she saw them exchange a fast, friendly glance in the rearview mirror. Then Nathan put a tape on, at full volume, ruling out the prospect of any further discussion.

Robin knew that if it wasn't for the accident, she would probably still be a hostage of that psycho in the Buick. But, as it happened, the car just ahead of them on the freeway collided with a truck, right before an exit, and when the psycho jammed on his brakes, she was able to jump out and run for it. "Stupid cunt!" she heard him say as she took off, even though the two drivers in the crash were both men. There was a lot of excitement, what with the broken glass and the drivers screaming at each other and all the horns honking. Other people got out of their cars, too, to rubberneck, so she wasn't that conspicuous running across the lanes to the off ramp, even when she tripped over a stray hubcap and skinned her knee. She didn't know where she was—they had been driving forever—and nothing around there looked familiar. But there was a gas station only a few yards away and she headed for it. An attendant came up to her and said, "Hey, were you in that accident, kid? Are you okay?" It must have been her tangled hair and her bleeding knee. Robin said, "Yeah, I'm fine, I just gotta use your phone, okay?" The guy said, "Sure, go into the office, and you'd better sit down, you're white as a ghost. Do you want a drink or anything?" Robin told him she'd have a Coke, and while he went to get it for her from the machine, she went to the office. She would have called Vicki to bail her out, but her mother had a stroke or a heart attack or something the other day, and she had gone to Akron to take care of her. So Robin called Rosalia, who wasn't home, and then, with her heart skipping madly, Lucy, whose line was busy, and finally, as a last resort, Nathan. By then the attendant had come back with her Coke and a bag of chips, and she was able to find out where she was and tell Nathan. He didn't sound thrilled to hear from her, but at least he didn't ask a lot of annoying questions, the way she knew Linda would later. He only cursed a little before he hung up. And he kept his promise not to give her away to Linda. They all rode home together in peace and quiet, except for Phoebe, who kept bouncing on Linda's lap and making these funny little chirping sounds.

15

The Kiss of Death

Madman Moe's ("Stop me before I sell again!") Used Car Emporium was on Valencia Boulevard, a few miles south of the airport, and directly in the flight path of incoming planes. As soon as Linda stepped out of Nathan's Z, with the sleeping baby glued to her chest and the diaper bag hung over her shoulder, a DC-10 came shrieking down through the cloud cover, setting off a frenzy among the plastic banners and threatening to shear off her head. She ducked, and shrieked, too, while Phoebe, who could sleep through anything except Linda's desire for her to sleep, stayed blissfully unconscious. No wonder Madman Moe screamed that way on his late-night commercials; he was probably deaf by now from all the noise. After the jet was gone, Linda looked up at the billboard above the trailer at the rear of the lot. A giant-sized Moe in his trademark straitjacket looked back at her with a lunatic gaze. *Stop me before I sell again!* he pleaded. Well, she certainly would if she could.

A moment later, Robin shimmied her way out of the shelflike backseat of the Z, and stood with her back to Linda and Nathan, staring avidly out at the gleaming rows of cars.

Linda sidled up to her and whispered, "Now remember, we're not made of money!" as a salesman came out of the trailer and strutted toward them. "Howdy, folks," he called in greeting when he was halfway there, a little middle-aged man in cowboy boots and a white jumpsuit. "Buenos días," he added when he got closer. "And what is your pleasure today?"

Before Linda could come up with some breezy reply, like "Just browsing, thanks!" or Robin could say God knows what, Nathan said he was looking for a no-frills car for the lady, just something clean with automatic, air, and a fair price tag.

Linda was impressed by the straightforward way he did business, without the digressive, delaying preamble of small talk. She could hardly ask the time of day of a stranger without commenting on the weather first.

"*Clean,*" she heard Robin mutter. "Give me a break." Red as fresh blood, she would have said, and faster than a rocket ship in orbit. Something slung so low you'd need limbo music and a shoehorn to get you in and out of it. Something like the Batmobile or Nathan's own car was probably Robin's pleasure today. But Robin was a not-quite-fifteen-year-old without a driver's license or any real money, and Linda was the customer here, even if Nathan was doing the talking. She nodded brightly to back him up, and then they all trailed the salesman across the lot. Robin dragged her feet past the later, slinkier models, the ones with little flames painted delicately on the doors, fancy chrome wheel covers, and finishes that gave back the blazing sun like mirrors.

Linda tried to distract and mollify her by handing Phoebe over. She was just starting to wake up, and would begin reaching for Robin soon, anyway. Phoebe truly worshipped her; Linda was merely a fill-up station on the highway to love. She suspected that Robin sneaked the baby sips of Coca-Cola when she wasn't looking. Phoebe's four tiny teeth had barely broken ground and were probably already riddled with holes.

Robin draped the baby across her shoulder and stayed just on the outskirts of their little scouting party. The salesman seemed to have read Nathan clearly; the cars he led them to were definitely sensible in appearance. Dull, matronly-looking sedans, clumsy station wagons, all the shy, homely wallflowers of the used-car world. Robin kept making strangling noises, as if she had a slab of steak stuck in her throat, and the salesman glanced anxiously at her from time to time during his spiel, which was peppered with Spanish phrases. "Miren, amigos! Check it out," he said, patting the stodgy rump of an '83 Fairlane, and Robin pretended to puke across its hood.

Linda nudged her and hissed, "Stop that!" Then she smiled amicably at the salesman. "Don't mind her," she said. "She just wants us to get something . . . spiffier."

That adjective only elicited more offensive noises from Robin, and Linda finally grabbed her arm. "Listen," she said. "I need a car to get me to and from work, not to show off to your little druggy friends." Maybe she should have just accepted Cynthia's offer of a loaner car from the studio. But she'd done so much for them already. Only the other day, she'd volunteered to take Phoebe for a few hours, while Robin was at the movies, so that Linda could do some housework without any interruptions. Robin wasn't happy about the arrangement, although the baby was perfectly fine at Cynthia's, and Linda got a lot done in the apartment, even enjoying the guilty pleasure of a short nap. Robin's general wariness of others reached new heights with its focus on Cynthia. "How come she gave you this?" she'd asked, referring to the pink jumpsuit Linda had worn home from that first private training session.

"My things were all sweaty," Linda explained. "And Cynthia was going to give it away, anyway."

"Why? It looks brand-new to me."

"I guess she didn't like it anymore," Linda said.

"I wouldn't take anybody's disgusting old hand-me-downs," Robin said. "I wouldn't take charity."

"You just said it looks brand-new," Linda said. "And it's not charity, it's a gift. *You* take gifts, don't you?" But Robin only gave Linda a pitying look.

Now she made a similar face, and yanked the diaper bag from Linda's shoulder. "Come on," she said to Phoebe, "let's you and me look at some *cars*." In moments she was tailing another sales-man and his customers, an androgynous young couple who seemed to be welded together at the hip, and were into much flashier models. Their confused salesman began holding car doors open for Robin and Phoebe, who slid right in, while the Siamese twins circled them, casing the exteriors.

Linda knew that Nathan was only being practical, but she couldn't help glancing wistfully at Robin, with Phoebe on her lap, wildly turning the wheel of a bronze, bullet-shaped Camaro, like the heroine of a car-chase movie. At the same time, Nathan urged Linda behind the wheel of a tan Delta 88, while he went off to tinker under its hood. It was a hot day, and ten times hotter inside the car. Linda left her door wide open, and she bounced around on the blistering vinyl seat so she wouldn't become bonded to it.

When Nathan finally banged down the hood, she jumped out. A few other salesmen and customers dotted the expansive field, but in a quick survey she couldn't locate Robin and Phoebe. Nathan and their salesman were going back and forth about cylinders and pistons and sparks. Linda cleared her throat and the salesman turned to her. "Want to give her a spin?" he asked, and Nathan shrugged and said, "Sure, why not?"

When the salesman headed back toward the trailer for the keys, Linda said, worriedly, "I don't see them anywhere, Nathan, do you?"

"Who, the kids?" Nathan asked. He hooked one arm around her neck and reeled her in. "They're probably closing a deal on a Vette." When Linda didn't even smile, he said, "Maybe they went to the trailer to use the ladies' room. Or across the street to get some ice cream. Don't worry, they're around here someplace."

"Why don't you take the car out yourself," Linda suggested, disengaging herself. "You know more about it, anyway, and I want to look for the girls."

"Come on," he said. "Robin is almost fifteen, and we'll be right back. This is gonna be your baby, Linda, so you'd better see how it handles."

But Linda's attention was divided, and it didn't really matter how the car handled. They were all lethal weapons she had not been properly trained to use, and the freeways were all minefields of disaster. Back in Newark, before Wright had taught her to drive, with such loving patience, on five of the last precious Sundays of his life, she'd taken buses or he'd driven her wherever she had to go. If she hadn't followed her instincts, like some poor dumb lemming, all the way to California, she might never have had to drive again. But it was impossible to live here without a car. Robin (where *was* that girl?) was right about that, at least.

The salesman came back and swung the keys to the 88 in front of her face like a hypnotist's pocket watch. "Las llaves, señorita," he said with painstaking enunciation.

"She speaks English," Nathan reminded him, and he grabbed the swinging keys and opened the driver's door. "Let's go," he said to Linda as he hustled her in. Then he dropped the registration to the Z into the salesman's waiting hand and got in beside her. The car was still an inferno. Linda had to pat the steering wheel several times before she could bear to grip it, and seat belts were completely out of the question. They rolled down their windows and let in more hot air, and then Linda turned on the ignition with a grinding screech.

"Let go of the damn key!" Nathan yelled at her.

The salesman waved to them as they pulled away. "Vayan con Dios!" he called gaily.

"Same to you, gringo prick!" Nathan called back, but his words were lost in the roar of the exhaust.

Linda drove slowly out of the lot and then around the block three times. "How is it?" Nathan kept asking her, and she kept repeating, "Fine, just fine," although the car felt exactly like the treacherous stranger it was. After their third rotation, Nathan motioned for her to pull over, and they switched places. He drove back to the lot, testing the air conditioner, the windshield wipers, the lights, the signals, and the radio on the way.

Their salesman was waiting to welcome them back. "Have you seen my stepdaughter and my baby?" Linda asked him. She held her hand up to approximate Robin's height. "Long blond hair, wearing cutoffs and an 'I've Seen Elvis' T-shirt?" It made her uneasy, describing Robin that way, as if she were actually missing and Linda was reporting her disappearance to the police.

The salesman looked blank for a moment, but then he said, "Oh, yeah. The blond kid, right?" He glanced around. "She was here a minute ago, I think. Maybe she's waiting for you in the trailer." He herded them in that direction, crooning a sales pitch, while Nathan recited a counterpoint of complaints about the car. Linda wondered if the salesman had actually seen Robin and Phoebe, or if he'd just said that to lure them inside. She wondered if Madman Moe would be waiting there, strapped into his straitjacket, ready to scream his insane slogan at them. She tried to bring up the matter of the girls again with Nathan, but another jet roared overhead, and he put his finger to her lips, probably afraid she was about to spoil his negotiations for the 88.

He'd warned her earlier that day, right after he'd picked them up, to let him handle the whole thing. He knew about cars and he knew about car salesmen, who, he seemed eager to inform her, were "the stinking bottom of the human shitpile." He'd worked briefly as a mechanic's helper at a lot in El Monte, so he knew. They all turned back odometers, he said, painted over rust and scuffed tires, and even fished out flood cars, polished them up, and sold them for new. "But isn't that against the law?" Linda asked, and Nathan whooped with laughter.

After the furious heat outside, the trailer was as cold as a meat locker. Robin and Phoebe were nowhere in sight, and no one in there resembled Madman Moe, either. A couple of salesmen played cards at a desk, while another one murmured into a phone, and a hard-looking woman with towering orange hair was speed-writing a contract for an elderly man.

Linda whispered, "Excuse me a minute," and ran to the door marked REST ROOM at the back of the trailer. She knocked and then opened the door, but there was no one inside. The faucet dripped into the rusted sink in a steady, ominous beat.

As soon as Linda returned, their salesman ushered them to a desk in the far corner, on which there was only a pad, a ballpoint pen, and one photograph, in a chipped plastic frame, of himself standing next to a big Cadillac. "Sit down, sit down," he said, taking his own seat. "Make yourselves comfortable." He patted his glistening brow with a handkerchief. "Boy, some scorcher, isn't it?"

"So how much?" Nathan asked, getting right down to business again, while Linda sat next to him, clasping and unclasping her hands in her lap.

"For you, my friend, only one sixty-five per month," the salesman said.

"The price, man," Nathan said impatiently, "I'm talking about the price."

"I told you, amigo, one sixty-five per month, and believe me, you won't get a better deal anywhere in the state."

"This guy's a riot, isn't he?" Nathan asked grimly, and Linda offered him a tentative smile.

The salesman began diddling with the pen and pad, making mysterious little markings and then crossing them out and making new ones. Finally he wrote something with a flourish on a fresh page and slid the pad across the desk to Nathan. "You look like really nice people, so I'm giving you a fantastic break," he said.

Nathan lifted his sunglasses, glanced at the pad, and slid it back, hard, across the desk. The corner of the pad caught the salesman in the gut, and he let out a little "Oof." "Hey, man," Nathan said, "I came here to do business, so don't jerk me around, okay?"

"That's an insider's price," the salesman protested, but Nathan stood up, and after a beat Linda took his cue and stood, too.

"Listen, amigo," the salesman said. "It's Sunday, right? The day of rest, right? I want to get home to my family, and I'm sure you want to get home with yours. *Lovely* family, by the way. I had a really good week, moved a lot of vehicles, so if I have to top it off with a cost-price deal, so be it." He wrote a new figure on the pad and this time he handed it to Nathan, who handed it right back.

"Get serious, *amigo*," Nathan said. "I didn't swim here yesterday, you know. We need brakes, we need springs, maybe we need a whole new car."

Linda had tried to read the salesman's latest figure, but the transaction had been too rapid. Their dickering was getting on her nerves; she felt like a spectator at some sporting event whose rules she only vaguely understood. She didn't even *want* that stupid car in the first place, and her mind kept wandering back to the children. Where could they be in this heat? She tapped Nathan's arm. "I'll be right back," she said, and hurried away before he could respond.

The torrid air slapped her as soon as she opened the door, and she had to shield her eyes with both hands to deflect the dazzling glare. The field of cars stretched and dissolved before her into a shimmering, multicolored lake. "Robin!" she called loudly across it, but there was no answering call. Linda's belly clutched and cramped. The down side of having people to love, of course, was the ever-present possibility of loss, a sorry lesson she had learned and relearned.

Sometimes, when Linda woke during the night in a state of dread, she got up to look at the two girls as they slept. Phoebe, spread-eagled in her crib, as if she'd landed safely there after falling from some great height, and Robin, disarmed by sleep, with a silvery web of drool in one corner of her open mouth. Both of them breathing, in and out. Linda would inscribe them once again on the credit side of her heart, and Wright and Manny on the debit side.

Standing in the middle of the used-car lot, revolving slowly, like a lighthouse beam, she suddenly remembered that name

Robin had once called her: the kiss of death. How could she have said such a thing! It certainly wasn't true in a literal sense. She wasn't anywhere near the liquor store when Manny was shot and killed in the holdup, an event so alien and horrific she still couldn't fully imagine it. And although she'd been at Wright's hospital bedside when he slipped from his life, and hers, in what seemed like a trick conjured by the doctor, she had never associated his death with her presence on the scene. *The kiss of death.* A spasm of shudders rode her spine as she thought of all those kisses freely given and taken in love, the fevered, wet, urgent, sucking pleasure of them. Could you draw out someone's life force that way, leaving him vulnerable to speeding bullets or stray embolisms? But that was ridiculous. Superstitious. Completely *crazy*! Afterward, the doctor told her that Wright's heart had probably been a ticking time bomb for years. And Manny had said only weeks before his murder how lucky he was to have found her.

When the baby allowed Linda to vent her maternal passion in a feast of kisses up and down her luscious self, Linda understood that it was a privilege, and a finite one. But she had never dared to examine exactly what she meant by that. Robin, of course, refused to suffer any demonstration of Linda's affection; she could barely stand her company. Yet Linda was sometimes compelled to kiss her, too, quickly and lightly, on the forehead or cheek while she slept. If Robin ever found out, she'd have a fit. "Robin," she quietly implored, "where *are* you?" She began to jog up and down the aisles between the rows of cars, the hysteria rising from her belly to her throat, which threatened to close around it. They *couldn't* be in the sealed microwave of one of the cars all this time. Robin was headstrong and careless, but she wasn't stupid.

Then Linda remembered that odd-looking couple Robin had been shadowing when she and Phoebe disappeared. Some kind of perverts, maybe. Drugs, sadism, cults, sacrifices. There were so many maniacs out there waiting for a fatal connection with someone innocent. The papers were full of stories. But would Robin go off with strangers after all the lectures she had endured on the subject, all the milk cartons at all the breakfasts of her life, with the faces of other people's missing children smiling their waxy, helpless smiles? And would she ever put Phoebe in real jeopardy?

Oh, why had she ever kissed them!

In Newark, once, just after she'd gotten her driver's license, Linda drove alone to the Garden State Mall to buy Wright a birthday present. Delighted by her success at getting there in one piece, she resolved not to think about driving back until she had to. Instead, she succumbed to the pleasure of planning a little surprise party for Wright that evening. She would try to get Robin involved, too, although the girl still barely acknowledged her, almost four weeks after the wedding. Maybe doing something nice together for their mutual beloved would draw them closer.

Shopping malls tended to be a natural backdrop for Linda's anxiety—all that space and all those people were so confusing and intimidating. And this one featured a parrot jungle and an artificial waterfall that would make anyone nervous. But that day Linda was propelled by her joyful errand and felt perfectly relaxed. She went from store to store, buying gifts and balloons and funny paper hats and birthday candles you couldn't blow out. She chose a handsome blue sweater for Wright, and a pair of silk pajamas she would present him with privately. On an extravagant but inspired impulse she bought something for Robin, too, a little tree-shaped lamp, with spaghetti-like branches that quivered with red liquid light when you plugged it in. Linda would have loved something like that at Robin's age.

Burdened with her bulky purchases, but feeling lavishly happy, she made her way back to the mammoth parking field, where she soon realized she had no memory of where she had parked the car. She walked up and down a couple of aisles, and then began to zigzag around like a cornered animal, murmuring, "Where?

Where?" It started to rain about ten minutes into her panic-ridden search, and by the time she found the Mustang, crouched in a row of similar cars, she was soaking wet and sobbing uncontrollably.

Later, Wright laughed fondly at her—why, you couldn't lose that one-ton pile of metal and rubber if you *tried*! All she had to do was get one of the mall's security guards to drive her around on his scooter until she found it. And everything was fine, now—why was she still so upset? He stuck a party hat on her head and locked his arms around her. Linda submitted to his embrace, but she couldn't explain herself or completely shake that feeling of doom. As if to give her nameless anxiety meaning and substance, Wright died a couple of weeks later. And a few weeks after that, when she and Robin were cleaning out the apartment in preparation for their trip West, Linda watched sadly as Robin tossed the little tree lamp into the trash.

That day at the mall was just a dress rehearsal for this day at Madman Moe's. Here she was, running again, with the stench of her own fear rising in a mist around her. But all her other losses were nothing now; she was cured of them, completely relieved of them, as in a revival tent-show miracle. There was only this in the world, only this new, raw, impossible absence. "Robin!" she bleated. "My Phoebe!"

It was getting late. There wasn't anybody else out on the lot. The latest jet that thundered over, drowning out her voice with its own, and casting her in its long shadow, had visible lights, like rubies and emeralds. It was carrying people home in time for supper with their families, for blessed sleep in their own beds. Without meaning to, Linda thought of all those lonesome nights when Robin had segregated her with spiteful silence, and the baby had screamed non-stop, because of colic or teething or some other wordless baby misery, until Linda was driven to fling herself facedown on her bed and whisper into the white darkness of the pillow, "Stop it, go away, why don't you both just go away and leave me alone!" And she remembered looking for-

ward to leaving Robin in Glendale, and the brief but grave con-
sideration she'd given to ending her pregnancy when she first
learned about it.

Now she wished that she could turn off her restless thoughts,
that she could simply pray instead. But she'd given up on God
after Wright's death, as both saviour and scapegoat of her puny,
scattered life. He was only a makeshift, pickup God, anyway, the
kind invented by children without religious training, a white-
bearded cross between Santa Claus and Charlton Heston playing
Moses. But maybe she should try praying, even without the
license of faith, just in case. Before she could carry that thought
any further, she glimpsed a distant figure through the blurred
vision of her despair. "Robin!" she cried again, but she saw in a
moment that it was only Nathan, running toward her and calling
her name. By the time he got to her, she couldn't speak at all,
only gesture at him in a jerky pantomime.

Nathan grasped her arms and shouted, "Linda! Calm down! Is
it Robin? You still can't find her? Dios mio!" Then, quietly,
"Listen, it's okay. She's only playing a little trick on you, hiding
out someplace. Come on, we'll find them."

He took long, athletic strides, pulling her along with him, so
that she hardly had to move her feet, like Ginger Rogers being
carried by Fred Astaire through an intricate dance routine. Linda
felt as if she were flying, as if she were unraveling. Nathan had
put a terrifying new idea into her head. Maybe Robin had just
taken off with the baby so they could live somewhere else without her. It was something she had casually threatened to do.
Sometimes when she spoke to Phoebe as though Linda wasn't
there, she said things like "Maybe you and me should split,
Feeble, before we get wimpy like her." Linda remembered now
that Robin had grabbed the diaper bag from her shoulder before.
There was a bottle of apple juice in there, a few toys, and a stack
of diapers. *And* Linda's wallet.

Nathan kept on talking. "When we find her, you can break her
neck, okay? That brat. I give you permission. I'll even help you,

okay?" He pulled her skimming body through the lot and across the wide road, between moving cars, to the ice-cream parlor, but it was closed and shuttered for the day. She didn't even remember going back across the road, but now they were running up and down the aisles of the lot, peering into car windows and knocking on roofs and hoods. My life should be passing in front of me, Linda thought, but all she saw were those endless flanks of cars, flaunting their coyly false, seductive signs. *Take Me Home! Creampuff! One Owner! Easy Payments!* And high above them the looming, leering gaze of Madman Moe, still bound and imprisoned on his billboard. Linda found herself praying silently to him as if he were the demented but all-powerful god of this automotive kingdom. Oh, merciful Prince of Pontiacs! she prayed. Stop me before I kill again! Finder of lost Mustangs! Help me now to find my children!

Near the end of her pregnancy, when she was so frightened, Manny had said how spunky she was to go through with a thing like that alone. As if she had a choice! One man put the baby inside her and another one pulled it out. But of course that wasn't exactly true, either. It was just that she'd made her choices from limited experience and a dumb trust in ordinary luck. It wasn't spunky, it was *irresponsible* to give someone the terrible twin gifts of life and death. This was the finite condition of human love, the thought she'd refused to think when she was planting those delicious kisses along the baby's silky flesh. She looked across the aisle at Nathan, another mortal she had recently kissed—only last night!—and with such reckless rapture. I'm sorry, I didn't mean it, she wanted to say, but only her shallow, panting breath came out.

They found them a few minutes later, lying curled together across the seat of a shiny, red classic Thunderbird. *Dreamboat!* proclaimed the Thunderbird's sign, and Mad Moe cackled from his heavenly perch. The windows of the Thunderbird had been sensibly lowered, but Robin and Phoebe were pasted to the white leather. Their platinum hair was darkened by sweat and their natural pallor painted with an unnatural flush. They slept deeply and earnestly, like the good, artless children they were. The baby had her thumb jammed down her throat and the empty juice bottle clutched in her other hand. Robin was heat-drugged and bewildered and it was difficult for Nathan to wake her. "What?" she said groggily. "What?" She didn't recognize either of them for a moment.

The baby was so limp Linda's blood staggered and slowed. But when she lifted her, there was a fresh puddle of pee on the white upholstery, a thrilling circular stain of life. At any other time, Linda would have tried to mop it up with shredding Kleenex, and then hurried inside to confess the damage and make amends. Now she kicked the door of the Thunderbird shut and stood there unbuttoning her blouse. She lowered the flap of her nursing bra, and prodded and coaxed the baby until she fastened herself and began to weakly suck.

Robin slumped against Nathan in a way she never would if she were wholly conscious. She was reduced to pure animal need for once, without the usual, maddening argument of reason. Nathan lifted her as if she were an infant, too, and carried her, unresisting, back to the trailer, where he bathed her hot face with wet paper towels while the tough-looking saleswoman fed her sips of 7-Up from her own personal mug. "World's Greatest Mom," it said in bold black letters.

Linda sank into one of the chairs near their salesman's desk. The men tried to avert their eyes as she continued to nurse the baby, whose sucking had become loud and vigorous. Linda kissed and kissed her heavy, fragrant head, then lifted one tiny, drooping hand and kissed that, too.

"About the car, we'll come back another time . . ." Nathan began, but Linda said, "No, I want to get it today." She had never been this assertive before, and he looked at her with a cautious mixture of admiration and alarm. "Write it up," she instructed the salesman. "But we need the best possible price. I have these two children to support."

Not that Linda was kidding herself. A used-car salesman might be moved by her story, but only, she knew, within his particular limits. And no matter what price they settled on, the car would reveal its own hard-luck story before too long. All the things that could go wrong with it would start to go wrong, one after the other. There would be daily wear and tear, accidents, the mysterious machinery of fate. Who was to say how anything really happened, or why?

Robin, who'd recovered her sullen, controlled demeanor, scowled at Linda. "So what kind of faggy car did you pick out anyway?" she demanded.

I'd like to kill you, Linda thought, I really would. Even her teeth ached with restrained rage. She reached across the baby and grabbed that unpleasant pink face and glared at it.

Robin glared back. "Hey!" she said.

But before she could squirm away or say anything else, Linda leaned forward and kissed her fully and ruthlessly on the mouth.

16

Brunch

The following week, Cynthia Sterling invited Linda and Robin to Sunday brunch at her house. Linda accepted gratefully; Nathan was going down to Baja for the weekend, to visit his mother, and the Sunday gloom she'd suffered since childhood would be intensified by his absence. But Robin tried to get out of it, using every excuse in the book, none of which Linda bought for a minute. "You do *not* have cramps, Robin," she said, as the girl lay languidly on the sofa Sunday morning, pressing one hand to her stomach and working the remote control with the other. Sermon, tennis, something in Spanish, something in Korean, sermon, Spanish, golf. "You had your period last week, remember?"

Robin pushed the off button in disgust, and said, "Yeah, well, but I told some kids I might meet them later at the arcade."

"If you'd made any other plans, miss, you would have mentioned them earlier. And don't try to tell me you forgot about Cynthia's, either. I reminded you last night before you went to bed."

"Why do I have to go?" Robin said. "I don't even like her."

"How can you possibly not like someone you've never met?" Linda reasoned. And especially someone so terrific, she thought. Of all the people she'd ever known, only Cynthia seemed to have an understanding of Linda's offbeat fix on things. During their ritual meals together after the training sessions, Linda found herself opening up in ways she hadn't to anyone since she'd left New Jersey, and her close female friends, behind. Cynthia was so easy to talk to—she listened ardently and didn't ever seem to pass judgment. And she was an amazing source of unconventional wisdom, about everything from removing difficult stains to facing your emotional needs. When Linda confessed her dislike of driving, Cynthia said that driving was only a metaphor for living, and to think of entering a freeway as merging with the moving stream of life. While Linda was trying to absorb that idea, Cynthia continued, "Hey, I ought to know *something* after fifteen years on the couch, shouldn't I? Now tell me all about how you got to California, and in God's name *why*." She spoke a little too fast, and jumped from one subject to another. Linda wished she was jotting things down, especially words like "metaphor" that she intended to look up later in the dictionary. Cynthia wanted to know if she'd come out here to be discovered. When Linda looked blank for a moment, Cynthia laughed and said, "How refreshing!" Everybody else, she assured Linda, was trying to break into the industry, on one level or another. Waiters, parking attendants, supermarket clerks. Her own houseman took method-acting classes, and her secretary wrote screenplays in her spare time. Cynthia said she half expected her dentist to break into song and dance during a root canal.

Linda told her about her experiences at Paradise, and how she had to forfeit all that money to the rental agent for sneaking Robin in. "Why, that crooked bitch!" Cynthia exclaimed, sounding remarkably like Robin. "That smells like a swindle to me." She grabbed a notepad and a pen. "Give me her name and address, and I'll have our legal department look into it." She scribbled down the information and sighed. "I'm afraid you're actually too nice for this world, Linda," she said. "Sort of the way the saints are cracked up to be." But it was an innocence spoiling to be spoiled, she quickly added. "I think it's time for a makeover." Linda moved her hand self-consciously from her rubber-banded ponytail to her flushed cheek, but Cynthia said, "No, no, I mean an *intellectual* makeover. We can work on the body some other time. Right now let's attend to the mind and the spirit." She plied Linda with more books: novels, biographies, collections of poetry. Linda had started *The Catcher in the Rye* obediently the day Cynthia gave it to her, and then finished it in two more days, reading in bed and while she nursed Phoebe and between classes at the Bod, still wondering what Cynthia's promised questions would be. She thought it was a terribly sad book. Holden Caulfield reminded her of Robin, especially his cynicism about everything and everybody, except his little sister, Phoebe. Linda wished the story was more upbeat, but she thought it might be good for Robin to read about someone like herself, that it would help her to feel less alone, less different. She left the book on Robin's night table, without saying anything about it, the way her own mother had once left a booklet on menstruation for her, but a week later *The Catcher in the Rye* was still in exactly the same place, with a couple of empty Coke cans and a bottle of black nail polish resting on its cover.

Robin could be such a mule. "Can I drive there, at least?" she asked now.

"You mean 'may I,' and no, you certainly may not," Linda said. "Not until you get your permit."

"Big deal, my birthday's next month."

Linda shuddered. "Then Phoebe and I can count on surviving until then, can't we? Now, come on, make yourself presentable."

Robin continued to gripe—what did they serve at *brunch*, anyway, runny eggs or something?—but she got up, finally, put on a wrinkled pair of shorts and a T-shirt, and swiped at her hair with a brush.

As they approached the gate at Cynthia's house, Robin said, suspiciously, "What is this, a castle?"

"Wait until you see it, Robin," Linda said. "It's even more beautiful inside." She pressed the bell on the intercom and announced their arrival. When the gate slid open, they drove through. "There's a real gym, right in the house!" Linda continued. "And a bathroom you could get *married* in, it's so big and white and gorgeous." In her enthusiasm, she forgot how negative Robin could be about luxuries she didn't have herself.

"Some people in this world are starving, you know," Robin said piously.

Since when did she have a social conscience—or any kind of conscience at all? "Well, *you're* not," Linda said, as she pulled into the circular driveway and shut off the engine. "Now, help me with the baby's things." She pushed the lever to release the trunk lock—there was plenty of stuff inside she'd need help with. Traveling even a short distance with a baby required major preparation and equipment: extra diapers, of course, and other changes, supplementary bottles, toys, an infant seat, a stroller. Before long she'd be needing a feeding chair and a playpen, too. The other day Cynthia said she ought to buy some duplicate equipment for her house, now that Phoebe was becoming such a regular visitor. It was silly for Linda to have to lug so much each time she brought the baby there.

Robin was pulling the folded stroller from the trunk when the door to the house opened and Lupe came out, followed by the two joyously barking dogs. There was a piercing scream from Robin, and the stroller clattered to the gravel as she scrambled to get back inside the car before the dogs reached her. She just made it, practically slamming the door on poor Bismarck's snout, and in only moments she'd punched all the door locks down, as if the Rottweilers were potential carjackers.

Linda handed the baby to Lupe and rapped sharply on the 88's right rear window. "What are you doing?" she said over the racket the dogs were making. "Come out of there right now. They won't hurt you, for heaven's sakes—they're little *lambs*."

Robin was scrunched down low in the back, next to the baby's car seat, with her hands over her ears. She probably hadn't heard a word Linda said.

"Now stop it," Linda shouted, rapping on the window again.

"This is ridiculous. Robin!" She noticed, with further frustration, that the keys were still in the ignition.

And now Cynthia was coming out of the house toward the car. "What's the problem?" she called.

"I'm afraid Robin's a little nervous about the dogs," Linda said, apologetically. Robin was on the floor of the car by then, face-down, to avoid looking at the dogs leaping at every window for entry. Linda could hardly deal with her own embarrassment and disappointment. On the way here, she'd allowed herself to imagine an unlikely scene: Robin, whose hair Linda had mentally combed out of her eyes, and on whose face she'd planted a civil expression, even a smile, greeting Cynthia like a normal human being, shaking hands, saying hello. Why was that too much to expect? "I'm so sorry—" she began.

Cynthia whistled shrilly, twice, cutting her off, and causing the dogs' frenetic leaping and barking to subside. "Come!" she said, clapping her hands, and Bismarck and then Brunhilde reluctantly left their cornered prey. "I'll bring them inside and lock them up," she told Linda, and she started walking briskly toward the house with the dogs at her heels.

"They're gone, Robin," Linda called, but it took her a couple of minutes just to get Robin to sit up and look at her. "They're *gone*," she repeated when she had the girl's attention. "Come on, open up."

Robin clambered around inside the car, looking through each window in turn. Then, satisfied that the dogs were indeed gone, she opened one of the rear windows a crack. "Let's go home," she said in a constricted voice.

"What!" Linda said. "What do you mean? We just got here. Phoebe's inside already. And Cynthia's waiting for us. Come on, Robin, this is quite enough."

"I can't go in there," Robin said.

"Why not? I told you, those dogs are friendly."

"It's not that," Robin said. "I'm allergic."

"Since when?" Linda asked. "This is the first I've heard about it."

"Well, I am," Robin insisted, and she coughed dramatically. "Would you like me to choke to death? I want to go home!"

Linda didn't know what to do. And now she had a frightening new vision—of Robin climbing into the front seat, turning the key, and driving away. "This is so humiliating," she said, squeezing the door handle in vain. "Please don't do this to me, Robin."

Cynthia came back out of the house then, alone. She went to the car. "The dogs are locked up," she announced. "Come inside for brunch."

"How do I know they won't get out?" Robin asked.

"Because I said so," Cynthia said evenly, staring her down through the glass. "Now let's go." Without another word, she turned and strode toward the house. A few seconds later, Linda, who was watching her retreat, heard the pop of one of the car locks.

As she and Robin followed Cynthia, Linda said, "I didn't know you were that afraid of dogs, Robin. Were you ever bitten?"

"I'm not afraid," Robin said. "I *told* you, I'm allergic."

There was no point in arguing with her, so Linda changed the subject. "Wait till you see the kitchen," she whispered. "It's bigger than our whole apartment. Wait till you see the *refrigerator*."

Robin was knocked out by everything—electronic gate, kitchen, refrigerator, gym, bathrooms, skylights—just as she'd been by the Beverly Body Health Club and Spa, and by all those glitzy shops on Rodeo Drive Nathan had taken them to see. But it wasn't cool to show it, and she would never give Linda the satisfaction of knowing she was right about anything. She didn't even let on that she had seen that much of Cynthia's house. After establishing that the dogs were imprisoned in a laundry room on the main level (she could see their restless shadows through the frosted glass door), she had ventured upstairs before brunch to use the bathroom.

This was probably the one Linda had gone so bonkers about. Robin peed, flushing the toilet two or three times afterward. You did it with a button that you hardly had to touch before everything went swirling quietly down. Then she turned on both of the basin faucets for cover while she poked around the room. There appeared to be a second toilet a couple of feet from the first one, although she had never seen one like this before. It had its own faucets, gold-colored, just like the basin's, and no lid you could close to sit on. Weird. Rich people were all weird, and this one looked like a total witch, with that streaky black hair and those mean eyes. She may have called off her killer dogs, but she'd probably sicced them on Robin in the first place.

Robin opened the linen closet, which was neatly stacked with thick white towels and good-smelling soap. It was like a display in a department store. She picked up a bar of soap and tried to shove it into her shorts' pocket, but it was too big, so she put it back in the closet. Then she shut the faucets and went down the long hallway to the gym. She skated around the hard, glossy floor in there until she got bored and wandered out to the hallway again. Just to the left of the staircase she saw a pair of double doors, slightly ajar. She peeked in at another vast room, and then slowly pulled the doors open, just wide enough to pass through them. This had to be Cynthia's bedroom, with that enormous satiny bed, like a queen's, and everything in the same peachy color, including the carpet Robin sank into up to her ankles. She sniffed the faintly scented air; it *smelled* like her in here: rich and evil. Robin strolled around, touching things: a silk brocade robe at the foot of the bed, dresser drawers that slid silently open and shut as if they'd been greased, a pharmacy bottle on the dresser top. "One capsule at bedtime," the label on the bottle said. Robin opened the childproof cap; there must have been about fifty or sixty dark red capsules nestled there. She spilled several of them into her hand and, after only a moment's hesitation, put them in her pocket. She put the cap back on and shook the bottle to redistribute the remaining capsules. Then she messed around some more, bouncing on the bed and snooping in closets. One of the doors she opened led to a smaller, adjoining room, with a mirrored dressing table and a poufy chair, and a wall unit with books and stereo equipment and lots of gold trophies on its shelves. She found a second bathroom off the opposite bedroom wall, with a great big round sunken tub in the middle, and marble steps leading down to it.

On the bedside table, next to the telephone, which was blinking like a switchboard, there was a fat black fountain pen and a notepad with something written on it. It said "Lucinda Blake" in red ink, and there was a telephone number scrawled under it. Robin could hardly believe it—Lucinda Blake was the star of her favorite soap, *Love in the Afternoon*! She played Lady Audrey Finley, an English noblewoman married to an American cowboy named Duke Kincaid, whose stepbrother, Jake, just out of prison for rape and manslaughter, was trying to steal his ranch and his wife. Lady Audrey was a platinum blonde, like Robin, except she was gorgeous, with practically navy-blue eyes and dark eyebrows and lashes, and she had this snooty accent Robin liked to imitate when she was alone. Duke was rough and tough with everybody else, but he was always gentle with Lady Audrey, who he called "ma'am," even when they were in bed together, doing it. Did Cynthia actually know Lucinda Blake? Linda had said she did something in television, but Robin hadn't really paid attention.

Love in the Afternoon was on in the afternoon, right after school, so Robin was able to follow it pretty regularly. Lucy and Carmel used to like it, too. Sometimes, when they were still friends, they'd all watch the show together, sprawled across one of their beds, and then try to predict what was going to happen in the next episode. Carmel made up the best stories, which featured earthquakes, kidnappings, and cases of mistaken identity; she could probably be a writer if she wanted to.

If you actually knew one of the stars of *Love*, you could just ask her what was coming up next. You might even get to read the scripts in advance. Robin picked up the pen and copied Lucinda Blake's telephone number onto a clean sheet of paper. As she ripped out that page and shoved it into her pocket, she thought she heard someone calling her, so she put the pad and pen back exactly as she'd found them, slithered sideways through the double doors, and hurried downstairs.

The brunch was amazing. They ate in a huge dining room, at a long polished table, with oversized plates and napkins as big as tablecloths. There was so much great food Robin wondered if other people had been invited and then didn't show up. A humongous bowl of giant shrimps in a spicy green sauce. She ate about fifteen or twenty of them, ignoring Linda's frantic signals to stop. Fried chicken, without a bucket. A fruit salad with only the good stuff in it: raspberries and blueberries and mangoes. Bite-sized buttery biscuits. And a flat, dark chocolate cake that tasted like frozen Milky Ways, only better. Robin had to open the top button on her shorts, but it was worth it. Feeling sleepy and full, she turned to Linda and said, "That was good." Then she looked around the room and said, "Hey, where's Feeb?"

"Lupe's taken her out for a walk," Cynthia said. "Would you like to take the rest of the torte home, Robin? And some of the chicken?"

Linda didn't give her a chance to answer. She said, "Oh, no, thanks, Cynthia. Everything was lovely, but we've really gone off our diets today."

What diets? This was the best food Robin had ever had in her life. "*I'll* take it," Robin said. "But where did they go?"

"Just around the grounds," Cynthia told her. "They'll be back soon. More lemonade?"

Robin didn't know why, but she suddenly felt alerted. And her stomach was beginning to hurt; she wanted to either yawn or burp, or both. She swirled the remaining lemonade in her glass; sugar or something had settled on the bottom. Maybe she'd been poisoned or given a sedative. She examined the moist crumbs of chocolate on her plate, and then looked at Linda, who sat there unconcerned, sipping her iced tea. "I think I'll take a walk, too," Robin said, wondering if she would find her legs paralyzed when she tried to stand. She was only somewhat wobbly, though, and Cynthia didn't try to stop her as she left the room and stumbled to the front door. She heard Linda start to call something after her, but she didn't wait to hear what it was.

Probably "Have fun, honey," or something equally dorky.

She felt a little better as soon as she got outside. The grounds of the house were like a park, with tree-lined gravel paths that led to separate little gardens. Birds tweeted and flew out of the trees as she went by, and a pair of black squirrels chased each other back and forth across the path. Robin walked through a grove of palms and came upon a shimmering blue swimming pool shaped like an artist's palette. There were flower gardens around that, too, and a row of cabanas on one side. The whole thing was on a hill, overlooking the city, which was shrouded in smog, giving it an air of mystery. She didn't see what's-her-name, Cynthia's slave, anywhere, and there was no sign of Phoebe, either. There was a rustling noise and Robin looked nervously back at the grove of palms, half expecting to see Cynthia herself come through them, flanked by her snarling dogs, but it was only those stupid squirrels again.

Robin heard Linda calling her as she made her way back to the house. She began to run, and when she was almost there, she saw Linda in the doorway, holding Phoebe in her arms, and coo-ing, "Yoo-hoo, here we are!" Robin was washed with relief. She grabbed the baby from Linda and danced her around, saying, "Where did you go, punkhead, huh? Where were you hiding?" She carried her into the vestibule, where Cynthia was waiting with a fancy shopping bag dangling from one outstretched finger. "Pardon the expression," she said, "but here's your doggy bag."

Robin took it, reluctantly. She'd have to dump it somewhere, later; there was no way she was going to eat any more of that drugged food. She was just lucky that the fresh air had cleared her head and settled her stomach.

"Thank you very much, Cynthia," Linda said, like some ventriloquist, poking Robin, who remained silent. "We all had a wonderful time."

"Well, good, I'm glad," Cynthia said. "Maybe next time we can take a swim."

Right, Robin thought, and maybe you'll try to drown me.

17

Roadkill

Robin had to move the driver's seat of the 88 all the way forward in order to reach the gas and brake pedals, which struck Linda as valid evidence that she wasn't old enough to drive. Of course, Linda didn't really believe *she* was old enough to drive yet, either, at twenty-eight. Maybe she never would be. But Robin suffered no such doubts about herself. She had been sitting out in the driveway for at least an hour now, turning the steering wheel and honking impatiently. "Linda!" she yelled every few minutes. "Come on! Let's *go!*"

With the car keys safely in her jeans pocket, Linda went methodically about her chores, humming to herself and trying to ignore Robin, which was something like trying to ignore a screaming steam whistle. Still, she washed the breakfast dishes and made the beds, fed and diapered and dressed the baby, and even vacuumed a little before giving in. When she finally came out, carrying Phoebe and an armload of her paraphernalia, Robin leaned on the horn again, just for spite. "Stop that," Linda said. "It's not even nine o'clock, you're waking up the whole neighborhood. And move over, missy, I'm driving."

"What!" Robin said, outraged. "You said *I* could drive. You said—"

Linda interrupted her. "I *said* you could drive after we drop the baby off, remember? There's no reason to endanger her poor little life, too. Now, come give me a hand with this stuff, will you?"

Robin climbed out of the car and grabbed Phoebe. "Hey, Feeble, we're going to . . . *drop* you off!" she shouted, tossing the baby into the air and barely catching her on the emphasis.

"Robin!" Linda shrieked. "You could kill her that way! And, besides, she just ate." But the traitorous baby only laughed with rippling pleasure and kept her breakfast to herself.

Linda drove toward Cynthia Sterling's, where Phoebe would be looked after until the driving lesson was over. This was the *third* time Cynthia had volunteered to take her when Robin couldn't sit. She was turning out to be such a valuable friend. "Big deal," Robin had commented the night before when Linda was singing Cynthia's praises. "Ms. Rich Bitch will just get one of her slaves to babysit."

"They're not slaves, Robin, they're servants," Linda said.

"Same difference," Robin said. She had an answer for everything. And she was so paranoid; according to her, Cynthia intended to kidnap Phoebe and turn her into a "slave," too.

Now, all the way from Hollywood to Benedict Canyon, Robin heckled and instructed Linda. "Faster. *Faster*" was her steady refrain on the freeway, and when they drove locally, she kept urging Linda to run over anybody crossing against the light. She even opened her window and yelled "Roadkill!" at a couple of startled pedestrians, and then argued that they were just asking for it. She couldn't seem to sit still for a minute, and Linda worried that she was on speed or something. First, Robin turned on all four air-conditioning jets full blast in her own direction, so that her hair blew wildly around her face while Linda sweltered, only inches away. Then she pushed the radio buttons rapidly from one rock station to another, and bounced around to the noise that filled the car. She lingered longest, it seemed, on any number with a violent message and a grating beat. Linda wondered once again what she was doing trying to teach someone like Robin to drive. It was really criminal, like putting a loaded Uzi into the hands of a known serial killer. She thought of those amusement parks they'd stopped at on their trip West, at Robin's insistence, and her insistence that they try all the dangerous rides, monstrous contraptions with names like "Death Rocket" and "Trip to Hell" that spun you madly around, or turned you upside down and inside out until you were nothing but streaming hair and tangled guts and a sustained, high-pitched scream. Linda had begged off everything but the safe and sane Tunnel of Love, using her pregnancy as an alibi, but she wouldn't have been too willing under any circumstances. Robin went on the other rides by herself, anyway, while Linda stood there watching her and feeling almost as queasy as she would have been aboard. Even on the benign bumper cars, Robin had driven head-on into other cars with what seemed like malicious glee. But she was full of adolescent bluff and bluster; all the awful things she'd threatened to do since Linda had known her, and then hadn't, could fill a book.

The one thing Robin seemed sincerely determined about, though, was driving a real car. She had been talking for months about getting her learner's permit, and right before her fifteenth birthday, in early July, she'd signed up for the Driver's Ed course offered in summer school. Her grades in English and social studies had fallen off considerably the past semester, but driving was the only subject she'd volunteered to take during her vacation. Linda knew that if she opposed her, Robin would simply "borrow" the car one day without anyone's blessings, including the state's. She'd managed to pass Driver's Ed somehow and get her precious permit, but she definitely needed further instruction, and lots of practice.

Linda couldn't afford to pay for professional lessons, so Nathan had promised to do the teaching for her. He'd come up with several reasons why Linda was unsuitable for the job: she was too nervous, Robin didn't like or respect her, and her own driving stank, no offense. He said that she drove like a little old lady, stiffly and slowly, as if she'd once been reckless but had learned her lesson. He hunched over in cruel imitation of her, staring bug-eyed into an imaginary distance and holding an imaginary wheel in a steel grip. When Linda squealed in protest and swatted at him with a magazine, he tried to temper the insult by kissing her neck and shoulders. And when she mentioned, as tactfully as she could, that he'd been stopped for speeding *twice* recently, he brushed her off in that same exasperating way, telling her to just let him take care of everything, muñeca, okay? Nathan had once worked at a driving school in San Diego (where *hadn't* he worked?), and he claimed there wasn't a driver born he couldn't handle. Linda certainly wasn't looking forward to teaching Robin to drive, and Nathan and Robin did seem to be getting along much better. But when he took her out in the 88 the following Sunday, they came back less than an hour later, both of them grim-faced and ominously silent. "What?" Linda asked in alarm. "What happened?"

No one bothered to answer her. Robin slammed into her bedroom, and Nathan splashed some cold water on his face before he slammed out of the house and roared away in his Z. When Linda tried to raise the subject with him the next evening when they were alone, he muttered angrily to himself in Spanish, like Ricky Ricardo after Lucy had just pulled some crazy stunt, and she was afraid to press the matter any further. Robin was even less forthcoming. Linda asked her, "Did you have an accident or anything, honey?" and Robin looked right through her with slitted eyes and didn't deign to reply. Linda seemed able to read her mind, though, something that was happening more and more lately. Maybe it was a common phenomenon between people who lived together for a long time. What Robin appeared to say was, "I had an accident, all right, asshole, and you're it." Or, "Yeah, I had a terrible accident—I was born." Either way, Linda didn't want to hear about it.

So the driving instruction was left up to her. After they deliv-

ered the baby to Cynthia, they were going to a supermarket a couple of miles away, maybe the only one in all of Southern California
that wasn't open around the clock. For some reason, probably to
do with either religion or sports, the Food Bazaar didn't open until
noon on Sundays, and the huge, empty parking lot would be a perfect place for Robin to practice. And at twelve, when the market
opened, they could get some groceries. Margarine, milk, deter-
gent, oranges—Linda made a mental shopping list as she drove,
feeling marvelously efficient for once.

The approach to Cynthia's house, her *mansion*, still delighted
Linda; it was like entering an enchanted forest. But Cynthia was
hardly the fairy-tale ogre and slave driver Robin made her out to
be. If she was, they wouldn't be here now, would they? In the
driveway, Linda got out and struggled to the front door with the
baby and all of her gear. She rang the doorbell with her left
elbow, setting off the chimes and starting the dogs barking and
howling inside. Robin stayed safely in the car, just in case someone let them out again. In moments, Lupe appeared and whisked
Phoebe away. Cynthia came out next, followed by her handsome
young houseman/chauffeur (whose name, Linda had found out,
was Mitchell, not Mellors). He relieved Linda of the diaper bag,
the Muppets mobile, and the folded stroller, and carried them
inside. "So long, kids," Cynthia called, so as to include Robin,
who had moved over to the driver's seat of the 88 the second
Linda vacated it. "Remember—drive safely now!"

"Yeah, right," Robin called back as she revved the idling
engine, "and you remember who that baby belongs to!"

"*Robin!*" Linda said, and then turned to smile at Cynthia in
apology, but she had already gone into the house and shut the
door. "You're crazy, do you know that?" Linda said to Robin as
she got in beside her. "Now, don't forget to fasten your seat belt,
and are you wearing shoes?" But even as Robin pressed her bare
foot to the gas pedal and peeled out across the gravel, Linda
looked anxiously back at the many inscrutable windows of the big
house, suddenly longing for one more glimpse of her child.

There was another car at the Food Bazaar when they got there, a silver Chevy Caprice with a teenage boy behind the wheel, and a man, probably his father, sitting erectly beside him. The boy drove in slow motion past the 88 as it entered the parking field, and Linda could make out all the details of his long white face, the geography of his freckles and pimples and silky stubble, the way the sunlight shone pinkly through his protruding ears, and how his mouth hung open in absolute concentration. Linda thought he looked desperate, as if he were being kidnapped and couldn't signal for help with anything but his eyes, which rolled like a spooked horse's as the cars passed one another. The father and Linda were the real captives, though, and she sent him a telepathic message of empathy and courage.

"Oh, shit, *traffic*," Robin said. Of course she was only being sarcastic. She'd wanted to take her lesson on the freeway, but Linda wouldn't risk that in an armored tank with Robin driving.

"Don't be smart," she warned her, and leaned forward to shut off the radio, which Robin had allowed to settle on a rap station, adding to Linda's feelings of apprehension.

Robin flipped it right back on. Then she said, "Hey, I know that kid," turning her head in the direction of the Caprice. "What a retard."

Linda sighed. Robin always said she knew people when she clearly didn't. It was just a cover, Linda thought, for her own loneliness, an adolescent version of imaginary friends. "You do not know him, Robin," Linda said. "Now keep your eyes on the road, please, and don't forget to signal." Her head was beginning to ache. She turned the radio down a little.

"Road?" Robin said, snorting. "You call this a *road*?"

She was only doing about twenty, but it felt to Linda as if they were zipping past the light poles: A1, A2, A3; past the handicapped spaces, with their blue lines and universal wheelchair symbols; past the windows of the Food Bazaar with its advertised specials on chicken breasts and rump roasts; past the chained gang of shopping carts; and the silver Caprice with its retarded, wild-eyed, teenage driver.

Linda felt grudging admiration for Robin, who grasped the wheel and went forward with such unwarranted confidence. Linda would never have learned to drive if Wright hadn't gently but firmly nudged her toward independent flight, like a mother bird. If he had lived to teach Robin to drive, too, he never would have lost his temper, or his determination to have her succeed. That's the way he'd been with Linda, even after two trained driving-school instructors had declared her unteachable. The main trouble was that she would think too much, think: this is the brake, this is the gas, this is the clutch, and, oh, God, this is me driving! That would quickly lead to: this is me *married*, and a stepmother besides! And from there it was an easy leap to: a few weeks ago I was single, and not long before that, I was a child myself; once I never existed at all, and someday I won't again, forever and ever. Her mind often tumbled out of control that way, down into a spiral of black thoughts that inevitably ended in the grave. It wasn't something she could help doing, or comfortably confide to anyone—it seemed so neurotic and childish—so she never tried. When Wright rubbed her back and asked her what was wrong and why she couldn't just *relax*, she blamed it on her high-strung nature. "You know me," she'd say, and he would smile, although he didn't really know her, not in that most acutely intimate sense. And neither did Nathan, who was a sweetheart in most respects, except for his short fuse and his tendency to be bossy. He would never gently inquire of her what was wrong; he would probably shout orders and accusations in two languages, instead. She could just imagine the circumstances of Robin's aborted driving lesson last Sunday.

Again, Robin drove past the silver car, and this time the man in the passenger seat turned slightly to look at Linda, with what she perceived as interest. Like a swinger out cruising for women, instead of a father teaching his child to drive. In the brief moment of their passing, Linda noticed that he had thick sandy hair and a pleasant crinkly look around his eyes. Green eyes, or hazel, she thought. And he looked tall, if you could really tell that about somebody sitting down. Anyway, he was more her usual type than Nathan, who was compactly built and so exotically handsome, almost pretty, with his endless eyelashes and creamy mocha skin. God, what was she *thinking* about?

Just then, Robin began using the light poles as a kind of obstacle course, by zigzagging between them. "What are you doing?" Linda demanded. "Stop that this minute!"

"But this is so *boring*," Robin complained. "Why can't we go on the freeway?"

"Because," Linda told her, "I want to live to be twenty-nine. And slow down, will you?"

"We're practically standing still now," Robin said. "If I go any slower, we'll be going *backward* in this ugly, decrepit car." It was true that the 88 wasn't glamorous, with its dull tan finish and worn plaid seat covers, but it got you where you wanted to go, even if that was only in circles in an empty parking lot. Robin kept grumbling, but she slowed down and straightened the car out just as the Caprice passed them once more, going in the opposite direction. Again, Linda found herself arrested by the glance of the driver's father. This time he smiled, and before she could stop herself she smiled back.

"Who are you smiling at?" Robin asked immediately, as if she had a side-view mirror attached to her head.

"I'm not smiling, I'm gritting my teeth, you make me so nervous."

"You were smiling at that guy, weren't you—at that retard's father. God!"

"Don't be ridiculous," Linda said, more annoyed with herself than with Robin. She knew very well that her love life was a sore point between them; Robin often intimated that Linda was promiscuous—although that wasn't the word she used—and she couldn't understand why anyone was attracted to her in the first place, beginning with Robin's own father. Sexual attraction was a mystery Linda wasn't prepared to solve or explain, but she was certainly *not* promiscuous. If anything, she was absurdly faithful. It wasn't her fault that some of her relationships ended abruptly when the man in question died. Robin treated her like someone old and out of it, who should have been cremated along with Wright, or buried with Manny. But this was the prime of her life, even if she hadn't entirely gotten the hang of it yet.

Linda stole a peek at her watch—the dashboard clock was fixed forever at 2:35—and saw that it was only a little after ten. It actually *was* boring, riding around and around like this; she didn't know how much more of it she could take. There was no law that said she had to let Robin continue driving until noon, so she cleared her throat and said, "I think that's about enough for today, dear. You did very nicely, though."

"*What!*" Robin said, ignoring both the false tribute and the implicit order to stop. "I don't believe you! I hardly drove at all!"

"Tomorrow is another day," Linda sang out gaily, even though there really wouldn't be a lesson the next day, and she knew how much Robin hated that kind of cliché. "Let's pull over now, please."

"Tomorrow!" Robin said scornfully, as she continued to drive. "What's the matter? Can't wait to see your stupid boyfriend?"

"Nathan isn't even home," Linda said, hating herself for dignifying Robin's accusation by responding at all. "He's down in San Diego for the weekend, on business." What *kind* of business, she suddenly wondered.

"I meant *him*," Robin said, indicating the stranger in the Caprice, which they were passing again for the zillionth time. And to make matters worse, the man chose that moment to wave to Linda. She didn't wave back, although that took the effort of one hand holding the other one down in her lap.

"My, what an imagination you have!" Linda exclaimed. But it was her own imagination that was unleashed by Robin's remark, and by the man's friendly gesture. In her mind's eye she'd already eliminated Robin and her teenage male counterpart from the picture. The man, whose name, she decided, was either Mike or

Dan, was recently divorced—no, widowed—and he was having a terrible time dealing with his loss and his sense of isolation. All he really wanted was someone nice to talk to, someone who'd understand what he was going through, someone who loved to dance and eat Chinese food—someone, perhaps, whose favorite author was J. D. Salinger. The week before, Linda and Nathan were lying in his bed, pleasantly spent from lovemaking, when she asked if he'd ever thought she had named Phoebe for Holden Caulfield's sister. And Nathan, predictably enough, had said, sleepily, "Who?"

As Robin drove on, Linda was transported to a charmingly furnished house in the Valley, where she and Mike were sitting in front of a blazing fire, sipping wine. When he dipped his head to kiss her, she felt the pleasure of affection along with the sexual thrill. It was companionship Linda craved as much as love, a concept Robin would never understand, and would probably mock, as she mocked just about every important thing Linda tried to tell her. Linda had to admit that she dismissed a great deal of what Robin said, too. But that was because the girl couldn't seem to separate the truth from her fantasies anymore. That business about Cynthia plotting to steal Phoebe, for instance. Still, Robin's overprotection of her baby sister was kind of sweet. Their physical resemblance became more striking every day, especially now that Phoebe had some hair. Robin had really freaked out last week when they discovered that Cynthia had trimmed it just a teensy bit, had made a feathery fringe of bangs so it wouldn't get in her eyes, like Robin's always did. You would think Cynthia had performed major surgery on Phoebe, the way Robin carried on. In fact, that was what she warned Linda was probably coming next. "You'll go there," she said, "and Feeb will have, like, this *nose* job, and maybe she'll be a brunette or something. One of the slaves will come to the door with those killer dogs and tell you you've got the wrong place. No habla ingles, señorita. Adios!" It was a perfectly ridiculous scenario, and typical of Robin, once she got going. Hadn't she warned Wright that Linda was only after his money? What money, she'd like to know. The debts he'd left behind had almost depleted his meager savings, and now Linda was working overtime to support the family he'd bequeathed her. But when Robin spouted all that nonsense about Cynthia, Linda had shivered, involuntarily. That was the trouble—people with overactive imaginations tended to be contagious. Before she knew it, Linda began to have her own disturbing thoughts, which she didn't bother to share with Robin. Starting with the white cashmere blanket that came home with the baby the last time she stayed with Cynthia. It was clearly very expensive—amazingly dense and weightless at once, and the color of vanilla yogurt. "Where did this come from?" Linda asked, and Cynthia only smiled and shrugged, as if cashmere blankets fell from the sky. Maybe they did, if you lived in the right neighborhood. "We went shopping," Cynthia finally said, "and it was on sale, and you know our Bebe, she can never resist a bargain." They laughed together over that and Linda thanked her, profusely, but said she really shouldn't have, it was wonderful enough that she'd kept the baby all day like that. It was only after she got home and put the baby to sleep under the beautiful blanket, and finished dinner, that she allowed herself to remember that Cynthia had said, "Bebe," not "Phoebe."

Once, when Linda was a young girl, a neighbor adopted a dog from the local pound. The dog was about five years old and was named Rusty, which the neighbor decided didn't suit him. She wanted to call him Prince instead, but she knew that a mature dog wouldn't answer to a new name just like that. So she changed his name a little bit every few days. She called him "Dusty" first, which was so similar to "Rusty" he came running without hesitation. A couple of days later he became "Dustin," and then, after that, "Justin." Linda couldn't remember exactly how they ever got to Prince, but she was positive it took weeks, and that soon afterward the dog was hit by a bus and killed while running across the road in response to his final name. There really wasn't any connection between that awful story and what Cynthia had called the baby, although Linda was sure Robin would have thought of one, and, somehow, recalling it now made her unreasonably uneasy.

Robin had circumnavigated the parking lot so many times Linda was getting a little carsick. She'd memorized all the specials in the supermarket window and had completely forgotten her own shopping list. The Caprice was still stuck in orbit, too, and its horn tooted a little melodic greeting when it went by this time. "Honk back," Linda told Robin. "It's only friendly."

"That dweeb," Robin said, without complying. "He's the one I told you about, the one that collects stamps or dead butterflies or something." She had never told her anything of the sort. "I think his dad just got out of jail," she added, with a shifty little side-glance at Linda.

Linda refused to take the bait. "Why don't you just concentrate on what you're doing?" she said.

"Why don't *you*?" Robin said, one of her typically empty and insolent responses.

"Don't be fresh," Linda told her.

"Don't *you* be fresh," Robin retorted. And then, murmuring so low Linda could barely hear her, she said, "Slut."

"That's it, Robin," Linda announced. "Pull over. Let's go! Right now!"

"What did I *do*?" Robin said. "I didn't do anything!"

She went right on driving, and Linda wished the 88 was equipped with dual controls, like the cars they'd used back at the Ben Hur Driving School in Newark. When she'd taken her own futile lessons there, the instructor kept slamming on his set of brakes to keep their car from colliding with other cars and lampposts and trees. Now Linda wanted to put an end to this monotonous ride and to Robin's assumed command of the car and their lives. She pumped her foot furiously against the floor mat, but Robin only speeded up a little in defiance. "Slow down!" Linda said. "Do you hear me?"

"Did somebody say something?" Robin said.

"Young lady, you are in deep trouble!" Linda cried.

"Blah, blah, blah," said Robin, leaning forward as she stepped up the speed even more.

"You are grounded!" Linda shouted, thinking what an odd thing it was to say when they appeared to be flying. Now things were truly whizzing by, and she felt the same sort of panic she'd felt watching the whirl and plunge of those terrible amusement-park rides. When Robin careened around a corner of the lot, the whole car shook and seemed to lean perilously to one side. Linda kept yelling for her to stop, and when that didn't work she began to simply scream. Each time they sped past the other car, its driver and passenger blurred into a single two-headed, openmouthed creature. Her screams might have been coming from them, or from one or both of the cars' horns, or from the overwrought engine of the 88 as Robin took it to its limits. But over all the compounded noise, Linda could distinctly hear Robin yelling, "Linda, I can't! It's stuck! Oh, shit, fuck! Linda, help me! Help!" Linda looked down and saw Robin's black-painted toenails splayed against the accelerator. "The brake, the brake! Use the *brake!*" she cried, and when she looked up again, Mike, Dan, the man in the Caprice, was zooming toward her, staring with an intensity she had only seen before in the face of a lover closing in for a kiss. And as if he were a lover, she shut her eyes against the exquisite moment of impact.

The world seemed to come back into focus as suddenly as it had vanished. Linda was lying alone across the front seat of the car, with her feet through the open door, and the dashboard hanging above her head, which ached fiercely. The radio was still playing—some heavy-metal number pulsed diligently near her ear—but whoever was screaming had considerably moved away, so that sound, at least, was muted and bearable. "Jesus fucking Christ," she heard someone say. "Don't move," someone else warned, and she almost laughed at the notion of moving, bringing a searing pain to her ribs. "Robin?" she inquired.

A man leaned in over her. "It's okay, they're coming," he said mysteriously. And then the screaming turned out to be a siren that kept growing louder before it stopped abruptly on an agonized high note, as if someone had strangled the screamer.

In the emergency room, they crowded around her and asked her name, and did she know where she was and who the President was. Linda confessed that she hadn't voted for him, but that wasn't what they wanted to know. Her left leg had fallen asleep, and her mouth tasted as if she'd been sucking on pennies. When she tried to tell them that, they pricked her with needles and set up an IV. And when they turned her head to one side, she saw that the man from the Caprice was lying on an adjacent gurney, looking back at her with his crinkly green eyes—well, one eye, anyway, since the other one was swollen shut. "Listen . . . sorry, so sorry . . ." she murmured.

"You stupid bitch, I'm going to sue your ass off," he said loudly and clearly, just before someone yanked a curtain closed between them.

Linda woke again in the recovery room, to somebody else's moaning. Her own pain was everywhere, but it was blunted, like a memory of pain. A nurse told her where she was and that she was doing just fine. The leg had needed surgery, but the arm was a clean break and easy to set. Linda saw the casts then—right arm, left leg—and felt their onerous weight. With her free hand, she traced her inflated mouth; her nose, which seemed stuffed but intact; and the tightly taped ribs. "Robin?" she said thickly, and the nurse said, "Uh-uh, dearie, I'm Paula." It was much too much trouble to explain, so Linda croaked, "Hi. Linda," right before she faded out again.

And then she was in another, smaller room, with an old woman lying in a bed across from her, watching television. Robin was there, too, her round pale face hovering above Linda's like a full moon. "You okay, Linda?" she whispered. "I'm really, really sorry. But it wasn't my fault, I swear. It was an accident."

"How are you?" Linda asked through her rubber lips.

"Huh? Fine, I guess," Robin said. "Like my knees and elbows are scraped and stuff, that's all. I got thrown out of the car the minute we hit."

"Seat belt," Linda said.

"Yeah, I guess I wasn't wearing mine."

"The other car?"

"Totaled, just like ours. But you were hurt the worst." She said it almost proudly. "You know, your leg and your arm and everything. They think your head's okay, though."

"What time is it?"

"I don't know. Late. Like almost nighttime."

"Phoebe!" Linda gasped.

"It's okay, don't worry. I called Ms. Rich . . . I called Cynthia and told her. She's coming right over."

Before Cynthia showed up, though, Nathan did. He was supposed to be in San Diego, wasn't he? Linda wondered how he knew what had happened. She was sure Robin wouldn't have bothered to inform him, and she did seem as surprised to see him as Linda was. As Robin retreated to a corner of the room, Nathan came to Linda's bedside and stared down at her. "Holy shit," he said softly. Then he bent and kissed her forehead and her fingers, arching his body carefully away from hers. Linda attempted something like a smile. "Right," she said.

"What?" Nathan asked. "No, don't try and talk now, mi vida. Just rest."

"You were *right*," she said.

"Yeah, I know, but who wants to be right all the time?"

"You," she said.

"Shhh," he told her.

"Supposed to be . . . in San Diego."

"I missed you, so I came home early."

"But how did you . . ."

"You mean, how did I find out? I got worried about the two of you, so I drove over to the market where you said you were going."

He was probably planning to heckle her a little, to give unsolicited advice, to take over.

"I got there maybe twenty minutes after it happened," he said.
"It looked like a war zone—glass, oil, foam, the works. The tow
trucks were trying to separate the cars and hook them up. One of
the guys called on his radio to find out where they took you. I
figured the morgue, myself. I've been downstairs for hours, they
wouldn't let me up here until now." He turned toward Robin,
"So, how are you doing there, Andretti?"

"It wasn't my fault," Robin mumbled.

"I'll bet," Nathan said.

"Nobody *asked* you—" Robin began belligerently, and then
stopped when she saw that Linda's eyes had filled with tears.

"Hey," Nathan said, "hey, we're not really fighting." He
reached out and grabbed Robin and pulled her against his side.
She struggled to get away, but he held her firmly by the shoulder.
"See?" Nathan said. "Pals!"

"It's not th-that," Linda said, starting to sob.

"Are you in pain, Lindy?" he asked. "I'll go get the nurse."

"No," she blubbered, "no!" even though the pain *was* asserting
itself again.

"Is it the car, then?" he said. "But you've got insurance, right?
And you never liked that old heap, anyway, remember? Listen,
sweetheart, everything's going to be okay, I promise you."

How could he say that? Everything in the world was wrong.
The pain was becoming more and more demanding, and an itch
was starting to crawl somewhere under the cast on her leg. How
was she going to dance or walk, or do anything at all? How was
she going to earn a living? And Robin's school was going to
reopen before long—who would take care of Phoebe? God,
when had she nursed her last? She realized that her swollen
breasts were making their own minor contribution to her body's
major discomfort.

A nurse came into the room and hustled Nathan and Robin
out. She gave Linda a shot for the pain, checked her IV and her

catheter, and left. The woman in the other bed spoke for the first time since Linda arrived. "Is that your husband?" she asked.

"No," Linda said. "Just a friend."

"Some friend," the woman said. "He looks exactly like Rudolph Valentino. You wouldn't remember him."

"Not personally," Linda said.

"He died young. In a hospital," the woman told her.

"Mmm," Linda said, politely. She was glad when Nathan, and then Robin, came in again. A moment later, Cynthia arrived, too, with an armful of flowers.

"Oh, my," she said as she approached Linda's bed. "How does the other guy look?"

"Well, his eye was a little swollen—" Linda began, but Cynthia waved the flowers at Robin, and said, "Be a love and get a vase for these, will you?"

Robin gave Cynthia her darkest look, but she grabbed the flowers, shaking a few petals loose in the process, and marched out of the room.

"For I am born to tame you, Kate!" Cynthia called after her.

"It's Robin," Linda said. By then Cynthia and Nathan were eyeing one another critically across Linda's bed, and the woman in the other bed had shut off her television set and was observing them all, as if they were a spin-off of the show she'd been watching.

"Where's the baby?" Linda asked Cynthia.

"Off in dreamland, where you should probably be, too."

"Linda needs to feed her," Nathan said.

"She's been fed," Cynthia answered. "She's perfectly safe and sound and happy. Listen, Linda, we'll get you a breast pump, and you'll feel a lot more comfortable. I'm going to see someone in charge and find out what's going on with you, anyway. Maybe we can get you transferred to Cedars. I know the chief of orthopedics there."

"Maybe she wants to stay here," Nathan said.

"I beg your pardon," Cynthia said. "I don't think we've met."

"Oh, sorry," Linda said, as if she were a negligent hostess at a cocktail party. "Cynthia . . . Nathan." The painkiller was starting to take effect and she was too woozy to deal with their last names. She could hardly remember them anyway. Robin came in and took a neutral position at the foot of the bed, clutching a urinal crammed with Cynthia's flowers, and Linda felt like Snow White in her glass coffin, surrounded by the grieving dwarfs. Except that the people around her bed seemed more irritable than sad. A bell began chiming for visitors to leave. Linda heard it dimly, but gratefully, through the cotton batting of her brain.

After the goodbyes, Nathan said, "Come on, Robin, I'll drive you home," and Cynthia said, "*I'll* do it. She's sleeping at my place tonight." "I am *not*," Robin said. Cynthia said something back, and Nathan answered her, and then they all shuffled out, murmuring disagreeably among themselves.

Linda was almost asleep when she felt a presence nearby. She opened her eyes and saw Cynthia leaning over her. "Good God, Linda," she said, "where did you find macho man—at a border check?" Linda was still trying to make proper sense of that when Cynthia added, "Don't you worry about anything, sweetie. Just concentrate on getting well. Little Bebe is in good hands."

Linda struggled to stay conscious long enough to answer. "The name . . . is . . . Rusty," she said, and then gave herself back to the darkness.

18

Dioramas

Robin got away with sleeping at the apartment alone the first night after the accident. She had told that witch, who'd won the tug of war with Nathan over who would drive her home from the hospital, that she was going to stay with her best friend, Lucy Thompson, that it was all arranged. Cynthia wasn't as gullible as Linda, though. She asked a lot of nosy questions, and she made Robin take a card with her telephone number printed on it, in the event of a change of plans. Then, after watching Robin pack an overnight bag, she insisted on driving her to the Thompsons', too. Robin had to think of a way to keep Cynthia from walking her inside, like a police escort, because she'd given her a phony address a couple of blocks from Lucy's house. When they got there, Robin ran out of the car, yelling, "Thanks a lot! Goodbye!" But Cynthia didn't drive away, as Robin had counted on her doing. She stayed right there with her headlights on and the motor running, and Robin could feel those eagle eyes on her back as she went up the walkway of a strange house and knocked lightly on the front door. Somebody on the other side started fumbling with the locks, calling out in a high, shaky voice, "Who's there? Who is it? What do you want?" Robin waved Cynthia away, muttering, "Go, just *go* already," but the car didn't move, and when the door of the house finally opened, revealing a little old lady in a pink bathrobe, Robin pushed her way inside, slamming the door shut behind her.

"Help! Police!" the old lady screeched, backing up against a wall, where a shelf filled with knickknacks shook and clattered. "Go away! I have no money! Don't hurt me, don't kill me!"

"Take it easy, will you," Robin said, peeking through the venetian blind at Cynthia's departing Porsche. "I'm leaving right now, okay? I made a mistake, okay? This is the wrong house."

But the old bag was still going like a siren as Robin fled through the same door she'd come in. Without looking back, she walked swiftly away from the house and around the corner. There was no one out on the street, but she slowed down, trying to look nonchalant, as if she belonged there, as if she was an ordinary person on her way home. Before she knew it, she was in front of the Thompsons' house. All the lights were on inside, and the station wagon was in the driveway. Without thinking about it, Robin crept up the little strip of side lawn and, standing on tiptoe between two bottlebrush trees, looked in through the kitchen window. She was instantly reminded of those dioramas she used to make in elementary school, to show how the Pilgrims or the Indians used to live. Making a scene inside a shoebox stood on its side had been one of the few school assignments Robin ever willingly did. It was kind of fun gathering up pieces of her old dollhouse furniture, and tearing bits of tinfoil for mirrors, or red cellophane for the flames in a fireplace or campfire. Once she even went so far as to make a little cardboard book for the father of the Pilgrim family to read by candlelight as he sat at the table, smoking his cardboard pipe. And now there was Mr. Thompson, in the blue-white flourescent glow of his kitchen, sitting alone at the table. He wasn't reading a book or smoking a pipe, though. He sat very still, with his head in his hands, staring at the floral pattern of the plastic tablecloth. While Robin watched, as raptly as she usually watched television, he removed one of his shoes, rubbed his foot as if it ached, and then put the shoe back on and rested his head in his hands again. The second hand on the wall clock crawled slowly around the numbers. Robin wished Lucy would come into the room. She had seen her only once since school let out, at the mall, surrounded by other kids. She'd looked in Robin's direction, and Robin could swear Lucy saw her, but then she turned quickly away and led her new pack of buddies into a store. Who cares? Robin had told herself. Good riddance. She didn't need a friend who blamed her for every stupid thing that happened in the world. Robin hung out sometimes with other kids, too, from a much faster crowd. Most of them were having sex, or said they were, and Robin didn't let on that she was a virgin, a freak who'd never even made out with anybody, except, once in a while, herself. But she didn't get a lot of their private references and jokes, and she began to feel like an outsider again. One night she went to a party where there were no parents around and plenty of pot and booze, and where an older boy named Richie, who she and Lucy used to drool over in the halls at school, massaged her breasts and swabbed out her mouth with his tongue. It felt surprisingly good, but then he got sick and passed out, and she had no one to tell about any of it afterward, which made it seem sort of pointless.

Before long, of course, Linda noticed that Lucy and Carmel didn't come around anymore, and she began to bug Robin about it. "What happened to your friend, Lucy?" she'd ask. "You were so close and now I hardly ever see her. You didn't have a fight or anything, did you?"

Robin growled various answers as they occurred to her: Lucy was sick, away on vacation, dead. She didn't think Linda ever really listened to her, anyway.

But Linda put one hand to her heart and said, "My God! What do you mean, she's dead? What happened to her?"

And Robin had to think fast and say, "What are you, deaf or something? I didn't say she was *dead.* I said she's in *bed.* She hurt her foot and she can't walk."

You could put a lethal curse on somebody that way, Robin

knew. A boy in Newark had killed his own grandmother by saying she had pneumonia, just to get himself out of detention. The grandmother, who was as healthy as a horse when he said it, actually got pneumonia the next day and was dead in a week. According to some people Robin ran into, though, Lucy was okay—at least physically. But she and her whole family were really freaked out by the loss of their shop in the riots.

Mr. Thompson stood up and Robin saw that he looked older and shorter and sort of sick. His shoulders were slumped and his usually warm brown skin had a gray tint. Mrs. Thompson came into the kitchen then, hesitating in the doorway first, like someone coming on stage in a play. She was wearing a white uniform that made her look fat. She opened the refrigerator and stared inside before she took out a plate of something and began eating from it absently with her fingers. Mr. Thompson looked at her without saying anything, as if he couldn't remember his lines. Where was Lucy? Probably down the hall in her room, with Carmel, both of them lying on their beds, listening to music. Robin could almost see that scene, too—the Indian-print bedspreads, the pinkish light, the spill of books and tapes and shoes between the beds—another diorama, of her own past this time, from which only she, herself, was missing. She had a sudden urge to tap on the kitchen window, to say, Hey, it's me out here, let me in! But then Garvey walked into the kitchen and went directly to the window, as if Robin *had* actually tapped on it and called out, and she ducked down behind one of the trees and ran back to the street.

It took her forever to walk home, and when she got there, the phone was ringing. Lucy! she thought immediately, and ran to answer it. But as she was about to pick up the receiver, she remembered Cynthia, who'd most likely be shrewd enough to check things out, to make sure Robin hadn't sneaked home again. So she had to let the phone go on ringing, which it did for a long time (Linda must have forgotten to turn on the answering machine that morning), and when it stopped, the silence was spooky. Robin picked up the receiver and dialed the number on the card Cynthia had given her. She intended to just breathe and moan into her ear, but a strange woman answered, saying "Ms. Sterling's service. Who's calling, please?" That rich bitch had somebody else do *everything* for her, even answer her stupid phone.

Robin dialed a number at random next. After several rings, a man answered in a groggy voice and Robin said, "This is the telephone company. We're checking to see if your phone is working okay."

"At . . . what time is it . . . almost eleven o'clock?" the man said. "Boy, you people put in some crazy hours. The phone seems fine, though, doesn't it?"

"I'm not sure," Robin said. "You don't hear that little humming sound?"

After a pause, the man said, "Well, yeah, I think so, now that you mention it. Sort of like a fly or a mosquito or something?"

"That's it," Robin said. "I'm going to hang up now and look into it, and I'd like you to just wait right there until I call you back."

"It won't take long, will it?" the man asked. "I was actually asleep," he added apologetically.

"I'll get right back to you," Robin assured him. "Don't move, okay?"

"Okay," he said.

What a jerk. Robin wondered if he'd sit there waiting until he dropped dead. She wondered if the old lady whose house she'd busted into had a heart attack afterward. It was possible to kill loads of people without ever laying a hand on them. Linda certainly could have died in the accident, and for a few moments there, Robin thought she had. They were taken to the hospital in separate ambulances, for some reason. Robin kept telling them she was okay, she was fine, and that it wasn't her fault, but she couldn't stop crying, like some idiot baby, so they made her get checked out in the emergency room. What a nuthouse that was. All those old people with oxygen up their noses, and little kids screaming, and somebody behind a curtain saying "Help me, please help me" over and over again.

"Where's Linda?" Robin asked everyone in sight, and they all asked her questions back without answering, a tactic of evasion she recognized because she used it so often herself. They asked her shit like "How many fingers am I holding up?" and "In what direction was your car traveling?" If Linda had died, Phoebe would have been a whole orphan then, like Robin. Except that, technically, Robin still had a mother. And Phoebe would always have Robin.

Robin had memorized Lucinda Blake's telephone number, in case she lost the piece of paper it was written on. She'd called the number a few times, after watching the show (which was taped, according to *TV Guide*), but she kept getting a busy signal. Still, it thrilled her to know she could dial Lady Audrey Finley directly, that it was *her* very own busy signal she was hearing. Robin dialed the number again now and this time she heard ringing. Then there was a brief mechanical pause, and a recorded female voice saying, "You've reached 984-1218. Leave a message at the sound of the tone."

She didn't sound like Lady Audrey; she didn't sound English at all. And she never said who she was. It could have been a wrong number. Robin might have made a mistake when she copied it down, she had done it so quickly. Maybe it was off by only one digit, and she'd have to spend the rest of her life trying to figure out which one it was, and what it was really supposed to be. While she was thinking all this, the tape at the other end of the line ran out. There were three consecutive beeps and then a dead sound. Robin hung up; she would try again some other night.

Linda's personal telephone directory was on the table next to the phone, and she began browsing through it. All these people back in Jersey she never saw anymore were in it, and there was Robin's father's old phone number at work. Under the Gs she found Manny still listed, too. It was typical of dopey Linda to keep dead people in her phone book. Like if they ever came back, she could call them.

The first name in the H section was Robin's mother's, Miriam Hausner. It was shocking to see it written out like that in Linda's familiar, cramped handwriting. Miriam's address, in Glendale, Arizona, and her phone number were right under her name. Robin remembered the day, just about a year ago, when she and Linda pulled up to that house and rang the bell. Robin had no real memory of her mother then, only a mess of imagined scenes from her own babyhood, in which both her parents appeared in conventional roles. Her father never helped her embellish those scenes with details from his own memory. Her mother was gone and that was that; he didn't want to discuss it. But he hovered over Robin as if she, too, might take off and leave him one of these days. All that love and attention drove her crazy, but when Linda came along and took some of it for herself, it was even worse.

The person Robin had invented as her mother was both more and less beautiful than the real thing. Miriam Hausner wore tinted glasses, for instance, that hid her eyes from Robin's searching glance, and she seemed at a loss on the occasion of their reunion. Once in a while, on TV, on *Geraldo* or *Oprah*, other mothers and children were reunited, and they always ran into each other's arms, bawling like babies. Oprah cried, too. Adults who'd been abandoned, kidnapped, or just misplaced somehow, when they were little, were all ready to forget the trauma and forgive the parents who'd managed to lose them. Robin noticed that they were often fat, as if they ate a lot to make up for the normal childhood they didn't have. The mothers were usually thin.

In Glendale, Linda explained about Robin's dad, and how this had seemed to be the logical place to bring her under the circumstances, while Robin's mother and her second husband, Tony, sat there like a couple of statues, as if they were being hustled by some pushy salesman to buy something they didn't need or want. But what had Linda expected, barging in on them like that, with an overgrown teenager who had nothing to do with the baby Miriam had left behind all those years ago? Robin could have been anybody, a total stranger trying to stake a false family claim, except that she looked so much like her father, probably the last person Miriam wanted to be reminded of.

The blinds in the house were drawn against the desert sun that Sunday afternoon. It was dark and cool and uncluttered inside. At least there were no other, replacement children there, but Miriam admitted at some point that Tony's son from his first marriage had lived with them for a while. She might as well have stabbed Robin or shot her. She *felt* wounded, in her chest and her stomach, and she could have reeled around that big living room, whimpering and bleeding all over the white furniture and the fancy rug. Instead, she just yelled something at them, at the top of her lungs. Then Linda started acting like she'd never meant to leave Robin there, like they'd just stopped in to say hello because they happened to be in the neighborhood. Yeah, what a coincidence. But Robin's mother looked relieved, and she thanked Linda for coming by and reminded them both to keep in touch. Of course, that left Linda and Robin alone together, which didn't thrill either of them. And today Linda had almost died.

Robin picked up the telephone receiver again. She knew what she was going to do, but she didn't let herself think about it too much before she punched in the numbers. The ringing sounded far away, much farther than the very next state, and it went on and on. They probably weren't home, and she was half glad, half disappointed. As she was hanging up, the ringing abruptly stopped and a breathless voice near Robin's hip, that could have been coming from the pocket of her jeans, said, "Hello. Hello?" It was her. Robin brushed her hair back with her free hand and slowly raised the receiver to her ear. "Hello!" she heard her mother say again. "Hey, is that you, Brandy? Quit kidding around, will you. Don't I have enough on my mind without this? Hello?" And then she hung up.

Robin wondered what was on her mother's mind. And she

wondered who Brandy was, and if she made crank calls, too. The only Brandy Robin had ever known was a large German shepherd some neighbors in Newark owned when she was about three or four years old. The neighbors, a batty old couple named Klyster, kept that Brandy chained in their yard all day, and there were signs posted on the fence and the house warning you to beware of the dog. Robin was too young to read, but she was afraid of Brandy, anyway. She looked like the wolf in fairy-tale picture books, and she lunged to the end of her chain, barking furiously, choking and slavering, whenever Robin came anywhere near the Klyster house. There was a sick joke going around that Brandy had eaten a few kids in the Klysters' last neighborhood; that was why they'd had to move here.

One day, when Robin was playing inside her own tiny yard, with its chain-link fence, Brandy got loose. She must have pulled the lethal-looking, spiral steel stake right out of the ground, because she was dragging it behind her on the end of that long chain when she suddenly showed up right outside the Reismanns' fence. Robin's father had just gone into the house to make lunch for the two of them and Robin was alone, digging in the dirt with a teaspoon. She heard the low growling first, and when she looked up, Brandy was pacing outside the closed gate, with her head down between her muscular shoulders, her fur bristling, and her tail drooping moodily behind her. Robin tried to call to her father. The word "Daddy" was in her mouth—she could feel its particular man-shape and sound there—but it wouldn't come out. He would be looking through the window any minute now. He was always checking up on her. The dog flung itself against the fence and Robin dropped the spoon and covered her eyes. But she could still hear the hungry growling and the sound of shuddering metal. Brandy was going to eat her! She would be packed inside that swollen belly with all those other unlucky victims, with Red Ridinghood and her grandmother and the foolish little pigs. Robin's father would come outside too late, and find the dog smiling and licking its chops, and nothing left of Robin but her inedible shoes and the abandoned spoon. Brandy rammed the fence over and over again, until Robin found her feet and her voice at the same moment. She ran to the kitchen door and threw herself against it, the way Brandy was throwing herself against the fence, and she yowled to be let in. But when the gate gave way at last under the dog's obsessive butting, Robin was still working on the kitchen door, screaming now, a whole opera of terror and rage, and she was wetting her pants. Her father had left her here for good—for *bad*—and the dog, the wolf, was biting at her heels, her behind, her legs! And then the door opened suddenly under her limp weight and she was yanked inside, leaving Brandy out there, barking and panting for her lost meal.

The bites weren't very deep; Robin's thick denim overalls had protected her from really serious injury. But she had to go to the dreaded doctor to have her wounds cleaned, and to get a shot. Her father was beside himself with worry and remorse. He'd been in the bathroom when it happened, and he cursed his own stupid bowels as he held her down on the doctor's examining table to be tortured.

After that, Robin couldn't even look at a dog without feeling a rising panic. Even the playful puppy her father bought for her the following Christmas was terrifying, with its unpredictable moves and aggressive little needle teeth. Robin locked herself in the bathroom and wouldn't come out until he promised to take it back to the pet store. As she got older, she learned to mask her fear in front of other people, to cross the street when she saw a dog coming, to shut her eyes and clench her teeth, to say she was allergic. She did have trouble breathing when she was scared, which made the allergy alibi sort of true. Of course, she often worried that the fear itself would give her away. Animals were supposed to be able to smell it on you, even when people were fooled, and it was supposed to make them go nuts. Linda was always petting vicious-looking dogs, and trying to get Robin to do it, too. That day at Cynthia's, Robin almost had a hemorrhage, she was so freaked by those two big attack dogs. She was sure they could smell her fear right through the sealed car, and that maybe they could *eat* their way through all that steel and glass. What were their names? She couldn't remember, except that they both began with a B. Like Brandy. Maybe her mother's friend by the same name was a human reincarnation of that long-ago she-wolf. Then, in a rush, it came to Robin that her mother had a whole *life* she knew nothing about: friends she hung out with, favorite colors and songs, foods she'd eaten and movies and shows she'd seen, the bed she slept in, clothes, work, habits, and the way everything looked to her through her glasses. It was like another diorama Robin could only be on the outside of, peering in.

She was much too hyper to sleep now, or to even watch TV, so she went into Linda's room to snoop around. Aside from some wild lace panties tucked between her regular cotton ones, the only thing of interest Robin found was a pair of love chains, with Nathan and Linda's names engraved on them, in the night-table drawer. She brought them to her own room to compare them with the ones she kept hidden in her dresser drawer. Linda's bracelets were probably sterling silver; Robin's pair looked corroded next to them. It was just as well she and Lucy had never worn them. They both could have gotten blood poisoning.

She took the one with her name engraved on it, unclasped the chain, and looped it through Linda's bracelet, which was already attached to Nathan's. She yanked on the outer bracelets and the chains held. Then she added Lucy's bracelet to her own and yanked again. What if everyone was chained together like this, the way you were once attached to your mother before the cord was cut? Then you couldn't lose anyone your whole life, no matter what happened, an idea so dazzling she had to sit down on her bed with the connected bracelets gathered in a heap in her lap. It was odd that she'd never seen Nathan and Linda wear their love chains, had never seen them before at all. She sat there on the bed, joining and separating them, joining and separating them, until she suddenly realized how they were probably used.

19

The Secret Room

The morning after the accident, when Linda was still in a fog of painkillers, a social worker came to her hospital room and asked a series of questions in a weary, bored voice, as if he'd asked them hundreds of times before. Married? Children? Parents? Disability insurance? Savings? He wanted to know if she had any other close relatives, and if she was eligible for unemployment benefits. Linda wished she had better answers, as the social worker grimly shook his head and scribbled inside his manila folder. Then he closed the folder and explained that foster care was available for Robin and Phoebe until Linda recovered. He said it would be about ten or twelve days before she could go home, or to a rehabilitation facility, and she would need physical therapy and household help for several weeks after that. "You'd better apply for welfare assistance right away," he advised. "They take about a year and a day down there just to process the papers."

Linda was in tears when Cynthia walked in. "What's the matter?" she asked. "What's going on here?" The social worker began his recitation again, in the same rehearsed manner, but Cynthia stopped him in mid-sentence. "Ms. Reismann is *not* a welfare case," she declared. "I'm responsible for her and her family." She signed some papers to that effect and the social worker left.

Linda was too stunned and moved to speak. Cynthia patted her shoulder and said that she and Lupe would keep the baby until Linda was well, and that they would take her in, too, when she was discharged from the hospital. "Let's just call it workman's compensation," she added, and then stopped Linda's flow of feeble protests—"Oh, but I couldn't . . . I hardly *worked* . . . It's too much"—with that little wave of her hand, which seemed just as capable of stopping a speeding train.

"The only problem," Cynthia said, "is that stepdaughter of yours. She pretended to go to a friend's house last night—I dropped her off myself. But when I went back early this morning, there was only an old woman there, too terrified to even undo the chain on her door. She claimed she'd never heard of Robin *or* her friend."

"But did you find her?" Linda asked, worriedly. "Is she okay?"

"Oh, *she's* fine," Cynthia said. "She's down in the gift shop now. I sent her there to get you some magazines. But it took Hester over an hour to track those people—the Thompsons?—down, and then it turned out Robin hadn't been at their house for *weeks*. I finally found her at your place, fast asleep with all her clothes on and the stereo going full blast. She's impossible, Linda. You really have to put your foot down." But that was something she couldn't do at the moment, either literally or figuratively.

That afternoon, Jewelle Thompson called Linda to express her sympathy about the accident, and to offer to take Robin in for a while, if she had no place else to go. The invitation was gracious. "I'm sure she won't be any bother," Mrs. Thompson said, "and they'll all be in school again in a couple of weeks, anyway. Thank heavens for this year-round schedule, right?" It still seemed like an awful imposition to Linda, but what choice did she have? Vicki was in Akron taking care of her mother, Rosalia had been laid off at the factory and she'd moved in with her married son, and Robin swore she'd hitchhike back to Newark before she'd stay with Cynthia. She didn't seem all that happy about going to the Thompsons', either—the girls had obviously had some sort of tiff—but she, too, had no real choice in the matter.

Ten days later, Linda was brought by private ambulance to Cynthia's house and settled into a rented hospital bed in the guest suite on the main level. Mitchell, the houseman, had filled the place with flowers from the gardens, and Lupe carried in a welcoming tray of tea and cake. Linda knew how lucky she was to be in such beautiful and comfortable surroundings, with people to care for her and the baby, but she was heavyhearted about her scattered little family. Phoebe was just out of reach, upstairs, in the dressing room off Cynthia's bedroom, and Robin was at the Thompsons', miles away.

Linda's own physical limitations only added to her feelings of frustration and loss. She couldn't use crutches because of her broken arm, and had to hobble around leaning on a clumsy walker instead. She needed assistance with just about every-thing—dressing, bathing, getting to the bathroom. Someone else even had to cut up her food.

There was an intercom she could keep near her to summon Lupe or her sister, Maria, who came to help out now several hours a day. Sometimes Linda picked up random sounds over the speaker from other parts of the house: Phoebe babbling or crying in her crib, Lupe and Maria chatting in Spanish as they worked together in the kitchen, or Cynthia talking on the telephone. She always seemed to be arguing with somebody about something—taping schedules, budgets, idiot writers, money-grubbing agents, no-talent actors. "I don't care *how* we kill that slut off," Linda heard her say one evening, "as long as we do it before she's up for renegotiation." Linda knew she was referring to a character on one of her shows, but it still gave her the chills.

The baby had been weaned to a formula while Linda was in the hospital; it couldn't be helped. First, there was all the pain medication she took that could be passed on through her breast milk. And then, after the medication was stopped, it was unreasonable to expect anyone to bring Phoebe to the hospital several times a day to be nursed. The few times she *was* brought in, she fussed and fretted in Linda's good arm, which soon ached from holding her, and she firmly rejected the breast. Her pursy little mouth and squinched-up eyes reminded Linda of Robin refusing to try something new and exotic in a Chinese restaurant.

Cynthia was right—the breast pump eased Linda's discomfort, if not her sadness, and her milk dried up pretty quickly after that. The baby thrived on the formula, though; she looked positively enormous now, and so much more mature. In less than two weeks, she had cut another tooth, learned to sit up without support, and added some wonderful new jungle cries to her vocabulary. She seemed shy with Linda, who felt strangely shy herself, the way she did when they were first introduced in the delivery room. She wished Phoebe's crib could be kept downstairs, next to her own bed, so they could get reacquainted faster, but that was impractical. Lupe, who attended Phoebe when she woke at night, slept upstairs, and all the other baby equipment was up there, too. It was hard to ask for favors under the circumstances, and when Linda meekly suggested that Phoebe be kept near her during the day, in her playpen or stroller, Cynthia reminded her that the more she rested, the sooner she'd heal. "Doctor's orders!" she sang out in cheerful reproach.

Nathan had been against Linda's going to Cynthia's, but he couldn't come up with any real reasons for his objection, or any practical alternatives. He lived in a small one-bedroom apartment, and neither of them could afford to pay someone to stay with Linda and the baby while he was at work. The day before she was released from the hospital to Cynthia's, he asked, "Why is she doing all this for you? You hardly even know her."

The question had occurred to Linda, too, of course, but she didn't feel inclined to study it. "I don't know," she admitted. "She's just a very good person, I guess."

"Yeah," Nathan said, "a regular little Mother Teresa."

"Nathan, she does *lots* of good things," Linda said. "I mean, she's on all these Hollywood committees that raise money to fight drugs and cancer and AIDS."

"This is different, Linda."

"Not just that," Linda went on. "She's sort of adopted these two Guatemalan orphans through Save the Children—a little brother and sister? She supports them and they write her letters every month. Cynthia has their picture on her desk at home. They're really adorable."

"Big deal," Nathan said.

"You sound just like Robin," Linda scolded, but she didn't have the strength to continue arguing with him. And when Nathan left abruptly later, on Cynthia's arrival, and she said, "You can't really be serious about him," Linda didn't exactly rally to his defense. Now, propped on the leather recliner in the guest suite at Cynthia's, she watched television or tried to read rather than deal with the little personal wars swirling around her. She watched both of the soap operas Cynthia produced—*Destiny's Children* and *Love in the Afternoon* (the one Robin was so crazy about)—surprised by how readily she became involved in their elaborate and unlikely plot lines. Would Lady Finley succumb to her evil brother-in-law's seduction? Would his plan to pour fatal toxins into the cattle feed at Rancho Rayo succeed? Linda lived mostly for her brief visits with Phoebe, though, and for her intermittent phone contact with Robin, whose voice coming through the wires seemed to be leached of its usual volume and bravado.

It had been three and a half months since the riots and two weeks since the accident. Robin had never been able to memorize historical dates or details for school, but those two events were clearly fixed in her head. One marked the beginning of the end of her friendship with Lucy, and the other the end of her life as she knew it.

Being forced to stay at Lucy's house when they weren't talking to each other really sucked. For a minute or two, Robin had con-

sidered refusing to go there, but winding up in a children's shelter or some creepy foster home would be even worse; she had
watched enough television in her life to know that much. The
only way to save face was to show that she didn't want to be at
Lucy's any more than Lucy wanted her there. This was mostly
accomplished with a permanently pained expression, exagger-
ated sighs, and frequent complaints to Carmel, who tried her
best to be neutral, or at least fair. Sharing a bedroom with Lucy
and Carmel didn't help matters, especially since it was so small
that their twin beds and Robin's folding cot had to be jammed
together. It was a good thing Carmel was in the middle, so they
both had somebody to talk to.

Mr. and Mrs. Thompson didn't seem to notice that the girls
were having problems. Robin supposed it was because they had
so many problems of their own. The silent scene she'd witnessed
through their kitchen window the night of the accident was still
being played out, one way or another, every day. Mr. Thompson
moped around the house most of the time. He'd been unable to
find a job, and the insurance company was giving him a hard time
about collecting on the fire at the photo shop. It had something to
do with combustible chemicals and an act of God or something.
Mrs. Thompson was working as a home attendant for a paralyzed
old lady in Brentwood; that was why she wore that white uniform.
According to Carmel, who fed Robin most of her information,
Cynthia was giving the family money for Robin's keep, which
made her feel worse than ever. Now she was a charity case, just
like Linda, except that Linda was living in luxury, probably eating
jumbo shrimp and fried chicken for breakfast every day, while
Robin was a prisoner of Lucy's unspoken anger in this crowded
little house. She remembered idly wondering where everyone
slept here, and how they tolerated being so close all the time.
Now, to her regret, she was finding out firsthand. Mrs. Pickett—
Ga—and Aunt Ez, who didn't speak to anyone, it seemed (Robin
wondered if she *could*), slept together in the living room on a
convertible sofa. Garvey spent his nights in the alcove off the liv-

ing room, on a BarcaLounger, with the head and foot lowered as far as they would go. Mr. and Mrs. Thompson shared the other bedroom. There was just one bathroom in the house, and there was often a long wait to get into it. Standing in the hallway, jumping from foot to foot because she had to go so badly, Robin thought of how she used to hammer on the bathroom door at home while Linda sang in the shower, and how Linda did the same thing when Robin was in there, toking, or just daydreaming on the toilet or in the tub. That setup seemed like heaven compared to this, and Cynthia's house, with those king-size bathrooms, didn't bear thinking about. The worst thing of all, though, was not seeing Phoebe every day, and the feeling Robin had that they were drifting further and further apart, that Phoebe would gradually forget her without daily contact between them.

Robin had caught a bad cold a couple of days after the accident, and Cynthia took one look at her and said she couldn't see the baby until she was better. "I'm better," Robin announced on the phone the following day, but then she had a major coughing jag, and Cynthia said, "Why don't we wait until that cough is completely gone."

By then, Linda was out of the hospital, and Nathan picked Robin up one afternoon and drove her to Cynthia's house. "This place gives me the creeps," she confided to Nathan as they pulled into the driveway, and he said, "Welcome to the club." Robin stepped cautiously from the car, but at least the dogs were nowhere in sight, and their barking sounded distant. Linda had promised they'd be locked in their outdoor kennel or in the laundry room whenever Robin visited.

She and Nathan went in to see Linda first, with Cynthia trailing after them, even though Robin was itching to get to Phoebe. Linda was on this big leather chair with her leg in its plaster cast raised. "Oh, honey," she said, when she saw Robin, and she looked as if she was going to start bawling. She held out her good arm until Robin walked over and submitted to an awkward hug. "Where's Feeb?" Robin asked as soon as she could free herself.

"Upstairs," Linda said, and Robin headed for the staircase.

Cynthia blocked her way. "Just a moment, young lady," she said. "You'd better wash your hands first."

"Why?" Robin demanded. "She's my sister—we have the same germs."

"That's true, I've seen them," Nathan said.

"Never mind," Cynthia told Robin, completely ignoring Nathan. "There's a bathroom right in there." She pointed to a door, and Linda, that kiss-up, said, "It can't hurt, can it?"

Robin went into the bathroom and shut the door. Her hands were perfectly clean, so she just let the water run for a couple of seconds, splashed a little of it on the fresh cake of soap in the soap dish, smeared the wet soap on a towel, and came out again, eager to get upstairs. But Lupe walked into Linda's room just then, carrying Phoebe. "Hey!" Robin said in greeting, and the baby crowed something back at her and held out her arms.

"Look, she remembers you!" Linda cried.

"Why shouldn't she?" Robin snapped. "I look the same." The baby seemed different, though, heavier for one thing, and older, more like an actual *person*. She was wearing a beautiful new outfit. "Where's the stroller?" Robin asked. "I want to take her outside."

"Oh, stay here, please," Linda said. "I'd like us all to be together today."

You *would*, Robin thought, but she hung around for a while. Then, when Cynthia went into the bathroom, and Nathan and Linda started making cow eyes at each other, Robin slipped away with the baby into the kitchen. Even there they couldn't have any real privacy. Lupe and another woman who looked a lot like her were always nearby, watching, and getting all worked up in Spanish when Robin roughhoused with Phoebe, who obviously loved it. Robin did get to give her a bottle, though, and for that little while it felt as if they were alone. Phoebe alternately patted the bottle and Robin's dangling hair, and they gazed steadily into one another's eyes, until Phoebe's fluttered and closed, and there was nothing but a lace of bubbles left in the bottle.

"Sleepytime, nenita," Lupe announced, taking the droopy baby and going toward the stairs. Robin began to follow her, but Cynthia came by then and said, "Linda wants to see you now, Robin."

"You and I haven't even had a chance to talk yet," Linda said, as if that was something they'd done a lot of in the past. She asked an endless string of questions about Lucy and Carmel and how Robin was getting along at their house.

"Fine. Good. Okay," Robin answered at regular intervals. She wanted to go upstairs and see Phoebe again, to watch her sleep, the way she used to at home. Linda had her boyfriend and her bosom buddy there; what did she need Robin for? "I'm just going to check on Feeble," she said.

"That's not such a good idea," Cynthia told her. "She's become a very light sleeper, and you might disturb her."

"I won't," Robin said. "I'll just look at her for a minute."

"I don't think so," Cynthia said.

Robin turned to Nathan for support, and he looked at Linda as if to say, "Okay, now the ball's in your court." Linda's eyes were sympathetic, but she only sighed and said, "Cynthia's right, Robin. Just let her sleep now. You'll come back to see her again real soon."

Nathan glanced at his watch. "We have to get going, anyway, Robin," he said. "I've got a couple of early-evening classes."

"Can I get a drink of water first?" she asked.

"Sure," Nathan said, and Cynthia added, "There's spring water in the fridge and some Coke and 7-Up in the pantry. Ask Lupe or Maria if you can't find what you want."

Robin left the room, but instead of making a right turn in the direction of the kitchen, where she could see the two Mexican women busy doing something at the counter, she hurried to the stairs. She took them two and three at a time, and reached the top in only a matter of seconds. She was out of breath and excited; this was going to be a cinch. She was tiptoeing toward Cynthia's bedroom—Linda had mentioned that Phoebe slept in the room right off it—when a door down the hall opened and a woman stepped out. Robin gasped, and the woman said, softly, "Hi. Sorry if I scared you. You're Robin, aren't you? I'm Hester Foley, Cynthia's secretary." She shook Robin's hand, which was all sweaty by then, and went into the big white bathroom and closed the door.

The double doors to Cynthia's room were wide open this time, and Robin darted between them, pulling them almost all the way shut behind her. She went right to the dressing room and skidded to a halt at the threshold, staring inside in shock and bewilderment. It was completely changed! The walls that were a pale yellow the day of the brunch had Mother Goose paper on them now, and so did the ceiling. Little Bo-peep chased her lost sheep around and around the room. The mirrored dressing table, that poufy chair, and the big wall unit were gone. In their place were a crib, a chest of drawers topped by a changing table, a rocking chair, and open shelves filled with stuffed animals. The fancy white furniture all matched, and the crib was crowned by a ruffled canopy the same peachy color as Cynthia's bedroom. The world probably looked pretty rosy to Phoebe when she lay there, awake. Long ago, when Robin still had those stupid fantasies about living with her mother, this was the kind of room she'd imagined she would have. But how had Cynthia managed to decorate it so quickly? And why did she bother, if Phoebe was only going to be here for a few weeks? Linda had said that Cynthia was renting some basic baby stuff, that it was easier and cheaper than moving Phoebe's own things from the apartment. But everything here looked brand-new and expensive. And could you rent wallpaper?

Robin crept up to the crib. The baby lay sprawled on her back with her hands curled and her chest pumping away. She seemed like a tiny captive behind the bars. Robin's own breath sounded harsh and raw in the stillness, and she tried to quiet it, but Phoebe *wasn't* a light sleeper, the way Cynthia said. She didn't stir at all while Robin leaned over the railing and watched her, or when she gently touched one closed fist and whispered, "See you, punk."

Robin opened the double doors a few inches and looked both ways down the hall. There was no one in sight, and all the other doors were closed now. That woman, Hester, must have gone back wherever she'd come from. Robin went down the stairs as swiftly and silently as she had climbed them. She ran into the kitchen, past the two women still at work at the counter, turned on the faucet in the sink, and poured herself a tall glass of water. She was gulping it down when Cynthia came into the kitchen and said, "That's quite a thirst you had, Robin." Robin refused to take the bait. She wiped water from her lips and dripping chin and tried to stare Cynthia down. But Cynthia only smiled and said, "You'd better hurry up now—Nathan's waiting for you."

Linda was weary from the excitement of having company, although she began to miss them moments after they were gone. It had made her very happy to see Robin and Phoebe together again, almost as happy as they were to see each other. Nathan had seemed a little sad today, though, or especially thoughtful. He'd sat there for a while, stroking Linda's hand, before he said, "You've got a pretty nice cell here, chica. Do you think they'll let you out early for good behavior?" He was probably just feeling jealous and lonely. Everything's going to work out, Linda told herself, with time and patience.

Right before Nathan and Robin left, the girl bent down over Linda, who thought she was being surprised by a goodbye kiss. But Robin only whispered something hotly in her ear: The moon? The room? M*aroon*? Whatever it was, she wouldn't repeat it when Linda said, "What? I didn't hear you, Robin."

"Oh, forget it," she said, as Cynthia came in with a fresh pitcher of ice water.

"Leaving already?" she asked. "Well, thanks so much for coming by."

On the way home, Robin said to Nathan, "Do you remember when I went to get a drink before? Well, I snuck upstairs to see Feeb."

"Good for you!" Nathan said. "At least somebody in your family has guts."

Robin didn't pause to savor the compliment. "But *listen*," she said, banging impatiently on his arm. "I couldn't believe it—there was all this designer baby furniture and wallpaper up there!"

But Nathan was too worked up himself to really pay attention. "I'll bet," he said. "Like everything else in that place—her designer water, her designer clothes, her designer goddamn *air*! Linda just better not get used to all that."

20

I, You

Robin had never dreamed she'd look forward to going back to school, but it was the only place she could get away from Lucy for most of the day. Of course, there were still the long nights and the endless weekends. Not talking to someone was exhausting, especially if that certain someone was always around, flaunting an attitude. All the unsaid words were right there in Robin's throat, fighting to get out, and she had to hold them back. And she had to hold her hands back from making the gestures that usually went with the words. Carmel helped as much as she could, speaking for Robin whenever she couldn't speak for herself. Sometimes Carmel seemed like a mind reader, as if she knew at the same moment Robin did what she intended to say. "Do you want the light off?" she'd ask at night, when she and Lucy were reading in bed and Robin was sleepy and bothered by the glare. "More potatoes?" she would say at supper, as Robin eyed the bowl next to Lucy's elbow. Lucy's deliberate indifference was driving Robin crazy, but she had to admire her ex-friend's stubbornness. It was a perfect match for her own.

Once, on their way to California, Robin and Linda had stopped speaking, too, for several hours. For some reason that Robin couldn't remember now, they didn't speak to anyone at all.

She had decided she would croak before she'd give in, but Linda, usually so spineless, held out also, mile after mile after mile. It got really stupid—they ended up at a restaurant where they had to order lunch by pointing to different items on the menu—but Robin kept her silence, figuring she might eventually be a contender for the *Guinness Book of World Records*. She didn't get nearly that far, but she did win her battle with Linda, who finally couldn't stand it anymore and blurted something out. Lucy and Carmel's Aunt Ez, on the other hand, had never said *anything* in Robin's hearing. She asked Carmel about it one day, and she said that her aunt used to talk, a long time ago, but that something very bad had happened to her down in Georgia, where she once lived, something she couldn't talk about to anyone, so eventually she quit talking, period.

Mr. Thompson was still out of work. He looked through the want ads every day, and he'd signed up at a couple of employment agencies, but it seemed as if nobody was looking for a photographer. He drove Mrs. Thompson back and forth to Brentwood, to take care of that old lady, and once in a while he did an odd job for somebody—working on a paint crew or helping out on a moving van—but most of the time he was home, just hanging around waiting for something to happen. Aunt Ez and Ga did the cooking and the housework, with the girls' help after school, although Lucy complained to Carmel that it was sexist, that Garvey got away with murder. He only had to take out the trash and do a little yardwork, which he conveniently forgot about most of the time. Robin agreed that Garvey was a pain, although at least he'd stopped focusing his hostility on her. He was hardly able to focus on anything. Whenever you looked at him, he seemed to be half asleep. Robin wondered if he was using crack or something. But when she examined him discreetly for other telltale signs—like the dilated eyes and shaky hands listed in those fliers the school nurse sent home—he checked out clean. Maybe he was just feeling bad about everything that had happened. This was the first year, Carmel told Robin, that their family couldn't go to the big reunion in Virginia, and Garvey was really disappointed.

Robin had called Linda right after their visit to tell her again about the nursery upstairs, but Linda still didn't seem to get it. "She's got it all fixed up," Robin said, excitedly, "like Feeb always lived there!"

"Well, don't you think that's nice?" Linda said. "To go to so much trouble to make her feel at home like that?"

"Nice?" Robin said, totally exasperated. "*Nice?* It's a fucking Twilight Zone!"

"Don't use that language with me, miss," Linda said. "And try to remember how lucky we are, under the circumstances. Instead of being suspicious of everybody, we should just be grateful." Cynthia was probably drugging her food, too.

One Sunday morning, Mrs. Thompson tried to get Mr. Thompson to go down to their shop with her to clean things up and see if anything could be salvaged, but he said he didn't feel like it, he had a headache, and what was the use. He'd gone there by himself right after the riots to assess the damage. Mrs. Thompson had wanted to go with him then, but he wouldn't let her. He kept insisting that it would be too hard for her to bear.

"I looked at my daddy in his coffin," she reminded him. But he went out alone, and he'd come home, Carmel told Robin, looking like he'd seen a ghost, or as if he'd become one himself. "Gone," he said. Only that one word, and then he cried, right there in the kitchen, in front of everybody. He made Mrs. Thompson promise to stay clear of the area. There might be more trouble, he said. But she began talking right away about insurance, recovery, starting over again. Carmel said it was as if she was talking to herself. "Gone," Mr. Thompson said again, and then he refused to discuss it anymore. In some respects, he was as out of it now as Garvey.

"Maybe it's not that bad," Robin suggested to Carmel later on Sunday. "Like maybe we could go there and fix it up a little."

Lucy, who was on the other side of the room, with her face in a book, said, "Hah!"

Could that be considered the beginning of a conversation? Robin decided to take that chance. "Well, why not?" she said, still looking at Carmel, just to play it safe.

"Yeah, why not?" Carmel echoed.

"Are you deaf, girl?" Lucy said, not directly addressing either of them. "Because it burned down. Because it's *gone*."

After lunch Mrs. Thompson announced that she was driving to the shop, with or without her husband. She'd kept her promise to stay away until now, long after his warning made any sense, and she had a yearning to see things for herself. "I need my girls with me, though," she said. Carmel and Robin, and then Lucy, followed her to the car.

Robin knew that groups of volunteers had gone into South-Central after the riots for a massive cleanup. There was even something on TV one night a couple of months ago, showing movie stars and regular people working side by side, sweeping and shoveling up the trash in the streets. Linda had called her in to watch because Lucinda Blake, and Raoul Forrest, who played Duke on *Love in the Afternoon,* were there, wearing fatigue caps and coveralls, waving their brooms and smiling at the camera. Everything around them still looked like a gigantic mess.

But nothing prepared Robin for the slow drive through the actual streets where it had all happened, for the eerie emptiness, the charred and shattered remains of buildings, sometimes only skeletons, through which she could see other damaged buildings and bits of incredible blue sky, for the rows of burnt-out car frames resting against the curbs like dinosaur bones. Robin was reminded of the ghost town she and Linda had visited in Death Valley on their trip West, not because this actually looked anything like that, but because the same astonished thought had entered her head in both places: People once lived here!

The cleanup crews had made only a dent in the rubble of South-Central; the streets were still piled with junk. Mr. Thompson's word seemed to echo through them: *gone, gone.* Henry's, where they'd eaten lunch that other day, in March, had burned clear to the ground. The big Coca-Cola sign, the sizzling griddle, the red vinyl booths, and the chrome counter stools, where Carmel had spun herself dizzy waiting for their change. All that was left of the shoe store where they'd window-shopped were the empty windows, the gutted room beyond them. And Robin couldn't even locate the jewelry store. The three girls gaped out the car windows like tourists, pointing, exclaiming. Mrs. Thompson made little anguished sounds as she drove, hunched over and clutching the wheel.

The sign above the Thompsons' photo shop was badly scorched, but you could still make out the "I" of "Images" and the word "You." I, You. Like cavemen talking. The door to the shop was completely gone. You could step right inside, the way you did at the stores in the mall, the way Robin stepped out into space sometimes in her dreams. Mrs. Thompson had a flashlight in her handbag, but they didn't need it, with that big hole in the roof. Rain had come in, on other days, where sunlight did now, and a sludge of half-dried mud glazed the layers of debris on the floor. The shop, without any counters or shelves, and with only a partial ceiling, looked much bigger than Robin remembered. She thought briefly of the skylights in Cynthia's house, and of how it had felt walking in here that other time.

Mrs. Thompson found her voice. "Be careful," she said, because it was slippery and there was broken glass underfoot, and because it was what mothers said. She had brought gloves for everyone, and she made the girls put theirs on before they touched anything. She had a few garden tools in the trunk of the station wagon: a weeding fork, two spades, and a hoe, which she distributed, too, so they could rummage around to see if anything of value was left. But pretty soon they realized that all the cameras and frames and film had either been destroyed in the fire or stolen. There was nothing to save, nothing to reap in this dead garden, except for the burnt and trampled remnants of photographs that were strewn everywhere. Brides separated from their grooms, blackened babies, headless bathing beauties.

Robin remembered how upset one customer had been back in March because her pictures were late coming back from the lab. "I just hope they're not lost," she'd said anxiously to Mrs. Thompson. "They're the only pictures I have of my engagement party." Now Robin poked her hoe through the litter, and uncovered the ruined evidence of other special occasions, of weddings and anniversaries and christenings. She looked for the family-reunion portrait of the Thompsons she'd studied so hard that other day, and although she could see it clearly in her mind's eye—the smoking barbecue, the battling cousins—she couldn't find the photograph itself, or any part of it.

Finally, Mrs. Thompson said, "What are we doing here? This is hopeless. Let's go home."

Robin and Carmel were glad to give it up, to get away, but Lucy, who was caught somewhere between rage and grief, unable to surrender to either, kept digging through the wreckage, as if she were searching for the final, lost piece of a jigsaw puzzle. Carmel had to call her name a few times before she looked up from her work, startled.

Nobody said much in the car on the way home, so Lucy and Robin's war of silence wasn't as obvious. Halfway there, Carmel fell asleep between them, her head lolling from side to side. She seemed to still be trying, even in her sleep, to be impartial. When they got to the house, Mr. and Mrs. Thompson went into their bedroom together and shut the door. Garvey flopped across Lucy's bed, but she kicked him out of the room and threw herself facedown in the rumpled depression he'd left in the covers. Carmel turned on the stereo, but Lucy barked at her to shut it off. In the sudden quiet, Robin felt herself writhing with everything she wasn't saying. Carmel was lying on her bed, pretending to read a magazine. The turning pages snapped like somebody's bubble gum. Robin had no choice but to stretch out on her cot and gaze up at the ceiling. If she stared at its roughly spackled surface long enough, looking for the shapes of animals and trees, it might calm her. But then she suddenly remembered what

Linda had said to break their silence that day in the car in Kansas or Iowa or somewhere. "Shall I close the window?" she'd asked. "Is it too breezy for you?" Only a little while before that, Robin had tried to send a telepathic command directly from her brain to Linda's, to see if it was possible to communicate without speaking. The order she'd beamed Linda's way was to close the very window she was now offering to close! It might have been a coincidence, but Robin was positive at that moment that it wasn't. She thought she had powers she didn't fully know about yet or understand, and that would help her to survive this hard part of her life. Later, after they were in L.A., she tried to send other messages to Linda the same way, but they never seemed to get through. Maybe the smog interfered, or maybe Linda was just a lousy receiver.

Now Robin turned her attention and her mental concentration to Lucy. *Look at Robin,* she demanded. But Lucy lay there without moving. It was even hard to make out the rise and fall of her breathing. *Look. At. Robin.*

Carmel groaned and threw down her magazine. Lucy rolled over onto her side, facing in her direction, and Robin's. *Look at me,* Robin implored. *Please.* "Please," she said aloud, surprising everyone, especially herself. "I *hate* this, Lucy," she said then, the words flying out of her mouth like a flock of doves. "I really hate everything."

Lucy looked at her, coolly, appraisingly. She was a much tougher opponent than Linda would ever be. For the first time, Robin believed she felt the way Linda often did, urgently having to speak, to say almost anything, just to fill in the dangerous holes of silence around her. "I'm sorry," she said. But what did she mean by that? Was she sorry for her ancient argument with Lucy, which she could hardly recall? Sorry for the loss of the shop? I, you. Or sorry about something else she didn't know how to express, or even gather up into an exact thought? Lucy certainly wasn't going to help her figure it out, and Carmel, sitting between them, seemed to be less of a neutral country now, no longer a dependable refuge from the enemy. She and Lucy both gazed steadily at Robin, and the desire she'd had to be noticed, to be recognized, became one of those trick wishes in fairy tales that end up working against the wisher. "It's not my fault," Robin said, her old standby, which sounded both true and false to her this time around. "I mean," she said, "I didn't ask to be white." As soon as she said it, she knew that, given the way things were, and if there actually had been a choice, she probably would have asked to be white. Just maybe not *this* white. She also knew that she, personally, hadn't beaten anybody up or burned and trashed South-Central, but the whole long, stupid, complicated history of trouble and blame was more than she cared to think about. Still, Robin had spoken first, had apologized for something she couldn't really name and probably hadn't done. Well, she wasn't going to make things worse now by starting to grovel. "Black people aren't perfect, either, you know," she said.

"African-Americans," Lucy said sternly.

"Okay," Robin conceded, hardly able to contain or disguise her joy. "Okay!"

21

Convalescence

The full-length cast on Linda's leg was covered with inscriptions and drawings. Cynthia had written "Break a leg!" in her bold hand, with a black laundry marker, and Nathan drew two linked hearts toward the inside of Linda's thigh, bearing his own initials and hers. She could swear she felt the strokes of his ballpoint pen right through the plaster. Linda showed Cynthia the hearts that evening, hoping she'd be won over by Nathan's romantic gesture. It was awful when people you cared about didn't like each other. "How sweet," Cynthia said, smiling. "And how corny." Then she asked, "What's his name again? Nathan? That's strange. There's no *th* sound in Spanish, you know. Is that his real name?"

Robin wrote "Good luck from Robin" on the cast, as if she were signing the autograph album of a classmate she hardly knew. But she drew a happy face underneath her name, which Linda decided was a sign of affection and optimism.

For an invalid, Linda was kept very busy. There were all those books she was supposed to read, the vocabulary list she was reviewing, the laptop computer she was learning to operate, and the daily exercises she did to maintain the muscle tone in her uninjured arm and leg. Cynthia was determined not to let her stagnate during her confinement. She insisted that every new day offered fresh opportunities for self-improvement, even when you were wearing two heavy, bulky casts. First of all, she discouraged Linda from watching so much television. "Believe me, you wouldn't touch this junk," she said, "if you saw how it was made."

But television was an escape, a chute down which Linda could slide, away from her restlessness, her frustration, and the vague sadness that inched toward her heart around the middle of every day. The junkier the show the better, it seemed. She'd become almost addicted to the daytime soaps, with their real time and unreal characters, and to the game shows, on which improbable wishes were magically granted or denied by some genial, godlike host. Linda did watch other, more worthwhile things from time to time. Something on public broadcasting about the food chain that sickened and fascinated her at once. A late-night travelogue on which an anthropologist examined the mating habits of the Asmat of New Guinea. And she'd caught a little of the Republican National Convention, which made her feel like a child again, with a strict father and an absent mother.

Whenever Linda heard Cynthia coming, she'd quickly switch off the TV, grab one of the convenient bedside books, and open it at random. Cynthia wasn't fooled, though. She would pat the still-warm television set on her way into the room, pluck the book from Linda's hand, making her lose her "place," and sit down beside her. Then she would quiz her about her assigned projects for that day. And when Linda failed, as she often did, to demonstrate progress in one area or another, Cynthia would launch into one of her pep talks. You are what you read. The mind has a thousand eyes and the heart but one. And did Linda want to be a dance instructor all her life? She did, actually, but Cynthia made it seem like such a pathetic ambition, Linda was ashamed to admit it. And she was gradually losing confidence in her own idle body. Improving one's mind and broadening one's skills were reliable ways out of a dead-end existence, Cynthia declared; the rest period she had enforced those first couple of weeks was clearly over.

At eight months, Phoebe was on a crash course of improvement, too. She was allowed to cry herself to sleep sometimes, a discipline Linda had never imposed. Cynthia said it was for Phoebe's own good, that the world was a structured place, which she'd have to learn sooner or later. "Later would be better," Linda said, but she was overruled. That night she had to wrap the pillow around her ears to muffle the heartbreaking sound of the baby's wails.

Cynthia and Phoebe started going to Mommy and Me classes one afternoon a week at an analytic research institute. Two eminent child psychologists presided over a program of educational play, with an emphasis, Cynthia said, on coordination and socialization. "I'm only a substitute mommy," she assured Linda. "You don't want Bebe to miss a single step in her development, do you? Remember," she said, in a teasing tone, "it's dog-eat-dog out there." Cynthia and Phoebe went other places together: shopping, to the zoo, and even down to the television studios where Cynthia's soap operas were produced. "Tell Linda all about your life in the fast lane," she instructed Phoebe when they returned from one of their outings.

Linda wished that Phoebe could really talk, so they might share some of their separate experiences. When they had a few minutes alone together, usually at the beginning and the end of the day, Linda spoke to her anyway, the way she'd spoken to her mother after her stroke, when she was in a coma and it was impossible to know exactly what she could hear or understand. She chatted to the baby about her own day, and about Robin, and how lovely things would be when they were all home together again. Phoebe didn't respond in kind, of course, but her gaze was direct and intelligent, her delicate brow creased in what looked like thought. And Linda could observe her progress—those distinct vowels and consonants in her babble, and the way she got up on her hands and knees now, rocking back and forth as if she were preparing to catapult herself across the room and back into their old life.

Linda was even more troubled about Robin, who *could* talk, but mostly chose not to. Telephone calls between them were especially grueling. More than once Linda had to say "Hello? Are you there?" in the middle of a conversation, because the line seemed to have gone dead. But it was only Robin retreating into her usual punishing silence. For a little while, she'd been talkative, going on about Cynthia's supposed plans to steal Phoebe. But when Linda refused to take her nonsense seriously, Robin simply clammed up again. She still came to visit every Monday and Friday afternoon, though, with Nathan. She spent as little time with Linda as possible, running off to find Phoebe wherever she was, in the house or out on the grounds. Linda tried to make the most of her moments with Robin, but it was like interrogating a prisoner of war who'd been trained to reveal nothing beyond her name, rank, and serial number.

Linda's relationship with Nathan seemed to suffer the most of all. Their sex life had been sabotaged by the circumstances—her injuries, their lack of privacy. And he wasn't any more forthcoming than Robin about his days and nights away from Linda. Sometimes he took her out to the garden in her wheelchair, and they sat there, gossiping about the club, about the outside world. He held her hand and kissed her, and he brought her little gifts—flowers and sucking candy and a Chinese backscratcher to relieve the violent itches under her casts.

The day he gave her the backscratcher, he said, "For those hard-to-reach places. And you can always use it to defend yourself."

"Against who?" Linda asked.

"The Dragon Lady, who else?" he said.

"Don't start that again, Nathan," she said sternly. "I mean it." But then she softened her rebuke by raking his arm gently with the small wooden hand of the backscratcher.

He gave her a slow, sleepy smile. "And you can always use me for those *other* hard-to-reach places," he said.

"Don't start that again either," she warned.

It was like the beginning of a courtship that could still go either way. Linda told herself that true love didn't die in the absence of its greatest expression, and that they would pick up their passion where they'd left off as soon as she was fully healed. When he kissed her, she kissed him back, chastely, with a hint of more to come. For some reason, she kept forgetting to ask him if Nathan was his actual given name.

Linda had other visitors, too. Vicki's mother was recovering nicely from her heart attack, and Vicki was back from Ohio. "Just look at you," she said, sweeping into the orderly guest room, dropping shopping bags, her shoes, and an outsized purse in her path. "I leave town for a few weeks and you get into so much trouble." Linda had never noticed how potent her perfume was, or at least she'd never minded it before. Like Robin, Vicki seemed both impressed by and contemptuous of Linda's opulent new surroundings. She went around the room picking up and setting down various objects: a brilliant blue paperweight, a tiny bronze Buddha, one of Cynthia's or her husband's Emmys. "Oh, why didn't I wear that skirt with the big pockets?" she lamented. She signed Linda's cast across the knee with her waterproof, kissproof lipstick. "Stay cool in the Big House," she scrawled, followed by a series of Cherry Smash Xs. Linda realized she had used the same metaphor Nathan had, when he'd said all that stuff about her cell and being let out early for good behavior. She had finally gotten around to looking up that word "metaphor" in the dictionary, but she was still pretty far behind in her vocabulary list.

Rosalia arrived on a Sunday, bringing bags of fruit and cookies and her maternal presence, which made Linda ache for Manny, for her mother, for everyone and everything lost in her lifetime. She asked Rosalia to sign the cast, too. Rosalia sat there for a long time, chewing on the other end of the marker, thinking about it. Then she wrote something lengthy in Spanish that Linda couldn't translate, but she recognized the words for "God" and for "love," and they comforted her. What wonderful friends she had, old and new!

When she was getting ready to leave, Rosalia said, "I won't be seeing you for a while, Linda. I'm moving away, to Chicago."

Linda was dismayed. "But why?" she said.

"You know, it's hard times. My cousins in Chicago said I could stay with them, that they'd help me look for work there."

"Can't you find anything out here?" Linda asked.

"I've been trying, believe me, but there isn't anything. And I don't want to be a burden to my children."

"Oh, Rosalia," Linda said. "I'm going to miss you so much. I wish I could help you."

"Help yourself, amiga," Rosalia said, bending to kiss her good-bye.

Cynthia had hired a new personal trainer, an Arnold Schwarzenegger–type named Craig. His sessions with Cynthia lasted much longer than Linda's ever had, and they must have been more strenuous, too, because Cynthia always stayed upstairs afterward for a nap. Linda was in training of sorts herself. Twice a week, the physical therapist she'd worked with in the hospital came to the house to put her through her paces. He said she was lucky to have been in such good shape before the accident, and that her youth increased her chances for a good recovery. Linda, shuffling around the room with her walker, didn't feel very youthful anymore. She was merely childlike, someone protected, but with limited privileges and liberty. She could smooch with her boyfriend, but not go all the way; she could be a mother, but not take charge of her children.

One Friday, when Cynthia and Phoebe were at the studio and Linda was dozing before the television set with the prop of an open book in her lap, she heard the doorbell ring and the dogs begin to bark. She clicked off the TV and looked at her watch—it was only noon, much too early for Nathan and Robin. Either

Lupe or Maria came down the stairs, followed by the dogs, and walked toward the front door. Then there was a flurry of conversation, in Spanish, between a man and a woman. The woman was Lupe, Linda realized after a few moments; she had never heard the man's voice before. They both sounded excited, and Bismarck and Brunhilde's watchdog act had dissolved into an uproar of happy yelping. Soon there were more footsteps, approaching Linda's half-opened door. The dogs bounded into the room and a long shadow fell across the threshold. "Hello?" she called, and the door opened the rest of the way. A husky man with a speckled beard and gray, brush-cut hair was standing there. He seemed as surprised to see Linda as she was to see him. Lupe stood behind him, smiling ecstatically and wringing her hands.

"Can I help you?" Linda asked the man.

"That seems unlikely," he said, taking in her harnessed arm, the elevated leg. "I'm William Sterling. I used to live here." The Director! "And who, may I ask, are you?"

Why did that seem like such a hard question? "My name is Linda—Linda Reismann," she said. "I'm Cynthia's . . ." Cynthia's *what*? "Cynthia's . . . friend," she finished weakly.

"Did *she* do that to you?" he asked.

"What?" Linda said. "Oh, no, of course not! I had an accident. It's a very long story."

"I'm sure it's an interesting one, too," he said. "But I don't have a lot of time right now. I've just come to get a few of my things, and then I'll be out of here."

"Was Cynthia expecting you?" Linda asked.

"Ho!" William Sterling said. "That's a good one! No, I made very sure Cyn wasn't expecting me, and that I wouldn't be expecting her, either. I don't know how much you know about us . . . Linda, is it? But our parting wasn't exactly what you'd call cordial." As he spoke, he began taking various things off the shelves and putting them into two large Neiman Marcus shopping bags that had been folded under his arm. Linda watched that beautiful paperweight disappear, then several of the television trophies, and

some books and papers from a desk in the corner. It was like witnessing a robbery without doing anything about it. Except, of
course, this *wasn't* a robbery—these had to be his own belongings. The dogs lay panting near Linda's chair, blithely watching,
too. And Lupe still hovered in the doorway, looking pleased and
worried at the same time.

At last he was finished, at least in here. "Ciao and shalom," he
said to Linda. Lupe and the dogs followed him out of the room.
Linda could hear them all trooping upstairs, where, she imagined, he would add to his loot.

He came down several minutes later and stood in the guest-
room doorway again. "Is there a *baby* in this house?" he asked.

"Yes," Linda said. "I mean, she's staying here, but she's out
with Cynthia right now."

"Whose baby is it?"

"Mine," Linda told him. "Cynthia's just helping us out, until
I'm better."

"I see," he said, looking pensive. "You must really be good
friends." He paused, studying her. "Well, it's been swell," he said
at last, slipping the little bronze Buddha into his pocket, almost
as an afterthought. "Be more careful from now on, Linda, okay?"
And then he was gone.

Linda waited anxiously for Cynthia to come home, but Robin
and Nathan showed up first. Robin was beside herself when she
discovered the baby wasn't there. Linda called Cynthia's office,
and her assistant said she was just about to call Linda, with a
message from Cynthia. She and the baby had gone into Beverly
Hills for a while, to shop, and then they were going on to a wrap
party at Chasen's. They'd be back about sevenish.

"Sorry, kiddo," Nathan said to Robin, "but I can't stay that
long. I'll make it up to you on Monday, okay?"

"*Monday,*" she said scornfully, as if he'd mentioned the next
century. She seemed both forlorn and angry, and she began nag-
ging him to leave.

Linda had been looking forward to talking to Nathan privately about William Sterling's surprise visit, but Robin hung around them, sulking, until he agreed to go. "Wait at the door for me," he told her. "I just want a minute with Linda." And Robin stalked out without saying goodbye.

"Listen, querida," Nathan said, as soon as he and Linda were alone. "There's something wrong here, something fishy. Don't you feel it?"

"Well," Linda admitted, "something really strange did happen today."

Robin leaned on the doorbell then, and the dogs, locked in the laundry room since her arrival, began barking frantically. Nathan yelled, "Hold your horses, Robin, will you!" He turned to Linda. "Tell me," he said. "What happened today?"

Now Robin leaned on the horn of the Z, making the dogs go even crazier.

"Damn it," Nathan said.

"We can't do this now," Linda told him. "Why don't you go, and I'll call you tonight."

"Don't forget," Nathan said, and he blew her a kiss and ran out.

Cynthia didn't come home until almost eight o'clock. She perched on the foot of the recliner while Linda cuddled and kissed the baby, and then she buzzed Lupe on the intercom to come get her. "Oh, not yet!" Linda cried. "I've hardly seen her!"

But Cynthia said it had been a very long day for such a little person, and Bebe needed her beauty sleep. Lupe came in and signaled Linda behind Cynthia's back not to reveal their secret. Then she took the baby and left. "I'll be up soon to tuck her in!" Cynthia called after them. "And how was *your* day?" she said, turning back to Linda.

Linda's pulse quickened. "Okay," she said, her gaze wandering nervously around the room, to the places where the paperweight and books and trophies had been. "But Robin was terribly disappointed that Phoebe wasn't here."

"I know," Cynthia said. "That was naughty of me. I just wasn't thinking."

They chatted a little longer, and then Cynthia went upstairs. Linda waited and waited, unable to concentrate on the television program she'd randomly selected, or to read, or to even think clearly. She nibbled on the fingernails of her good hand, and clawed viciously with the backscratcher at an elusive itch under the cast on her leg.

Finally, the explosion came. It started with something like a war cry from upstairs, and soon Cynthia was shouting in Spanish and English. Linda could barely hear Lupe's muted response. Then Cynthia came tearing down the stairs and burst into Linda's room. "Why the hell didn't you call me?" she demanded. She stomped around the room, running her hands over the shelves. "Shit! Oh, shit!" she said. "My paperweight! That fucking bastard!" She was breathing heavily, almost sobbing, and knocking things off the shelves. Again, Lupe was in the doorway, but she wasn't smiling this time, and when Cynthia looked in her direction, she disappeared. Linda hadn't even thought to shut off the TV, and it blathered mindlessly in the background as Cynthia ranted and paced. "You little ninny! You ingrate!" she yelled at Linda. "Is this the thanks I get for taking you in? Is this the way you repay me for all I've done for you?"

It ended almost as quickly as it began. Cynthia dashed out of the room, Linda shut off the TV, and the whole house fell into stillness. Linda believed she could hear the beams settling, the grass growing outside the windows. She was reaching for the telephone with her trembling hand, not sure who she was going to call—Nathan, or Vicki, or even Robin, someone, *anyone* to take her and Phoebe out of there—when Cynthia came back into the room.

"Linda," she said. "I don't know what to say."

Neither did Linda. She eyed Cynthia warily as she came closer and sat cross-legged on the rug next to the recliner.

"Oh, sweetie, I'm so sorry," Cynthia said, her eyes bright with unshed tears. She took Linda's hand and squeezed it. "I didn't mean anything I said to you. Can you ever, ever forgive me?"

"I think we're too much trouble," Linda said in a hoarse whisper. "I think we'd better leave."

"Linda, Linda," Cynthia said. "You're not any trouble at all. You're my salvation, remember? I would probably die if you left me now, if I had to stay here alone. I *wanted* to die before you came. What I did just now . . . well, it was crazy. I was out of control. I'm so humiliated, I'm so very sorry. Please say you forgive me."

It was really odd having Cynthia sit at her feet this way, pleading for forgiveness. Why did that make Linda feel more helpless than ever on her reclining throne? "I don't know—" she began.

Cynthia's hand flickered upward and then fell over Linda's again. "Listen," she said. "Just give me a chance to prove myself, all right? To make it up to you. God, this has been the worst year of my life." How many times had Linda said *that* to herself?

"The horrible thing is, I guess I still love him," Cynthia continued. The tears spilled over finally and she wiped them away impatiently with the back of her hand.

Linda pulled a Kleenex from the dispenser and gave it to her. "My mother used to say that love was man's gain and woman's bane," she said.

Cynthia blotted her eyes and blew her nose. "She sounds like a natural-born sage to me," she said.

"She was, I guess," Linda said, with a rush of pride and longing. "She had lots of sayings, anyway." After a reflective pause, she asked, "Do you have a mother, Cynthia?"

"Well, she's still *alive*, if that's what you mean. But she's more of a natural-born . . ." For the first time since Linda had met her, Cynthia seemed at a loss for words. Then she said, "Let's just say we haven't spoken in years."

"But that's awful!" Linda exclaimed.

Cynthia shrugged. "You get used to it," she said. Linda didn't think she ever would, but she kept that thought to herself, and Cynthia sprang up, saying, "I almost forgot! Bebe and I have something for you." She hurried out, and Linda hardly had time to shift her position in the chair before Cynthia was back again, carrying a large manila envelope. "Here," she said, holding it out. "Wait till you see this."

Linda hesitated and then took the envelope. How had this happened so quickly? One minute she was getting ready to call out the troops, and the next minute she was accepting a gift from the enemy. She opened the envelope flap and withdrew a photograph of Phoebe, a black-and-white close-up. She was looking into the camera the way she sometimes looked into Linda's eyes. It was an amazing picture, so clearly focused you could count the hairs on her head, all standing on end in a staticky white halo. The photographer had captured nothing less than Phoebe's babyness—the silvery shimmer of drool on her lip, that expression of innocent knowingness, the perfectly poreless texture of her skin.

Cynthia waited while Linda took the image in, and then she said, "We were going to give it to you together at breakfast. But I really don't think she'd mind if you have it tonight. We'll have to buy a frame for it tomorrow. Antique pewter, I think, or maybe we'll just float it in Lucite."

"It's wonderful," Linda said. "Who took it?"

"My cameraman, Tommy Chin. He'll be very happy to hear that you like it. And, Linda? I want to make it up to Robin, too, for today, for not having the baby here in time. Do you think she'd like a private studio tour, maybe the chance to be an extra on *Love in the Afternoon*?"

"She'd kill for it," Linda said.

"Well, she won't have to, I'll set it up. Now, are you as exhausted as I am? Shall I send Lupe down to help you into bed?"

"Cynthia?" Linda said.

"Yes?"

"Don't let the baby cry herself to sleep anymore, okay?"

"Sure," Cynthia said. "Whatever you say. Mother knows best." She bent down and kissed Linda's forehead. Linda recalled Nathan doing the same thing the very first time he drove her here. Then she remembered that he'd crossed himself.

22

Fifteen Minutes of Fame

A silver stretch limo pulled up to the Thompson house at six o'clock in the morning, causing a mad commotion of last-minute activity inside. Carmel danced and wiggled her way into a pair of sparkly gold leggings, while Lucy and Robin elbowed each other for space in front of the bathroom mirror. "God, I'm so ugly!" Robin cried. "No, *I* am!" Lucy insisted. "Both ugly, you ax me," Garvey observed from the doorway.

Mrs. Thompson said to Carmel, "It's going to be a hundred degrees out there today. Why are you wearing those heavy things?"

Ga came to the bathroom door carrying a plate. "You going to eat these eggs?" she asked Robin. "You can't go on no TV without breakfast."

Neighbors across the street looked openly through their windows at the purring limo, and Carmel and Aunt Ez looked back at them. "I bet they think we're famous now," Carmel said, rapturously.

"Or that somebody died in here," Mr. Thompson said.

Robin was hardly ever up this early. When she stepped out into the pink and promising air, she yawned with blissful abandon, while Lucy and Carmel turned to wave at the less fortunate

Thompsons seeing them off. The inside of the limo was deliciously cool and dim, like a movie theater before the lights go all the way down. Robin sat between her friends in the plush backseat, hoping that people in passing cars were speculating about the celebrities hidden behind the tinted glass of the limo, the way she used to when she was an ordinary person riding in an ordinary car.

On the freeway Lucy turned on the built-in TV, but there was nothing but news and aerobics at this hour, so she shut it off again. Robin took three cans of Pepsi from the little refrigerated bar and passed them out. The girls popped the cans and clinked them together in a wordless toast. As they sipped the Pepsi they peered through the glass partition at the back of the distant driver's head, which struck them as hilarious, with its jutting ears and stupid monkey cap.

After a while, Robin withdrew into a reverie. She had been torn between going to the studio alone and bringing her friends, which Cynthia had reluctantly agreed to let her do. On the one hand, Robin would have the satisfaction of riding off in glory while they watched enviously from the curb, and she could always tell them about it later—tell them forever and ever. On the other hand, they could be witnesses to her triumph, and help her tell everyone else about it afterward, like the Supremes backing up Diana Ross. The witnessing won out in the end, probably because Carmel had such a flair for storytelling. Now Robin allowed herself to imagine what it would be like at the studio. Cynthia had said she'd have a good time, but to remember that it wasn't Schwab's Drugstore, whatever that meant. Robin didn't know why Cynthia was doing this for her, but she was so excited she didn't really care.

Last year, when she'd told some girls back in Newark that she was moving to L.A., one of them said, sarcastically, "Yeah, maybe you'll get on TV," and they all laughed. Well, this would show them. *Love in the Afternoon* was on all over the country, in New Jersey, in Ohio . . . in Arizona! Robin was slightly worried, though, that they might ask her to do something she didn't know how to do, like cry on command or sing or something. After all, she had no acting experience. Still, the director or somebody might say, "Who's that blond kid? She's kind of cute, isn't she? She's the image of Lucinda Blake, isn't she?" And then they could work it out that Lady Audrey had this baby girl fifteen years ago, back in England, and that she had to leave her there because her first husband died . . .

Lucy said, "Earth to Robin! Come in, please!"

When they got off the freeway and began traveling through local streets, the girls gave up the thrill of being mysterious for the thrill of being seen, and the potential thrill of star-gazing. They slid the back windows down and hung out of them, hoping, in vain, to see someone they knew or someone well known. They waved and yelled at everybody they passed, anyway, just for the fun of it.

At the studio gate, their driver told the guard who they were and where they were going, and after making a brief phone call he motioned them inside. As they were pulling into a parking space, Robin spotted a great-looking guy in tight jeans, walking across the lot, carrying a paper bag. "Oh, my God, look!" she shrieked. "It's Christian Slater!"

"Where? Where?" the other girls chorused.

The driver's voice came to them loudly through a speaker in the rear of the limo. "Nah, that's not him," he said. "That's only some lousy gofer." Had he heard every word they'd said? And who asked him, anyway?

He escorted them to a reception desk in a large white building, where they were given visitors' badges and told to wait until someone came for them. The driver tipped his hat in a mock salute and left, saying he'd see them later. Robin gave Lucy and Carmel some final instructions. "Don't stare at anybody," she said. "It's not cool. And don't go to the bathroom."

Carmel said, "What do you mean? Why not?"

"Because that's not cool, either," Robin told her.

"But what if I have to?" Carmel asked. "I think I have to already!"

After a while, a woman who looked like she might be somebody took them down a long corridor lined with celebrity photos, to Cynthia's office. The girls pinched and socked one another all the way there. The office wasn't as fancy as Robin had envisioned, and Cynthia herself, who Robin had described to her friends on another occasion as "this Hollywood bitch goddess," looked disappointingly plain. She was wearing jeans and a white T-shirt, just like Robin, and hardly any makeup at all. "Hi, there," she said, when Robin peeked into the office. "Are you ready for your fifteen minutes of fame?"

She walked them further along the corridor, and then down a ramp to a cavernous, windowless area of the building. "These are the studios," Cynthia said, and then, in a hammy voice, "The place where dreams are born and hopes are shattered." Wasn't that the way *The Windswept World* opened every day? Or was it from *Destiny's Children*?

"Do any of you ever watch *Tilt*?" Cynthia asked. It was Robin's favorite game show, the one where contestants had to work their way, by answering trick questions, through the maze of a giant pinball machine. "They're taping in there right now," Cynthia said. She indicated a door with a lit red light overhead. The door opened briefly as they passed it, to let a man carrying a tangle of wires out, and a burst of audience applause hit them like machine-gun fire.

The *Love in the Afternoon* set was brightly lit when they arrived, and there were several people sitting around a table looking at scripts. A woman standing behind one of the seated men— Duke!—was unrolling toilet paper and winding it around his neck, while another woman put blusher on his cleft chin with a big brush. Robin didn't recognize Lady Audrey right away. She was draped with a plastic cape, the kind that women at cosmetics counters wear during makeovers. Her platinum hair was in fat rollers and she was wearing glasses. Like a disguise, like Robin's mother.

Cynthia took the girls over to a short man with earphones on and a T-shirt that said: *Don't Talk to Me Unless I Cue You.*

"Frank, this is Robin, the kid I told you about," Cynthia said, sharply nudging Robin, whose gaze was fixed on Lady Audrey. "Her friends are just along for the ride," Cynthia explained. "Robin, this is Frank Golden, my floor manager. Do what he tells you. I'll be back for you later." And she sauntered off.

"How're you doing?" Frank Golden asked, not really wanting to know. He ushered them to some folding chairs on the shadowy sidelines, where a well-dressed elderly couple were already seated, and he told Robin to sit tight until he called her. "Want anything in the meantime?" he asked. "Coke? Perrier? A banana daquiri?" The girls were all struck dumb, able only to shake their heads.

There were a few small café tables and some chairs in the center of the big room. The tables were set with tablecloths, flowers, and wineglasses. A couple of men wheeled in a wood-paneled wall, complete with paintings and light fixtures, and placed it behind the tables. Lucy poked Robin, who poked Carmel, who squeaked with delight. They all gaped as Lady Audrey's hair was combed out, as her glasses were removed, and extra touches of makeup were applied. When her plastic cape was yanked off, a tight black dress cut to display about a mile of cleavage was revealed. Duke leered at her. "Forsooth, my lady," he said, "is that what you're wearing to lunch?" The guy sitting next to him in a fancy cowboy outfit said, "I think she *is* lunch," and she reached over to slap him with her script. Robin realized that he was the actor who played Jake, Duke's evil stepbrother.

Frank Golden strode to the middle of the floor and clapped his hands. "Okay, everybody, take your places," he said.

Jake and Lady Audrey sat down at one of the little tables, and the elderly couple settled themselves at a table close by. Frank Golden beckoned to Robin, who stood up and, after a shove from Lucy, stepped into the hot splendor of the lights.

"Who's the blond kid?" demanded a booming voice from

above, like God's, or that voice at the Planetarium that named all the stars in the Milky Way. Robin looked up, but all she could see was a small window, high on the wall, with a grid of lights behind it.

"She's a friend of Cyn's," Frank said, in conversational tones. "We're gonna use her in the scene."

"Is she AFTRA?" the voice asked.

After what? Robin wondered.

"Nah," Frank said, "but she's only gonna be atmosphere."

Atmosphere—what did that mean, that she was like *air* or something?

"Shouldn't she see wardrobe? It's supposed to be an upscale bistro."

"She's just a kid, Sy," Frank said, "and it's the nineties, remember? Anything goes."

"Well, give her some color, for Chrissakes, she looks like a corpse. No offense, kid," the voice thundered.

Frank led Robin to the table where the old couple sat. He pulled a chair from another table and put it at theirs. "Say hello to your grandparents," Frank told Robin, sitting her down. The old lady gave her a dirty look. "You're their little honey, and they're treating you to this boss lunch. You'll sit here, sip some water, nibble something, and chat with them during the scene."

"What do I say?" Robin said.

"Doesn't matter," Frank told her. "You're not on mike. Just look natural." But she had never been able to figure out exactly what that meant.

The makeup woman came over and did some things to Robin's face, which immediately began to itch, first here and then there. "Don't touch," the woman warned when Robin tried to scratch her nose. She wished she could look in a mirror. Over on the sidelines, as far away as the moon, Lucy and Carmel sat primly on their folding chairs. And at the table right in front of Robin's, almost near enough to touch, sat Lady Audrey and her step-brother-in-law, Jake. Robin couldn't stop looking at her. Three big video cameras on dollies circled around them, and the set buzzed with conversation.

"Okay!" Frank called. "Let's settle down now, people!" Like the principal at a noisy assembly, only here everyone actually paid attention. It grew quiet. Frank yelled, "Stand by, kids, we're gonna do this!" He raised his hand. "Five. Four. Three," he said, holding up the right number of fingers for each count. For the final two counts he just signaled silently, and then dropped his hand. Instantly, a man dressed as a waiter marched up and began pouring ice water from a pitcher into the glasses at Robin's table. Someone had already put three plates down, with some gloppy brown-and-yellow food on them. Robin picked up a fork and poked at her plate. "Could I get pizza instead?" she asked the waiter, but he was already walking away.

"Why did they saddle us with her?" the old man at Robin's table said to the old lady, smiling while he said it.

The old lady sipped some water. "She knows the executive producer," she said, smiling back. "It's all who you know in this shitty town."

"I don't even know why I've come here," Lady Audrey said to Jake.

Jake gazed into her dark blue eyes, after a quick peek down her dress. "Because I willed you here, my love, that's why. Didn't you know you're under my power?"

"Don't say things like that, Jake, please," she murmured, with a sexy little shiver.

The voice from above bellowed, "Cut! Cut!"

"What's the problem, Sy?" Frank Golden asked.

"That kid, she's gaping at Lucinda. She looks like she's catching flies."

Frank ambled over to Robin's table. "Sweetheart," he said, "don't stare, okay? It's not polite. Look at Grandpa here, instead, and maybe he'll buy you a pony. All right," he announced to the room at large. "Take two!" And he began counting down again.

Three takes later, Robin's jeans were stuck to the seat of her chair, and her face had to be powdered for the umpteenth time. She was still trying hard not to look at Lady Audrey, who was still having a heavy conversation with Jake. He kept suggesting they continue talking elsewhere, as if this was all real and Robin's staring had ruined their privacy. The couple at Robin's table continued to talk only to each other, mostly bitching about how they never got a break in this rotten business. Robin had no intention of talking to them, but the last time Frank came by, he said, "Move your lips, will you, kid, this isn't Madame Toussaud's!" So now she was saying anything that came into her head. "Testing, one two three four," she said. "Knock knock, who's there? What's up, doc? Shazam! Abbadabbadoo!" It made it hard to listen to what Lady Audrey and Jake were saying, but she couldn't seem to stop herself once she got started.

At last the scene was completed. Frank yelled, "Cut! It's a buy!" and everybody got up and started moving around. Cynthia had come back onto the set and was talking to Frank. Robin was burning with thirst, even though she'd finished her whole glass of water and sucked all the ice down to nothing. That "waiter" had never returned to refill the glasses or take away those yucky plates of food.

Carmel and Lucy rushed over. "You were *great!*" Carmel said, hugging Robin.

"I didn't do anything," she said modestly.

"I know," Carmel said, "but still."

"They look a whole lot different than on TV, don't they?" Lucy said, ogling the stars, who were getting ready for their next scene, in what looked like a motel room.

"Bigger," Carmel said.

Cynthia walked over and said, "I heard all about your debut, Robin. I'd hang on to my day job if I were you." Then she took them to lunch in the basement cafeteria, where they didn't see anyone they recognized, except for that Christian Slater look-alike, who was leaving with a box of takeout as they came in.

Later that day, the girls watched *Love in the Afternoon* in the

Thompsons' living room. It was a pretty boring episode that focused mainly on some business dealings at the ranch. But near the very end Jake phoned Lady Audrey and in a harsh, seductive whisper asked her to go out with him. He'd been asking her, in more or less the same way, for weeks.

"Don't do it, don't go!" Carmel pleaded, inches from the screen, while Lady Audrey bit her lip and pondered the invitation.

"What is *wrong* with you, girl?" Lucy said. "This show is *taped*, remember? She went out with him already! Robin was sitting right *next* to them, remember?"

But Robin was more tolerant of Carmel's confusion. The show she was on today wouldn't be aired for two more weeks, and even in real life, the order of events could get all jumbled up inside your head. Love ebbed and flowed in every direction. People died or disappeared—like *that*! Robin could hardly keep track of things—they happened so crazily and so fast—much less understand why they were happening. Maybe that was why they had soaps, where one thing slowly and carefully followed another, where dreams were born and hopes were shattered in neat and comforting succession.

23

Love in the Afternoon

Neither Linda nor Cynthia spoke about their awful encounter again, and Linda didn't tell Nathan, or anyone else, the whole story. That Friday night, when she called him as she'd promised to do, all she mentioned was William Sterling's surprise visit, the various items he'd taken from the house. She was afraid Nathan wouldn't buy Cynthia's defense of temporary insanity, or her own catalogue of excuses for staying on: The casts would be coming off in a couple of weeks. The baby was used to everyone here. Where else could they go? And Cynthia had *said* she was sorry. They were all reasonable excuses, but Linda suffered a lingering anxiety she barely managed to dull by watching television or listening to the top-forty tunes on her bedside radio. The only useful thing she did during the long hours of the day was to practice her word processing. She would be walking again way before she'd be able to dance, and Cynthia had promised to help her find an office job if she mastered some clerical skills. Still another favor—Linda's debt kept growing and growing. Only a few days ago, Cynthia dropped an envelope in her lap, saying, "Here you go, sweetie, Paradise regained!" There was a check inside, a rebate of Linda's security deposit on the Paradise apartment— plus interest. She tried to hand it right back, to defray a small portion of her expenses here, but Cynthia wouldn't even consider it.

As Linda pecked out the business letter in her workbook with one hand—"In re last week's shipment of six thousand barrels of crude oil"—she couldn't help thinking of Cynthia's bitter words: "Is this the way you repay me for all I've done for you?" But she *did* seem genuinely sorry for losing control like that, for saying all those terrible things. The very next morning, Linda had awakened from a restless sleep to find Phoebe in bed with her, investigating her eyelids. Cynthia was sitting on the edge of the bed, watching them with a sad little smile on her face.

She became less strict in her monitoring of Linda's activities after that, and more attentive in other ways. She brought glorious gifts home from a shopping spree: an Hermès scarf as a sling for Linda's arm, a beautiful French bisque doll for the baby's toy shelf. And she'd kept her promise to get Robin on her favorite TV show. The episode would be aired next week; Linda could hardly wait to see it, even if Robin had already told her every plot turn. And she was looking forward to her visit with Nathan and Robin today, hoping they could all spend some pleasant time together, for once.

But from the moment they arrived, Nathan began contriving to be alone in the house with Linda. "Why don't you take the kid for a little walk?" he said to Robin when she came downstairs, with Phoebe riding piggyback. He assured Linda they'd have lots of time to be together later. "In fact, take her for a big walk," he amended, as Robin put the baby into her stroller. He gave Robin some money and suggested she pick up a treat for everybody at the gourmet shop they'd passed on their way here, less than a mile down the road from the house. "I'll buzz you out at the gate," he said. "And take your time getting back, okay?" Then he went into the kitchen, where he held a brief but lively discussion in Spanish with Lupe and Maria, soon after which they left, too, carrying their purses and string shopping bags. Linda heard the slamming of car doors and the muffled roar of the Jeep's engine.

"Where are they going?" she asked Nathan when he came back into the room and began to lower the blinds.

"Who knows?" he said, shrugging.

"Well, what did you say to them?" Linda persisted.

"That immigration is on the way. That I'd planted a time bomb in their kitchen. That I didn't want them to hear your moans of happiness."

"You didn't!" Linda exclaimed, and felt an agreeable little swoop in her belly. Mitchell was probably driving Lupe and Maria to the Farmer's Market. The women could spend hours there, pinching the produce, assessing the baked goods, and haggling over the prices, while Mitchell read *Variety* or practiced his method-breathing in the car. Three birds with one stone, Linda thought. And Monday was Hester's day off, she suddenly remembered, the day she stayed home and worked on her screenplay.

"What time does Vampira get in?" Nathan asked.

"Do you mean Cynthia? She said she had meetings today right through dinner."

"Well then, alone at last," Nathan said, with a villainous smile.

"Oh, *you*," Linda said, and her belly took another roller-coaster dip. Of course they couldn't do very much with all that plaster in the way, but it would be fun just to neck, to let herself become aroused, to have a mini preview of the coming attractions.

Nathan found a continuous-music station on the portable radio. They were in the middle of a golden-oldies program— Artie Shaw was playing "Stardust" when he tuned in. She could hear the dogs start to yelp in the laundry room as Nathan closed and locked the guest-room door. He might have let them out until Robin got back, although they did tend to growl at him whenever he got too close to Linda.

Soon he was very close to her, kneeling next to the recliner where she lay, placing sweet, slow kisses up her good leg, starting at the sole of her foot. "What are you doing?" she asked, when he reached her knee, which jerked under his lips as if the doctor had hit it with that little rubber mallet.

"You're like Sleeping Beauty, niña," he said. "Maybe I can

wake you up this way." He rose to his feet and wedged himself next to her on the recliner. He began kissing her mouth, while he slid his hands under her flowered kimono, like someone searching blindly under furniture for a lost button. Linda hadn't meant to get *this* aroused. She tried to push him away, murmuring, "Stop, Nathan, come on, don't, oh, please . . ." the last words melting into those moans of happiness he'd joked about before. What was he thinking of? What was she? She was in no condition, it was physically impossible. The dogs were howling in their prison. Robin could come back any minute. Lupe and Maria. There could be a fire, a flood, an earthquake . . .

It was like their first time together—the hair-raising friction of his touch, the rush of blood to her head and then away from it, that delirious struggle to be joined. Except he couldn't seem to lie on top of her without crushing her good arm. It was already prickling with pins and needles. And when he pulled her over on top of him, with a great, grunting effort, her casts immobilized him. They tried lying on their sides facing each other, and then with her back to him, but none of these arrangements worked, either; it was much too awkward, or painful, or both. Nathan kept sliding off his side of the recliner, and Linda felt in danger of falling, too. If only she had broken the *same* arm and leg!

"Come on, sweetheart," he whispered, getting up and holding out his arms. "We'll have more room on the bed." That was true, but lack of space wasn't the main problem, and the sight of the hospital bed, with its chrome side rails and starchy white sheets, was discouraging. Linda allowed him to help her up, anyway, the least romantic of maneuvers, with her saying, "Hold it a minute, I need my shoe. Let me get my balance, let me get my walker," and him lurching around under her dead weight. Violins poured like syrup from the radio as she dragged herself toward the bed, leaning on the walker, with Nathan right behind her. "This isn't going to work," she told him breathlessly, when they were less than halfway there.

"Okay, rest a minute," he said, nuzzling her hair, and then lifting it to kiss the back of her neck. "God, you smell so wonderful."

"But I'm not wearing any perfume," she said.

"I know," he said into her neck, "it's you." He pressed himself against her—it was like having a gun at her back—and all the bones of her spine seemed to liquefy. Nathan supported her with one hand and lifted the kimono with the other.

"Oh, Nathan, not *here*," she said, and realized as she was saying it that the radio was playing that haunting old love song, "Where or When." Her left knee forgot its confinement and tried to buckle along with her right one. "We can't," she said, but she was already cooperating as best as she could, bending and shifting precariously.

"I won't let you fall," Nathan said huskily, as he moved against her, and he said it again as he entered her, all his years of dancing paying off in an amazing display of agility and strength. This was something like dancing, like a bolero, Linda thought, in its slow sensuous movement, its precise tempo. The walker continued to creep forward toward the bed, Linda's left hand holding on with the determined, trembling grip of a weight lifter pressing more than his limit. The kimono slipped off one shoulder and then the other, and slid down until it's silky fabric was all gathered loosely at her waist. "Oh, love," Nathan moaned against her neck, the wings of her naked back. She could hardly hear him over her own raucous breathing, her answering cries, and the baying of the banished dogs. Neither of them heard the sounds of a car's tires scattering the gravel in the driveway.

Robin did take her time walking to the gourmet shop. It was hot out, for one thing, and it was so great being alone with Feeb for a change, away from that dungeon. This was something like her old daydream of the two of them living on their own somewhere. She had never worked out the details—what might have happened to Linda, for instance, or where they would live, or how Robin would support them. It was enough just to vaguely picture them together, two sisters against the world.

This whole stupid separation would be over soon. On the phone last night, Linda had said that her casts would be coming off in a couple of weeks. She'd be going back home as soon as she could get around on her own, and Robin and Phoebe would go with her. Robin had mixed feelings about leaving the Thompsons'. What she mostly felt at their house was a sense of safety, as if she'd fallen from a circus high wire into a net, a net filled with family. She didn't belong there—any idiot could see that—and there was hardly enough room for the people who did. They were so nice to her, though, except for Garvey, and even he'd been easier to take lately. Not that they were friends or anything, but with Lucy and Carmel on her side, he'd become a more tolerable enemy. And everybody else in the family closed ranks around Robin, like the walls of a fortress. She had come to them out of the blue and they'd taken her in, no questions asked. The cot had been dragged up from the basement, dusted off, and unfolded. Aunt Ez set a place for her at the table each day, Ga shoveled food onto her plate. To Robin's surprise, she was starting to get used to all the activity and noise of the household. She especially loved the give-and-take of Mr. and Mrs. Thompson's voices, and the slap of cards as they played two-handed gin rummy at night in the kitchen. Routine card-playing conversation, like "I'm knocking with five," and "That's it, sugar, you got me on the schneid again," took on as much mystery and power as that sexy stuff Duke and Jake were always whispering into Lady Audrey's ear. Robin could fall asleep to the sounds from the kitchen. When Mr. and Mrs. Thompson argued, you knew they would make up again. They had troubles—really bad ones—but they kept on living through them.

By the time Robin reached The Sensual Gourmet, she was overheated and dying of thirst. Nathan had given her twenty bucks to get them all a snack. She could buy plenty with that, starting with a couple of Cokes and a big bag of barbecue chips for herself. It was nice and cool inside the shop, and pleasantly dark after the glare of the street. When Robin's eyes adjusted to the change, she saw that the only chips in the store were made of *vegetables*, and they cost eight dollars for a tiny bag! Were they kidding? And they had all these designer drinks in the refrigerated case, like seltzer mixed with mango or passion-fruit juice, but there wasn't a plain Coke in sight. Robin stared into the deli case, with its disgusting fish salads and greasy olives, looking for something edible, while the sales clerk stared suspiciously back at her. Like there was really something here she'd want to steal. She ended up buying a bag of those chips and a bottle of fruit-flavored seltzer for herself, and she bought a small container of something pink and fluffy, called salmon mousse, for Nathan and Linda. That killed almost the whole twenty. She poured half the seltzer into the baby's bottle—her apple juice was practically gone—and they went out into the brilliant day again.

Robin decided to take a different, shadier route back to Cynthia's. There was a street she'd passed before that looked interesting, sort of twisty and with lots of those tall palm trees tilting toward one another, and she headed in that direction, eating and drinking as she went along. It took her quite a while to get the foil bag of vegetable chips open. They tasted a lot like regular potato chips, and the seltzer wasn't bad, either. But what a rip-off.

Nathan and Linda both heard the front door close. She almost pitched forward over the top of the walker; he caught her just in time. "Christ," he whispered. "Who's that?"

"I don't know," she whispered back. "Oh, God, I hope it's not *him* again."

"Him? You mean her husband?" Nathan asked, fumbling with his clothes. "Why would he come back?"

"I don't know," she said. "Maybe he forgot something." She glanced down at the kimono—more bounty from Cynthia's closet—tangled around her waist and the walker. "Never mind, just help me put this on, okay? And get me back to the chair—no, wait, we're closer to the bed. Nathan, hurry up!"

Cynthia called out, "Hello, I'm home! Lupe? Maria?"

Linda and Nathan froze in place as they listened to her footsteps—going toward the kitchen and then up the stairs—before resuming their slow, frantic progress to the bed.

Nathan was propping Linda's foot up, and she was fussing with the ties of the kimono and trying to calm her hectic heart, when Cynthia knocked on the door. "Linda? Are you in there? What's going on? Where *is* everybody?" she said, rattling the knob.

"Just a minute!" Linda trilled, patting Nathan's curls, and then her own disheveled hair. At least the bedsheets were still pristinely smooth. "How do I look?" she asked. "Am I completely wrecked?"

Nathan laughed. "Hey, I'm not *that* good," he said. "You look beautiful," he added, gazing at her with serious eyes.

"*Quit* that," Linda ordered. "And go open the door."

Cynthia took stock of things as soon as she walked in. You could see it in her face, in her rigid posture. Linda was as mortified as a teenager caught on the living-room couch by her parents. "You're home early," she said, in a high, cracked voice.

"So I see," Cynthia said. She opened the blinds to let the sun gush in, and Linda and Nathan both had to shield their eyes.

"Where's everybody else?" Cynthia asked.

"Mitchell took Lupe and Maria shopping," Linda said. "I guess they were running low on a few things. And Robin took the baby for a walk."

"A walk?" Cynthia said. "Where?"

"Just in the neighborhood. Right, Nathan?"

"She was going to that little shop down the road," Nathan said.

"Who gave her permission to do that?" Cynthia asked. "It's hot as blazes out there."

"She had the parasol on the stroller," Linda said. "And I'm sure she took some apple juice along. Robin is really sensible about the baby." But she was thinking of that day at Madman Moe's, of running around in the sizzling heat, cold with fear, searching for them.

"Wait a minute," Nathan said to Linda. "They're *your* kids. Why are you letting her grill you like this?"

"I don't remember speaking to you," Cynthia said.

"No, you didn't," he said. "I'd probably remember that myself."

"This is my house," Cynthia told him, "and I'll thank you to leave right now."

"That's it, Linda," Nathan said. "I'm out of here. Are you coming with me?"

"How *can* I?" she said, wishing at that moment he would simply pick her up and carry her out. But the casts, the weight of her situation, had never seemed heavier. She might have been a mobster's victim, set in cement and sent to the bottom of the sea.

Nathan headed for the door.

"Don't, Nathan, wait a minute. *Please*," Linda said. He paused in the doorway, and Linda turned to Cynthia, hoping she'd say something to smooth things over, the way she did on that terrible Friday, but she just stood there with her arms folded and a resolute expression on her face.

"But what about Robin?" Linda asked Nathan.

"I'll wait for her in the car," he said, and was gone.

"I know you're upset, Linda," Cynthia said, after a moment. "I am, too, so we'll talk about it later, when we both feel calmer and more reasonable. Right now, I'm going out to look for those children."

As she was about to leave, though, Robin announced herself at the gate and Cynthia buzzed her back in. A few minutes later, Linda heard Cynthia and Robin talking in the vestibule but couldn't make out what they were saying. Then Robin came into the guest room, carrying a small shopping bag. "What's going on?" she asked Linda. "How come Nathan's in the car already? And what's the matter with *her*?"

"It's kind of a misunderstanding," Linda said.

Nathan beeped his horn.

"Why are you crying?" Robin said.

"I'm not, really," Linda said, wiping her eyes. "I'm just feeling a little emotional."

Nathan beeped his horn again, and Robin said, "I gotta go. Here." She took a sweaty-looking plastic container from the shopping bag, pecked Linda on the cheek as she handed it to her, and left. Linda put the container on the table next to the bed, and touched her cheek, where she could still feel the startling pressure of Robin's lips. She could still feel Nathan's imprint, too, everywhere on her body, and she knew she'd be crazy to stay here any longer, even crazier than Cynthia appeared to be. She would call Nathan, as soon as everyone in this house was asleep, and ask him to rescue her, as he had that day in Culver City. If she didn't think too much about it in advance, they could work things out, somehow, together.

Much later, after Lupe and Maria came back, and Phoebe had been fed and bathed and put to bed, Cynthia came into the guest room, carrying two trays of food. She set one on Linda's lap and sat down on the edge of the recliner with the other. Linda wasn't hungry, even for that modest soup-and-salad supper. "Cynthia, listen," she said, and Cynthia put her soup spoon down. "Nathan and I made a mistake today," Linda continued. "I mean, we used poor judgment, I guess, but you were really awful to him. Why do you hate him so much?"

"I don't hate him," Cynthia said. "That would require more effort than he's worth."

"How can you say that—he's been wonderful to me!" Linda said.

"What do you really know about him, Linda?" Cynthia asked.

"All I need to know," Linda said. "That he's kind and funny and good . . ." And beautiful and a fabulous lover, she might have added, but didn't.

"Hmm," Cynthia said. "How about his background?"

"Well," Linda said, "he was born in Baja. His father died when Nathan was a teenager, and his mother still lives down there. He has two older sisters, in Nevada." Cynthia waited. "He's had many interesting jobs, and he's been dancing forever, just like me."

"Does he go to San Diego a lot?"

"Not a lot. Sometimes, on business. Why?"

"Did he ever mention anyone named Delila Diaz to you?"

Why did that sound so familiar? "Who's that?" Linda asked. "His sister? A cousin?" Her heart was beating very fast.

"Why don't you try 'wife'?" Cynthia said.

Linda's arm twitched and the soup splashed all over the tray. Cynthia put her own tray down and got up to take Linda's from her. "What do you mean?" Linda said. "Nathan's not married!" It occurred to her then that she'd never asked him if he was, at least not directly. She had once asked if he'd ever been in love before and he'd said yes, but that it was a long time ago, and was something he didn't like talking about. That was the same night he first told Linda he loved her, and when she told him all about Wright and Manny.

"I'm afraid he is," Cynthia said, sitting down on the side of the bed.

"I don't believe you. Where did you get that idea?" Linda demanded.

"From Paragon Private Investigators. Or one of their special agents, to be more precise. Would you like to see his report . . . on Natalicio Diaz?"

"You put a private detective on *Nathan*?" Linda said. "But *why*?"

"Because I'm concerned about you and the children, and I don't want you to get hurt. Because you're charmingly naïve, Linda—easy game for any fast-talking Romeo. You need someone to look out for you."

"No, I don't," Linda said. "I can look out for myself." Who was Cynthia to talk, anyway? She'd been sleeping with that new, muscle-bound trainer of hers from day one. It was something Linda had known for a while, but had never acknowledged before, even when Craig came down the stairs after their sessions, whistling and buttoning his shirt, and let himself out the front door.

"I believe the evidence indicates otherwise," Cynthia said. She stood. "What's this?" she asked, picking up the plastic container Robin had left. She pried the lid open, sniffed at the contents and recoiled, snapping the lid shut again. "Good God!" she exclaimed. "Did he bring you this? Is he trying to poison you?"

Linda didn't answer. The real poisoner, the liar, the evil witch, was in the room with her.

Cynthia stacked the trays, dropping the offending container on top, and carried everything to the door. Then she turned around. "Linda," she said, "listen to me. I know you're very angry and distressed by all this. But don't let your anger get misdirected. Just remember that I'm here for you, that I'm on your side, okay? I'll see you in the morning."

Linda was shaking so hard the bed rattled. When Lupe came in later to help her get ready for the night, she pretended to be asleep, and Lupe covered her, shut off the lights, and tiptoed out. Linda waited until the house was completely quiet and then she reached for the phone and dialed Nathan's number. It rang four times before he answered, sounding drowsy. "Hey," he said, when he recognized Linda's voice. "I didn't think the warden still let you make outside calls. Well, have you come to your senses yet? Are you ready to be paroled?"

"Nathan," Linda said. "Are you married?" She hadn't meant to say it that bluntly, and the ensuing silence seemed to go on forever and ever. She was about to hang up when she heard him say, "Linda, mi amor, listen, it's not as simple as that." Then she did hang up, and lay there, acutely awake, while the room gradually turned from lavender to pink to gold.

24

What Are You Wearing?

Right before her casts came off, Linda felt the way she had at her high-school graduation—terribly excited about her imminent freedom, and a little scared. "This is gonna cost you an arm and a leg, ha-ha!" Dr. Marcuvitz shouted over the screaming of his hand-held saw. Linda wanted to scream, too, like poor Phoebe did when her doctor came at her with a hypodermic.

Dr. M. slipped on his mask and worked on her leg cast first. A vacuum attachment on the saw sucked up the plaster dust as he cut a perfect seam down the length of one side and then the other, so that the pieces came off neatly, like the two halves of an oyster shell—Nathan's blurred blue hearts on one half, Cynthia's indelible black message on the other. And there, under the matted padding, was Linda's pearly, skinny, hairy leg, stained with Betadine, and wearing an impressive pink scar down its shin. She remembered taking her roller skates off as a child and experiencing this same airy lightness in her feet and legs. The unveiled leg itself seemed to be a relic of her girlhood, before she'd developed those dancer's calves, before the razor's first scrape. Dr. Marcuvitz asked if she wanted to save any part of the cast as a souvenir—one of the autographs, perhaps, or a drawing? Another patient of his, he told her, a well-known country-and-western singer, had his whole cast glued back together and shellacked, and then kept it as a piece of fun sculpture in his living room. Linda tried to imagine something similar in her own apartment, where Wright's landscapes were currently the only works of art. "Thanks, but I don't think so," she said, and watched as the doctor sliced up the remains of her plaster prison and tossed the fragments into the trash. Then he proceeded to liberate her arm.

Back at Cynthia's, Linda limped around, leaning on a cane, and still using the Hermès scarf as a sling for her stiff, tired arm. It would take several weeks of intensive therapy before she'd be completely healed. She had known this all along, but now that the casts were off, she was impatient to move freely again. Sometimes she stood at the foot of the staircase, wishing she could run up and see Phoebe whenever she felt like it, but she wasn't allowed to climb stairs yet, even slowly and with care.

One afternoon, Cynthia watched Linda's painstaking progress from the garden to the kitchen and said, "Well, you're almost human again. It's time for a makeover."

Linda sighed. She felt far from human. She had become more and more dispirited since she'd learned of Nathan's deceit, as if her very soul had been punctured and suffered a slow but steady leak. Lately, she found it simpler to yield without debate to Cynthia's bulldozing, and save everybody's time and breath.

This time Cynthia meant a cosmetic makeover, the sort of major renovation the women at the Bod indulged in whenever they grew restless, or dissatisfied with who they were. Linda had been raised to realize she was no beauty, and that vanity was a foolish waste of time, in any case. But when she tried to convey the gist of this to Cynthia, she was treated to that hand-waving gesture again. And then Cynthia went to the phone and called a famous, full-service salon on Rodeo Drive. "Believe me, Luba darling," Linda overheard her say. "She needs *everything*. Just bill my account."

Despite all the personal attention she received at The Essential Me, Linda was reminded of an automatic car wash, of a chained car being dragged through an assembly line of hoses and brushes. First, a huge Russian woman slathered green wax onto her eyebrows, upper lip, underarms, forearms, bikini area, legs, and even down that fine line of fuzz below her navel she'd had since her pregnancy, and that Nathan had assured her was sexy. She hoped it wasn't all going to grow back dark and bristly, which her mother had always warned her would happen if she used a depilatory on her legs, but she felt too embarrassed to ask. Instead, she yelped with each brutal yank of those hair-lined linen strips, while the Russian woman sternly insisted, "Doesn't hurt, doesn't hurt one bit."

At least the sea-salt bath and herbal massage were nice and relaxing. As she was being gently slapped and kneaded, Linda realized how much she'd missed being touched, and that her longing wasn't strictly sexual. Between the mud mask and the European hydrating facial, someone creamed her hands and feet and slipped heated mitts and booties on them, leaving them to sauté inside. Then a team of four miniature Asian women, one at each of Linda's hands and feet, performed a simultaneous manicure and pedicure, while some models paraded past, for her benefit, in beachwear.

Her hair was attended to next, by a couple of specialists who added some russet highlights and gave it a stylish, layered cut. The grand finale (the equivalent of simonizing, Linda thought) was a meticulous application of makeup. She had hardly ever used more than a little lip gloss, but now a cosmetician primed her face and neck with a creamy foundation and "brought out" her cheekbones with strokes of blusher. Layers of shadow and mascara were applied to her eyes, and her lips were carefully outlined and then painted the same Chinese red as her nails. Linda was astonished by her own reflection, and even Mitchell did a double take when he picked her up. "Whoa," he said. "For a minute there I thought you were some glamour babe." Linda had been given samples of the various beauty products to take home with her, but she didn't think she'd be able to achieve the same effect herself, or that she'd really want to. It was glamorous, all right, but impractical; her eyelids were starting to droop under the weight of that glop, and she probably couldn't eat a thing without ingesting some lipstick, too. And as Mitchell had hinted, she was still her plain old self underneath it all.

Cynthia pronounced her gorgeous, though, and said that some cosmetic dentistry was the obvious next step. Linda hadn't thought about her overbite since that horrible experience with Dr. Leonard in Culver City. But here she was, as Cynthia pointed out, practically in the job market again, and needing to look her very best. Once more, Linda gave in without a struggle, although she had a flashback of Nathan saying she was like Sleeping Beauty, needing to be awakened by his kisses. She made herself think about something else in a hurry, something less disturbing. Nathan had tried to call her for days after their last, disastrous conversation, but she hung up immediately the first time, and instructed Lupe to answer the phone after that and say she wasn't available.

Vicki brought Robin to visit now, only once a week, and she wasn't ever left completely alone with the baby anymore. She complained about that, and she remarked that Linda looked and acted even weirder than usual—sort of hypnotized or stoned. "What happened to Nathan?" she demanded. "Did you bump him off, too?" Her own dental retainer had finally been removed a few months ago, and she was amazed to see Linda sporting braces now. Vicki was, too. "I don't believe this," she said. "Do you have a date for the junior prom yet?"

"There's nothing wrong with making the most of yourself," Linda said, trying not to lisp or drool as she said it. It was less trouble to echo Cynthia's attitudes than admit how defenseless she was against them.

"Do you remember the Moonies?" Vicki asked. "If you keep this up, we're going to have to call in a deprogrammer. Or set you up selling flowers in the airport."

"Stop it," Linda said.

"Well, Lady Bountiful's spent a bundle on you, hasn't she?" Vicki said. "What's in it for her?"

"I intend to pay her back someday," Linda said, evading the question.

"Like in the year 3000?" Vicki said. "Listen, I've been picking up some extra cash doing piecework at home. It's easy, I just glue some shi—some glitter onto Christmas cards. You can practically do it in your sleep. If you want in, I'll speak to the boss lady."

Cynthia had said she'd help Linda find a real job, something better paying and more interesting, she hoped, than making Christmas cards. But she didn't want to hurt Vicki's feelings. "Well, maybe," she said. "I'll see." Linda hadn't told Vicki or Robin the entire truth about Nathan, either. That was still too painful to talk about. She would only say they'd had some "differences" and had gone their separate ways. "Which way did *he* go?" Vicki asked, and Robin said, wistfully, "That was one awesome car."

Robin's television debut had come and gone in a twinkling. Linda had hoped they'd watch it together, but Robin elected to be with her friends at their house. She kept calling Linda for days beforehand, though, to remind her she would be on that Thursday afternoon. Cynthia was at a casting call, but Linda lured Lupe, Maria, Hester, and Mitchell into the guest room to watch it with her. Robin didn't appear until almost the end of the half hour of that episode of *Love in the Afternoon*. And then she was only in the blurred background of one scene for about a minute, sitting at a restaurant table behind the stars of the show, along with a handsome and pleasant-looking elderly couple. Robin's hair was in her face, as usual, but you could tell that she was scowling. The elderly couple smiled and chatted while Robin glared at her food and seemed to be muttering to herself, like some crazy street person. The camera concentrated on the stars, and she never got a close-up or came into full focus. Still, everybody in the guest room applauded politely when it was over, and Linda felt foolishly tearful and proud. Robin called immediately afterward, to collect her kudos. "Wasn't that the crappiest show you ever saw?" she asked gleefully. "Didn't I suck?"

.

As she had promised, Cynthia arranged a few job interviews for Linda, and she was finally hired by a small law firm in the Beverly Center mall, as a front-desk receptionist. Her duties included answering a multiline telephone and doing some filing and typing, all of which taxed her healing arm and her tentative office skills. Albano and Murphy was mainly a personal-claims practice, and Mr. Albano, the partner who hired Linda, decided to overlook her clerical deficiencies because of her lameness. He thought it added a nice touch to the place, making it seem more "simpatico" to their injured clients. He offered to handle her case, too, for next-to-nothing, although she'd said she didn't really have one. In fact, the man in the Caprice had sued Linda, just as he'd threatened to do, and her insurance company had already settled with him. "It was completely our fault," she told Mr. Albano.

He shook his head. "Rule number one," he told her, wagging his forefinger too close to her face. *"It's never your fault."*

"Oh, but it really was," she said, pulling back a little. "My step-daughter—"

"You're adorable, do you know that?" he said. But all she knew was that she was going to have to try to stay out of his way.

Mitchell drove Linda to and from work and her physical-therapy sessions, which were taking place at the hospital again, on an outpatient basis. In a few more days, he would be driving her home. Cynthia came into the guest room one night to discuss the transition. "I've been thinking," she said. "You and Robin really ought to get used to the apartment and each other again before the baby joins you."

"What?" Linda cried. "Oh, no, Cynthia! I want all of us to be together right away. That's what I've been dreaming about, what I've been *living* for."

"I'm sure that would be good for you," Cynthia said, "but what about Bebe? Remember, she's gotten used to things here, used to Lupe and me and the house."

"She'll adjust," Linda said resolutely. "Babies are very adaptable." This was one time she wasn't going to just fold under pressure. And she didn't need anyone to kiss her awake, either.

"Of course she'll adjust, eventually," Cynthia said, "but the change should be gradual. We've discussed it at length in our Mommy and Me class, and I've talked it over with Jocelyn, too." That was Cynthia's shrink, Linda remembered, the one who charged two hundred and fifty dollars a "pop." There were probably whole *families* who lived on less than that for a week. And then Linda recalled craving some teenage fad back in the seventies—Sea-Monkeys, a Mood ring, or the latest Bee Gees album—and her mother reminding her of all the starving children in remote corners of the world. "By the way," Cynthia continued, "Jocelyn wants to speak to you. She's completely booked, but maybe we can schedule a phone session after hours tomorrow."

Linda couldn't imagine talking to a total stranger about her personal life, especially on the telephone. It made her think of phone sex, of all those lonely people out there making sad, imaginary connections. "What are you wearing?" they'd say into the darkness. "What would you like me to do to you?" And Linda's mind was definitely made up about Phoebe. But when Cynthia said, "Just talk to her once, Linda, okay? As a special favor to me, *please*?" she felt obliged to do it. After all, Cynthia, bestower of uncountable favors, had never asked one in return before. And what harm could a single phone call do?

Jocelyn called Linda from her car. She was on her way to her beach house in Malibu for the weekend. First, there was a staticky silence, broken by the sounds of rushing traffic, and then this bright, friendly voice said, "Hi, Linda? It's Jocelyn. This is a pretty funny way for us to meet, isn't it? But I feel as if I know you already!"

Linda was taken aback. Her notion of a psychotherapist, gleaned mostly from television and the movies, was someone staid and forbidding who always made you talk first. She'd barely said hello back before Jocelyn went on, in that same cheery tone. "I hear the casts are finally off," she said. "How are you feeling?"

"Better, thanks," Linda said. "A little better every day." She wondered if she should ask how *Jocelyn* was. It seemed impolite—unnatural—to talk about herself without asking anything about the other person, about her health, or how her day had gone.

"Well, good!" Jocelyn said. "That's exactly what I wanted to hear. Now, when are you planning to go back to your own place?"

"By the end of this week," Linda said. "Phoebe and I are *both* going home," she added, defiantly, and braced herself for an argument.

But there was only a roar of static that made her hold the phone away from her ear. And then Jocelyn said, "Oops! Just a little dip in the road. So you and the baby are going home to resume your lives. I think that's terrific."

"You *do*?" Linda said.

"I certainly do. As I've told Cyn, the mother-child bond works best in its natural environment."

"Thank you," Linda said, gratefully. "I think so, too."

"Are you able to take care of the baby yourself yet, Linda?" Jocelyn asked. "She seems like such a little handful."

Had Jocelyn ever actually seen Phoebe? "Not exactly," Linda said. "I mean, my bad arm isn't strong enough to lift her yet, but it will be soon. And she'll be at day care every day until Robin, that's my stepdaughter, comes home from school. She's fifteen and very, very capable."

A horn honked noisily. "Oh, blow it out your nose!" Jocelyn yelled. "Sorry, Linda, but there seem to be all these maniacs out on the road today. Let's see now, where were we . . . Oh, yes, Robin. She's quite a handful herself, from what I hear."

"Well, yes," Linda admitted, "but she's just wonderful with the baby."

"That's really great—I happen to believe that sibling attachments are extremely important."

"Oh, me, too," Linda said, feeling more relieved and gratified by the minute. Maybe it wasn't that difficult to understand what people got from phone sex.

"You and Robin and the baby are a tightly knit little family, aren't you?" Jocelyn said.

"We are," Linda agreed. "We've been through an awful lot together."

"I know. And it must have been very hard. Hard to make ends meet on your salary, hard dealing with the loss of your husband—the children's father—and with all the added stresses of relocation and frustrated romance . . ."

Didn't Cynthia ever talk about *herself* during therapy? "It *was* hard," Linda said. "It still is. But everybody has problems, don't they?"

"Hmm, yes, but you seem to have had more than your fair share." She was so sympathetic, and so *nice*. There was another burst of static and then Jocelyn was saying, ". . . separation anxiety?"

"Pardon?" Linda said.

"I was just thinking out loud," Jocelyn said. "This is such a vulnerable stage in your baby's development, and she's made other, recent ties that are pretty important to her, too, am I right?"

"I guess," Linda said.

"And the way she'll handle separation for the rest of her life is rooted in what she experiences now, in this formative period."

Linda tried playing therapist herself then, by keeping quiet, and it worked.

"Death, lovers' quarrels," Jocelyn continued. "Why, even leaving home for the very first time . . ."

"I don't see how—" Linda began, but Jocelyn interrupted. "Linda," she said, "trust me on this, will you? It's my specialty. Grown men and women are often emotionally paralyzed, stuck in bad relationships, in bad jobs—you name it—all because of early-separation trauma."

"But you said that Phoebe and I should go home—"

"I know I did, and I meant it. You belong together in your own little nest. I'm talking about your working hours, the hours Robin is in school. Is sending the baby back to some institutional day care in her best interests?"

"Kiddie Kare is smaller than most places. And it's practically right around the corner. These two really nice older women who've raised their own families—"

"I'm sure," Jocelyn said, "but they must be strangers to Bebe by now. What is she, eight months old already?"

"Nine, almost nine and a half," Linda said, staggered by the fact. A whole chunk of Phoebe's babyhood had flown by in this house.

"So she'd be right on target for stranger anxiety. And then there's this other condition called marasmus—a failure to thrive—that we sometimes see among infants who don't get adequate one-on-one attention. How many children are there in that day-care center of yours?"

Linda took a deep breath. "Ten," she said in a ragged whisper.

"What did you say? I couldn't hear you."

"Ten!" Linda shouted. "Ten!"

"Look," Jocelyn said, "all I'm suggesting is that your child be allowed to retain some object constancy in her life while she's making this big change. That makes sense, Linda, doesn't it? And it would be to your financial advantage until you get on your own two feet again—no pun intended!—wouldn't it?"

Linda didn't feel like answering. She waited for the further intervention of static, for the blaring of those maniacs' horns, but all she heard was the constant whoosh-whoosh of weekend traffic and Jocelyn's patient, inquiring silence.

25

Home, Home

Nathan must have been staking out Linda's apartment, watching it for signs of life. On Friday evening, only a few hours after she and the children came home, and soon after Robin helped her put Phoebe to bed for the night, the doorbell rang. Linda was in the bathroom, brushing her teeth—a tricky business since she'd gotten the braces—and she called, through a mouthful of toothpaste foam, "Robin! Can you get that? I'm in the bathroom!" But Robin's stereo was booming away behind her closed bedroom door, and she didn't hear a thing. Linda spat hastily into the sink and went down the hall to the front door. She opened the peephole, expecting to see Mitchell standing there. He had brought them all home earlier and was supposed to come back soon with more of Linda's and the baby's things. But it was Nathan's framed face she saw, and she quickly shut the peephole and held her hand against her rapid heart. He pushed the bell again immediately, and he seemed to be kicking at the door. She was afraid he'd wake Phoebe with all that racket, so she undid the locks and opened it.

It had been a long, mysterious, and thrilling day. All Linda could think of, from the moment she'd awakened at five that morning in Cynthia's guest room, was "Home, home," with a yearning she hadn't experienced since she'd first landed in L.A. She had packed her belongings the night before, with Lupe and Maria's assistance. There was nothing to do now but get ready for work and wait for the day's events to be set into motion.

Cynthia had an early taping scheduled, and she was going to a spa in Palm Springs for the weekend right from the studio. She came into the kitchen when Linda was finishing breakfast and said, "I'm running late and I hate mushy goodbyes. This isn't really goodbye, anyway—we'll be in very close touch." She gave Linda a quick hug, and left.

Linda didn't have a chance to deliver the little speech of gratitude she'd rehearsed, and the words had to be stored in her overcrowded head for a later date. At the office, she made even more typing errors than usual, and she accidentally disconnected Mr. Murphy in the middle of a long-distance call. He came out of his office screaming, but Mr. Albano calmed him down and made excuses for Linda. "This little girl just has too much on her plate," he explained, and then he suggested she leave for the day, although it was only three o'clock. He kept stroking her back while he said it, and she had to squirm out of his reach while she was thanking him. But she was glad for the extra time to shop for a gift for the Thompsons, and to be able to pick Robin up at their house before supper.

She went to a shop in the mall right near the office and looked at the usual hostess gifts—the salad-bowl sets and silver nut dishes—thinking they were *too* usual to repay such extraordinary kindness. Then she considered some exotic plants at the florist's, and was reminded that her own homely house plants, her asparagus ferns and ficus, were still at Nathan's apartment. He'd taken them there the day after the accident, so they wouldn't die of neglect. She left the florist's and went into the next shop, a place called Sun and Moon that specialized in celestial toys. Nothing there was very practical, but almost everything was beautiful, from a hand-painted chart of the planets to a glass gadget filled with silvery stuff that illustrated the moon's pull on the tides. After much deliberation, Linda chose an illuminated globe of the heavens for the Thompsons. It was expensive, almost two hundred dollars, but when the salesclerk plugged it in and all the stars blinked on together, like street lamps, Linda was hooked. "It'll look even better in the dark," the clerk promised.

Mitchell met her at the entrance to the store, and they went directly to Cynthia's to get the baby. There was a minor scene there, with Lupe kissing Phoebe from head to toe, and weeping when she finally had to release her. Maria stood behind them in the doorway, alternately mopping her own eyes and fluttering her handkerchief in farewell. Linda said, "This isn't really good-bye, she'll be back Monday morning, remember? Phoebe, say bye-bye, Lupe, bye-bye, Maria, adios, muchachas, see you soon!" But by the time she got into the car with the baby, Linda was feeling pretty weepy herself.

She recognized the Thompsons' yellow bungalow even before Mitchell spotted the house number. She had driven there enough times in the past, to drop Robin off or pick her up, but she had always been in too much of a hurry to get out of the car. Now she walked up the path to the front door, with Mitchell right behind her, toting Phoebe and the gift-wrapped box. As Linda was about to ring the bell, the door flew open to reveal Robin standing there, next to her suitcase and a couple of loaded shopping bags. And before Linda could say a word, Robin grabbed the baby from Mitchell and said, "Okay, I'm ready, let's go."

"Well, just give me a chance to say hello to everybody, and thank them for having you," Linda said, going around Robin into the hallway.

Mitchell put Linda's package down and picked up Robin's luggage. "I'll wait for you in the car," he said. "Take your time."

"I thanked them already," Robin told Linda, trying to block her way.

But then a plump, pretty woman in a white uniform came into the hall and said, "Linda, hi, I'm Jewelle Thompson. Come on in and meet everybody." She patted Phoebe's head, saying, "You, too, buttercup," and she led Robin and Linda into the living room. The rest of the family was already gathered there: Mr. Thompson, the girls, Mrs. Thompson's mother and sister, and a very cute little boy, who Robin managed to jab with her elbow as she went by him. The house looked pretty small to hold this many people; having Robin here, too, must have really been an inconvenience.

Phoebe didn't seem to be suffering from stranger anxiety today. The women passed her around the room like a tray of hors d'oeuvres, and she laughed and crowed as she grabbed for their noses and earrings. They all made such a happy fuss over her you would think *she* was the gift Linda had brought for them. "Robin," she said. "Mitchell left a big package out in the hall. Would you bring it in here, please?"

Robin jumped up, glad to have an excuse to leave the room. She had been worried all day that Linda might try to come into the house and meet the Thompsons. It gave her the same queer feeling she used to get back in elementary school whenever her father showed up for some parent-teacher thing, with that pale, pitiful face of his. She would try to pretend she didn't see him, and if he insisted on talking to her, that she'd never seen him before. On *Destiny's Children*, there was this guy with two separate families—a bigamist—who was going to be found out any day now. Especially since his daughter from one family and his son from the other one had met out of town and were starting to fall in love. The father was always writing in this journal he kept—things like "Dear God, please don't let my two separate worlds, my two perfect lives, collide." Which was total bullshit, but Robin could still relate to it, especially right now. She was positive that Linda was going to do something embarrassing. She already had, just by showing up, and by having a spaz over a dumb lamp as soon as she got into the living room. Robin couldn't wait to get out of here. But when she picked up the package in the hallway, with its fancy gold-foil paper and bouquet of curly ribbon, she realized it was a gift Linda had bought for the Thompsons, something that would probably be the greatest embarrassment of all. The box was big and heavy. Robin thought of that dorky sculpture Linda had gotten for what's-her-name— Stephanie's—birthday slumber party. If this was anything like that, Robin was out the door. She shook the package, but it only made a little hollow, rattling sound.

As she approached the living room, she heard Linda say, "I wish there was some way I could really repay you for all you've done for Robin."

"Don't mention it, Linda," Mrs. Thompson said. "It's been our pleasure."

"A real experience," Mr. Thompson added.

"I wish she could stay here forever," Carmel said passionately.

In the thoughtful silence that followed, Linda turned to Aunt Ez and said, "Have you always lived in Los Angeles?"

Robin burst into the room and thrust the box at Linda, saying, *"Here!"*

"Thank you, dear," Linda said. She held the gift out to Mrs. Thompson. "This is just a small token," she began, feeling suddenly discomfited. It *was* just a small token; almost any gift would be, under the circumstances. But as she looked around the neat, shabby room, the globe seemed like a cruel and exorbitant joke. She might at least have gotten something useful for all that money, like a microwave oven or a clock radio.

During a chorus of protests from the elder Thompsons—"You shouldn't have. Really. It wasn't necessary"—the boy, Garvey, ripped off the wrappings and opened the cardboard box. Robin held her breath as he reached in and pulled out this big, black ball. For one horrified moment she thought it was a bowling ball, but then she saw that there was an electric cord dangling from it. God, was it a bowling-ball *lamp?*

"Well, well," Mr. Thompson said, taking the globe from Garvey and spinning it on its axis. "Shut the blinds, son," he said.

Linda had noticed that the big trees right outside the living-room windows already filtered out most of the daylight. That's why the lamp with the painted glass shade was on. When it was turned off, and the venetian blinds were drawn shut, it was practically dark in there. The baby had been chattering away, but she grew quiet in the shadowy room, along with everyone else. Garvey had to pull out the lamp plug, so his father could plug in the globe. "Is everybody ready?" he asked, his voice wonderfully deep and theatrical. And then the galaxies lit up all at once, just as they had in the store. But now they glittered more brilliantly, the way they did in the real heavens, or the way Linda remembered they did on those velvety summer nights in Newark, when she and Wright used to walk hand-in-hand beneath them. When had she last looked up at the sky, except to assess the thickness of the smog, or to see if it was going to rain?

The baby clapped and pointed and exclaimed in her own musical language. "*Stars,*" Lucy said, carrying her close enough to touch the glowing globe. "See the *stars*?"

"How did you ever know?" Jewelle Thompson asked Linda. "Astronomy is one of Lee's real interests."

"Back in Virginia, anyway, where they still have stars," Lee said.

"They have them in Jersey, too," Linda told him, with an unexpected swell of homesickness.

"*I* never saw any there," Robin said.

"Honey, you probably never looked," Lee Thompson said.

When it was time to leave, when Jewelle began asking them to stay for supper, and her sister went into the kitchen to begin preparing it, Linda didn't want to go. She couldn't exactly define the way she felt in this energetic household, except that it was the opposite of lonely. But she believed that her family should have their first meal together, after such a long separation, in their own home. Jocelyn would probably agree.

Robin, who had been in such a hurry to leave when Linda first got there, started dawdling now, suddenly remembering a pair of sneakers she'd left under her cot, and that her favorite jeans were still in the bathroom hamper.

Carmel wasn't helping matters. She clung to Robin, saying, "I'm not letting you go, and that's final."

Lee said, "Watch out, little sister, or you're going with her," and Carmel said, "Can I? Please?"

Everybody clustered together near the front door to say good-bye. "You be good, child, hear?" Mrs. Pickett said, trying to smooth Robin's rumpled T-shirt.

"Come back soon, all of you," Jewelle said, as her sister held Robin in a long, silent embrace. The girl had never let Linda hold her like that.

Then Lucy grabbed a hank of Robin's hair. "Call me the minute you get home, or else," she threatened.

"Lord," Mrs. Pickett said. "You're going to see her in school on Monday."

"If not sooner," Mr. Thompson said.

"Shut the door, will you," Garvey growled. "You're letting all the bugs in."

The apartment might have been closed up for a century, the air was so stale and so still. Dust lay over everything like finely sifted flour. Cynthia had wanted to send a cleaning crew in here first, but Linda was superstitious about anyone else setting foot inside the door before she and Robin and Phoebe did. "Home," she said, as she crossed the threshold. Mitchell came in a few minutes later with the luggage. He opened some windows for them and then left. Linda went from room to room, turning on all the lights, even though it wasn't really dark out yet. The double-wedding-ring quilt was folded at the foot of her bed, where she'd left it the morning of the accident, and a rainbow was still trapped in the prism on the kitchen windowsill. A few cockroaches scurried for cover when the fluorescent lights flickered on. On the way here from the Thompsons', Linda had asked Mitchell to stop at a 7-Eleven, where she'd bought some essentials—milk, bread, eggs, baby food—and the fixings for a supper of some of Robin's favorites: macaroni and cheese, and instant butterscotch pudding. Now Linda made a shopping list that included Pledge and Combat. The words "Home, home" hummed like music inside her head as she and Robin bathed and fed the baby, as they set the table and ate their own delicious, starchy dinner. Then Robin helped her put the baby to bed and do the dishes. Phoebe didn't settle in as easily as Linda. She kept standing on her knees in her crib—a recent mastery—rattling the bars and crying in a constant and desperate way. Robin had put the night-light on for her, and she and Linda had sung an assortment of lullabies. They had to take her out again after a while, and Linda rocked back and forth with her in the rocking chair, feeling so tired she was afraid she would fall asleep first. But she finally prevailed, and Robin lifted the limp baby from her arms and put her carefully into the crib. They tiptoed out together, exchanging conspiratorial glances, and Robin went to her own room, shut the door, and turned on the stereo.

It was a few minutes after that, while Linda was brushing her caged teeth, that the doorbell rang, and she went down the hallway and looked through the peephole and saw Nathan. As she opened the door, she had a vision of the first time he ever came to the apartment, of how he'd grabbed and kissed her, and propelled her backwards in that ardent sexual dance. She became weak-kneed and furious at the memory, and limped back a few steps on her own, just in case. But Nathan wasn't doing any grabbing this time; his arms were completely occupied by Linda's ferns and ficus. They had grown rampantly since she'd last seen them, and they looked like some untamed jungle foliage instead of common domestic plants. If it wasn't for their familiar blue and yellow pots, she might not have recognized them as her own. "Hello, Linda," Nathan said. "Can I bring these guys in? They've really missed you."

Linda looked behind her, hoping and not hoping that Robin

would appear. "You can put them down right here," she said, "and then leave, please."

He stood there, a beautiful garden statue overrun by vines. "What happened to your teeth?" he asked, and when she didn't answer, he said, "Just give me a chance to explain, amor, okay? I'm going to tell you the truth."

"It's too late for that," she said. "I already know the truth."

"Only a little of it," Nathan said. "It's a long story."

"Well, I don't want to hear it," Linda said. "Just go." She turned and limped away toward the kitchen. He followed her, still carrying his burden of greenery.

"I'm married," Nathan said, lining the plants up neatly on the kitchen table, "but in name only." Linda stood on the opposite side of the table and the plants formed a protective boundary between them, like a hedge, like the wall in a confessional. She could hardly see him. She leaned against the table and covered her ears, but his voice came through clearly, anyway, and the fronds of one of the ferns moved slightly with his spoken breath. "We've been separated for over two years. The love ended even longer ago than that. She lives in San Diego. We were dance partners there once, too. Delila and Diaz, I told you about that."

La, la, la, la, Linda said to herself, trying to blot out his words.

"I should have told you. But it was so good between us, right from the start, and I was afraid it would spoil things. It was stupid, maybe, but it's what I did. Linda, I'm sorry." He paused, and then went on. "I've been going down to San Diego to see her, to talk about getting a divorce. She wants us to try again, but I don't want to. I only want to be with you."

How sincere he sounded, and how contrite. And when had they last been this close without touching? She could simply reach through the fern and bestow her forgiveness. But working in a law office had given Linda a new perspective on ways the truth could be bent, on how language could be used to seduce and manipulate. She knew now that Nathan had been in San Diego the night of the riots, when she was rushing to his rescue in her bathrobe, like an idiot. And how many other nights had she spent alone and restless because he'd said he had "business" to take care of? Monkey business, her mother would have called it. What do you really know about him? Cynthia had asked, and Linda's answer was based more on feeling than on fact. The essential and incontestable fact was that he had lied to her. Something like a coiled spring came loose inside her chest, and she swallowed deeply, past dregs of affection, longing, and even sympathy. "Go away, Natalicio," she said in a flat and unfamiliar voice. "I don't want to be with you."

Then the baby began to whimper in her sleep. Linda went down the hall to the bedroom and leaned over the crib railing to pat and rub her back, murmuring, "Shhh, it's okay now, Mommy is here, we're home. It's okay, lovey, shush, shush." She could barely hear Nathan's footsteps, or the sounds of the front door opening and closing behind him.

26

Like a Virgin

Robin didn't get it. Linda had split up with Nathan, for no good reason, probably, and now she'd gone out with this geek from work, who had a mustache that looked like he painted it on and a big, ugly brown Cadillac. He also had his picture inside a matchbook cover that Robin found in Linda's purse. On the outside it said, "Have you been disfigured in an accident?" When you opened it, it said, "I'll help you collect big $$$. Dial SUE-5555," right above his face. *He* looked disfigured, if you asked Robin, but Linda went out to dinner with him the other night. The stuff that went on between men and women was probably the craziest and most interesting thing in the world, although Robin still had no love life of her own to think about. That guy, Richie, who'd kissed her and felt her up that one time, must have been whacked or juiced when he did it, because whenever their paths crossed now in school he acted as if he'd never seen her before.

To make things worse, Lucy had gotten herself a boyfriend, a really cool, good-looking dude named Shay Cunningham. One minute she was just talking to him near the bus stop, and the next she was telling Robin, in this fake-dreamy voice, "Girlfriend, I think I'm in love." A week later Shay's picture was hidden in

Lucy's wallet, under her cafeteria pass, and his name was scrawled in ink on the palms of both her hands. She had to scrub them thoroughly every day before she went home. Carmel was the only one in their family who knew about Shay—she said her parents would think he was *too* cool—and she was sworn to secrecy. She covered for Lucy in exchange for some of the hot details, like how far they'd gone (not that far, yet), and what it was like. Robin was upset because *she* wasn't Lucy's main confidante anymore. Carmel told her every last thing, though, which only made her feel worse.

It was a double-edged pain for Robin—she was jealous of Lucy's sudden new status and happiness, and jealous of Shay, who had stolen her away and turned her into someone unrecognizable. Chickenshit Lucy, who would never cut classes with Robin, skipped out sometimes now with Shay, and then lied about it to her mother, without blinking those big, innocent brown eyes. She lied to Robin, too, canceling plans with her at the last minute by pretending to be sick, or busy doing something at home. And she never wanted to know anything about Robin's life anymore; it was only "Shay and me" this and "Shay and me" that. It seemed there was some law that said you couldn't have a boyfriend and a best friend at the same time. Lucy even *looked* different. She'd started wearing makeup to school and she'd developed this funny walk that made everything on her skinny body stick out and jiggle. Her sudden new favorite performer was Madonna; if Robin heard her sing "Like a Virgin" one more time, she was going to kill her.

It had been hard enough for Robin to leave the Thompsons' house and go back to live with Linda, without this added grief. If it wasn't for Phoebe, she didn't think she'd be able to stand it. Just weeks ago, she and Lucy and Carmel had been like *that*. When Robin's episode of *Love in the Afternoon* was finally on, they'd all watched it together at their house, pummeling each other and screaming so loud when Robin appeared on the screen they didn't hear any of Lady Audrey and Jake's dialogue.

Carmel was as loyal as ever to Robin, but without Lucy around, she wasn't a complete and satisfying friend. Her babyish habits were much more noticeable and annoying lately. Robin hated the way Carmel kept touching her arm when they talked, and how *bouncy* she was. But there was nobody else to hang out with, nothing else to do.

One afternoon, when Lucy was out somewhere with Shay, Robin lay across Carmel's bed, polishing her nails and listening to Bon Jovi sing "In These Arms." Carmel plopped down beside her, making the whole bed shake, and tipping over the polish. She poked Robin in the ribs and said, "So just guess where they are today!"

Robin jumped up and shouted, "Keep your hands to yourself! And if I hear one more word about your asshole sister and her asshole boyfriend, I'll gag!"

Carmel's eyes immediately filled with tears, another thing about her that drove Robin crazy. Her feelings got hurt if you looked at her the wrong way.

"I'm going to the mall," Robin said, and Carmel's tears spilled out. She looked as if she'd just been hit by a bus. "So, do you want to come?" Robin added grudgingly.

"I can't," Carmel said, sniffling. "I've got too much homework to do. And I have to vacuum in here. It's actually Lucy's turn, but I'm switching with her."

"Well, goody-goody for you," Robin sneered, bringing on another flood of tears, and then she took off.

She caught a ride in a florist's delivery van to the Glendale Galleria. It occurred to her as she strolled around there, eating a beef burrito and looking into the shop windows, that she might run into Lucy and Shay. She'd already seen other kids from school, all of them traveling in cliques, like herds of sheep. Some of them said hi to her, but nobody asked her to hang out. Big deal—she didn't need to hang out with a bunch of sheep. And at least this wasn't the mall where Linda worked; the last thing Robin needed right now was getting the third degree from her:

"Where are all your friends? How did you get here? You didn't hitch, did you?" How did she think Robin got around, in a private jet?

Robin wished she had Phoebe with her, but she was at Cynthia's house until Linda got home from work. That whole setup was ridiculous. Linda said it was just until the baby got over her "social anxiety," whatever that meant. It was probably only some more bull that Cynthia made up and Linda swallowed. There was nothing wrong with Feeb and there was nothing wrong with her old day-care center. Robin used to be able to walk over there and pick her up right after school. Now she had to wait until Mitchell delivered her to the apartment every evening, like a package.

Robin went into the five-and-dime and skimmed one hand over a counter display, right near the entrance, of small plastic toys: monsters and robots and dinosaurs. Without really thinking about it, she snagged one of the dinosaurs, a pinheaded purple freak with a spiky spine and a forked tail, and shoved it into her knapsack. This was the part of shoplifting she liked best—that instant rush and the thought: I did it! But it was usually followed fast by a letdown: So what, who cares? Sometimes she wondered why she was never caught, except that once. Maybe it was because she *didn't* think before she took something, didn't start acting suspicious while trying to act nonchalant. It was all pure impulse—wham, bam!—and then it was over. Or maybe it was because she'd never taken anything really worthwhile, from one of the swankier shops. She put her hand into the knapsack and fingered the dinosaur's spikes as she walked through the electronically monitored doorway, with her ears burning and her skin tingling, but without setting off any alarms. The dinosaur probably wasn't valuable enough to have one of those security tags on it. She would give it to Phoebe tonight, to remind her that Robin was her real family, and that not only rich people give presents.

There was a fancy gift shop next door called Happy Hands that boasted the works of "noted American artisans." That meant things like faggy handmade sweaters and teakettles with wings, but Robin wandered in anyway. There were just a few other customers, and nobody her own age, which made her pretty conspicuous. Two women in saris were unfolding a tablecloth between them, a fat man played with some wind chimes, and a salesman was showing a tray of jewelry to a platinum-blond woman in dark glasses. He eyed Robin over the woman's shoulder, and Robin turned away and looked into a showcase of miniature crystal objects: animals, flowers, musical instruments. Everything good in this place seemed to be locked up behind glass. It was sort of a personal challenge. Robin stared at the dazzling array in the case for a couple of minutes before she noticed the small silver key stuck into the sawtooth lock. Was it some kind of trap? She stepped closer to the glass, pretending to get a better look at something inside, and her breath left a patch of moisture that came and went. The key looked like a regular key. There were no strings or wires attached to it. Robin slid her right hand up her own chest before letting her fingertips graze the icy glass. Then she walked them carefully across and down toward the key, shifting her torso to cover her maneuvers. The key turned with the slightest click, but Robin's heart bumped as if a bomb had gone off inside the showcase. She glanced around behind her, trying to stay calm, to seem casual. Luckily, that fat guy was still hitting the chimes; they were ding-donging like mad. The two women were going through a pile of woven shit now, and the salesman was showing the blonde more jewelry. No one seemed to have heard the key in the lock or Robin's runaway heart. She pressed the flat of her hand against the glass panel right near the lock and started to slide it open. There was a faint rumbling, but no squeaking, as she had feared, and the panel moved smoothly along its track. Robin grabbed the nearest piece of crystal, a little harp, her fist quickly smothering its brilliant light. It made her think of the magic harp in "Jack and the Beanstalk," her favorite childhood story because it was scary, and because Jack's mother was so proud of him in the end for making them rich and happy. But first Jack had to take a lot of chances: stealing the giant's hen, then his money bags, and finally his magic harp. The harp called out "Master, master, master!" to warn the giant that it was being stolen, and he came roaring down the beanstalk after Jack. The harp in Robin's knapsack only made a little ping against something, her keys or that plastic dinosaur, when she dropped it in, and nobody seemed to notice anything.

The important thing, she knew, was to take her time leaving, not to arouse suspicion by being in a big hurry. She even strolled a little further into the store first, and faked an interest in some boring silk scarves in another case, while she silently and slowly counted: One banana, two banana, three banana . . . all the way up to thirty. Then she started walking toward the doorway at a nice, leisurely pace. An earsplitting alarm went off as she passed through it, but she kept going. She'd barely made it out into the mall before a big black guy in cutoffs and a mesh T-shirt grabbed her by the arm. "Yo, baby," he said. "Where *you* off to?"

"Hey!" Robin said, trying to get free. "Let go of me!" But instead he hooked his arm tightly through hers and marched her back into the store, setting off that stupid alarm again.

The salesman was waiting for them near the front counter. "Thank you, Michael," he said.

"Yeah, Michael, thanks a *million*," Robin said, and the guy laughed. She glared at him. Weren't security guards supposed to wear uniforms?

"Let's have it," the salesman said to her, holding out his hand.

"Have what?" Robin said. "I don't know what you're talking about." But she was only playing for time. This was different from the shoelace incident—this was genuine trouble—and she had no idea what she was going to do next. She looked around and saw that a little crowd had gathered. The fat man, the women in the saris, and a saleswoman who'd come from the back room were all gawking at her, in that disgusted and fascinated way people gawk at the victims of a car wreck. Only the blond woman in the sunglasses ignored the whole scene; she was busy writing something at the cashier's desk. In profile, she looked familiar to Robin, like someone famous seen in person for the first time. Her hair reminded Robin of Lucinda Blake's. But it couldn't be, could it?

"You've tried to pull this sort of thing here before," the salesman said to Robin, which wasn't true. She'd never been in this place—she *hated* stores like this. "We've had our eye on you for a long time," the salesman continued. Then he nodded, and the guard wrested the knapsack from her and began pulling things out of it and piling them up on the counter: the crystal harp, the plastic dinosaur, a bottle of blue nail polish, Robin's keys, the matchbook with that geek's picture inside, one of Feeb's pacifiers, a few chewed-up pencils, some loose change, a tampon, a bag of Gummi Bears.

"Hey!" Robin said, before he was finished, just to say it. Out of the corner of her eye, she could see the blond customer approaching. Great. Why didn't they sell tickets?

"What's your name, miss?" the salesman demanded.

"Lucy Thompson," Robin said promptly, "and you'd better let me go. My father is a big-shot lawyer and he'll probably sue you if you don't." Why did she say "lawyer"? She'd meant to say "cop."

"Her name is Robin Reismann, Julian," someone else said, "and she doesn't have a father."

Robin whirled around. It was the blonde who'd spoken, and in a voice Robin knew very well. The woman removed her sunglasses. Her dark eyes flashed, and her mouth was cruelly amused. Robin's mouth dropped open, as if its hinges had broken off.

"Do you *know* this girl, Ms. Sterling?" the salesman asked.

"Close your mouth, Robin," Cynthia said, "before something flies in." She turned to the salesman. "I certainly do know her," she told him. "Her mother works for me." She glanced at their rapt audience. "Could we take this inside, please?" she said.

In the office in the rear of the store, the salesman offered to let Robin go, if Cynthia would vouch for her. "We've got the merchandise back, so we'll just forget the whole thing—that is, if you say so, Ms. Sterling," he said.

"Thanks, Julian," Cynthia said. "But it wouldn't be very instructive for Robin to simply walk out of here as if nothing happened."

That *witch*, Robin thought, she's going to have me arrested. "Listen—" she began.

"No, *you* listen, for a change," Cynthia told her, "and keep your little trap shut." She put her sunglasses back on. They were really an amazing disguise, along with her hair. It used to be so black, with those gray streaks in it. When did she bleach it? It *was* the same color as Lucinda Blake's now. Or Robin's own hair, or Phoebe's.

"Do you want me to get the police involved in this?" the salesman asked. If Cynthia gave the okay, he would probably send Robin to the chair.

"No," Cynthia said. "I don't think we have to go that far, at least not this time. But I would like this episode to go on your own permanent records. You said that she's been in here before, and I think it will serve as a future deterrent."

"He's a liar! I was never here before!" Robin said indignantly, and Cynthia lowered her sunglasses and threw her one of those killer looks.

"As I was saying, it will be a deterrent to future crime," Cynthia said. She wrote everything down on the salesman's pad: Robin's name and age and address. "Linda wouldn't be very happy to hear about this," she told Robin. "So I might just keep it to myself, for her sake. But you'd better shape up, lady, or else." Then she looked at her watch. "I have to get back to the studio," she said. "You'll be sure to send my purchases out this afternoon, Julian, won't you?"

"Of course, Ms. Sterling," Julian the brown-nose said. "I might even drop them off myself on my way home. And I'm very sorry

you had to be delayed like this. Kids today, what can you do?"
He scurried behind Cynthia like a mouse, reaching out with one
paw to push the office door open for her. "But it's always a pleasure to serve you, Ms. Sterling. See you again soon, I hope. Have
a nice day now!" Blah, blah, blah.

Robin should have been relieved, about the police part anyway, but she felt a simmering, restless anger, even when she was
out in the mall again, free, and with all of her belongings (except,
of course, for the crystal harp) back in her knapsack. It was hard
to breathe right and hard not to talk to herself. She was angry
with that jerky salesman and that fink security guard for humiliating her like that, angry with Cynthia for being such a control
freak, with Linda for a thousand different reasons, with Lucy for
choosing stupid love over friendship, with Carmel for not being a
good enough substitute for Lucy, and with Nathan for not sticking around when things got rough. Robin was even angry with
Lady Audrey for dumping Duke in favor of his evil stepbrother.
But she was angriest, practically to the point of stormy tears,
with her father and Manny for being dead.

27

Rocket Man

Linda ventured out on her lunch hour to get some panty hose at The Broadway. They were having a buy-three, get-one-free sale on her favorite brand, and she was down to her last pair. She planned to go right back to the office afterward and eat the tuna-salad sandwich she had brought from home and stashed in her desk drawer. The mall seemed especially crowded today, with a lively, festive air beyond the usual Friday afternoon shopping fervor. Linda noticed a number of American flags hanging in the doorways of stores, and people hurrying by carrying smaller flags, and signs and balloons that said things like *Vote Clinton/Gore* and *Bill and Al '92*. Bill and Al. That sounded so friendly, so *real*, like the names embroidered on the coverall pockets of the men who pumped gas at the Chevron station. Someone at work had mentioned that Governor Clinton was in Los Angeles and that he was scheduled to make a speech at the mall that afternoon, but Linda had forgotten about it. That was what happened when you were caught up in the trivial details of your own life, like buying panty hose and dodging your lecherous boss.

Mr. Albano and Mr. Murphy were both voting for President Bush again. Linda heard Mr. Murphy tell someone on the phone that he didn't need some tax-and-spend Democrat to change *his* country, he liked it just the way it was. And the other night at dinner, when Linda mentioned to Mr. Albano that she was thinking of voting for Bill Clinton, he said he didn't trust "Slick Willie" any further than he could throw a piano. Linda hadn't actually been thinking about voting for anyone; she hadn't even gotten around to registering yet. Mr. Albano was the person *she* didn't trust, and she was just trying to make conversation that wasn't too personal.

Linda had agreed to their dinner date against her better judgment, and only after trying earnestly to get out of it by telling him that she didn't mix business with pleasure, and that she'd recently broken up with someone and wasn't ready to start dating anyone else. This last was certainly true. Linda hadn't heard from Nathan again after he delivered her plants that night. Not that she expected to hear from him, or wanted to, but there was the sense of unfinished business between them, of a wound that hadn't properly closed over so that it could begin to heal.

Mr. Albano wore down Linda's resistance with arguments he might have made in the courtroom, piling up evidence for his own innocent intentions. "I'd like to get to know you better," he said, "but strictly as a friend. I just got out of a bad relationship myself, and believe me, I'm not ready to get burnt again either. Hey, it's only dinner, anyway, with all four hands on the table. We both have to eat, Linda, don't we?"

Linda told Vicki she was dreading the date. "Then why didn't you just say no?" Vicki demanded. "Didn't you learn *anything* from Nancy Reagan?" But Mr. Albano had been so persistent. The only thing he couldn't convince Linda to do was call him Vince. As long as she didn't cross that crucial border into familiarity, she told herself he wouldn't get the wrong impression.

He took her to Hoofbeats, a steakhouse in the Valley that had tufted, red-leather booths and flickering carriage lamps on the paneled walls. As they were being seated, waiters went by bearing trays laden with bloody slabs of beef. It seemed you got to choose your own raw steak at Hoofbeats, before it was carried away to be grilled to order. From time to time, Linda had considered becoming a vegetarian, mostly for reasons of health—hers *and* the animals'—but her meat hunger always won out in the end. As their elderly waiter hovered with his burden of glistening flesh, and Mr. Albano leaned across Linda to make his selection, she became almost ill with revulsion. This evening was about sex, plain and simple, no matter what he'd said about all four hands on the table, and not wanting to get burnt again. She could feel it in the pressure and heat of his arm and leg against hers, and she could smell it in the faint but vulgar perfume of the quivering steaks. "How about you, honeybun?" Mr. Albano said. "Which one gets your juices flowing?"

"You choose," Linda gasped, with her eyes closed, and she slid a couple of inches away from him on the cold leather seat of the banquette. But she knew that she'd only be fighting him off in a few more hours on the cold leather seat of his car, and she wondered if she should force herself to eat a big, rare steak, just to build up her strength. She hardly ate anything, though, and she did have to fight him off, desperately, at the end of the evening. That was how her next-to-last pair of panty hose got ripped.

Things became more congested as Linda approached The Broadway. A wooden platform had been erected near the entrance to the store, and someone was setting up a cluster of microphones on it. There were television cameras all around—kids were mugging for them already. Behind the platform, a band of uniformed musicians had assembled and were taking out their instruments. And several people milled around two folding tables draped with red-white-and-blue bunting, one on either side of the aisle. Linda was glad she'd taken her cane with her, as she worked her way through the crush and into The Broadway. The area around the panty-hose counter was exceptionally busy, too, because of the sale, she supposed, and a general overflow from the mall. By the time Linda made her purchase and left the store, the band was tuning up in that boisterous way that makes you want to cover your ears and gives you a thrill of expectation at the same time. The crowd had grown considerably and everyone was surging forward, toward the platform. Linda was pushed forward, too, as if by the ocean's tide; it would be really hard to try to go in the other direction now. And if she stayed to hear the speech, she could just skip lunch, or pick up some yogurt or a taco to eat on her way back to the office. She really needed something more fortifying, though, after staying up so late again, pasting glitter onto those Christmas cards. Robin had helped for a while last night, until she realized it wasn't much fun. She was too careless, anyway, strewing glitter way outside the prescribed areas, and stopping to read the verses aloud, breaking Linda's concentration and her assembly-line rhythm. "With jingle bells and Yuletide smiles, we send our love across the miles," Robin read in a mocking singsong, and then she grabbed her own throat and croaked, "Oh, gag me!"

"I'd love to," Linda said. But she was already speeding backward across the miles and years to some childhood Christmas that couldn't possibly have been as happy as she remembered or imagined it was. Why was the past always sweetened by memory? Would she think of *this* tiresome night someday with a similar wrench of nostalgia? The work was more boring than strenuous, but the glue stank and the glitter got into everything. It stuck to their fingers and hair and eyelids, and was scattered in their clothing and even in their food. At night, there was a trace of phosphorescent glitter on Linda's pillow, like a sprinkling of stardust. The extra money would certainly come in handy, though.

Linda decided in favor of staying for the speech, more out of curiosity than anything else. She had never seen a Presidential candidate in person before. It would be something to tell Robin about later, although she'd probably be a lot more impressed by some television or rock star.

The bandleader raised his baton and the band broke into a loud, brassy rendition of "Don't Stop." An older couple near Linda did a few steps of the fox-trot, practically in place, to scattered applause, and several people began singing along with the music: "Don't stop . . . thinkin' about to-*mor*-row!" Then, under the din, Linda felt something like an electrical current move rapidly from one person to another. "He's here! It's him!" she heard. "Bill, Bill! We love you, Bill!" a man yelled, and the woman right next to Linda flapped her arms and emitted a joyful, wordless shriek, like an exotic bird about to take flight.

Linda was reminded of the time she and Dee Dee Mueller, her best friend at Coatesville High, traveled by bus to Pittsburgh for an Elton John concert, the first concert either of them had ever attended. They'd saved some of their baby-sitting money for an entire year for this expedition, and each girl had told her mother she was staying overnight at the other's house to study for finals. It was the most daring thing they'd ever done. They were remarkably innocent for the late seventies, truly believing that sucking Pop Rocks made you high—why else did they start giggling like that when the candy exploded its sweet tartness in their mouths?—and that they would be best friends forever.

The arena was packed when they got there. Linda and Dee Dee grasped hands as they went toward their seats, in ecstatic anticipation of the music, and in terror of being separated. After the opening act (awful Beatles imitators called the Termites) had overstayed its welcome, Elton John—himself!—leaped into the fiery lights, wearing a gold-lamé jumpsuit and those cool glasses, setting off a charge of excitement that traveled from body to body around the arena, until everyone was united in one gigantic, screaming mass.

Linda hadn't seen or heard from Dee Dee Mueller in over ten years—they'd drifted apart soon after graduation—but now she wished Dee Dee was beside her again, to hold onto and scream with as Governor Clinton went by, only a few yards away, huge and handsome and familiar, and radiating his own heat and light. It was too bad Vicki wasn't there, either. Just the other night, she'd said that Clinton might be the first winner she ever voted for. "And if he fucks up," she added, "well, at least he'll be *our* fuckup for a change, instead of theirs." But Vicki was off in Acapulco, catching a few days with her married lover.

Standing by herself, Linda felt shy and separate from the merriment around her. The governor shook hands and patted babies, lifted high by their parents as if for a blessing from the Pope, and kept smiling that generous, boyish smile. Linda wasn't close enough to touch or be touched, and she had to use her cane as a kind of pogo stick to see what was going on, but she was thrilled anyway. The crowd went crazy, just as that other crowd did at that long-ago concert in Pittsburgh. The speech they waited to hear was already singing in their hearts and brains. It was like that at the concert, too, Linda remembered, the words and music to "Rocket Man" running through her even before Elton John took the stage.

Clinton stepped onto the platform, and a chant began: "We want Bill! We want Bill!" Flags and signs were waved about, and the band played one more jazzy chorus of "Don't Stop." What happy chaos it was! Bill Clinton had to hold his big hand up for several minutes before the noise abated. Then, when he said, "My fellow Americans," in his eager, raspy voice, the crowd went wild again. Even the few hecklers—a man shouting, "Stop killing innocent babies!" while waving a blowup of a bloody fetus, and someone else who screamed, "Go back to Arkansas!"—were easily drowned out by the roars of affection and approval. Linda was still too self-conscious to join in; she stood quietly, her entire being poised and listening.

"My fellow Americans," Governor Clinton said once more, and this time there was a respectful hush. He spoke about California first, how it had been especially hard-hit by the recession, and said he was here to offer hope for change.

Linda thought sadly of Rosalia, who wasn't doing much better in Chicago than she had in L.A., and remembered that she owed her a letter.

"Do we have the courage to change for a better tomorrow?" the governor asked, and a tremendous cheer went up. He went on to talk about racial division, saying that we all needed one another, that we could only achieve a stronger America by working together. And then he said, "There's been a lot of talk in this campaign about family values; I know something about that. I was born to a widowed mother, but we were still a family. A family involves at least one parent, whether natural, adopted, or foster, and children. A good family is a place where people turn for refuge and where they know they're the most important people in the world. I've seen the family values of all these people in America who are out there killing themselves working harder for less. And I think the President owes it to family values to show that he values America's families."

He seemed to be speaking directly to Linda, assuring her that the haphazard choices she'd made were all right, that her odd little family was legitimate and valuable, and that if she just hung in there, help was on the way. Fourteen years ago, when Elton John leaned across the lights and sang, "My gift is my song, and this one's for you," Linda knew that he meant *her*, and not Dee Dee, who was crying and seemed to be eating her hands, or the thousands of other teenage girls around them, holding up lit matches and flaring cigarette lighters as an expression of their devotion.

Governor Clinton stepped down from the platform, and men in suits and dark glasses immediately surrounded him, but he worked a determined path through them to his enraptured audience, extending both hands to be gripped and wrung on the way. Linda felt herself being borne by the human tide in his direction. She knew, from the sudden escalation of noise and the rush-hour press of bodies, that she was very close to him, although she couldn't actually see him. She hooked her purse and shopping bag over the wrist of the hand that held the cane, and she waved her other hand high in the air, as if it held a political sign. The glitter under her fingernails sparkled gaily, like the match flames at the Elton John concert. "Hello!" her hand said. "Thank you, Bill! I love you, too!" And then an amazing thing happened: in passing, Bill Clinton reached out and took Linda's waving, chattering hand in his, *enveloped* it in one of his soft, warm paws for what must have been only seconds. The source of contact was unmistakable, the shock of it stunning. She would not have been surprised if her hand had disconnected itself from her arm then and floated upward, like all those liberated helium balloons dancing high above the heads of the mob. But the rest of her was solidly, safely rooted to earth. This was what the laying on of hands probably meant, an infusion of spirit and hope from one person to another with the simple, miraculous application of touch.

He was there, and then he was gone, and once again Linda was transported with hardly any effort of her own, this time toward one of the bunting-draped tables, where other people were already lined up, registering to vote. She looked at her watch; her lunch hour was over, and she hadn't eaten a thing. But a different hunger invaded her now, a hunger to remain a part of this magical, encompassing crowd, a hunger to belong and to participate. She took her place in line and waited to register, too.

Mr. Albano was very angry with her—"pissed off" was the way he put it—and the elation Linda had sustained all the way back to the office was severely threatened. Her rejection of his advances the other night was something he clearly wasn't going to accept with grace. She had hoped he would pretend the whole thing hadn't happened, so that everyone's pride could be discreetly restored. But when she saw him at work the next day, he was hostile and sarcastic. He criticized her typing in front of Mr. Murphy's snooty secretary, saying that if she paid as much attention to her work as she did to her makeup, she might remember that "sincerely" was spelled with two "e's." It was not only cruel, it was completely unfair. Linda had given up a while ago on those cosmetics from The Essential Me, because they were, essentially, *not* her, and had gone back to just using lip gloss. She worked up the nerve to knock on Mr. Albano's office door later that day, to complain about the way he'd embarrassed her.

"And what did you do to me?" he rejoined. To her bewilderment, he blamed *her* for turning him on, for being "so damn sexy" all the time he couldn't think straight. The way she walked, the way she smiled.

What was he talking about? She walked with a limp and she wore braces. "I didn't. I'm not," Linda protested. "I thought we were going to just be friends. What happened to all four hands on the table?"

"Oh, come on, sweetkins, be serious," he said. He began walking toward her with that lustful look in his eye, and she fled his office. Since then she'd been trying to do her job properly and stay out of his way—no small endeavor.

She was over an hour late getting back to work after the Clinton rally. As soon as she walked in the door, carrying her shopping bag of panty hose and a cup of half-eaten frozen yogurt, Mr. Albano strode out of his office and said, *"Read my lips, Linda!* I am really pissed off this time!"

"I'm sorry—" she began, automatically.

"Sorry doesn't cut it," he said, interrupting her. "This is your wake-up call, doll. You'd better start toeing the line, because I'm not gonna alibi you anymore."

"You don't have to alibi me. You can just dock my pay," she said, and took a spoonful of the yogurt to cool her burning mouth. He looked at her in astonishment. Linda was pretty astonished herself; she had never spoken to him this way before, or to anyone else in authority. Her telephone rang, and without dropping her defiant gaze she reached for it and sang out, "Good afternoon! Albano and Murphy, attorneys-at-law. May I help you?" Mr. Albano stared at her for another moment before he slunk back to his office.

Linda retained that surprising new sense of confidence and purpose all day. By five o'clock, other urgent thoughts had bullied and shoved their way to the front of her consciousness. Their main theme was that it was time to resume responsibility for her own life. She had to get another car soon, even if it meant making payments on it for years to come. Dr. Marcuvitz had said she could start driving again, but she'd put it off, out of fear of driving and because it was easy to put off. He'd also said she should try becoming less dependent on the cane, something she'd really been intending to do. She had to think about getting another job, too, although she hadn't logged much experience at this one, and she certainly couldn't count on getting a reference from either of her bosses. Then there was the matter of the baby. Linda had taken her to visit her old friends at Kiddie Kare last Saturday, and Phoebe had literally *leaped* from Linda's arms into Rose Petrillo's. There was no reason in the world she couldn't stay there again while Linda was at work, even if it made things tighter financially. And even if Cynthia objected. Linda had been relocated, she realized, to the outskirts of Cynthia's world. There were no more cozy lunches, no more intimate conversations. Linda hadn't seen her for almost two weeks, and they spoke only briefly on the phone, mostly about some delay on Mitchell's part in delivering Phoebe.

"This is your wake-up call," Mr. Albano had said, and it was as if a warning bell had gone off inside Linda's head. She thought of Governor Clinton urging courageous change, and she heard Nathan's voice again, offering to kiss her awake from her enchantment, and Robin asking if she was hypnotized or stoned. Linda was wide awake and buzzing with plans as she covered her typewriter and gathered up her purse and cane. It wasn't until she was ready to leave the office that she noticed the two pink telephone messages, almost hidden under a stack of letters on her desk. "Call Cynthia Sterling at studio," the first one said, and the second one said, "Call Cynthia at home." They had both come in during her squandered lunch hour and they were both marked "Urgent."

28

St. Francis of L.A.

Robin was napping on the living-room sofa with a pillow clutched to her belly when the doorbell rang. Shit. She had cut out of school right before lunch and come straight home to sleep off her monthly attack of cramps. She'd made herself a peanut-butter-and-raisin sandwich and turned on the TV, to help her relax, but every single channel had this speech what's-his-face, Clinton, was making at the Beverly Center mall. There wasn't even a game show on. Politics bored Robin almost as much as social studies, so she killed the TV. After she ate her sandwich, she closed the blinds, turned off the telephone, and curled up on the sofa. She couldn't have been asleep for more than a few minutes when the stupid doorbell rang.

Still clutching the pillow, she tiptoed to the door and looked through the peephole, which Linda was always reminding her to do, in case a serial killer decided to pick their bell to ring. Robin wasn't afraid of opening the door to some schizo stranger, though. She was more worried about letting an attendance officer in, or someone she knew and didn't want to see. Right then, that included just about everybody. But there was only a young, good-looking guy she'd never seen before standing out there. "Who is it?" Robin asked, and the guy said, "Is Linda Reismann home?" What was this, *another* boyfriend?

"Who wants to know?" Robin said.

"Mercury Messenger Service. I have a delivery for her." Robin undid the locks and opened the door.

"Are you Linda Reismann?" the messenger asked, looking at her skeptically. He held up a manila envelope. "I'm supposed to deliver this directly to her."

"Yeah, that's me," Robin said, yawning. He hesitated and then handed the envelope over, and when he extended a clipboard with a pen attached to it by a string, she scribbled Linda's name in perfect forgery. She'd had enough practice, signing cut slips she was supposed to bring home from school.

This was no cut slip; the envelope was way too thick. As Robin carried it inside, she saw the words "Personal" and "Confidential" stamped all over it. She looked at the name in the upper left-hand corner—William Sterling—followed by a Hollywood address. Who was he? The only Sterling Robin knew was the Rich Bitch. She yanked off the stubborn, sticky mailing tape, using a pair of scissors and her teeth, and pulled out a bunch of papers held together by a big clip. There was a handwritten letter on top. Robin plopped herself back down on the sofa to read it.

Dear Linda,

We met briefly (but memorably) at my ex-wife's house a couple of months ago. I'm going out on a limb here because I was favorably struck by you, by your rather touching ingenuousness, and because I believe you're about to be in deep trouble. My own post-marital experiences with Cyn (hell hath no fury, etc.) have sharpened my suspicions, and the enclosed papers only confirm them. Kobrin's specialty is child custody and he's a killer.

If you need a lawyer yourself, as I imagine you will, you might contact John Freed of Freed, Westman, Upshaw, and Gofstein in Beverly Hills. And use my name; he owes me a favor. Good luck— you're probably going to need it.

Sincerely,
William Sterling

Robin read the letter twice, and she still wasn't perfectly sure what it meant. She pulled out the next sheet of paper. It was another letter, typed this time, and addressed to Cynthia, from somebody named Arthur Kobrin, Esq. Robin's own name popped out at her from the middle of the page. "Surveillance of her step-daughter, Robin Reismann, has also proved fruitful." Surveillance. That was a word Robin knew, from school or television, or maybe just by instinct. She glanced at the first page of the bundle under the second letter. The heading said: *Paragon Private Investigators, 50 Years of Efficiency and Discretion, Edmund J. Riley, Director*. Somebody, a private detective, had been following her, *spying* on her! Hadn't she felt a spooky presence nearby lately, something that made her scalp prickle and her skin crawl? She tried to think. The substitute Spanish teacher they'd had last week, who threw chalk and erasers at all the kids who didn't pay attention. The guy with the twitch playing Super Mario at the machine next to Robin's at the video arcade the other day. That jerk batting the wind chimes at Happy Hands. Anybody, or everybody.

Robin turned to the report itself. It was too long and complicated to read word for word, so she just skimmed it, searching for key phrases. There were plenty of those. Linda's name, for instance, and Nathan's ... and Manny's! "Sexually active," she read. "Widowed white female." Further down, Robin found her own name again, followed by paragraphs including phrases like "frequent truancy," "serious vehicular accident," and "appre-hended while shoplifting." There was even something about Phoebe! Her age and how long she'd been at Cynthia's house. Did they follow her, too, when she was out in her stroller? Robin went back to the second letter and read the whole thing.

Dear Cyn,

   As we've discussed, this is a long shot; birth mothers almost always have the edge in these cases. But you'll be happy to know that our investigation has proved to be very productive. Ms. Reismann has demonstrated an unsavory lifestyle, and there are serious incidents of negligence in re her minor children. Most crucial are her promiscuous sexual behavior, erratic work patterns, and casual assignment of child care.

Surveillance of her stepdaughter, Robin Reismann, has also proved fruitful. I believe we have some strong evidence to support a charge of unfit motherhood against Ms. Reismann, and to help boost your own custodial suit. I can't make any promises, of course, but we'll give it the old college try. Lunch sometime next week for further discussion? I'll phone on Monday.

> Aff'ly yrs,
> Arthur

The letter was dated September 16. That was about two weeks ago, when Linda was still living at Cynthia's! Robin sat there for several moments, as if the physical weight of the papers on her lap was pinning her down. She'd been right all along. All the things she'd accused Cynthia of, that Linda had called Robin's "paranoid delusions," and that she herself had only half meant—had said mostly to get a rise out of Linda— were true. Her first instinct was to grab the phone and call Linda at work, to scream the news at her. But when she'd told her about the nursery, Linda only accused her of being ungrateful and of using bad language. There was no guarantee she'd get *this* either.

Robin flung the papers aside and searched under the sofa for her sneakers. She shoved her feet into them, ran into Linda's room, and rifled through the stuff in her drawers and her closet. She didn't know yet exactly what she was going to do, but whatever it was, she was positive she'd need some money to do it. "Shit, shit, shit," she said, as she dumped the contents of two of Linda's purses onto the bed, scattering loose pennies, used Kleenex, and supermarket coupons. That stupid glitter was everywhere, and all she got for her trouble was about six dollars in change. Then she remembered Linda saying she had to get to the bank on Saturday to cash a check from the Christmas card company for last week's work. Where was it? Did she have it with her? Robin went into the kitchen and looked in the most obvious place first, the place robbers probably learn about in robbery school—the sugar bowl—and hit the jackpot. In addition to the check, which was for thirty-three bucks, there was a five-dollar bill and three singles. She stuffed the money and the check in her knapsack, then filled two of Phoebe's baby bottles with milk and another one with apple juice. She tied the bottles together, around a frozen cool-pack, using a big rubber band, the way Linda always did before a trip to the mall. That all went into the knapsack, too, along with a couple of jars of baby food. As an afterthought, she threw in some cookies and an orange for herself. Before she left the house, she dialed Cynthia's home number, to make sure she wasn't there. When Lupe answered, Robin asked, in a kind of German accent, to speak to Ms. Sterling. "Not home," Lupe said. "Who is calling, please?" And Robin hung up.

The bank Linda used was only about five blocks away from their apartment. Robin ran all the way there, but she found herself at the end of a long line. She danced impatiently in place; anything could be happening to Feeb while that old lady deposited chicken feed in her Christmas Club and the Chinese guy pushed roll after roll of coins through the slot at one of the other tellers' stations. "C'mon, c'mon, let's go," Robin muttered, until it was finally her turn. The teller—his lapel pin said Mr. Boncourt—looked at the check and then at Robin. "Is this yours?" he asked.

"Yes," she said. What did he think she'd say, that she had found it in the street? Written it herself? Stolen it from her stepmother's sugar bowl?

"You forgot to endorse it," he told her, passing the check and a ballpoint pen to her through the slot under his window.

Robin flourished Linda's signature for the second time that day and passed the check back. Without thinking, she pocketed the ballpoint pen.

"Do you have any photo ID with you, Ms. Reismann?" the jerkoff asked.

"No," Robin said, "I left it in my car." What she wanted to say was, "No, but you'd better give me the thirty-three bucks or I'll have to kill you."

"Do you have a signature card on file with us?" he asked.

What the hell was that, and how should she know? "Of course," she said, tapping her fingers on the marble counter.

The teller left the cage and went to a file cabinet, where he flipped through a gang of cards until he found what he was looking for. She watched him compare her imitation of Linda's signature with the real thing for what seemed like hours. Then he walked slowly back to the cage, still examining the check, and said, "How would you like it?"

Robin exhaled. "Whatever you have," she said, and watched as he counted out two tens, two fives, and three singles, each bill snapping between his fingers like a small firecracker.

As soon as she stepped to the curb outside and held up her thumb, a BMW pulled over with a squeal. Robin barely had time to cram the money into her jeans pocket. The driver, a woman about Linda's age, said, "Where you heading?" Robin told her the name of a street near Cynthia's, the street that fancy deli was on, and was invited to get in.

The car stank of pot. "So, what did you do, pull a stickup?" the woman asked.

"Yeah," Robin said, and was surprised by the major laugh that got.

It was the easiest ride she'd ever hitched. No other questions asked, no conversation at all after that, and they sped through the streets with Megadeth screaming away on the tape deck. Why couldn't she have gotten a stepmother like *her*?

Robin got out right in front of the deli. "Thanks!" she called, and the woman yelled back, "Hey, it was mythical!"

As Robin began walking swiftly in the direction of Cynthia's house, she remembered the dogs. Fuck! They wouldn't be locked up today, when she wasn't expected. She stopped under the nearest palm tree and leaned against its bristly trunk. She had only worked things out loosely in her head on the way here: somehow, she was going to sneak up to the house, get inside without anyone seeing her, grab the baby, and leave. She intended to handle any problems of interference—from Lupe or Maria or Mitchell—as they came up. There were plenty of excuses she could make if she was caught in the act, and at least everybody in the house knew her, knew she was Phoebe's sister. The dogs were another matter; there was no talking her way around them. Robin tried to blot out their gruesomeness, the way they had leaped at the car that first time, as if they wanted to eat her alive. If she had thought things out more carefully, she might have been prepared. There were those sleeping pills she'd swiped from Cynthia's bedroom. She had swallowed one of them a few weeks ago, before she went to bed, just to see what would happen. Mrs. Thompson had to shake her awake for school the next morning, and she kept dozing off all day during classes. She might have wrapped the rest of the pills in hamburger and thrown them to the dogs as soon as they approached her. It was something she'd seen in a movie once and it worked great; the dogs, a couple of really mean Dobermans, keeled over in about a second. But she had nothing with her at all to divert or calm Cynthia's vicious dogs.

Robin walked back to The Sensual Gourmet and peered through the window. Maybe they had some dog biscuits she could toss around to keep those beasts busy. She went inside and the same snotty clerk who was there the last time gave her the same snotty look. "Do you have any dog biscuits?" Robin asked.

"*Hardly,*" the clerk said with a nasty little snort, as if he thought she wanted them for herself. "Would you care for anything else?"

Robin scanned the counter for some other possible dog bait, and then just grabbed a bag of those vegetable chips she'd bought the last time. It killed her to shell out eight bucks for something she wasn't even sure would do the trick, but those damn dogs looked like they'd eat anything they could get their jaws on, even overpriced people snacks.

The most important thing, she reminded herself as she hurried toward Cynthia's, was not to let the dogs smell the fear on her. She sniffed one of her armpits, wishing she had that deodorant stick Linda was always trying to make her use; she would have rubbed it over her whole body.

Robin was so concerned about the dogs she didn't even think about the gate until she was in front of it. Of course it was locked, and much too tall to scale. Not to mention the spikes on top. Robin considered ringing the bell on the intercom and using some excuse, like a UPS delivery, to get herself inside, but she didn't want to arouse anyone's suspicion. She was standing there, trying to come up with something better, when she heard the sound of tires on gravel. She crouched against the wall as the gate opened and the Jeep, with Mitchell at the wheel, drove out of the grounds and down the street. Still in a crouch, so she wouldn't be seen in the Jeep's rearview mirror, Robin scrambled through the gate like a giant crab before it slid shut again. Then she sprinted up the winding road, darting through the trees. When the house was in view, she stopped to catch her breath and to survey the scene. There were no cars in the driveway, no gardeners' trucks in sight. Robin ran around to the back of the house and pressed herself against the stucco wall beneath the kitchen window. She could hear the dogs making a racket inside. "Please, *please* don't let them out," she whispered to no one in particular, and of course she started to sweat buckets.

The window ledge was just above eye level, and there was nothing around to stand on. Robin jumped as high as she could and got a quick glimpse, through the open window, of Lupe sitting at the center island, reading a magazine. She had a flash of herself looking through the Thompsons' kitchen window the night after the accident. Once again she wanted in, badly, but for a very different reason. She jumped again, and this time Lupe was yelling at the dogs, who leaped and clamored around her. "Basta, locos!" she yelled, swatting at them with her magazine. Robin jumped a third time and the kitchen was empty. Then she heard a door slam and the two dogs were right there, snarling and backing her against the wall. There seemed to be a hundred of them. Robin squeezed her eyes shut. She was drowning in perspiration, and her belly was clenched in a cramp worse than any period she'd ever had. The dogs brushed restlessly against her legs, snorting and growling low in their throats. Robin crossed her arms over her chest, something her father had once told her was a way of letting an animal know that you aren't a threat. "Daddy, Mommy," Robin murmured. She was still holding the unopened bag of chips when she crossed her arms, and the crushed foil thundered against her thundering heart. "Nice dogs," she said hoarsely, "good dogs," the way the guy in that movie did before he tossed the Dobermans the doped meat. She wished she could remember the names of these monsters—it might fool them into thinking she was an old friend—but she could hardly think of her own name right then. "I come in peace," she added weakly, but that was from another movie, she realized, about cowboys and Indians.

Robin would have stood there forever, not moving at all, until she died, or the dogs did, if it wasn't for Phoebe. She *had* to get into the house, she had to save her. Taking a deep, whistling breath, she opened her eyes and lowered her arms to her sides. One of the dogs sniffed her clenched fingers with its slimy nose, while the other one checked out the bag of chips. Up close like this, Robin could see the terrible and fascinating details of their faces: the way the whiskery hairs on their brows twitched, and the flickering smiles on their ragged, glistening jowls. Slowly, slowly, she moved her hands until they were both gripping the bag. She tried to tear the foil across the top, but it probably would have been easier to crack a safe. The last time she'd bought a bag of this stuff, she remembered, she'd worked on it forever before it gave. She didn't have that kind of time now. Maybe she should just throw the sealed bag on the ground and let them tear it apart with their fangs. The thought of those fangs made her shiver, and she tugged once more, with all her might, and the bag ripped apart. Some of the chips flew out, and the dogs scrambled for them like pigeons chasing bread crumbs. She started to walk away from the wall in the slow motion of dreams, absently eating one of the chips herself as she went. The dogs followed her, with their heads down, while birds swooped overhead between the trees and a couple of squirrels came out of hiding to look for a handout. Robin was like that statue in front of the St. Francis Academy back in Newark, the one with all the stone animals around it, and the birds, real and fake, perched on its head and outstretched arms. St. Francis of L.A. It wasn't that she'd lost her fear. It still made her sick to look down at the dogs on either side of her, at their broad, rippling backs, their dangling, dripping, wolflike tongues. Her mouth was so dry she almost choked on the vegetable chip, and she counted her steps aloud as she walked, to keep herself from going too fast, to keep from screaming. If one of the dogs had started barking then, or made a sudden move toward her, she would probably have taken off in a panic. But they didn't, and she didn't.

Now she just hoped that Lupe had left the door unlatched when she let the dogs out. Robin put her hand on the knob and turned it. It went all the way around and the door opened with only a little shove. The dogs scooted in ahead of her and ran to the kitchen. She waited anxiously with her back against the door, expecting some exclamation of surprise from Lupe, but all she heard was the muffled roar of the vacuum cleaner, coming from the direction of the guest room.

Robin tiptoed toward the stairway, the way she had the day she discovered the nursery. The dogs came out of the kitchen and caught up with her before she was halfway up the stairs. She felt her heart pitch when they reappeared, and she could hear it beating in her ears the rest of the way. The hallway was empty. That woman, Hester, was sitting in front of her computer, tapping on the keyboard. Robin silently ordered her not to turn around and she seemed to get the message. Cynthia's bedroom door was half open and Robin and the dogs slipped inside. The blinds in the nursery were closed. Robin was afraid to look in there, afraid to discover that Cynthia had taken the baby with her on location, or that Maria had her out somewhere for a walk. Phoebe was right there in the beautiful white crib, though, fast asleep, with her little butt in the air. "Shhh," Robin whispered to the dogs, to the sleeping baby, to herself. If the baby cried, if the dogs barked. *Master, master, master!*

Robin snatched a handful of Pampers and a folded blanket from the changing-table shelf and jammed them into her knapsack. When she bent over the crib, Phoebe rolled onto her back and opened her eyes abruptly, the way a baby doll blinks awake. "Shhh," Robin said again. "It's only me." Phoebe smiled, sat herself up, and raised her arms. Robin picked her up and cuddled her for a moment. Her skin was still warm from sleep, and sweet-smelling, although her diaper felt heavy to Robin's experienced hand. "Wanna go bye-bye?" Robin said.

She'd almost forgotten about the dogs, who circled her excitedly now, to Phoebe's great amusement. Robin carried her to the doorway of the bedroom and glanced up and down the hallway. All clear. And all quiet, too, she realized. When had the vacuum stopped droning? Holding the baby tightly against her chest, as if they were dodging gunfire, she ran down the stairs to the front door, with the dogs running alongside her. *"Stay!"* she said, and pulled the heavy door open. The dogs looked at her longingly, but they obeyed. Robin didn't even take the time to close the door behind her, and as she raced across the driveway toward the trees, she could hear Lupe cry out, "Hey, muchachos! Who let you in, eh?"

At the big gate, Robin reached one hand through the bars to ring the bell on the intercom. Long moments passed before she heard a crackle of static and then Lupe saying, "Hola! Quién es?"

"It's me—Linda!" Robin shouted. To her surprise, Linda's voice was almost as easy to do as her signature.

"Linda!" Lupe exclaimed happily, and after several heartbeats, the gate began to slide open.

29

Crazy Like a Fox

Linda steadied her shaking hands and dialed Cynthia's number at work. The voice-mail message came on at the other end: "You've reached the office of Cynthia Ster—" She hung up before it could play itself out. She dialed Cynthia's home number next and Lupe answered the phone, shouting and crying something in Spanish, and then Cynthia came on the line. "Who is this?" she demanded.

"It's me," Linda said. "What's wrong? Has anything happened to the baby?" She started to cry in anticipation of Cynthia's answer. Of *course* something had happened to the baby. What else could this be about?

"Linda, did you take her? Is she with you?" Cynthia asked.

"What do you mean, is she with me?" Linda sobbed. "I'm at *work*. Oh, God, she's not missing, is she? Cynthia?"

But Cynthia only said, "You'd better get over here," before she hung up.

Linda's hands flew around her face now like terrified birds. She clasped them together and wrung them into submission. Then she dialed her own apartment number. Let Robin be there, she prayed. Let her answer the phone and say something insolent and relieving at once. *Sure, I took the baby—she's right here with me. What's the big deal? She's my sister, isn't she?* But Linda only heard her own idiotic taped message. "Hi, this is Linda. Robin, Phoebe, and I are all busy right now, but—" She slammed the receiver down, grabbed her purse, and went limping out of the office.

Mitchell was waiting next to the car in the parking lot, exactly where she expected him to be. It was a habit of privilege, she realized, like expecting someone else to cook and serve your meals, to do your laundry, your every bidding. She had learned to take things from others with only a few pangs of conscience, to say thank you graciously in two languages: Thank you for everything, Cynthia. Muchas gracias, Lupe, Maria. Had she made some unspeakable bargain?

"Mitchell! What happened?" she said, and he shook his head and said, "I don't know. Jesus. Lupe went upstairs and the baby was gone from her crib." He gave Linda a sympathetic glance as he opened her door, and they didn't speak again as he zipped in and out of traffic all the way to Cynthia's.

The gate to the estate was wide open. As the car went up the gravel driveway, Linda remembered her mother saying something about closing the barn door after the horse was stolen. Or did she remind Linda to close the front door behind her, saying that they didn't live in a stable? What difference did it make *what* she'd said, and why was Linda thinking about that now? She knew that her mind was traveling everywhere but in the direction of disaster, that she was only, barely, keeping herself from hysteria. *My baby, my baby.* Mitchell pulled up to the house and Linda jumped out and ran into the vestibule, where the dogs bounded up to greet her. She shooed them off. What kind of watchdogs were they, anyway, if they let a kidnapper in and out? Lupe and Maria were standing there, weeping and clinging together. "Where is Cynthia?" Linda asked. "Donde está la señora?" Her voice was as high and thin as a bat's.

"Ahí," Lupe said, pointing behind Linda.

Linda turned around. She didn't recognize Cynthia at first.

The blond hair, her own state of panic. It was a moment from a bad dream, or from an even worse movie, the kind where the insane murderer, clutching a butcher knife by then, turns out to be the heroine's best friend, or her boyfriend in drag. If human blood could simply stop dead in its circular route, Linda's did right then. Those familiar eyes, so darkly intense, so unfriendly, were even scarier than the unfamiliar blondness. "Where is my baby?" Linda said. "What have you done with her?"

"Don't be a fool," Cynthia said. "I told you I don't know where she is." Her expression hadn't changed, but when Linda walked purposefully in her direction she flinched, as if she expected to be struck.

Linda went right past her to the stairway. Of course she had left her cane at the office in her haste, and she hadn't climbed any stairs, with or without assistance, since the accident. It was as if she had forgotten how; she paused, looking down at her own two feet. *Right, left. I left my wife and forty-eight kids! Left, right. Right in the middle of the kitchen floor!* She hadn't thought of that silly marching rhyme since childhood, when it had helped to prod her reluctant feet toward school every day. I'm losing my mind, she decided, as she gripped the banister and pulled herself up onto the first step. Her bad knee buckled a little, but she held on and went up another step, and then another.

"Don't you understand English?" Cynthia yelled from the foot of the stairs when Linda stopped midway for a moment to rest. "She's not up there!"

Linda resumed her climb. It took a long time to get to the top, and she was exhausted and slick with sweat when she got there. "Phoebe!" she called, and she lurched through Cynthia's bedroom to the dressing room. *God.* She felt woozy and had to shut her eyes for a moment and lean against the wall, the wall with its nursery-rhyme paper. When she opened her eyes and looked around her, everything was still there—the wallpaper, the shelves of dolls and toys, the Mother Goose lamp, the beautiful, empty, canopied crib. This was a carefully planned room for a permanent tenant. Linda ran her hands over the crib sheet, hoping to catch some of the baby's warmth there, but the sheet was cool, even to her icy hands. Oh, Robin, Linda thought, forgive me.

Going downstairs was just as difficult as going up, and in her reckless rush Linda tripped and almost fell headlong down the whole flight. Cynthia was waiting for her in the kitchen. "Well? Are you satisfied?" she asked. She was actually smiling, in a grisly way. Then she reached for the cordless phone. "I'm calling the police," she said.

"No, don't!" Linda said, putting her hand over Cynthia's. "Maybe—"

Cynthia shook off Linda's hand. "Maybe *what*?" she said. "Who are you trying to protect—your Chicano boyfriend? Your JD stepdaughter? Those *people* she's such pals with?"

Everyone Cynthia mentioned with such obvious disgust, Linda longed to see, to speak to at that moment. "Maybe you'd better think about protecting *yourself*," she said. She wasn't certain what she meant by that, but Cynthia grew pale at her words and slowly lowered the telephone receiver. Linda picked it up and called home again. Again, her own recorded message. She called the Thompsons' next, and Jewelle answered the phone. Linda said, trying to keep her voice under control, "This is Linda Reismann, Robin's mother? Is she there, by any chance?"

"No, she's not," Jewelle Thompson said. "In fact, I was just going to call *you* and ask if you'd seen Lucy. Maybe they're together somewhere."

Linda began to cry again. "Jewelle," she wailed. "My baby's missing!"

"What do you mean, missing? Did the girls take her somewhere? Now hold on, Linda, don't cry, okay? Lee and I will be right there."

"I'm not h-home," Linda said. She recited Cynthia's address. "Please come and get me. *Please*," she begged. She hung up and dialed Nathan's number next, hoping she'd find Robin hiding out there, but he didn't answer. "Oh, God, what will I do?" she murmured, pacing the length of the kitchen with the phone in her hand.

"Why don't you try and pull yourself together," Cynthia said sharply.

"Why don't you get out of my life!" Linda shouted back at her, and flung the phone across the room. It hit the refrigerator and then bounced to the floor at Cynthia's feet, where it lay, humming ominously.

By the time the Thompsons arrived in their station wagon, Linda was waiting outside for them, pacing again and shivering. They put her between them in the front seat and sped away. Lee drove and Jewelle kept her arm around Linda's shaking shoulders, saying, "It's all right, honey. You'll see. Everything's going to be all right."

At first Linda thought the apartment had been robbed, with the dresser drawers pulled out and emptied like that, and those papers all over the sofa and the living-room floor. Was Robin kidnapped, too? She combed through the mess in the bedroom, with Jewelle's help, feeling completely confused and crazed with anxiety. All the thoughts she didn't want to think started crowding into her head: the story of the Lindbergh baby; the little boy who disappeared years ago on the way to school in New York City; that whole *busload* of children, somewhere down South, taken on a terrifying joyride. And every week, it seemed, there was a television movie based on another family's tragedy.

Lee Thompson walked slowly into the bedroom. He had picked up the papers in the living room and was scanning and sorting them. "What's this detective stuff about?" he asked Linda. He handed her some of the papers and she sank onto the bed with them and began to read. None of it made any sense at first, and then, suddenly, it all made total, horrifying sense. The letter from William Sterling. The letter to Cynthia from her lawyer. And the detective's report: five pages that summarized Linda's entire recent history. Her job at the Newark Fred Astaire's. Her marriage to Wright, his death, and her trip West with Robin. Their illegal stay in Paradise. Linda's pregnancy. Her various, short-lived jobs. Her affair with Manny, and then with Nathan, and even her one horrendous date with Mr. Albano! Various purchases were noted, including the lacy thong panties she'd bought on a silly impulse at Frederick's of Hollywood, soon after she got the job at Cynthia's. It all sounded so sordid the way it was written. Sexually active widowed white female. A pregnant dance instructor, cocktail waitress, and cashier in a liquor store, sleeping around on short acquaintance. Men practically dying at her feet, one of them violently. *The kiss of death.* A sentence in the middle of one page read: "On April 29, 1992, the first night of the riots in South-Central L.A., subject left minor children in the care of a neighbor she hardly knew, and drove, in her nightclothes, to that troubled area for an assignation with her current, married paramour." That information could only have come from Regina Clark, who still acted so neighborly near the mailboxes. But how did they know about Mr. Albano, and the panties? Linda must have been followed, maybe everywhere, without ever becoming uneasy or suspicious. So much for feminine intuition.

There was a lot of information about Robin, too—her habitual truancy, her hitchhiking, something about shoplifting, and, of course, the accident and its aftermath. The wording implied that Linda left her children with just about anyone handy, that she'd turned Robin over to the Thompsons without ever having met them, and that Cynthia, another virtual stranger, had complete charge of Phoebe for months. It also mentioned that Linda had accepted numerous gifts of cash and material goods from Cynthia while the infant was in her care, as if a trade of some kind had been arranged. I can explain everything! Linda thought, and then wondered if she could, if some impartial judge or jury would stay impartial very long in light of her seemingly wayward past, her less-than-impeccable present. What would anyone think of a pregnant cocktail waitress in hot pants and cowboy boots, a woman who slept with someone else's husband and made impulsive decisions without any apparent regard for her children's welfare? Linda sat dispiritedly on the bed with the papers strewn around her, reading the last page. She would not have been surprised to discover they'd gone even further back into her life, and nailed her for the juvenile offenses of loneliness and daydreaming, for lying to her mother and going to a rock concert, for wishing herself into a grownup future. Well, here she was, here she was.

Linda read the letter from William Sterling again and wondered how he'd gotten hold of the other letter, to Cynthia from her lawyer, and the detective's report. It didn't matter, though. The main thing was that Cynthia was crazy—dangerously so— and here was further evidence of it. But she had money and power, unlike most crazy people, who couldn't hire expensive lawyers to plead their case, or to help them steal someone else's child. Crazy like a fox, Linda's mother used to say about anyone slyly irrational. The phrase suited Cynthia far better than her platinum hair.

No one had broken into the apartment; only Robin had been here. She had read the letters and the detective's report, and she'd ransacked the closets and drawers, looking for money. Then she'd gone to Cynthia's house to rescue the baby—in defiance of the dogs, the electronic gate, of Cynthia herself—an act of such singular heroism Linda's eyes ached at the very idea of it. She went to the kitchen and looked in the sugar bowl, and as she'd already guessed, the money she kept there for a rainy day was missing. The check from the greeting-card company was gone as well, but she doubted that Robin would be able to cash that.

Jewelle called her own house and found out that Lucy had come in a few minutes before. They had a brief conversation that sounded tense and angry to Linda. It seemed that Lucy claimed, at first, to have spent the afternoon with Robin at the apartment. When Jewelle challenged that story, Lucy backed down. There was something about Carmel, and then something about a boy, but Linda was too distraught to listen, once she realized that neither of the Thompson girls knew where Robin was. Jewelle hung up and went into the hallway to talk quietly with Lee. Their heads were together, he was touching her arm. Linda watched them for a moment with utter envy. Then she dialed Nathan's number again, and this time he answered, sounding so surprised and pleased to hear Linda's voice her hope plummeted. "Nathan, have you seen Robin today?" she asked.

"No, of course not. I haven't seen or heard from her since . . . since you and I broke up. Why? What's the matter?"

"Are you *sure*?" Linda said, feeling a flood tide of fear rising in her chest. "Then where can they be?"

"Who? Who's 'they'?"

"Robin and Phoebe!" she cried. "They've disappeared!"

"Hey," he told her, "take it easy. Remember that day at Madman Moe's?"

How could she forget? She had been lucky that once, a warning from the gods, she believed now, not to be so careless ever again. "This is different!" Linda cried. "She's run away. She took the money from the sugar bowl. And the check for the glitter job." She couldn't seem to stop babbling. "There were all these papers at the house. Letters. Cynthia hired a detective—"

"Chica, listen, I'm coming to you," Nathan said. "Wait for me, okay? And we'll find them again, safe and sound, just like the last time. I promise you that."

But she knew that no one could really promise her anything of the kind.

30

And Leave the Driving to Us

The bus had almost pulled away—the door had wheezed closed and the motor was thrumming like a giant heart—when someone pounded on the door and the driver opened it again. Robin, who was slumped down in her seat near the rear of the bus, with the baby asleep across her lap, peeked nervously out into the aisle, half expecting to see a cop coming toward her with his gun drawn. But only an old lady carrying a bunch of shopping bags climbed aboard, saying, "Whew! Oh, boy! What a rush! Thank you very much!" in one of those megaphone voices. Yeah, Robin thought, and thank *you* for nearly giving me a coronary. The old lady took a seat up front, right behind the driver. She was the kind who'd talk to him for the whole ride, annoying everybody, even though there was a sign above the windshield that said: "Do not speak to driver while vehicle is in motion." Robin let out an exasperated sigh, but she was also weak with relief, and with hunger. She hadn't had anything to eat since that peanut-butter-and-raisin sandwich, practically a lifetime ago. She should probably try to sleep now, too, so that she could stay awake with Phoebe later. But she felt too keyed up from everything that had happened that day, and everything that lay ahead.

After she'd cleared the gate at Cynthia's, with the knapsack on her back and the baby in her arms, Robin started running down the street. In Newark, on such a warm afternoon, there would have been about a hundred witnesses to her getaway—people sitting on stoops and cars, or hanging out their windows hoping to grab a little breeze. Whenever something happened in the old neighborhood, a robbery or a fire or a murder, everybody wanted to be on the news that night, blabbing about it. "I live right next door," they always said. "It's just terrible," they'd add, smiling into the camera. Or "I'm shocked. He's such a nice, quiet guy— you know, friendly, helpful," while the cops carried the body bags out of the house behind them.

But these streets were almost empty. A black maid in a pink uniform walked a little white poodle, and a couple of gardeners worked on the perfect borders of a perfect lawn with electric edgers. And that was it. Robin slowed down as she went past the gardeners, in an effort to seem normal, casual. She even managed to crank up a smile when one of them smiled at her. The hardest thing of all was not looking behind her as she walked. She knew that she had to get herself to a main thoroughfare, and soon, before anyone got suspicious. If she tried to thumb a ride in this graveyard, she'd probably make headlines.

Standing at a busy intersection about half a mile from Cynthia's place, she imagined the BMW, with its cool driver, coming by once more and stopping on a dime for her; she even *willed* it to appear. But fifteen or twenty minutes later, no one had stopped, except at the traffic signal, and they all zoomed right off again as soon as the light changed. Robin could feel her face getting hotter and redder, and there were strands of hair sticking to her forehead and the back of her neck. The baby's head felt hot, too, like a boiled egg, and Robin had to keep shading it with her hand. By then, she'd have settled for a ride in a garbage truck or in a station wagon full of nuns. What she got instead was a big, rattly old blue Lincoln with someone who looked older than God behind the wheel. He opened his window and peered out at her. "You looking for a ride, young lady?" he asked. No, she wanted to say, I'm just standing here catching some rays. "Yeah, thanks," she said, and she pulled the passenger door open and climbed in before he could change his mind.

The old guy was the opposite of the BMW lady; he drove about five miles an hour, as if he was keeping time with the Mickey Mouse music playing on his radio. And he started quizzing Robin the second she sat down. "Is that your baby sister?" he asked. "Cute little gal, carbon copy of you." Like Robin had never heard *that* before. When she said she wanted to go to the bus station, he asked her where she was off to, and why in the world she was leaving "beautiful, sunny Los Angeles." He could have been Linda's grandfather. Robin told him she was going to a family reunion in Montana, a state pulled at random from all the geography lessons she'd ever suffered, although she couldn't exactly place it on the map or think of the name of a single city there. Then he wanted to know if she was going to a ranch, and if she liked horses. Why not? Robin thought. It was as good as any story she could have made up herself. "Uh-huh," she said. "I ride all the time. My mother and father are both in the rodeo." And then this weird thing happened. She actually *saw* a ranch in her mind's eye, with people on horseback galloping toward it from a distance, and other people sitting around a campfire, waving to them. Before she could make out anyone's face, though, the old guy was telling her how he'd once had this little Arab, a real high-spirited beauty. Robin wondered if he was some kind of pervert. Not that she was worried; if he tried anything funny, she'd simply deck him. He was so ancient he'd fall over if you blew on him. The only old person Robin actually knew was Lucy's grand-mother. Everyone else seemed to die or disappear before they had a chance to get old. And Ga was only old in her body. There were times Robin believed she could straighten out her comma-shaped back if she decided to, kick off those ugly orthopedic shoes, and race Garvey around the block and win.

At last they were at the bus terminal and the game of Twenty

Million Questions was over, or almost over. "Are you going to be okay, young lady?" the old gasbag asked. "Do you need any money or anything?" Robin would never understand it if she lived to be two hundred herself, but she said, "No, thanks, we're fine," and got out of the car.

She waited on one of the ticket lines inside the terminal, her eyes darting restlessly around her. It was twenty of two, just about when Feeb usually woke from her nap. Robin wondered if Lupe had gone in to check her yet, or if she was still listening for waking sounds on the baby monitor. And what did she make of Linda never showing up after announcing herself at the gate? Maybe they'd discovered everything by now and the terminal was surrounded by cops. All the people here, though, seemed to be burdened by crappy luggage or bratty kids, or both. A cop would have stood out in this place like a . . . *rich* person.

When it was Robin's turn at the ticket window, she asked what the fare to Newark was. She had already seen, on a timetable, that an express bus going there would leave in a little less than an hour. Perfect. That would give her enough time to go to the bathroom and change Feeb's diaper, and to get something sub-stantial—like a hot dog or a burrito—to eat, with time left over to wait on a couple of other ticket lines and leave a phony trail behind her. Robin glanced at the humongous map of the United States hanging on the far wall, for inspiration. She could inquire about tickets to Florida, Minnesota, Kentucky, Vermont . . . When the cops questioned everybody later, they'd never be able to pin down her actual destination.

"When do you want to leave?" the woman behind the ticket counter asked.

"On the next bus," Robin said.

The woman punched some computer buttons and then she said, "That will be $159.50."

Robin was stunned. "But I only want to go one-way," she said.

"That *is* one-way," the woman told her. "The round trip is $319. It's pretty far, you know. Now if you purchase your tickets twenty-one days in advance, there's a fifty percent discount, and if you purchase them fourteen days in advance, there's a thirty-five percent . . ."

But Robin had stopped listening. She stood there, trying to figure out the difference between the fare to Newark and what she had in her knapsack. She was about $120 short—it was hopeless. And she could still hear herself saying, "No thanks, we're fine," to the old guy in the Lincoln. The baby squirmed in Robin's arms and started to whine, and a booming voice over the loudspeakers called out all the stops on a bus to Sacramento that was ready for boarding. The man behind them on line tapped Robin on the shoulder, scaring the life out of her. "Miss," he said, "my bus is leaving in a few minutes. Get the lead out, will you?" A couple of other people behind him started grumbling, too, and Robin had to step aside. She walked over to the map and stared up at it. Newark *was* pretty far from Los Angeles, almost as far as you could go without falling into the Atlantic Ocean. She'd picked it because it was familiar, because you didn't need a car to get around there, and because it was where she, and Feeb, had first started out. Now she surveyed the country looking for someplace closer, and cheaper, to get to. Her gaze traveled upward from L.A. to Nevada, and further north to Oregon and Idaho. Hey, there was Montana, just above Idaho! Robin looked south from there, across Wyoming and Colorado and New Mexico, and then she hung a left and came to Arizona. It was right next door to California, where it had always been. If she could have reached that high and spread her fingers wide, she was sure they'd span the distance from Los Angeles to Glendale. Maybe it was the dumbest idea she'd ever had (except for not taking money from the guy in the Lincoln), but it was fixed in her brain now and she couldn't get it out.

She took her place at the end of another, shorter ticket line. At the window, the man said she'd missed the only direct bus to Glendale for the day, but that she could go to Phoenix and make a connection there. The one-way fare was $32.50. The next bus was leaving in fifteen minutes. Robin bought her ticket and hurried to the bathroom, where she peed, with the baby sitting on her lap. Then she changed Feeb's smelly diaper on the changing table, clearing the room of the women combing their hair and gabbing at the mirrors nearby. There was no time afterward to make any phony inquiries about other buses, or to get anything to eat, except for a couple of candy bars from a vending machine. At Gate 7, the driver stood next to the sleek silver bus marked "Phoenix." Cupping Robin's elbow in his hand, he helped her aboard.

Nobody took the seat next to her—that was the beauty of traveling with a baby—although the bus was almost full. Robin couldn't have stood it if she had to make conversation with one more stranger today. She and Feeb were finally alone, the way she'd always dreamed. It was much harder and scarier than she had imagined, though. As if she'd had the same thought, Phoebe grabbed one of Robin's fingers and held on, a source of comfort to both of them. Robin began to think of all the things she hadn't taken with her and wished she had, a list she knew would keep getting longer as the trip progressed: baseball caps to cover their conspicuous hair, her watch, her Walkman, a toothbrush, a jacket, some grass, some gum, a pacifier for Feeb, more food . . . The knapsack was on the empty seat and she reached across the baby and took out the orange and began to peel it. The juice ran down her fingers, stinging the skin around her bitten nails, and her stomach growled in anticipation of being fed. The trip was going to take over eight hours—she guessed her hand couldn't *really* have spanned the distance between L.A. and Glendale— and she had to make her provisions last. She intended to save the cookies and candy for much later, although it would be hard to eat them in front of Feeb, who had a big sweet tooth already and shrieked when she wanted the cake or ice cream you were eating. She had finished a whole bottle of milk before she conked out. Robin was thirsty, too, and dying for a Coke, but she was going to have to settle for some pukey water from the fountain next to the closet-sized bathroom in the very back of the bus.

The orange was gone in only a couple of minutes, and it hardly made a dent in her appetite. She found herself scraping off the bitter white part inside the rind with her teeth and eating that, too. She decided to just count the cookies, but she discovered that they'd been reduced to a pile of crumbs by the stuff she'd wedged on top of them. There was no point in saving crumbs, so she began picking at them, popping them into her mouth until they were all gone. She shook the knapsack, unable to believe she'd eaten every last little bit. Suddenly self-conscious, Robin glanced across the aisle to see if anybody had been watching her scarf down the orange and cookie crumbs like that. But the couple sitting directly opposite had a big coat thrown over them, and were doing something underneath it Robin didn't want to know about. She looked out her window, instead, at the moving landscape. Trees, signs, cars, other people's houses. They were still in California and all she had left to eat were the two candy bars. And to make things worse, everyone else on the bus, it seemed, was busy unpacking a five-course meal. Various smells, of garlic, onion, pizza, egg salad, and coffee, mingled and wafted their way to Robin. She wanted to rush up and down the aisle and grab anything she could and gobble it down, even the egg salad. Instead, she clamped a corner of Phoebe's blanket over her nose and shut her eyes.

Robin didn't know how long she'd been asleep, but when she woke, Phoebe was sitting on the adjoining seat, screaming her head off. The bus was dark, except for the little beams of the reading lights above some of the seats. Over the baby's screams, Robin could hear the old lady up front telling the driver the long, boring story of her life, and a child somewhere in the middle of the bus chattering in Spanish. Phoebe's diaper needed changing again for sure, but Robin decided she'd better feed her first. She reached into the knapsack for a jar of mashed bananas. It took her only a couple of seconds to realize she'd never packed a spoon—another item for her list of left-behinds—but Phoebe was working up to a major fit by then. Robin twisted the cap off the bananas, stuck a finger into the jar, and held it against Phoebe's lips. "Here you go," she said. "Yummy yummy, down the tummy." Where did that come from? Robin wondered. Maybe she was getting to be a poet.

With hardly any hesitation, Feeb sucked the finger clean and then opened her mouth for more, like a baby bird waiting for the next worm. She did it so matter-of-factly she might have always eaten this way. Robin stuck her finger into the banana mush again and again. She could feel the pull of Feeb's sucking all the way down to her toes; did nursing feel something like this? When the jar was empty, Robin said, "All gone!" as cheerfully as she could. Phoebe's mouth and chin began to tremble immediately, but before she could let go, Robin took out the second bottle of milk and stoppered her with it.

Much later, after they'd both slept again, they shared a candy bar, the Milky Way, the one without the nuts. Phoebe went back to sleep in minutes. But Robin stayed awake from then on, although everyone else, except for the driver, seemed to be dozing. Even the old lady had finally shut up. With the dark and quiet world going by in rapid-rewind motion, Robin allowed herself to think at last of Linda, and of Lucy and Carmel, of how she was rushing away from them, mile by mile by mile. And then, for the first time, she thought about Glendale and who she was going to see there.

31

Prisoners of Love

Once again, Linda was beside Nathan in the Z. But this was nothing like the old days, when the car was a speeding chariot and the only emergencies seemed to be sexual. They drove slowly, scouting the streets and not speaking, like a long-married couple who had run out of things to say to one another. They had been driving around the neighborhood for over an hour, and now they were heading toward a local video arcade that was one of Robin's favorite haunts. Lucy and Carmel had gone with their father to check out the malls, and Jewelle had stayed at Linda's apartment, in case Robin decided to call home.

Walking into the sudden, artificial night of the arcade, with its barrage of noise and lights, was like stepping into a war zone. Most of the people seated or standing at the rows of machines were teenagers—their hands gripping the throttles, and their entire selves fixed on the electronic images flashing and stuttering before them. It didn't take long to establish that Robin wasn't among them. But Linda continued to study that surreal scene, while Nathan went to talk to the man in the change booth.

Linda had never been in an arcade before, had never watched Robin sit, like these other children, mesmerized by a blitzkrieg of animated violence. When she'd tried to limit Robin's visits to this sort of place, she had always lumped it with television, as a general waste of time and bad for the eyes. But she could see that it was far worse than television, or the mindless, deafening music Robin lived by, despite the "participation" here, the clench-fisted manipulation of the bleeping blips on every screen in the room. These kids, with their tensed bodies and vacant eyes, were all shooting themselves in the brain, so they wouldn't have to think for a while, so they wouldn't have to even *be*.

The man in the change booth hadn't seen Robin and Phoebe that he could remember, and neither had anyone in the next arcade, or in any of the stores along the strip that catered to adolescent taste in audio and video tapes, in cheap jewelry and grunge clothing. As they walked back to the car, Nathan put his arm loosely around Linda's drooping shoulders. It was only a sympathetic gesture, but Linda couldn't stand to be touched, and she stepped out of his reach. "How could she have just gone off like this?" she said angrily. "I'm going to wring her neck when we find them!" She turned and saw his pitying face before he had a chance to rearrange it. "Oh, God, Nathan," she said, "what if we *don't* find them?"

"We're going to," he said gruffly. "Didn't I promise you?"

Lee Thompson let them into the apartment, with Lucy and Carmel right behind him. "No luck," the two men said simultaneously, and Carmel's eyes glittered with tears. Both girls looked like those teens you see on the evening news, huddling at the funeral of a slain classmate.

Jewelle came in from the kitchen, drying her hands on a dish towel. "If it was *my* kids," she said, "I'd call the police. I'd want all the help I could get, and fast."

"But if we sic the police on Robin, it's liable to help that lunatic's case," Nathan said.

"Lunatic is right," Lee said. "What is she, one of those baby freaks or something?"

"Oh, no," Linda said. "I mean, she wasn't ever really that *affec-*

tionate with Phoebe." She thought about it for a moment. "I think she just wanted to outdo her husband, her ex-husband. He's going to have a baby, so she wanted one, too, and first."

"Well, why did it have to be *your* baby?" Jewelle asked. "Why didn't she have one of her own?"

"Maybe she can't," Linda said. "Maybe she's too old."

"It would take too long, anyway," Nathan said. "It's like impulse shopping, you know? She sees it, she wants it, she takes it."

"More like shop*lifting*," Jewelle observed.

"She probably could have adopted a kid," Lee said.

"Those two little Guatemalen orphans . . ." Linda murmured.

"Too dark for her money, I'll bet," Nathan said. "She saw this pretty, healthy, blond baby and figured: why not? But I think you faked her out, Linda. I think she's afraid to call the police, too. The baby disappeared from *her* house, remember, and she'll want to keep her own record clean."

Linda nodded absently. Cynthia seemed so remote and irrelevant now. What was a custody case without a child, anyway? By not calling the police, Linda was only protecting Robin, just as Cynthia had accused her of doing. If the girl were caught now, it would be one more strike against her. She might even end up in some juvenile detention center—not for kidnapping her own sister, maybe, but for breaking and entering, or something else illegal she must have done that day, out of desperation. Linda knew that *she* was the one who should be locked up, for criminal innocence, although she was reformed now, once and for all. After the horse had escaped through the open barn door. She tried to console herself by remembering that Phoebe was with Robin, who loved her, and not some unimaginable stranger.

Nathan cursed quietly in Spanish as he looked through the detective's report, but at least he didn't say "I told you so," in any language. He just said, "Let's try to think like Robin. Where would she go?"

"Back to Newark, maybe," Linda said. "She always used to

threaten to go there when things were bad around here. Maybe we should check the airlines."

"That's a pretty expensive ride," Lee said. "How much money do you think she has?"

Linda calculated. "Not much, I guess," she said. "She was supposed to get her allowance tomorrow. Even if someone was crazy enough to cash that check for her, she'd still only have about forty dollars."

"That's not enough to get her to Newark," Nathan said. "Unless she tries to hitch her way there."

"She wouldn't, not with the baby," Jewelle said quickly. "Robin is much too smart for that." Linda gave her a grateful glance.

"Do you have all your credit cards?" Nathan asked.

"I only own one," Linda said, shuffling through the junk in her wallet, "and it's still here. But maybe she borrowed extra money from somebody else."

"It better not be my girls," Jewelle said. "They're in enough trouble with me already." She glared at Lucy, who lowered her eyes and shook her head.

"What about some of her other friends?" Lee asked.

There was a long, uneasy silence. "Well?" Jewelle prompted.

"Robin's not really that close to anybody," Lucy said finally, and that awful but familiar truth struck Linda with new force. She remembered Robin and herself at some amusement park long ago, disappearing together into the pitch-dark Tunnel of Love. Linda had wished fervently, foolishly, for a miracle then— the two of them restored to daylight in a bond of friendship, if not of love.

"Everybody just sort of hangs out," Carmel added to her sister's blunt judgment, a touching and transparent defense of Robin's separateness, her lack of social charm.

Still, Linda went to the telephone and tried calling a few kids whose names Robin had spat out derisively over the past months: Stephanie Kraus, Marybeth Nixon, a boy named Richie Darr. As Linda expected, neither Stephanie nor Marybeth had seen Robin recently—except in passing, at school—and the boy claimed never to have heard of her.

Jewelle had made sandwiches and coffee while the others were out, and now she urged them to sit down and eat something. Linda was surprised to see, by the kitchen clock, that it was way past suppertime. She wasn't hungry, at least not in the usual sense—the hollowness at her center was more emotional than physical. She picked up a teething ring from Phoebe's high-chair tray and gazed at Robin's empty place at the table, wondering if they had enough food, if they were comfortable and safe somewhere. "Let them be safe," she said aloud. They were all standing around the small table, and it was as if grace had just been said.

There weren't enough chairs for everyone, but Lucy and Carmel shared the step stool, and Nathan perched on the edge of the counter. Lee held a chair out for Linda and said, "You come sit by me." When she did, Jewelle started coaxing her to take a few bites of a sandwich, saying it would give her the energy she needed to go on with the search. But Linda could only get some milky coffee past the obstruction of dread in her throat. It was getting dark out. Jewelle had put on several lights in the apartment, prematurely, but she couldn't ward off the night. The sky had already dimmed, and the trees outside the kitchen window were gradually losing their color and definition. It was that time of day when the world is cleanly divided between those with shelter and those without it. For all her bravado, Robin was afraid of the dark. Not that she would ever admit it. But hadn't she moved a little closer to Linda in the absolute blackness of the Tunnel of Love? And sometimes, when Linda came into her room in the morning to wake her for school, she'd find the bedside lamp still burning weakly from the night before. The memory of such ordinary, unsung mornings was more than she could bear, and she got up abruptly, making the coffee slosh and the silverware jump. "I can't just stay here like this!" she cried. "I've got to keep looking for them."

Nathan stood, too. "Let's go," he said, putting his cup in the sink. "We'll start at the bus station, where the fares are cheapest. Who knows, she might even be planning to sleep in their waiting room tonight."

"I'll take the girls home and then go to the airport," Lee said. "Just in case."

Again, Jewelle volunteered to stay at the apartment and cover the telephone.

As soon as Linda and Nathan walked into the bus station, a baby started to cry, making Linda stop short and spin around. But it was a tiny black baby, worn like a flower on the shoulder of a young man waiting on a long ticket line. He patted and patted her without noticeable effect. It was much too bright in that big room. Linda had a headache, and a loud, staccato announcement coming over the P.A. seemed to be hammered directly into her skull: "The bus for Salt Lake City, with stops at San Bernadino, Barstow, Baker, Las Vegas, and Provo, is now boarding at Gate 5." All of them places where Robin and Phoebe might or might not be. And the enormous map on the wall offered a bewildering feast of other possibilities. Linda had to hurry to catch up with Nathan, who was making his way rapidly past the map to an office in a far corner of the terminal. Her limp had deepened in the past few hours, and her whole leg felt strange, numb and painful at once.

The agent at the desk inside the Customer Service office was attending to someone else when they got there, a woman whose luggage was apparently lost. She was filling out a claims form and remembering aloud the contents of her suitcase. "My good blue dress," she said mournfully. "The shoes I borrowed from my sister for the wedding. My bathrobe. Oh, and my slippers."

My *children*, Linda thought, with a fresh wave of misery. She had the wild notion that she might have to fill out a form, too, that she'd be asked to provide detailed descriptions of her missing items. A parade of pictures marched through her throbbing head: Phoebe's lopsided and swollen beauty, moments after she was born; Robin's rare smile, lighting on her face like a bird on a branch before it flew off again; the way both girls looked asleep, and just coming awake.

When it was their turn at the agent's desk, Nathan flashed his open wallet and said, "Ed Riley, Paragon Investigators. We're looking for a runaway kid." He went on to describe Robin in practical detail: age, height, weight, coloring. He said she had a baby with her, and that they might have been in the terminal sometime in the afternoon. Linda looked up at the clock on the office wall just as the minute hand moved. It was nine thirty-seven. She thought of that opening to the evening news back in Newark: It's 10 p.m. Do you know where your children are?

The agent picked up the telephone and typed something into his computer with his free hand. Linda heard him murmur an echo of Nathan's description into the phone as he typed. Then he said, "It will take a little while. You might want to get yourselves a cup of coffee or something."

There was a coffee shop right in the terminal, but they went around the corner to a quieter, darker place and sat in a booth. Linda put her head down on the table between them. "How did this happen?" she asked. It was a genuine question, and a complicated one. She meant this current crisis, but also everything that led up to it. She wanted to be comforted, but not absolved.

Nathan seemed to understand. "Lousy luck," he said. "A few wrong moves. Fate. The story of everyone's life." He put his hand out to touch her hair, and it hovered briefly above her head before he drew it back again.

The black coffee and the doughnut they shared dulled Linda's headache a little, and she was better able to tolerate the cruel lights of the bus terminal when they returned there, if not the disappointing news. The agent told them that a girl fitting Robin's description had inquired about the fare to Newark, at about one-thirty that afternoon. The ticket seller remembered her because she looked something like her own kid. The girl didn't buy a ticket, though, and her trail ended there.

"But if she was right *here*," Linda pleaded, "a girl with a baby . . ."

The agent held up his hands, as if to demonstrate that they were empty. "Lots of girls," he said. "Lots of babies." He conceded that Robin might have gone to another window and bought a ticket for somewhere else, but if she paid cash for it, there wouldn't be any way to trace it. And maybe she decided to just leave the terminal, he said, and spend the night somewhere in L.A.

"That's true," Nathan said. "She could have done that." He leaned dejectedly against the wall.

"Look," the agent said. "I know what you're going through. I'm a father myself."

"Hey, I'm not the father," Nathan told him.

"Sure," he said, "I almost forgot. You're Eduardo Riley, private eye. Maybe it's none of my business, pal, but why don't you have the police doing this for you?"

"It's a long story," Nathan said. "But listen, man, thanks for your trouble." He straightened up and shook the agent's hand. "Come on," he told Linda. "I have an idea."

He drove them only a few blocks to an all-night movie house, and parked at a meter just down the street. Linda glanced up at the marquee in horror. It was a double bill: *The Pink Panter* and *Pussy in Boots.*

"They wouldn't sell Robin a ticket to this place," she said, "would they? I mean, she's a minor."

"Are you kidding?" Nathan said. "They'd sell one to *Phoebe* if she had the dough."

Nathan said something to the ticket-taker, and he let them inside. They walked up and down the aisles together, scanning each sparsely populated row. The men sitting there, most of them alone, slithered lower in their seats and averted their faces. All that time, a pornographic struggle was being thrashed out on the screen, accompanied by assorted gasps and moans—from the sound track, and from the audience. For some crazy reason, that song "Prisoner of Love" started playing in Linda's head, and she couldn't stop it until they were out on the street again. She felt so discouraged she wanted to lie down on the sidewalk and bawl, like that baby in the bus station who would not be soothed by her father's gentle patting.

Nathan walked Linda to the car and locked her inside, while he went to check a couple of other theaters of the same ilk, on the same street. She did scream a little after he left, tentatively at first, and then really loud—a kind of savage howl—like someone being murdered. She was astonished that several people walked right by the car without seeming to notice or hear her.

When Nathan came back, they rode around near the bus terminal a while longer, stopping to look into laundromats and fast-food places. Then they drove all the way west on Wilshire to the Santa Monica Pier. Linda remembered taking the children there last winter, and how they'd all ridden the carousel, with its thrilling lights and music and speed.

The carousel was still and dark now, and most of the concession stands were shuttered. A man who sold souvenirs said it had been pretty slow for a Friday night—there was too much of a breeze—and he didn't remember anyone resembling Robin and Phoebe passing by. Linda sagged with disappointment, and Nathan said, "Let's try the beach." He didn't sound very hopeful, though, and Linda guessed he was just trying to keep her going.

They took off their shoes and walked onto the damp, cold sand. The chill seemed to travel from the bottom of Linda's feet to all the bones in her body. As they walked among the blanket-wrapped figures lying there—the homeless and the fugitive lovers—she felt like an intruder in someone's bedroom. And the sight of one blond girl (not really like Robin) entwined with a dark-haired boy squeezed her heart shut. "They're not here," she said wearily. "They're not anywhere. Let's just go back."

At the apartment, Jewelle was sitting on the sofa with her shoes off. She had the dazed and disheveled look of someone startled awake. Nothing had to be said; she and Linda each read the absence of news on the other's face. For the first time that day, Linda realized that Jewelle was wearing a white uniform, that she must have just come in from work when Linda called her, all those hours ago, begging to be picked up at Cynthia's. "It's past midnight. You must be exhausted," Linda said. "Do you have to go to work tomorrow?" She spoke in a hushed voice, as if someone else in the apartment was still asleep. Her mother had worn a uniform like Jewelle's whenever she went away, and when she came home again.

"No, no," Jewelle said, speaking softly, too. "The weekend woman is on." She yawned and shivered. "I'd better call Lee to pick me up."

"Don't bother. I'll take you home," Nathan told her. He turned to Linda. "Lie down while I'm gone, niña, okay?" he said. "I'll be right back."

"I feel terrible about leaving you, Linda," Jewelle said as she put on her white shoes. "But there's nothing else to do tonight, is there?" She hesitated, and then she blurted, "Girl, you ought to call the police!"

Linda slumped in the doorway of the living room, overcome by fatigue, and giddy almost to the point of tears, or hysterical laughter. Her headache was back in full force and her leg was killing her. She wanted to go to sleep, she wanted to wake up. "Jewelle," she said, "tell me something. Where would *you* go if you were Robin?"

Jewelle didn't hesitate for even a second this time. "Family," she said with complete conviction.

Linda moaned and slid down the doorway to sit on the floor. "But Robin doesn't *have* any family," she said despairingly. And then she looked up, blinking in surprise, and said, "Oh."

32

Mother

The bus arrived in Phoenix on schedule, a little after 10 p.m., and the connecting bus, to Glendale, wasn't going to leave for more than an hour. Robin watched as other passengers were met at the gate by friends and relatives. All that hugging and kissing—some of them even took pictures—and then they vanished together into the night. There were only a few people left in the terminal, either sleeping on benches in the waiting room or standing around, staring blankly into space. The baby was asleep, too, and Robin shifted her from one weary arm to the other, like a sack of potatoes, which was what she was starting to feel like. Robin had carefully counted out what was left of her money as they were pulling into Phoenix: four dollars and seventy-five cents. She blew all the change on a vending-machine Coke and sat down on a bench to wait for the second bus. While she waited, she ate the other candy bar she'd bought in L.A. and drank the Coke. But her snack didn't give her the quick sugar high she'd hoped for, and she had to pinch her fingers bloodless to stay awake.

When the Glendale bus arrived, she climbed stiffly aboard. Only two other passengers, a couple of blue-haired women, got on. They both sat down—near the front, of course—while Robin asked the driver if he knew where Cornelia Street was. He was about to consult a street map when one of the blue-hairs announced that she knew exactly where it was. She leaned over and patted the seat directly across the aisle from hers. "You sit right here, young lady," she told Robin. "My sister and I live just three blocks from Cornelia Street. We'll see that you get there safely."

"It's only about a twenty-minute ride," her sister added. "We'll be there before you know it."

In the meantime, Robin had to endure another series of nosy questions, starting with why she was out so late with such a little baby. This was definitely her day to be bugged by old people. It was too late to pretend she was mute or couldn't speak English. Instead, she mumbled something about having missed an earlier bus.

"What a precious child," the woman nearest Robin remarked, about Phoebe, and the other one said, "Is it a boy or a girl?"

Was she blind? "A girl!" Robin said indignantly.

"Oh, really? How old?"

This was turning into a *relationship*. "Thirty-five," Robin said, under her breath. How old are *you*? she was tempted to add, and when did your hair turn blue? But when the same woman offered to hold Phoebe for a while, Robin handed her over, and then stretched and flexed her liberated arms. Of course, that left her open to a whole new round of cross-examination. She was getting better and better, though, at making things up on the spot. This time she and Feeb were the daughters of a very wealthy, recently divorced couple—a doctor and a lawyer. Their mother, the doctor, had just relocated to Glendale from Phoenix, and Robin (a.k.a. Stacy) and her sister (Tiffany Marie) were going to live there with her, after spending several months with their father. Robin could have said she'd dropped in from Mars or the moon and gotten the same reaction, the two women were such pushovers. They clucked in sympathy about poor Stacy and Tiffany's broken home life, and about how thoughtless their father was, not to drive them to Glendale himself at this hour, or send them in a hired car. Robin toyed with the idea of saying, "Yeah, he's so thoughtless, he went and *died*," but she only shrugged bravely and yawned.

She was poked awake at Glendale and led blindly off the bus, the way her father used to lead her to the bathroom at night when she was little. Before she dozed off, she'd sent a repeated ESP message to the blue-haired sisters: *Shut up. Shut up. Shut up* . . . And out on the sidewalk in Glendale, when they started to escort her to Cornelia Street, she insisted she could find it herself. They argued and fussed and finally gave in. But after they'd pointed the way and gone off around the corner in the opposite direction, still calling their goodbyes, Robin wanted to run after them, like some brainless baby duck chasing its mother.

She had been around here once before, but somehow nothing looked familiar. Of course that other time was more than a year ago, and she and Linda had arrived by car on a bright Sunday afternoon. She remembered a group of children running through a sprinkler on one of the front lawns and a man reading a newspaper on his porch. You could sense it was Sunday, the way you always can, no matter where you are. Now it was about midnight; the street lamps were pretty dim, and there were lights on in only a few of the houses.

Robin was freezing. Wasn't the desert supposed to be hot? And it was so quiet, everybody had to be either asleep or dead. Phoebe was awake again, wide awake. She screeched like a set of bad brakes and pulled on the reins of Robin's hair, commanding her to go. "Shhh, ouch!" Robin cried. Then she wrapped the blanket around the baby's shoulders and started to gallop with her, chanting softly as she went along: "Giddyap, giddyap, giddyap, horsey." Phoebe laughed merrily and jiggled in her arms, still gripping the reins of hair. The moon seemed to be keeping pace with them, bouncing over the rooftops and trees. After a minute or so, a dog started barking somewhere, making Robin pause breathlessly, but it sounded safely distant and too shrill to be very big, so she resumed her gallop all the way to Cornelia Street.

"Well, here we are, Feeble," she said in a whisper. The baby yanked hard on her hair again, but Robin eased it out of her fist and walked slowly up the pathway of the two-story, white-shingled house: number 1418. Until that moment, she hadn't realized she knew the address by heart. There were no lights on inside, at least none that she could see, but the moon had faithfully followed them here, and it threw its pale, silvery glow over everything. The last time, there was a neat yellow Corvette in the driveway, with one of those canvas bug-covers over the front end, but now there was only a naked white Taurus parked there. Maybe the Vette was in the garage or out being fixed. Or maybe it was the wrong house. She walked back to the street to recheck the number painted on the curb. It was the right house. Robin approached the front door, hoping they hadn't decided to get themselves a dog since the last time she was here.

The last time, *he* came to the door in his bathrobe, looking like a handsome gangster, with his great tan and that big head of styled gray hair. Her mother's husband. He thought that Robin and Linda were a couple of religious nuts trying to convert him. "Forget it, sisters," he said. "We're already saved." He almost slammed the door in their faces, but Linda stopped him. Robin couldn't say a word; she was so weak she could hardly stand up. She could still remember the way the chest hairs sprang out of the gap in his robe, and the neck chains and turquoise rings he wore. Linda said some stuff to him about who they were and he let them into the cool, shaded entry of the house, calling upstairs that they had company.

Minutes later, she came slowly down the stairs, rumpled and drowsy. She was wearing a loosely tied green silk bathrobe, just like his. They had been in bed together, Robin understood, and they hadn't been sleeping. She wasn't sure how she knew this, but she did, and with horrible certainty. Her mother was like no one she had ever met or even imagined in all those years of imagining. She was too short and young to be anyone's mother, and she wore glasses. Robin didn't look anything like her. Her name was Miriam, but he called her Mim.

She was perfect.

Robin rang the doorbell. The chimes pealed out, startling Phoebe, who stiffened and whimpered. "Take it easy," Robin told her, told herself. There was no barking and there were no footsteps—only silence and the tinny echo of the chimes inside Robin's head. She tried to look through the peephole, but all she could see was the reflection of her own eye. She was positive she'd see him—Tony—again, as if he was the butler or the doorman and it was his *job* to open the door. It would probably take him a while to get there, but she was marking the seconds, using the pulsebeat in the baby's temple, and this was taking much too long. Robin was shivering from the cold, and maybe a little from nerves, too. What if they were on vacation? What if they'd moved? She didn't know why this hadn't occurred to her before, with the wrong car in the driveway and everything. She pushed the bell again, hard, several times. The chimes kept going, like a thousand Avon ladies calling. In the middle of all the noise, the porch light suddenly flicked on and the door opened. Robin almost fell inside. But it wasn't him standing there; it was *her*, without her glasses. She looked older, less glamorous. Her dark hair was cut short, like a boy's, instead of shoulder length. It was flattened on one side and stood up in horns on the other, probably from sleeping on it. She was wearing a different bathrobe, a kind of ratty blue one, and she had a pistol in her hand, aimed shakily at Phoebe.

"Don't," Robin said, backing away and trying to shield the baby at the same time.

Her mother lowered the pistol. "God," she said, softly. "Is that *you*?"

"Yeah," Robin croaked.

"What in the . . ." She came closer and squinted at Robin and then at Phoebe. "Oh, boy," she said, shaking her head. "Just what I needed." She hustled them inside, switching on an interior light, and shut the door behind them. In the little vestibule, she gave them another once-over. "She's yours, all right," she said. "Who's the father?"

Robin was completely confused for a moment, before she understood with a terrible jolt what her mother meant. During the last few miles of the trip to Phoenix, she'd worked up an alibi to explain her surprise appearance here. She was going to say that Linda had died, of some brain disease, leaving Phoebe and her alone in the world. In a sense, Robin decided, it was actually true. But this was an even better story, she realized. Linda hardly had to come into the picture now, and Phoebe belonged to Robin in every possible way. Her mother was standing there with the drooping gun in her hand, waiting for an answer. "I don't know," Robin said, finally.

Her mother let out a long, whistling breath and then she turned and went into the living room, beckoning Robin to follow her. This was the room where they'd all sat that June afternoon, when Linda told Tony and Miriam about her short marriage and about Wright's death, expecting them to welcome Robin into their lives with open arms. It would have been a whole lot easier for her to get into heaven. Not that they said no, exactly. It was more that they, that her mother, didn't seem very enthusiastic about the prospect of Robin staying. She acted like somebody trapped by a really slick door-to-door salesman. She might buy the set of encylopedia he was pushing because she didn't know how to resist the sales pitch, but she would never look at it once it was on her shelf. Robin was stupefied: she had fallen in love and been jilted, all in a matter of minutes. And then, to make things worse, her mother mentioned that stuff about Tony's son having lived with them for a while. That was when Robin came to sudden, agonized life. "I wouldn't stay here if you gave me a hundred million dollars!" she yelled. Like they were offering her a bribe to stay. At least Linda went along with her, for once, babbling about how they'd really just dropped by to say hello. And then she took Robin's hand in hers and they walked out of there.

Out of here. This was the same room, and these were the same white couches, only they were a little soiled now and a little less plump. And he was missing—her mother's henchman, her doorman, her partner in crime. Robin looked nervously toward the stairs, expecting him to come lumbering down them any minute. Fee, fi, fo, fum! She remembered how big and muscular he'd seemed next to tiny Miriam, how deep his voice had been. There was still no sign of him; he was probably sleeping. But wouldn't her mother have woken him up when the doorbell rang this late? He was so protective of her last year, like Robin had busted into her life just to ruin it. Of the two of them, wouldn't *he* be the one packing a gun? Maybe they'd split up since Robin was here. That idea cheered her considerably. In her old dream of being reunited with her mother, it was always just the two of them. It would be a lot easier to accommodate Phoebe into the revised dream than Tony. Robin put the baby down on the blond carpet and relaxed into the sofa cushions. Phoebe took off at a high-speed crawl toward a low table loaded with breakable stuff.

"Where is . . . what's her name again?" Robin's mother asked. "Donna? Rhoda?"

"Linda," Robin said. "I don't live with her anymore."

"Do you mean . . . because of the baby?"

"Uh-huh."

"Well," her mother said. "Like mother, like daughter."

"What?" Robin said, startled.

"I had you when I was young, too. Not as young as you, though. And *I* was married, by the skin of my teeth. But my mother was ready to throw me—no, no!" she said to Phoebe, who was on her knees next to the table, reaching for a little glass candy dish.

Phoebe screwed her face up to cry, so Robin grabbed the baby blanket and tossed it lightly over her head. "Where's my Feeble?" Robin said. "Where's that little punk?" It was a game they'd played on the bus, and Phoebe still remembered it. She pulled the blanket right off and crowed with delight at the magically returned room. Robin threw the blanket over her again, with the same happy results. Using her other hand, she removed the candy dish and put it on a higher table, out of Phoebe's sight and reach.

Then Robin scooped her up and, turning to her mother, said, "Do you have any milk? And a place where I can change her?"

"Into what?" her mother asked. But then she said, "Come on, we'll fix her up." And she took them into the kitchen for the milk, and then ushered them up the stairs. Halfway to the top, Robin heard something odd, over Phoebe's contented sucking, a kind of gurgling sound, like the filter in a fish tank. Her mother hurried ahead of her and shut the door facing the landing, but not before Robin caught a glimpse of a room faintly lit by an orangy night-light and a hospital bed with somebody propped up in it. That's where that weird noise was coming from; you could hardly hear it now through the closed door. She didn't say anything about what she'd seen and heard, and neither did her mother. She led Robin into the small room next door and put on the light. There was a daybed in there, a small table with a digital clock on it, a pinball machine, and an exercise bike. The carpeting was green and shaggy, like an overgrown lawn. Was this where Tony's son had slept when he lived with them? Robin put the baby down on the daybed and began changing her diaper.

"You can sleep on that tonight," Robin's mother said. "But where will we put her?"

"She can sleep with me," Robin said. "We always sleep together."

"If you say so," her mother said. "The bathroom's down the hall on the left. Are you hungry? Do you want anything to drink?"

Robin shook her head. "Could you just hold her for a couple of minutes?" she said. "I'll be right back."

Her mother took Phoebe from her. "So now I'm a grandmother," she said, in amazement, returning the baby's frank scrutiny. "What next?"

A few seconds passed before Robin realized what she'd said, and that it wasn't true, that it could never be true; you had to be a *mother* first. She went to the bathroom and emptied her bowels and bladder. After she'd washed her hands and dried them on the lone skinny towel hanging there, she found a tube of toothpaste in the medicine chest and rubbed a dab of it over her gritty teeth with one finger. She stared at the closed door near the landing before she went back into the little room. If that was Tony on the hospital bed, he had to be really sick. It was true that Linda had used a bed like that for only a couple of broken bones, but in the moment before her mother shut the door, Robin got the impression of serious gloom. The gurgling, that funny orange light, and especially the motionless figure on the high bed. She couldn't bring herself to ask about it, though, and her mother still didn't volunteer anything. She merely handed her a pillow and an afghan, and said, "Good night, Robin. Sleep tight. We'll discuss all this in the morning."

Her name spoken in her mother's voice was a pure wonder. Robin supposed she should call her something back, like "Miriam," or "Mom," or even "Mother," but she couldn't manage to get any of those words out. So she said, "G'night, Mmm . . ." as if she were only humming to herself, or falling asleep standing up, before she could finish her sentence. She was actually pooped enough to drop off like that, but after she lay down she kept thinking she was still on the bus. There was a persistent replay of rushing landscape behind her eyelids, and she'd jerk awake before the bus could crash into something. The daybed was much too narrow for two people, even if one of them was a midget, and she'd left the back cushions in place as a bumper for Phoebe. "Now remember, don't smother yourself," Robin had told her as they settled in together under the afghan. It was scratchy and it smelled of mothballs and old sleep. In the creepy silence, Robin thought she could hear that gurgling noise again, and she pressed her ear against Phoebe's murmuring chest to drown it out.

33

Tarzan and Jane

A bell rang and rang and Robin fell out of the bus onto the grassy strip at the side of the road. She groped around in the dark and found a baby bottle, a bicycle pedal, and then a sneaker. Her *own* sneaker, by the feel and smell of it. She lay there in a half doze, not sure where she was, until the overhead light came on and her mother's bare feet appeared at eye level in the shaggy green carpet. The feet were exactly like Robin's own—small and chubby, and with the second toe longer than the first. "Is it time to get up already?" she asked, struggling to her knees. That had to be one lousy mattress; she didn't feel the least bit rested. The baby, she saw, was still dead to the world, hogging the middle of the daybed.

Her mother hiked up her nightgown and climbed onto the exercise bike. "No," she said. "It's only about one o'clock."

"You mean, in the *morning*?" Robin asked, rubbing her irritated eyes, her whole numb and tingling face. "Then I just went to sleep."

Her mother began pedaling the bike. "I know," she said, "but we have to talk."

"About *what*?" Robin said. What was so important that it couldn't wait a few hours, after all these years?

"About Linda. About you. About the baby," her mother said, pedaling faster with each pronouncement. The bicycle chain made a loud, clackety noise, but Phoebe didn't stir. "The telephone rang before, Robin, didn't you hear it? It was Linda."

"Oh, shit," Robin said.

"Yeah," her mother agreed. "You've got quite a lively little imagination, haven't you?"

"You don't understand," Robin said. "I really had to do it."

Her mother jumped off the bike and the wheels kept spinning. "Well, sometimes you gotta do what you gotta do," she said. "God knows I can appreciate that."

"Is she coming here?" Robin asked.

"Who—Linda? Of course she's coming. What did you think?"

Robin sank to the edge of the daybed, making the baby bounce a little, but she still didn't wake up. "I think some people don't care about their children," Robin said into her chest, and in such a low voice she could hardly hear herself.

After a moment, her mother said, "That was the worst thing I ever did."

"But *why*?" Robin said. It sounded more like the cry some zoo animal might make than an actual, human word.

Her mother sighed. "It would be really hard to explain," she said. "I'd need a lot of time."

Robin didn't say anything, and her mother signaled her to wait as she went out of the room. She came back a few minutes later, carrying a wooden chair. She pushed it against the daybed so that its ladder back made a barrier for Phoebe, and she put Robin's pillow on the floor alongside the chair. "Come with me," she said. "I want to show you something."

Robin followed her into the hallway and to the door of the next room. Her mother opened the door and went in, but Robin stayed on the threshold. The filter noise was louder now and there was a strong, sweetish odor she didn't recognize and didn't like. The man on the bed was Tony's shriveled old father. He had the same nose and ears, only bigger, and a few strands of that steely gray hair. Robin couldn't tell if he was really tan, like Tony, or if it was the orange light that made him look that way. His mouth was open, and he didn't seem to have any teeth. Something clear ran down an IV tube into one of his hands. Both the smell and the gurgling came from him. Robin saw another, regular bed on the other side of the room, with a blue robe across the foot of it, and she realized this was *their* bedroom. And that was Tony on the hospital bed. Her mother picked up the robe and put it on. Then she adjusted the clip on the IV tube, and said, "Let's go downstairs."

In the kitchen she put a kettle of water on to boil and set two ceramic mugs on the breakfast bar. They were bright red with a pattern of green vines; one said "Me Tarzan" on its side, and the other, "You Jane." She spooned instant coffee into the mugs. "Decaf," she said. "I hope that's okay. It's all we drink around here."

Robin sat on one of the two stools near the bar. There were two of everything here. She never drank coffee at home—she didn't like it—but when the steaming water hit the granules in her mug, the one marked "Me Tarzan," the aroma was irresistible.

Her mother sat next to her and picked up the other mug. "I guess you were my crime, Robin," she said. She looked upward. "So that must be my punishment." She took little sips of her coffee. "It's weird, but we found out he was sick right after you and Linda were here last year."

"What's the matter with him?" Robin asked.

"The big C," her mother said. "Prostate first, and then everywhere, fast as a forest fire."

Robin had only a vague notion of what and where a prostate was—something bean-shaped down there in men, she thought, but her vision of a raging forest fire was vivid. "Will he get better?" she said. A little kid's question.

"No. He's almost gone." Her mother said it calmly, but her hand trembled and she had to put the mug down carefully on the bar. "He was in the hospital for weeks this last time—nightmare city—and I decided to take him home to die."

To her own amazement, Robin identified the intense ache she was feeling as envy. Why weren't they talking about *her*?

Her mother seemed to have read her mind. "This is really incredible," she said. "I mean you, sitting here like this."

"Didn't you ever, like . . . miss me?" Robin asked.

"Of course I did. You were such a cute baby, actually an awful lot like . . ." She gestured toward the ceiling.

"Phoebe," Robin said.

"But I was this wild kid, madly in love, and I wasn't ready to deal with all that responsibility yet."

"So you just made believe I didn't exist?" Robin said.

"No. No, that's not true. Do you remember my telling you last year that I called a couple of times when you were little? To see how you were doing, and maybe to speak to you? But your dad wouldn't put you on. He hung right up on me."

"A couple of times," Robin said sadly.

Her mother said, "I had the idea I'd come and get you some-day, when you were older, when *I* was older, and you'd fit in more with our lives."

"You never came," Robin said.

"Time just kept going by. And Tony wasn't ever really keen on it. He gave up his family, too, you know."

"But you took *his* kid in!" Robin cried.

"Oh, God, yes, Kevin." She made a face. "Tony's ex practically dropped him on our doorstep after she remarried. He was about thirteen then, and a holy terror. Stole things, set little fires, hot-wired cars . . . You name it, Kevin did it. Believe me, he didn't last very long around here."

They were silent for several moments after that. Robin sup-posed it was her turn to say something about herself, but she couldn't think of anything to say. It was as though she'd had no significant history from the time she was abandoned until this reunion.

"I don't blame you if you hate me," her mother said. "I had my second chance with you last year and I blew it, royally." She ran one hand through her cropped hair, as if she was looking for the rest of it. "But when you showed up tonight . . . I don't know, I thought maybe I was being given a *third* chance."

"That's not what you said when you saw us," Robin reminded her. "You said, 'Just what I needed.'"

Her mother smiled. "Well, that was my initial, *gut* reaction. I mean, you definitely caught me off guard. But later, after I got back into bed, and had a chance to think about it, I felt really happy you were here."

All the murderous and adoring thoughts Robin had ever harbored about her mother clashed in her head, but the word "happy" clanged and clanged there like a church bell. She knew she was much too tired to think straight. "When is Linda coming?" she asked.

"I'm not sure. She's driving here with a friend, and they were going to sleep a little before they started out. She sounded wiped out—they've been looking for you for hours."

"*What* friend?" Robin said. If the Rich Bitch was heading this way, she and Feeb were heading out the back door. Anyway, they weren't going back to L.A. with Linda until she came out of her coma and got real.

"I didn't ask," her mother said, "but I think it was a he." She stood and stretched, like a cat. "Let's go back to sleep now, too, okay?" She put her hand lightly on Robin's shoulder and they went up the stairs together.

Phoebe woke Robin later that morning by trying to crawl across her chest. According to the digital clock, it was only six-thirty. Robin groaned. "Give me a break, punkhead, will you?" she said. But aside from being hungry and wet, the baby seemed completely refreshed and ready to begin the day. Robin could hear voices coming from downstairs. Was Linda here already? She changed Phoebe, using the last diaper, and carried her and the empty bottle down to the kitchen. Robin's mother and another, older woman were sitting at the breakfast bar, drinking coffee. The other woman had brassy blond hair and a big, mannish body.

"Robin," her mother said, "this is my next-door neighbor and dearest friend, Brandy Moore. Brandy, this is my . . . Robin."

All Robin could think of was the dog named Brandy that bit her so long ago. If this Brandy had bared her teeth and growled, she would not have been completely surprised. But she only smiled and said, "Hi, there, how're you doing?"

Robin went to the refrigerator and took out the carton of milk. "Fine," she said, although the question hadn't really required an answer.

Her mother rinsed Phoebe's bottle and filled it from the carton. "Brandy is my lifesaver," she explained as she handed the bottle to Robin. "She comes every morning and every evening to help me with Tony, to turn him and sponge him down."

"Oh, yeah?" Robin said. Phoebe grabbed the bottle from her and plugged it in, curling her toes around it.

"The hospital sends a visiting nurse three times a week. But she comes in the middle of the day, for only a couple of hours. I'd be lost without Brandy."

Brandy blushed. "Please," she said. "I don't do a thing. But *this* girl here is an absolute saint."

"I'm no saint," Robin's mother said.

In the harsh morning light, Robin saw tiny lines around her eyes, and a few strands of gray in her dark hair. And you're no girl, either, she thought, but all she said was, "Feeb's going to need diapers and some real food."

"What does she eat?" her mother asked.

"Baby food, of course," Robin said. But how would you know?

"I'm kind of low on that stuff right now," her mother said. "How about a mashed banana? Or a scrambled egg?"

She ended up feeding Phoebe bits of egg and toast while Robin ate her own breakfast. The baby was distracted by the circles of sunlight on the bar, and the way Brandy's armload of bracelets crashed together every time she took a sip of coffee. "Hey, you," Robin's mother said. "Open up. Yummy yummy, sliding down the tummy." Robin looked up sharply and stopped breathing.

Later, after Brandy went home and Phoebe was napping, Robin asked her mother what happened to the Corvette she remembered seeing in the driveway.

"I sold it after Tony stopped driving. It was his toy, anyway, and we needed the cash. Tony is—*was*—in insurance. He was tops in his company, he could sell flood coverage to an Arab. But he was on straight commission, so our income did a nosedive after he got sick."

"Did you work, too?" Robin asked, still trying to fill in the blanks of her mother's secret life.

"On and off, at a travel agency. And I got my real-estate license a couple of years ago, just in time for the bust. I'll have to do something when this is over. Right now, we're living on interest, and chipping away at the capital."

While her mother was in the shower, Robin went upstairs and into the room where Tony lay. She couldn't stop staring at him, couldn't stop searching the living corpse on the bed for traces of her terrible enemy of that summer's day. He opened his eyes and looked back at her. She gasped, whispered "Hi," and fled.

Downstairs again, Robin asked her mother why Tony was still so tan if he was in the hospital for such a long time. "That's not a tan," her mother said. "It's jaundice. His liver." Prostate, liver, a whole stew of rotten beans.

At about eleven o'clock, the door chimes rang. Robin hid out in the kitchen with Phoebe, while her mother let Linda and Nathan in. She could hear their murmuring voices, and then Linda burst into the kitchen, with her eyes shining. "Robin honey, Phoebe, I'm here!" she exclaimed. Like she was the one who'd been missing all along.

Robin endured an embrace, with Phoebe in the middle,

before Linda gathered the baby up and danced around the kitchen with her. Nathan stuck his head in the doorway. "Hey, Christopher Columbus," he said to Robin, "qué pasa?"

"Shut up," she said.

Robin's mother came in and Linda said, "I can't thank you enough, Miriam."

"Forget it, Linda," Robin's mother said. "I should really be thanking you."

They were so polite to each other Robin wanted to puke. And then, to top it all off, her mother invited everyone to stay for lunch.

"That would be lovely," Linda said. "Are you sure it's no trouble?" Then she handed the baby to Nathan and proceeded to help Robin's mother make the salad and the sandwiches. Robin had to set the table. She did it as noisily as she could, so she wouldn't have to listen to the stupid conversation about which was the fastest route back to L.A.

Just as they were sitting down to eat, Brandy showed up to join them. Linda and Nathan didn't seem to know about Tony, and nobody wised them up; nobody even mentioned him during lunch. It was so freaky; him up there dying, and the rest of them down here eating ham-and-cheese sandwiches and saying things like "This is really delicious," "It's so warm for September," "More coffee, anybody?" They talked all around Robin's adventure, too, which made her feel both relieved and neglected.

Linda had brought the diaper bag along, filled with baby supplies. Robin took her upstairs to the room where she'd slept, so she could change Feeb's diaper and clothes. Linda stopped in the doorway, listening hard. "Do you hear something?" she asked.

"Fish," Robin said. "They've got this huge tropical fish tank in the other room."

While Linda was putting a clean outfit on Phoebe, she said, "Robin, that was a crazy thing you did. But I understand why you did it."

"You were crazy, too," Robin said.

"I was," Linda admitted.

"So what's going to happen?"

"You mean with Cynthia? I'm going to call that lawyer her husband suggested. Don't worry, we'll work it out. And if we can't, I guess I'll have to shoot her."

Robin laughed. Then she picked Phoebe up and kissed her cheek, her neck, and her fingers before handing her to Linda.

"Speaking of husbands," Linda said, "where's Miriam's? I didn't want to ask before, just in case, well, *you* know."

"Playing golf," Robin said smoothly. "With some of his insurance buddies." Tony was her mother's business, not Linda's.

They went downstairs to the kitchen, and Nathan said, "We really have to get going, girls. It's a long ride."

"That's a heck of a lot of driving for one day, isn't it?" Brandy said over the rush of water. She was at the sink, with rubber gloves on, washing the dishes.

"I'm used to it," Nathan said. "I once did a stint of long-distance hauling."

"I could always spell you when you're tired," Linda told him. She turned to Robin. "Have you got your stuff together, honey?" she asked. "I think it's time to say goodbye."

Brandy shut the water and peeled off the rubber gloves. Robin was standing next to the breakfast bar, where the Tarzan and Jane mugs had been set out to dry, side by side. Her mother was leaning against the refrigerator, hugging herself. Robin felt as if she'd been running. She took a powerfully deep breath, the way you do before you jump into a pool. Without looking at anyone, she said, "I think I'm going to hang out here for a while."

34

Tony vs. Death

October 10

Dearest Robin,

Can you believe it's still Indian summer here? Phoebe and I went
out yesterday with only our shorts and T-shirts on! (But we're not
complaining!) How is the weather there? We all miss you very much.
I hope school is good in Glendale. Do you have to take a bus? Have
you made some new friends yet? I know you must be very busy, but
I really hope you can find the time to drop us a line and let us know
how you're doing. Or you could call collect. Phoebe says hi. I mean
she actually *says* it. Nathan says it's really *ha*, that she's only laughing
at us for trying to teach her to talk. Well, that's all for now. Please
give my best regards to your Mom and Tony.

Lots of love,

Linda

P.S. Guess what? I don't need my cane anymore!

P.P.S. Write!

One of the good things about Glendale was that Robin didn't
have to go to school, at least not while Tony was still alive. The
subject didn't even come up. She and her mother were together
all the time, in the kitchen or the sickroom, or out at the super-

market and the mall when the visiting nurse was there to take care of Tony. Her mother bought Robin new clothes and a few things for herself as well; sometimes they tried on the same outfits in the store's dressing room.

Her mother let Robin drive the Taurus home from the mall one day, after Robin said that she had her license but not much experience. "What have we got to lose?" her mother said, handing her the car keys. "You only live once, right?"

And Robin saw Linda lying still and bloody across the seat of the 88. She shook her head free of the image and said, "Right." Her mother was so cool she didn't even ask to see the license.

Brandy was in the backseat of the car, and as they drove away she kept yelling things like "Watch out for that truck!" and "Oh, my God!" Horns blared all around them, and Robin said, "She's going to make me have an accident."

Robin and her mother discovered that they liked many of the same foods, and that they were both addicted to the same daytime soaps. They ate Chicken McNuggets and fries on snack tables in front of the television set in the living room. Her mother couldn't believe that Robin had really been on *Love in the Afternoon*. She had missed that particular episode, and she let Robin act out the whole thing for her.

Brandy hung around a lot in the beginning, ruining things by sitting between them and talking back to the TV during their shows—by just being a third wheel, the way Robin had usually been with her schoolmates. "Why doesn't she get a life?" she grumbled when the door chimes rang first thing one morning.

"Don't be like that," her mother said, on her way to the door. "She's lonely, poor thing." She'd already told Robin that Brandy had been a widow for years, and had no children.

"I once knew a dog named Brandy," Robin said. She'd decided that this Brandy was doglike—not vicious, maybe, but slavish, the kind of dog that *licks* people to death. "Woof, woof," she said, when Brandy came in, and her mother laughed.

Some afternoons, after the nurse arrived, Robin and her mother tiptoed out to the car, giggling and shushing each other, and took off before Brandy could ask to go with them. She finally caught on, of course, and her feelings were hurt. Robin overheard her mother on the phone saying, "Well, I'm really sorry you feel that way, but I think you're being oversensitive."

After that, Brandy stayed away, and her retreat meant that Robin had to pitch in with caring for Tony. He was as helpless as Phoebe, but without any of Phoebe's appeal. His dark urine spilled down a tube into a clear plastic bag that had to be emptied twice a day, and he wore a grownup diaper for the other stuff. At least there was very little of that, and either Robin's mother or the visiting nurse cleaned him up; Robin was grateful that they covered his private parts while they worked. Despite the sheepskin pad over the bottom bedsheet, he'd developed ugly, oozing bedsores on his heels and elbows and bony behind that needed to be smeared with a special ointment. The two women took care of that, too. Robin got into the habit of watching everything they did, carefully, like there was going to be a final on it one of these days. And she learned to help sponge Tony, and turn him from one side to the other every few hours. He only weighed about ninety pounds, but it felt like ninety pounds of lead. After they turned him, they used an aspirating machine to suck out the mucus that kept accumulating in his throat; the gurgling noise stopped for a while whenever they did that. Tony opened his eyes and looked around from time to time, but he always closed them again right away, as if he didn't like what he saw. The nurse, Roberta, said he probably didn't see anything, that he was semi-comatose. "One foot in this world and one in the next" was the way she described it. "His biggest problem right now," she told Robin, "is his strong heart."

Linda wrote to Robin often—chatty letters, mostly about Phoebe and the weather. She enclosed snapshots of the baby she must have taken herself, because they were either out of focus or overexposed. Robin kept them on the shelf in the closet of her room, on top of her new clothes. Her mother offered to fix the

room up for her, to take out the bike and the pinball machine
and put in a chest of drawers and a comfortable chair instead.
But Robin said she liked it just the way it was, and she did.
Sometimes, when she couldn't sleep, she got up and played the
pinball machine in the dark. Or she put on the light in the closet
and looked at the snapshots of Phoebe.

Finally, there was news in one of Linda's letters about Cynthia
and her custody suit. "We went to family court this morning,"
Linda wrote, "and the whole case was thrown out." Robin had a
satisfying vision of Cynthia, her lawyer, and all those stupid
papers being flung through a window of the courthouse by somebody like Bull Shannon, the goony bailiff on *Night Court*.

That afternoon, when her mother was out buying milk, Robin
went to the phone and dialed Linda's number in L.A. After the
third ring, she heard Linda's super-friendly "Hi," and said, "Hi,
it's me!" back, before she realized Linda's greeting was taped,
and that it was continuing right over her own breathless reply:
"This is Linda. Nathan, Phoebe, and I are all busy right now. If
you'll leave a message at the sound of the tone, we'll get back to
you soon. Thank you!" That only confirmed what Robin already
knew—that Nathan lived there now, and she didn't—and she
hung up without leaving a message.

Tony died two days later, almost a month after Robin's arrival
in Glendale. Nobody, including his doctor, had expected him to
last that long, even with his terrific heart. Robin had been hoping
it wouldn't happen during one of those rare times she was alone
in the house with him. She imagined it would be something like
hand-to-hand combat—Tony vs. Death—a battle that might
shake the walls and overturn the furniture. Every scary image of
dying she'd hoarded from years of television-watching came back
to haunt her. Gangsters writhing around for about a week after
being peppered with bullets. Some guy on his deathbed in a soap
opera, sounding like he'd swallowed a rattlesnake. Maybe the
worst pictures she'd kept in her head were of cartoon cats and
mice who *wouldn't* die, even after they were pitched over cliffs

or ground up by a cartoon machine into cat-or-mouse burger. They made Robin think of Tony magically restored to his healthy, handsome, dangerous self, to his intimacy with her mother that would forever exclude her.

As it turned out, she was in his room, but not alone with him, when he died. Her mother and Roberta were both there, too. They had just finished the ritual of cleaning and turning him, and were about to do the thing with the aspirating machine, when Roberta realized the gurgling in his throat had stopped on its own. "Uh-oh," she said. She pressed two fingers to his neck, her eyes shut in concentration. Then she took out her stethoscope and listened to his chest with it. She folded the stethoscope and put it back into her pocket. "It's all over, dear hearts," she said. "Let's be glad."

Robin moved instinctively toward her mother, who went past her into Roberta's open arms. Her mother cried quietly, almost politely, while Tony lay there turning gray under his jaundiced tan. Robin tried to feel something—pity, grief, the kind of gladness Roberta had meant, or even vengeful joy—but the whole event was sort of a letdown.

The house became busy within minutes. Brandy was the first to show up, before the doctor or the undertaker, and Robin's mother let herself be bear-hugged in forgiveness and consolation. Other neighbors, who Robin had never seen before, came over, too, and their gentle murmurs gradually grew to a swarming hum. Her mother became a celebrity surrounded by fans and Robin couldn't get near her. Not that she knew what she'd say if she had the chance. "Sorry," which all the visitors whispered, like a password, seemed both inadequate and phony.

In the early evening, after everyone else was gone, Brandy sat down at the kitchen telephone and made some long-distance calls, from a prepared list. Robin's mother sipped coffee at the breakfast bar and stared bleakly into the future, or the past, while Robin stood in the doorway and listened to Brandy's end of the phone calls. They seemed to be mostly to Tony's relatives back East. She opened with the same lines each time, varied only by the names of the people she was calling. "Is this So-and-So? Well, I'm a close friend of Tony and Miriam Hausner's, and I'm afraid I have some bad news for you."

Robin took the coffeepot from the stove and silently offered her mother a refill, but she covered her cup with one hand and closed her eyes. She didn't open them again until Robin had replaced the coffeepot and gone back to her station in the doorway.

Two of Tony's four children—the middle ones, his daughter Jennifer and his son Kevin—flew in from New Jersey the night before the funeral. The older daughter was traveling in Germany and couldn't be reached. And when the younger son, in Cleveland, was asked if he could make it to the services, he said, "I think he owes *me* a visit," and hung up. Jennifer and Kevin stayed at a motel nearby and arrived just in time for the chapel service the next morning. The minister was brief. He said only a few things about Tony, about his devotion to his wife and his concern for his children, and how much he'd loved his work and golfing and his cactus garden. There was a prayer and then a woman played "Moon River" on a keyboard organ. Robin kept stealing glances at Kevin, sitting at the other end of her row, almost surprised to see that he wasn't an angry thirteen-year-old boy anymore, someone who might set a fire in the chapel rest room or take the hearse on a joyride. He was about twenty-five, and average-looking, except for his acne-scarred skin and the way he kept blinking. Tony's daughter was pretty in a boring way, with the kind of looks they were always making over in women's magazines. She was only about five years younger than Robin's mother, who had once told Robin she had a "thing" for older men. That was during Robin's earlier visit to Glendale, with Linda, and the only time they'd ever discussed Robin's father. Her mother explained that he had smothered her with a love that quickly snuffed out her own, and she had to escape or die. Robin knew firsthand about his smothering affection, but she'd felt ferociously protective of him then, of what was left of him: his ashes still waiting for disposal in a plastic box in the trunk of the Mustang. Right after they left her mother's house, Linda drove to this wooded rest area off the highway. Dorky Linda couldn't get the box open for the longest time. She finally had to hit it with a rock. Then she said something about Wright Henry Reismann, that he was a good man who would be missed, and she spilled the ashes all around them. On the other side of the trees, a family was sitting at a redwood table, opening their picnic basket.

Robin's mother broke down at the cemetery. As the coffin was being lowered into the grave, she called pleadingly to Tony not to go, not to leave her all alone. Brandy started sobbing, and then Kevin, and finally Jennifer let loose, too. Robin was rattled by this unexpected display of emotion. Things had been so calm until then. It had seemed to be just a matter of getting through the terrible, necessary steps of the day. She had been on the fringes of her mother's plans for the funeral, and now she felt more out of place than ever. The only one in the family group not mourning, the only one who didn't belong. The pitch of weeping and wailing had grown alarmingly, and at its very peak, there was suddenly a much louder, more piercing cry, like when the lead singer grabs the melody in the final refrain of a song. Everyone turned around to see who was making that racket, and no one was more astonished than Robin to realize it was herself.

A few days later, Robin's mother announced that it was time they stopped fooling around and got serious about their lives. That meant she was going to look for a job, and that Robin should register for school. The two of them, and Brandy, drove about three miles to Goldwater High. Classes were just changing when they entered the building, and the halls flowed with mobs of noisy, jostling students who all knew one another. A secretary in the office said that she would send to Northside for Robin's records. In the meantime, she wanted to know if Robin had a birth certificate with her, or any other official document of identification, to get the ball rolling. "Why don't you show her your driver's license, hon," Brandy said.

35

Lucky Life

On Monday, October 26, three days after Nathan's divorce became final, he took Linda and Phoebe to a Chinese restaurant on San Pedro Street for a celebration supper. He hadn't been in the mood to do much of anything over the weekend. When Linda asked him if he was feeling sad, he'd said, "Nah, just a little off." But he had to be in mourning for his lost marriage, no matter what he said, and she kept a cautious and respectful distance from him until Monday morning, when he woke, cheerful again, and exuberantly horny. They both had early classes at the Bod, but they lay there after making love, dozing in each other's arms, until Nathan suddenly said, "Do you feel like Chinese food?"

Linda raised her head to look over his shoulder at the alarm clock. "At seven-thirty in the *morning*?" she asked.

"No, chica," he told her. "*Tonight.*"

"Okay, chico," she said.

At some other time, with some other man, she might have been hurt if he began to think about food so soon after lovemaking. But there was an uncanny pleasure in planning *anything* ahead with Nathan: meals, movies, even the dullest domestic chore. Later, in the shower, after she'd scrubbed his lovely back and turned around so he could scrub hers, the sight of his shampoo alongside her own in the shower caddy gave her an absurd rush of happiness. His shirts and trousers crowded her clothes in the bedroom closet, but she didn't mind. She even liked watching the wild mingling of their underclothes in the dryer.

With Robin gone, they had a lot more time and privacy for their passion. Phoebe was sleeping in the second bedroom now, but it was also a sort of shrine to Robin's former occupancy. Her posters of rock stars still hung on the walls, and there were a few articles of her clothing in the closet and drawers that Linda hadn't gotten around to mailing to Glendale yet. Her sole attempt at nursery decor was the installation of a Kermit nightlight. Linda went in to check on the baby a few times every night. In Kermit's gentle green glow, she looked extraterrestrial. Like Robin, only a tourist on this planet.

Linda thought of Wright as soon as she walked into Yum Luck's, because their wedding had taken place in the back room of a Chinese restaurant in Newark a lot like this one—with similar red-flocked wallpaper, a golden-dragon motif around the padded bar, and a big, murky aquarium in which carp swam listless laps. She remembered how festive the platters of sizzling rice had seemed on her wedding day, and how hilariously funny Wright was when he tried to eat with chopsticks. Linda had worn a blue linen suit and a matching picture hat she had to take off during dinner, so she could see what she was much too excited to eat. The eight guests they'd invited, co-workers and friends, toasted them into a long and glorious future with champagne and Chinese beer. Only Robin had put a damper on the merrymaking, by scowling and tapping her foot during the ceremony, and then picking suspiciously through the special Happy Family entree Linda had ordered for the table, like a Board of Health inspector.

At Yum Luck's, they were seated next to the aquarium, to Phoebe's delight. From the perch of her booster seat, she had fish to ogle and point at while she tried to master her slippery noodles.

But again Linda was reminded of Robin, of the fish tank in her mother's house Linda heard bubbling that day but never got to see. The girl hadn't written or called once in all these weeks. When Linda decided to swallow her pride and call her, Robin wasn't there. The woman who answered the phone, someone named Roberta, took Linda's message, but Robin never returned the call.

Linda pulled the teapot and the soy sauce out of Phoebe's reach. She started to protest and Nathan gave her his key ring—her new favorite toy—to play with.

Linda kept stirring her bowl of soup, so that the wontons sank and rose and sank and rose in the fragrant broth. Nathan said, "Do you want to switch? Would you rather have the hot-and-sour?"

"Do you know what she once called me?" Linda said. "Robin, I mean. She called me the kiss of death."

"Why did she do that?"

"Because, you know, first her father, and then Manny . . ."

"That's crazy," Nathan said. "That's really crazy."

"Well," Linda said. "I kissed them, didn't I? And then they both—"

"Hey, I'm still here," Nathan said, "aren't I?"

"I think you'd better pinch yourself," Linda told him, "just to be sure."

Instead, he pinched her, under the table. "Yep, I'm still here," he said.

"Maybe I should have acted more hurt and surprised when she said she wanted to stay there," Linda said. "Maybe she was only testing me."

"It wasn't you she was testing," Nathan said.

"And I could have told her more about the thing with Cynthia, how scary it really was. I made it seem like settling a parking ticket."

"Linda mujer," Nathan said. "Sometimes you have to just let go."

It pained her to think he might also be talking to himself, about his once-wife. What if Linda hadn't been so bold that night of their search for Robin and Phoebe? What if she had simply thanked him at the end and sent him on his way again? After they'd phoned Robin's mother and discovered the children were there, relief and fatigue had overwhelmed them. Linda, fired up by the relief, wanted to battle the fatigue and leave for Glendale right away, but Nathan talked her out of it. It was a long drive, he said, and it had been an even longer day. They both needed to sleep for a while, and Robin and Phoebe probably did, too. He was going to take Jewelle home and then head for his place to catch a nap; he promised he would be back to pick Linda up in a few hours. Jewelle was in the bathroom while he was saying all of this. Linda found herself listening for the toilet's flush, for the sound of an opening door. The seconds were beating away. She could practically hear them, as if her egg timer was running. "Nathan," she said, in a voice thick with sleepiness and emotion. "Don't go home tonight." This was the new Linda speaking, the recent convert to action, to choice, the swimmer who would no longer simply float on her back through the currents of life. She and Nathan looked at one another with deepening attention. When Jewelle finally flushed the toilet, it roared like Niagara Falls.

They didn't make love that night; Linda was asleep when Nathan came back and got into bed beside her. She turned to him so naturally, and without fully waking, he might have been her lifelong husband returning from a midnight trip to the bathroom. They wound themselves together in knots that would have stumped Houdini and double-dove into sleep. In what seemed like minutes, she was shaking him to get up, to get going.

On the way to Glendale, they talked and talked. Robin was going to be in the car with them on the way back, which would certainly limit their ability to speak freely. Linda paid close attention this time while Nathan told her about Delila. "We met in Baja in 1985," he began. "She'd come down from San Diego to visit relatives. We became dance partners first—in fact, we met at a dance-hall contest. I was just hanging out with some buddies.

Delila was supposed to be in the contest, but her partner stood her up." He paused for a moment, remembering. "We fooled around on the sidelines before the thing started, flirting a little, trying out a few steps. We were in perfect sync, the way it sometimes happens, and her friends and mine started daring us to enter the contest as a team."

"Did you win?" Linda said, already knowing the answer.

"Yeah," Nathan admitted, "and it was a real high. Delila put off going home, indefinitely, and we started working together— developing routines, getting a few local gigs. Pretty soon we got close in other ways and . . . well, marriage seemed like the inevitable next step."

"You don't have to make it sound as if you didn't love her," Linda said.

"Did I do that?" Nathan said. "I didn't mean to."

"What happened then?" Linda asked, trying to ignore the crowded sensation in her chest.

"Life happened," Nathan said. "You know, disappointments, jealousy, money problems. We had this big dream of making it professionally, but we stayed small-time. When we moved up to San Diego, I had to take a string of low-paying odd jobs—off the books—just to get by. But once I got my green card, I wanted to settle down and teach somewhere, maybe open our own studio, and start a family. But Delila wouldn't let go of the dream."

They had been cruising in the middle lane on the freeway during this entire conversation, and now he cut sharply over into the fast lane, making Linda's heart swerve with the car. "Then, later," he said, "when things were completely bad between us, she wouldn't let go of me, either. That's what I was working on when I met you."

Why did it bother her so much that he'd had an amorous past? What did she expect—he was thirty-three years old. And she had her own considerable history in that department. She had been married, too; she might have been married *twice*, if Manny hadn't died before it could happen. Her feelings were unreasonable, but love itself was unreasonable. "Did you still sleep together?" she made herself ask.

He hesitated, and then he said, "Yes, before I met you. I guess we were breaking apart kind of slowly. But after I met you, we stopped. I stopped." Linda felt her chest expand.

In the restaurant, Phoebe squished rice between her fingers and threw it at the fish tank. "Nice fishies," Linda said, patting the tank. "At my wedding," she told Nathan, "somebody asked for rice, you know, to throw at Wright and me when we left the restaurant? The waiter brought steamed rice in one of those little takeout containers."

Nathan laughed. Then he described his own wedding, which sounded much more elaborate and romantic than hers. It took place in somebody's courtyard, he said, with a lot of family and friends present. There was a fountain splashing. Strings of colored lights had been threaded through the trees, and a mariachi band played all night.

"What did she wear?" Linda asked, and Nathan smiled with indulgence at what he obviously considered a "woman's" question.

"A traditional Mexican wedding dress," he said. "Long and white, with embroidery all over."

Linda shut her eyes and envisioned someone named Delila, in a long white dress, whirling with her handsome new husband under colored lights. For the first time, she felt kinship with that bride, and sympathy; there were so many other ways to lose a man besides death.

Linda was the one in mourning when she and Nathan came back from Glendale. She had never expected Robin to stay with her mother; all she'd ever heard from her about Miriam was sorrowing rage. And Linda was surprised that Miriam was so willing to take Robin in. That other time, she and Tony had seemed like a club no one else in the world was qualified to join. Maybe the biggest surprise of all, though, was Linda's own acute feeling of loss. Robin had always been so difficult, and at the Beverly Body and elsewhere Linda had heard the real mothers of other adolescent girls wish they would just disappear. But the family she and the children had forged, had *invented*, was broken by Robin's choice. And all the work of argument and willful affection seemed wasted.

Linda wrote to Robin regularly, the way one might write to a child away at camp or boarding school, with lighthearted gossip of home, and every expectation the child would eventually return there. In the letter about Cynthia, Linda decided to maintain the same breezy, carefree tone, to just give the news of victory and not a rundown of the battle.

On the day of the hearing, Nathan had dropped Linda and Phoebe in front of the courthouse before he parked the car. At that precise moment, Mitchell pulled up in the Porsche and helped Cynthia and a handsome, beefy man out of the backseat. Linda began running up the steps, as if she were being chased, as if she believed Cynthia or the man with her—her bodyguard?—would try to wrest the baby from her arms. She had to pause on the top step to compose herself, and Cynthia and her escort went past her into the building, without even a glance of acknowledgment. Linda had once seen a movie star go into a restaurant with the same inward focus, while the traffic of everyday life streamed by. She was tempted to run back down the steps and keep going, Robin-style. But she saw that Nathan was already coming up them, toward her.

The hearing was held in something like a high-school classroom, with a blackboard and a flag and a large desk up front. The judge was a cranky woman in a slightly soiled robe; it looked as if a baby had spit up on her shoulder. She kept muttering to the clerk sitting alongside her, as she flipped through the pile of pages on her desk so quickly they crackled. Cynthia was sitting with that man, who seemed to be her lawyer, at one of two tables facing the judge. Teacher's pet, Linda thought. She and Nathan sat down in the last of three rows of chairs set up behind a brass railing. Cynthia and her lawyer leaned together, whispering and smiling, while Linda tried not to stare at the stain on the judge's robe. She turned to look at the open door behind her, wondering where her own lawyer was. Then she wriggled lower into her seat. She noticed that Nathan was slumped in his, too; they were like a couple of unprepared schoolchildren who don't want to attract the teacher's attention. Not that Linda was completely unprepared. Her lawyer, Mr. Freed, had met with her once at his office, and he decided, within minutes, that his legal strategy was for Linda to state the truth, in her own words, in her own way. Vicki and Lee and Jewelle had all volunteered to stand up for her in court, as character witnesses, but Mr. Freed insisted that wouldn't be necessary. He didn't even tell her what to wear, the way lawyers in the movies always did. Still, she'd tried on four outfits before she decided on the freshly ironed white blouse and navy pleated skirt. The blouse was rumpled now, after the car ride and Phoebe's gymnastics in her arms, but that didn't matter. The problem was that Mr. Freed wasn't here yet, and the hearing was about to begin without him. The clerk stood with his hands folded and cleared his throat. A court stenographer took her place at one side of the judge's desk, with her hands poised over the keys of her machine, like a pianist's. Linda looked behind her one last time and saw a uniformed officer close the courtroom door, as the clerk began to speak in a strong monotone: "Sterling versus Reismann, Case 1734 of '92. Judge Margaret Place presiding." Phoebe babbled in response and the judge glared at her.

"Shush, poopsie," Linda said. She hoped the baby wouldn't start crying or head-banging, a habit she'd picked up recently, which made her seem retarded or disturbed.

The clerk continued. "Lawyer for the respondent has submitted a motion to dismiss the petitioner's claim for custody of female infant, Phoebe Ann Reismann."

"I've read the papers submitted by both parties," the judge said. "Is there anything further to be added before I rule on the motion?" Phoebe bounced on the trampoline of Linda's lap and hollered. Everyone but Cynthia looked at her. She hadn't looked at her, or at Linda, once.

Cynthia's lawyer raised his hand. "If your Honor please," he said, "surely it's premature to rule on the—"

The judge interrupted. "I'll decide whether or not it's premature to rule on a motion in my court," she said.

Linda realized she'd had a history teacher very much like her, in the eleventh or twelfth grade. Miss Chute, her name was, although behind her back she was alternately called Miss Shit and Miss Cootie. The main thing about her was that she had no pets among her students; she seemed to hate everyone equally, and she did a great deal of name-calling herself, right to people's faces. If you didn't know the answer—or worse, if you didn't *care* about the answer—you were a "Neanderthal," a "cretin," or a "microcephalic." Whenever Linda was called on to recite in Miss Chute's class, her voice thinned out to a barely audible thread before it disappeared altogether.

Cynthia's lawyer stood. "But, your Honor," he said, "in her answering papers the petitioner requested that certain hearings be held in order to determine what merit, if any, is contained in the respondent's motion. Pending these hearings, and in the child's best interests, the petitioner also asks that present custody be transferred to her."

"I can read, Counselor," the judge said dryly. "Sit down." Then she pointed her finger at Nathan. "You!" she said. "Are you representing the respondent?"

Nathan untangled his feet from the rung under his chair and sprang to a standing position, almost crashing sideways into Linda and Phoebe. "No, ma'am, I'm not. I'm her . . ." Linda watched as he scrounged helplessly for a word that would sound respectable in court. "We're going to get married," he said at last.

That information didn't seem to interest the judge, one way or the other, but Cynthia's lawyer said, "For the record, your Honor, this . . . this *consort* of Ms. Reismann's is already married."

"I've filed for a divorce," Nathan shot back.

"This is absolutely fascinating," the judge said, "but I don't have all day. Where *is* the respondent's counsel?"

Linda raised her hand timidly and then stood, with Phoebe in her arms. "Maybe he's stuck in traffic," she suggested. As soon as she said it, she knew it was exactly the sort of obvious and useless answer that would have brought Miss Chute's wrath down on her like a storm of hailstones.

Sure enough, Judge Place said, "Thank you *so* much," with searing sarcasm.

Cynthia's lawyer rose again. "Perhaps, your Honor, respondent's counsel has chosen to simply submit his papers rather than expose himself to the court's probing questions on the matter."

Linda, still standing, said, "That's not true! He definitely said he'd be here."

"Are you the child's mother?" the judge asked her.

"Yes!" Linda said, in a voice that carried to every corner of the room. "Yes, I am!" It was the only absolute truth she knew.

Cynthia's lawyer jumped up. "Your Honor, she may be the mother in name—" he began.

"I'm her mother in every way!" Linda shouted. "I gave birth to her and I nursed her and I . . . Oh, what do *you* know about it anyway!"

"Objection!" Cynthia's lawyer proclaimed. "This hysterical outburst—"

"No, *I* object," Linda said, turning to look hard at Cynthia, who finally looked back at her with glinting, gun-metal eyes. "I object to all of this, to anyone thinking, just because they have money, that my baby is up for grabs . . . for sale!"

"Ha!" Phoebe yelled and flung herself hard against Linda, head-first. Linda cupped Phoebe's head while the baby commenced to bang it, with the persistence of a butting goat, against Linda's breast.

"She's tired," Linda explained, still cupping Phoebe's thrusting head.

"So am I," the judge said. "Motion granted. Petition dismissed."

There was a hiss of whispering at Cynthia's table, and then her lawyer said, in a weary voice, "Your Honor, would you entertain an oral application for reargument?"

"I wouldn't entertain it if you made it in tongues," the judge told him. "There is nothing left here for argument, Counselor, and you know it. If any further frivolous applications are made before this court, I will seriously consider sanctions."

The last Linda saw of Cynthia was her furious white profile going by in a blur of motion. If only Robin had been there.

At Linda and Wright's wedding dinner, the dessert was a platter of sliced oranges, honeyed walnuts, and fortune cookies. Somewhere, Linda still had the little paper slip from the fortune cookie Wright had chosen for her and placed in her hand. "Lucky life," it said. She'd had it laminated a couple of weeks later at a stationery shop. Now she no longer believed in simple, blind luck. The story of her life so far had persuaded her that, despite certain unavoidable events, you still had to make your own luck, good and bad. Yet at Yum Luck's she rotated the little dish with its two folded fortune cookies until she had an intuitive sense that the one meant for her was closest at hand. She picked it up and snapped it in half and pulled out her fate: "The struggle is its own reward." She handed the slip to Nathan. "What do you think this means?" she asked him.

He read it and shrugged. "I don't know," he said. "But it sounds like something my mother would say."

"Mine, too," Linda said.

When they got back to the apartment, lugging the baby, the diaper bag, and a doggie bag of leftover lo mein and kung po chicken—in a perfect impersonation of an average American family—they found Robin crouched on the front step. "Where have *you* been?" she asked.

36

The Disappearing Act

Nathan's actual name, the name on his voter registration card, as well as his birth certificate, driver's license, and naturalization papers, was Natalicio Julio Diaz, the same as his father's and his grandfather's. On the way to the polls on Election Day, he told Linda that his mother had almost died when her labor with him suddenly stalled after eighteen strenuous hours. She was at home at the time, in her own bed, where her two older children had both been safely delivered by a midwife. During the quiet eye of that third storm, Nathan's father took her to the community hospital, and a doctor there named Nathan Glass committed some medical wonders, including turning the baby around at the last minute, so that he wouldn't land feet-first into his life. So it was Natalicio on all the official documents, in honor of family tradition, and Nathan everywhere else, in honor of Dr. Glass.

There was an explanation to be found for almost everything, Linda decided, if you looked hard enough for it. After she and Nathan arrived home from the custody hearing, she'd phoned Mr. Freed, her no-show lawyer, to tell him about the outcome and to ask where he'd been. He explained that he *had* been stuck in traffic—he'd called the courthouse from his car phone, but the message had never been delivered—and that he would waive his fee in light of his delinquency. A few weeks before, when Linda called William Sterling to thank him for the referral to Mr. Freed and for all his other kindnesses to her, she worked up the nerve to ask how he had happened to come across those confidential papers and letters. "Oh, I have my sources," he said mysteriously. And then he added, "There's hardly anything you can't get in this town in return for reading a screenplay, or giving somebody an audition." Hester, Linda thought immediately—or Mitchell. The only puzzle she still couldn't solve was Robin, but she was willing to settle for simply having her here.

Robin had never written back to Linda while she was in Glendale. She didn't write to Lucy or Carmel, either, although they both wrote to her several times before giving up. Robin believed she had to sever herself completely from her old life before she could truly live her new one. But she couldn't turn off her thoughts of home, of Phoebe and Linda and Nathan and the Thompsons. They would all go on living, she supposed, as if she had never existed. The way her mother had before Robin found her again. Without meaning to, she envisioned the apartment in L.A., everyone sitting at the table without her, talking and eating. She remembered doing the same thing here, in her mother's house, when Tony was upstairs, dying.

Robin walked around with an ache in her body she couldn't exactly define or locate. It seemed to travel from her chest to her throat to her belly to her head. It wasn't that her mother had proven to be imperfect—nobody's really perfect—or that her attention kept wandering away from Robin to other people and things. Robin was hungry for attention, but she had learned how to wait for it, or to do without. The problem lay mainly in herself, in her inability to forget. She longed for the sudden, convenient amnesia of soap operas, but she couldn't forget the fact of Phoebe, no matter how hard she tried. She looked and looked at the pictures Linda had sent, and felt a growing panic of loss. And sometimes, when she was trapped in the shower with a headful of suds, or on the exercise bike, going nowhere fast, she would swear she heard Linda calling her, over the pounding water or the churning wheels.

The day before she was supposed to begin classes at Goldwater High, Robin was in the house, waiting for her mother to come back from her new job at a car-rental agency. She had been told to start supper, to defrost a package of chicken parts and cut up some potatoes and onions. But she lost herself in a series of daydreams about Lucy and Carmel. In one of Carmel's letters, she'd said that Lucy had broken up with Shay after her mother found out about them, but there was an ongoing intrigue of notes passed in school, and "accidentally on purpose" meetings at the mall, all of which fascinated Robin, despite her decision to be disengaged.

Her mother came home and the chicken parts were still united in a block of ice, the potatoes and onions uncut. A lecture ensued, not very different from the ones Linda used to dispense, about responsibility and maturity. "I can't do everything around here," Robin's mother said. "Don't you ever think of anybody but yourself?" And Robin mumbled, "Big deal" and "Who cares?" whenever she could get a word in. The crazy thing was, the whole business only made her homesick. After a supper of tough, pinkish chicken and lumpy potatoes, she lay on the daybed, with that migrating ache settled firmly in her gut.

In the morning, she put her new looseleaf book into her knapsack, along with a couple of sandwiches and the money she'd been filching from her mother's purse, and Brandy's, for days.

"Good luck today," her mother said, "and don't forget your keys."

Robin gazed at her for a long moment, with the stillness and focus of a photographer. Miriam was drinking coffee, bending daintily over the sink so as not to spill any on her car-rental-agency uniform. It included a perky red bow tie that set off her dark hair and eyes, and her name was embroidered in red on her white blouse.

"So long," Robin said. Then she went out the door and past

the school-bus stop on the next corner. About a mile away, she hitched a ride to the Greyhound station in Phoenix.

There was a long line outside the elementary school designated as Nathan and Linda's polling place. Nathan had only become an American citizen in January, so he was going to be voting for the first time, too. In honor of the occasion, he'd bought a small flag for Phoebe that she waved with reckless patriotism in everyone's face, when she wasn't chewing on it. Robin had come along with them because she had nothing else to do that morning. School was closed and Lucy was at the dentist's. They'd spoken for hours on the phone the night before, until Linda threatened to pull the plug.

The line into the school moved very slowly and Robin began to complain after about ten minutes: the sun was in her eyes, she was thirsty, she was tired of standing, and she had a blister on her foot. She offered to take Phoebe around the corner to a coffee shop, where they could sit down for a minute and Robin could get a Coke. "I'll be back before you get inside," she promised.

Linda hesitated, but Nathan took a ten-dollar bill from his wallet and handed it to Robin. "Bring us something cold, too," he said. The whole scene seemed vaguely familiar to Linda, but she was too focused on the children to really think about it. She watched them go down the street until they disappeared around the corner. The line into the school stopped for a while before it started creeping forward again, but the mood of the prospective voters remained patient and upbeat. They were like ticket-holders waiting to get into a hit Broadway show. After about half an hour, Linda and Nathan were almost at the school door. Linda said, "They should have been back by now. Save my place, okay? I'll just run around the corner and see what's keeping them."

Nathan held her firmly by the elbow. "No," he said. "Don't worry, they're okay." He made a visor out of his hands to protect her crumpled brow from the sun, and in the slanted shadow he kissed her lightly on the lips.

In the school's gymnasium, they were directed to the registration tables for their precinct. Nathan went to the table marked A–L, Linda to the one marked M–Z. After she signed the register and was handed a ballot, she waited on a short line to get into a voting booth. It was a narrow, three-sided cubicle that reminded her of those boxes magicians use to make their assistants vanish, except that there was no curtain here. How could anyone have any privacy? When the man right in front of Linda went into the booth, she turned and saw Robin standing in the doorway of the gym with Phoebe in her arms, surveying the place. "Yoo-hoo! Robin! Over here!" Linda called.

In moments the man came out and gave his ballot to the inspector. Now it was Linda's turn. She waved to her children, who were coming toward her, and stepped inside the booth. It was the most private and mystical place she'd ever been. Her body had become the missing curtain, shutting out the room and all the people behind her. In here, she was the magician, the magician's vanished girl, and the audience waiting to be wowed. Earlier that morning, she and Nathan had lingered in bed to look at the election pages in the newspaper, but Linda had known for a long time who she was going to vote for, and why. She put her ballot in the slot and punched in her choices with the stylus, carefully and hard. Then she removed the ballot and stepped out of the booth, delivering her votes to the system and herself back into the living world.